PRAISE FOR SHARDS OF HISTORY

"*Five out of five stars!*—One of the most beautifully written novels I have ever read. Suspenseful, entrapping, and simply . . . well, let's just say that *Shards of History* reminds us of why we love books in the first place."

—Good Choice Reading

"Fast-paced, high-stakes drama in a fresh fantasy world. Rebecca Roland is a newcomer to watch!"

—James Maxey, author of *Greatshadow: The Dragon Apocalypse.*

"A must for any fantasy reader. Prepare to be taken by storm with Rebecca Roland fever."

—*Plasma Frequency Magazine*

"A passionate tale that will engage both young adults and more weathered fantasy readers."

— *NewMyths.com*

"A captivating tale of a deadly clash between matrilineal and patriarchal cultures in a pseudo Native American setting replete with dragons!"

—Susan Abel Sullivan, author of *The Haunted Housewives of Allister, Alabama.*

"Roland's beautifully woven, suspenseful debut novel draws readers into a groundbreaking fantasy panorama and resonates in the heart with its genuine, personal portrayal of loyalty, relationships, and sacrifice."

—David J. Corwell y Chávez, author of "Encounter at Boca del Diablo" (*Tales of the New Mexico Mythos*)

Other titles by Rebecca Roland

Shards of History Series:
Shards of History
Fractured Days
Shattered Fates

Short Stories:
The King of Ash and Bones
featuring a story from the Shards of History series

The Necromancer's Inheritence Series:
The Graveyard Girl
The Necromancer's Return
The Necromancer's Book of Magic

FRACTURED DAYS

Shards of History, Book Two

REBECCA ROLAND

World Weaver Press

FRACTURED DAYS

Published by World Weaver Press
Albuquerque, NM
www.WorldWeaverPress.com

Edited by Sarena Ulibarri
Cover designed by World Weaver Press

ISBN: 069242928X
ISBN-13: 978-0692429280

Also available as an ebook.

For the women in my life who have shown me what true strength is about: Tiffany K., Mary D., Julie J., and last, though certainly not least, my mother.

ACKNOWLEDGMENTS

When I wrote *Shards of History*, I initially meant for the novel to stand alone. But not long after it came out, I found myself thinking about the characters I'd left behind. What were they up to? How were they getting along? Were their troubles over? The more I thought about them, the more I realized I wanted to find out what happened next. So I came back to the Taakwa Valley and Malia, and the Maddion and the Jeguduns. Sometimes characters and places won't leave you alone, in a good way.

As always, I was fortunate to have beta readers who pointed out problem areas and offered great solutions, including Sarah Bartsch, Beth Cato, Peter Simonson, and Susan Abel Sullivan. Without their keen insight, this book wouldn't be quite the same. I worked with editor Sarena Ulibarri for the first time on this book. Her suggestions were extremely helpful, and as a fellow Corgi owner, she pretty much rocks. As always, it's been enjoyable working with the talented and brilliant Eileen Wiedbrauk and Elizabeth Wagner.

For general support and encouragement, I owe thanks to Codex, which is a great writing community. I'm also grateful that I had the chance to attend the Odyssey Writing Workshop back in 2007, which is where I wrote the short story that led to *Shards of History* and thus the novel you're currently holding in your hands.

I want to thank my friends, who have always been supportive and who talk up my books with anybody and everybody. I owe a huge thanks to Nate for his constant support. And as always, big hugs for Miles, who helps me look at the world anew every day.

FRACTURED DAYS

CHAPTER ONE

Malia crested a rolling hill and stopped just before reaching the summit. Near the Big River, which flowed to her left, the bones of a dead dragon curved through the spring grass. On the other side of the rushing, wide river lay more bones. Their riders had been gathered into massive pyres and burned, but the dragons had been too large. They'd been burned where they had fallen when the magic barrier rose around the valley.

She had done this. She'd pulled the magic through her hands, and the Jeguduns' hands, and repaired the shattered barrier. She'd killed thousands of Maddion men and their dragons.

And she couldn't remember it at all.

She rubbed at her forehead as if that could shake loose the thick fog that hung around those particular memories. Anything that had happened to her in the seasons leading up to the Dragon War was gone. Vanished, as if she'd never lived that time. When she looked at her brother, Vedran, standing a half-pace behind her, it was as if he'd grown into a man overnight. He'd gone from a pesky, scrawny boy who left frogs in her sleeping pallet, into a braided man, carrying a hunting dagger at his hip, a bow and quiver against his back, and a dragon's tooth on a leather strap around his neck.

Then there was the man who walked on her other side, also slightly behind. Enuwal, the healer. He'd prodded her on after she came out of the long sleep. All winter he'd given her work, both physical and mental, pushing her until she felt a semblance of normality. And now, proclaimed healthy, she was on her way home. She could return to her training to become her village's next clan mother. She'd have to start over, or nearly so, but then again, almost everybody had to begin anew after the war, all because of the Maddion tearing down the magic barrier protecting their home.

Home. She recalled Selu, her village, but would it look the same? The people wouldn't, or at least, not all of them, just as Vedran looked to her as if he'd aged overnight. Her stomach was a mess of knots. With sweaty palms, she gripped the leather strap of her travel sac, slung across her torso. Selu lay just over this rise. A few tendrils of cooking smoke rose in the distance. If she took a few more steps, she'd see the village. Then, she only had to get through the evening meal with her mother, perhaps with the clan father, and she could rest. It wasn't only the day's fatigue, or even the trail's fatigue, that exhausted her; it was the weight of all that had happened to her, and the daily battle to try to reclaim any lost memories she could. Maybe, once she was home, she could push this fog aside and remember. Enuwal and the Jeguduns claimed it wasn't possible, but nobody had ever before worked magic like she had. Maybe . . .

She took a deep breath.

"Are you all right?" Enuwal asked. He was tall and lanky, with gray touching the hair around his temples, and lines that cupped his mouth. His eyes, the color of rich soil after a rain, flickered as he studied her face, his brows furrowed. He stood close. Malia enjoyed it when he stood close to her. She enjoyed it even more when he touched her, sending shivers from the base of her neck to her fingers and toes.

"I'm nervous," she admitted.

"Well, I'm starving," Vedran said. "I can't wait to get home."

When the wind blew just right, it brought the smell of roasting meat and baking bread, and a hint of something sweet. Malia's stomach grumbled appreciatively.

"You'll be fine," Enuwal said. He took her hand and squeezed gently, then let go.

Malia nodded. "Of course. It's just been a while." A *long* while, if she included the time missing from her memories.

She adjusted her tunic and her skirt, plain deerskin for travel. Beneath her skirt, she wore a thin leather belt that held her dagger, its weight comfortable and familiar against her hip. She patted her dark hair, tucking a few loose strands behind her ears, and ensuring the rest of it remained in a knot above the nape of her neck.

Then her hands went to her necklace. Two Jegudun feathers hung from it. One was worn, old, sable. She'd earned it when she began her training as clan mother. Putting that necklace on for the first time was one of the last memories she had. She recalled the surge of pride when it settled against her skin. She could hardly wait to resume her training, to prepare to lead her village.

The other feather was a dark, glossy gray. It belonged to a Jegudun named Tuvin, who had shown her the truth about his kind and the real history of her people, the Taakwa. Those memories lingered behind the fog in her mind, but always the feather brought a bittersweet ache to her heart.

Last, her hands went to the beads hanging from her hips, red mingled with black; red for her clan, and black to indicate she was in mourning. Her husband, whom she didn't remember at all, had died during the war. She wasn't sure how to mourn a man she couldn't recall. She'd brought him up several times with her mother and Vedran, and each time they'd carefully changed the topic after a brief mention of his hunting prowess or how he helped provide families with meat during the previous summer's drought. Maybe they were scared of hurting her somehow, or maybe, given her feelings toward Enuwal, they thought it unwise. She just wanted to give the man's memories their proper due.

"I'm ready," she said. She straightened, pushed her shoulders back, and took the last few steps that carried her to the hill's summit. Her legs ached from days of traveling. She wasn't sure if she'd sleep in her mother's home tonight, or her own. Hers would be strange to her, but maybe it would help. Maybe it would bring about some flicker of recognition.

Selu stood in the bottom of a shallow bowl, surrounded by grass on three sides, and crops on the fourth. The crops stretched to the Big River, some lines already green with leafy plants. Usually, men worked in the fields from dawn to dusk, but although there was still daylight, the fields were empty. The knots in Malia's stomach twisted tighter.

"There's something wrong," she said. "Where are all the men?"

"I'm sure nothing's wrong," Vedran said, but he was frowning.

Selu itself formed a large circle, with mud-brick homes two and three levels high. A smokehouse stood apart from the village. It was a long, squat building with tendrils of smoke rising from its flues, the wind carrying the smell of wood smoke and salty meat with it.

Additions had been made since Malia had last seen the village, or rather, since her memory left off. At some point, she had built one of those additions herself, on the occasion of her marriage. She searched her mind for any inkling of that time and came up against the same dense fog. A dull throb began in the back of her head. If she pushed herself any further, she'd end up with a headache, and the world would start to spin. She forced her thoughts away from the immediate past and toward the moment.

"Tulah beat us here," Enuwal said.

Tulah, a Jegudun, perched on one of the village's highest points. She let out a long whistle, then dove into the air. Her wingspan was wide as four men laid in a line, and her brilliant white feathers shimmered almost painfully in the setting sun. Most Jeguduns' coloring ranged from light cream to ebony, but Tulah was the only one with feathers so bright.

Her wings beat the air and sent strands of hair whipping around Malia's face, stinging her cheeks. When Tulah landed and tucked her wings behind her, their apexes rising above her shoulders, she stood no taller than a young child.

Her figure was human-like, short and stocky, and covered with white down. Her snout was elongated and wolfish, and sharp teeth lined her mouth. Tufted ears pointed forward, and her eyes, blue as a clear winter sky, shimmered with intelligence.

She waddled forward on short, muscular legs. Jeguduns were meant to grace the skies, not walk on the ground. She greeted them with a slight nod and a happy trill.

"Tulah, is everything all right?" Malia asked. "Nobody's working in the fields." And now that she noticed, no children played outside the village, and no women were coming in from gathering foodstuff in the woods or bathing in the river. It was strangely quiet.

The Jegudun nodded, then fell in with them as Malia led the way down the slope toward the nearest alley that led into the village center.

Home. So much was familiar, like the warm mud-brick walls glowing in the sun, the river rushing past and snaking out of sight around the next hill, the woods stretching west, mostly made up of pine, fir, and aspen. An eagle circled above the plains south of the village, then tucked its wings and dove. It came up a moment later with a small, squirming figure in its talons, most likely a rabbit.

A few narrow alleys led into the village center. Malia walked into the nearest alley's cool shade, intent upon all that she had to relearn, and so it took her a few steps into the village center itself before she realized that the entire population stood within the clearing.

She pulled up, gasped. Her mother—Selu's clan mother—stood in front of the crowd, hands clasped before her ample figure. She wore strands of all of Selu's clans woven around her hips, along with a light skirt and tunic embroidered with leaping fish around the skirt's and sleeves' hems. Gray liberally sprinkled her hair, pulled back into a tight bun. Lines creased her forehead and her mouth. Malia had seen her mother after she'd woken from the long sleep, but her mother had left soon afterwards to tend to village business.

The crowd standing behind her was made up of faces both strange and familiar, and evidence of the Dragon War was everywhere. Many of the young men wore dragon teeth around their necks, as Vedran did. A young, braided man with burns on his right arm and neck stood tall, and approaching the crowd came an older man with a limp. Several women wore black beads mingled with their clans' own colors. Some men wore tunics with black squares sewn over their chests. There were children missing. That family there . . . Malia struggled for the woman's name. *Jessa*. Jessa had had five children. The oldest, a boy who would have soon earned his braid, was gone. A lump rose in her throat. The throbbing in the back of her head intensified.

Her mother stepped forward, shoulders back, a somber expression on her face. The crowd shuffled, a baby cried and was silenced quickly, but otherwise, utter quiet held reign.

"Malia," her mother said. "Selu welcomes you back home. We are proud that the war's greatest hero came from our very own village."

She flinched at the words. Greatest hero? She recalled none of it. All she knew was what others had told her, and the memories the Jeguduns were able to share with her. And even if she *could* recall her actions, she wouldn't have called them heroic. She had done what needed doing.

As if he knew she needed him closer, Enuwal took a small step and, though he remained behind her, brushed his fingers against hers. She leaned back ever so slightly. This was not the homecoming she'd imagined. She'd expected a warm dinner, a comfortable place to sleep, and easing back into village life. Instead, the weight of all those stares threatened to propel her right back out the alley and into the darkening plains.

Most of the crowd smiled at her, or at least looked upon her warmly. They were glad to have her home. But a few looked far from pleased. One man in particular, a hooked nose his most prominent feature, scowled heavily enough to carve deep lines around his mouth and along his forehead. He stood beside a pregnant woman, the swell of her belly small. Malia racked her mind for his name, but there was nothing familiar about him. The woman's name was Kima.

Her mother stepped forward, arms out. Malia hesitated. Her mother had never been a very affectionate woman. To embrace her in front of the entire village heightened the oddity of the situation. But, the people—*her* people—were leaning forward, expectant. So Malia met her mother halfway and wrapped her arms around the shorter, plump woman, careful not to disturb the beads around her hips.

"I'm sorry," her mother whispered. "The council started talking about a homecoming, and the next thing I knew, it had gotten out of control. Everybody was so eager to have a celebration."

She squeezed her mother. "It's all right. If I can survive dragons, I'm sure I can survive this."

Her mother pulled back, a relieved smile on her face. It made her look younger all of a sudden. There was something in her eyes, too. Pride? Yes, her mother's eyes shined with the emotion. It hadn't happened all that often in Malia's life. A lump rose in her throat.

"Do you think you can say something?" her mother asked. "They'd love to hear you talk."

The hooked-nose man scowled deeper. *Most* would like to hear her talk. She'd have to find out who that man was.

Wings fluttered. Tulah flew up to perch on a roof. More wings whispered in the air, and other Jeguduns joined her until they formed a rough circle all around. Perhaps a dozen Jeguduns in all crouched on the roofs, wings folded, watching, like huge condors eyeing carrion, or like a hungry pack of wolves. Malia mentally shook the image free. That was her old way of thinking. She knew better.

When she had come out of her long sleep, she'd been shocked to find how much time had passed and how much her brother had changed, but she'd been even more surprised to discover that her people now counted the Jeguduns as allies. She'd been raised to fear them and mistrust them, and somehow she'd helped bring them and the Taakwa together.

Not everybody counted the Jeguduns as allies, though. A few men and women in the crowd shifted their weight, eyeing the Jeguduns suspiciously, hands twitching near their daggers. Only a year ago, these Jeguduns' presence would have meant war. It took time to change people.

Malia handed her travel sac to Vedran. The crowd parted as her mother led her to a tree stump set in the center. The sky was a deep purple, the harsh day giving way to a velvety night where stars twinkled in the sky like mica in pottery. Several children went around lighting torches that had already been spaced around the village. The flames sputtered and hissed, and the smell of wood smoke and burning sap danced across the air.

The odor tickled at Malia's mind. The fog hiding her memories shifted for a minute, just long enough for a tiny crack to appear, and the image of a massive fire, eating at the forest, flashed through her mind. Her steps froze, and she gasped.

"Are you all right?" her mother asked, laying a hand on Malia's arm.

"Yes, yes," she said, struggling to follow that tiny crack, but the wall of fog had already closed in again. The throbbing at the back of her head intensified. She looked around, blinked, wondered what she was doing here. Where had all these people come from?

Then she remembered. She was home. She had to speak to them. Many of these people were wounded far worse than her. She caught the young, braided boy's gaze. The burn scars twisted the skin of his right arm and neck, and part of his face. He was familiar somehow, the same age as Vedran. One of Vedran's friends? She tried rolling back time, imagining the boy smaller, with the last vestiges of baby fat around his cheeks, and it came to her. Herule. He was Vedran's closest friend, and she hadn't recognized him. How could she not recognize him when he'd spent long days in their home?

She walked the last few steps, wishing she could have Enuwal beside her. But when she climbed the stump and looked out over the crowd, she spotted his tall, lanky figure at the edge. He smiled, and a pleasant warmth passed through her. Beside him, Vedran grinned and nodded. They were glad to have her home, too. And when she got past the strangeness of it all, she admitted she was happy to be home. A genuine smile formed.

"I am happy to finally be home," she began, her voice echoing off the walls. She made sure to turn one way slowly, and then the other as she spoke, so that everybody could hear her well. "I'm sure those of you who fought thought the same thing when you finally walked into the village and saw the same loving, welcoming faces that I see now."

Her mother smiled and nodded. In the back of the crowd, the scowling man turned away and made to leave, but Kima grasped his arm, leaned toward him, and whispered something. He stayed, every muscle in his body tense. Malia turned from them.

"My mother called me the war's greatest hero, but I don't deserve that title. For one thing, I can't remember the war. Although I can't remember what I did, I'm sure I was terrified the entire time. With dragons and Maddion flying overhead, and fires burning all around, who wouldn't have been?

"The greatest heroes are standing in this crowd," she continued. "Despite your injuries, you are home again and working, tending the crops, hunting, fishing, mending clothes, caring for your children, cooking, building homes. Some of you were directly injured in the war. Others were injured because your loved ones never came back home. Some of us have holes in our bodies, others in our heads," she said, tapping at her own and drawing a few wry laughs with the gesture, "but all of us have holes in our hearts. We all miss somebody or something." Her own missing memories stretched before her. Her people hurt because they had lost husbands or wives or children or siblings. She should have hurt . . . she'd lost a husband, after all. And yet, she was oddly numb.

Somebody sniffled. Malia stood straighter, scanning the Jeguduns who silently watched them. "But for all of our losses, we have also gained some things. We've gained new friends in the Jeguduns. We've regained our magic. We are stronger than we were only a year ago. We'll never stop missing the people we've lost, but we'll continue to live, and we'll add children to our families, and we'll create beautiful things, and all of that will soothe the sting of what we recently endured. The worst of it will fade as the dragon bones fall apart in our fields." She nodded, her lips pressed tightly together, and stepped down from the tree stump.

Her mother moved forward. She gestured a young woman forward. "This is Ayeelah, my attendant. There was so much to do after the war, I needed some help."

Malia nodded a greeting at the woman. She had high, round, flushed cheekbones. She carried a wide basket covered with a blanket woven in geometric patterns in deep red, black, and white.

"The village wanted to show their appreciation," her mother said. "They all put this together for you."

Malia took the basket. She let out a quick grunt at its weight and quickly set it on the tree stump she'd been standing on moments before. The blanket was soft and thick, better than any of hers by far. "It's lovely," she said.

"Look under it," Ayeelah said. She bit at her lower lip as if trying to hide a smile.

Malia folded back the blanket. Nestled into the basket was a smooth spade for digging in clay, new paintbrushes with fine bristles, and in all sizes, and tiny jars of paint ready to use.

"Oh," she said. She ran a finger over the bristles, over the jars, and at that moment, she felt solid and whole and as if she'd truly come home.

Enuwal had insisted she work on pottery during her recovery. It was something she'd enjoyed before. Her hands remembered what to do and enjoyed burying themselves in wet clay, but she'd found herself numb whenever she'd worked on it. But this made her want to hide away somewhere and create a bowl, or a cup, or a vase, and paint something on it . . . maybe lilacs like the ones she'd spotted two days before. She sighed.

"It's lovely," she said.

Wings flapped, the crowd stepped back, and Tulah landed nearby. She held something rolled in her hands, tied with a leather strap. She stepped forward and held it out.

Malia gingerly took the item. It felt like leather, but smoother, and thinner. At Tulah's urging, she untied the strap and unrolled it to reveal a painting of Tuvin's Falls, the misty water glistening, and Jeguduns in flight around it. Her lips slightly parted.

"This is amazing," she said. "It's so vivid. Who made this?"

Tulah sketched a small bow, and when she straightened, she gave a wolfish grin, her eyes twinkling in amusement.

"Thank you," Malia said. She wanted to spend more time looking at the painting. She wanted to sneak away and dig for clay and begin working on a new piece of pottery. But everybody was watching her, and waiting. They wanted their celebration. She carefully rolled the painting up and tied it, placed it in the basket, and then handed everything to Ayeelah. "Would you put this somewhere safe for me?"

"Of course."

Somebody started shaking a beaded gourd. Another joined, and another, until the sound echoed off the mud-brick walls and seemed to come from everywhere, including inside Malia's head. The throbbing at the base of her skull flared. She rubbed at her forehead.

"What is it?" her mother asked.

"A headache. Too much excitement."

"After you greet people, you can slip home and rest."

"And which is my home?"

Her mother flinched. "Stay with me and Vedran tonight. Tomorrow your brother can show you where you lived before the war. Then you can decide where you'd rather stay."

Enuwal joined them. "That was a lovely speech." He grinned. "I can't say that about too many of the speeches I've heard in my lifetime."

Her mother nodded. "It was heartfelt. Thank you. Everybody has been looking forward to your homecoming for such a long time."

Warmth flushed Malia's cheeks. Though she'd been training to be the next clan mother, she had never been one to enjoy standing in front of a crowd. Still, she had a duty to her people. Her own discomfort was nothing compared to the discomfort of those who had been injured in the war, or who lost loved ones.

Her mother led her through the crowd. Some people were dancing, playing the beaded gourds and wood pipes. It was like the harvest celebration, except nobody was wearing masks, and the atmosphere was lighter, more casual.

Others had brought out food. The rich smell of roasted duck filled the air, along with fish and root vegetables. There were bowls of fresh spring greens, mugs of tea and the warm chocolate drink the Jeguduns had introduced them to, and blueberries.

Malia spoke with the clan father, Paski. Skin crinkled around his eyes from long days squinting in the sun, and more lines formed a web around his mouth from smiling often. He was beaming now, clasping his hands before him as he said, "My life in your hands," the formal greeting of a man to a woman.

She spoke with the members of the women's council, six in addition to her own mother, and then with the men's council. Soon their faces and words blended together, as intrusive as the beaded gourds she usually enjoyed, and she began looking for her mother, who had wandered off to speak with somebody.

She excused herself and weaved her way through the crowd. A woman, dancing, bumped into her and nearly toppled her over.

"Oh, excuse me," she said without a glance at Malia, laughing as a man pulled her back into a small cluster of people.

Malia sighed. Even though she wanted a quiet night, her mother was right. Things had been too tense since the war's end. A celebration was in order. After tonight, they could all put the war a little further behind them.

At some point, the Jeguduns had flown off. In most of the villages, they made visits lasting a day or two, sometimes three, as they shared information with the Taakwa, but their presence still made some Taakwa uneasy enough that they felt it best to keep their visits short and to make their camps outside the villages. Tulah was a closer friend to Malia than most of these people. Everybody had changed so much. Or perhaps she was the one who had changed. Sometimes she caught her reflection in the water and startled. She was too young to have faint lines fanning around her eyes, or those strands of gray in her otherwise dark hair, or such stooped shoulders, as if she carried the entire valley on them.

Her mother was talking with Paski, huddled in a dark space where the torchlight didn't reach. She was using her hands quite a bit, unusual for her mother. Most of her conversations were calm and orderly, no matter what the subject. Malia headed toward them.

Kima's husband, the man with the hooked nose, stepped in front of her. Malia nearly ran into him, drawing up short at the last moment. He wore the same scowl, and between the angry glint in his eyes and the sharp bend of his nose, she felt as though she were facing down a bird of prey.

"You don't even recognize me, do you?" he asked. His voice trembled with anger. His fingers twitched, as if they longed to curl into fists.

Malia took a half step back. "I'm sorry, but I don't recognize many people these days." Out of habit, she racked her mind for this man's identity. The throbbing sharpened, and sent a spike of pain through her skull. She moaned, but the rattling gourds and voices and laughter covered the sound. "Perhaps you could remind me who you are." She pushed against the fog, demanding access to her lost memories.

He followed her, pressing too close, looming. "I'm your dead husband's brother, Andrij."

The fog in her mind roiled like angry storm clouds. "I . . . I'm sorry, I don't remember you."

"You don't remember me, or your husband, do you? His name was Dalibor."

"I know." She scanned the crowd for Enuwal's tall form, or Vedran, or her mother, but she and Andrij might as well have been alone in the village center for all the attention anybody paid them.

"Looking for Dalibor's replacement?"

Her gaze snapped back to him as anger, fueled by his words, surged like the agitated fog surrounding her lost memories. "I remember nothing of the past few seasons, not even my husband, I'm sad to say. I wish I did. I wish I remembered the man for whom I wear mourning beads." She took a step toward him, forcing him back. "How dare you approach me in such anger?"

For a moment, the fury melted from his face, leaving only sorrow. She almost felt sorry for him. She was about to ask what he wanted of her when the world started to spin. The fog in her mind slipped forward, lapping up new ground like a swollen river swallowing anything along its edges.

"No," she gasped. She wasn't using magic. She wasn't even anywhere near a Jegudun. Her memories . . . She reached out a hand as if she could grab them and keep them from slipping away. Instead, she grabbed Andrij's tunic. He pulled out of her grasp with a silent snarl.

She fell, the fog rolled over her, and the world went dark and silent.

CHAPTER TWO

Malia first became aware of the faint smell of wood smoke and burning oil, then came the crackle of wood in a dying fire, followed by voices murmuring nearby. Her mind was fuzzy, her head throbbed, and her limbs were heavy. She was lying on a sleeping pallet. A blanket that smelled faintly of lavender covered her. The scenario reminded her all too much of coming out of her deep sleep after the war. Confusion. Pain.

She cracked open an eye, not sure where she'd find herself, but certainly not expecting the familiar surroundings of her mother's private room. Her head spun.

Wooden shelves lined the mud-brick walls, holding folded clothes, baskets filled with beads and strips of leather, and gifts from the villagers, such as finely woven blankets, paintings done on vellum, and delicate wood carvings. On one shelf, standing alone, was a vase that Malia recognized as one of her own, and one of the first she'd made. It was lopsided, a crack ran down one side, and the river scene she'd painted looked painfully childish, but her mother had smiled when Malia gifted it to her.

Her father had died when she was young, just after Vedran had been born. His things had gone to Vedran, or to others in his family, and all traces of him were long gone, his face only a wisp in her memories. And then her grandmother had died soon after, of a broken heart, her mother had said. Malia had only the faintest recollection of arms simultaneously strong and soft, and the smell of wild roses, and eyes much like her father's. She pushed aside those memories. She hadn't thought of her grandmother in a long time.

What was she doing here? The last thing she remembered was packing camp with Vedran and Enuwal and setting out for Selu, and then . . . nothing.

She pushed the blanket aside and sat up. The room tilted, slowed, then steadied. Carefully, she climbed to her feet. She wore her travel skirt and tunic, but no shoes, and no belt or dagger. She still wore her necklace, the two Jegudun feathers warm and light against her skin. Her hair was tied back, but tendrils had come free. She patted them down, tucking the ends into the twisted knot at the nape of her neck. Her mother's sleeping pallet, rolled up, stood in one corner, and Malia's travel sac sat on the floor beside it.

Once she was convinced her legs wouldn't buckle, she stepped gingerly through the blanket hanging in the door and into the main, public room where her mother held council or entertained guests.

A few bits of wood smoldered in the hearth. The light mostly came from two lanterns standing on shelves on either end of the room, made of thin, beaten metal with stars and moons carved around them. Metalwork was the Jeguduns' specialty.

More shelves lined this room, holding other gifts, bowls and plates, utensils, mugs, and baskets of herbs for cooking and some for tea. Her mother leaned against a pile of pillows beside the hearth, dark half-circles beneath her eyes. Vedran sat, his hands fiddling with a small pile of arrowheads. Enuwal leaned in one corner, his elbow against the wall, and his lowered head resting in that hand.

"How did we get here?" Malia asked.

They all whirled toward her as if a dragon had crept into the room, eyes wide and bodies taut. Enuwal was the first to move. He hurried toward her, cupped his hands on either side of her face, and tilted her head up. He scanned her eyes, not as a lover might, but as a healer, searching for something wrong.

Dread coiled in the pit of her stomach like a rattlesnake about to strike. "What's the matter? What happened?" She raised a hand to her head as the throbbing spiked momentarily.

"You don't remember arriving in Selu?" Enuwal asked.

"No."

His hands, cool and dry, trembled ever so slightly on her face. "Do you remember me?" he asked.

"Of course I do." She took his hands and gently lowered them.

He closed his eyes and breathed a deep sigh. "Clan mother be praised. I would hate to go through that again." He opened his eyes. "Or for *you* to go through that again." He steered her to another pile of pillows. "Here, sit. I'll get you some tea. Does your head hurt?"

"Yes."

Enuwal rummaged through one of her mother's baskets. Malia held out a hand. "But please, no willow bark. I just want something light and sweet."

He hesitated, frowned, then his face relaxed. "Of course." He set some dried herbs in a mug, then poured water from the kettle tucked in the hearth. Moments later, the scent of lemon balm reached Malia.

"What happened?" she asked again.

"What's the last thing you remember?" her mother asked.

She probed her memories like a tongue probing a loose tooth, cautiously, afraid it might hurt. "I think I remember this morning. We broke camp. We had slept near the river, on a little mesa jutting over the plains. There were ducks in the water . . . mallards. And a pair of geese, with goslings."

Enuwal nodded. "That was this morning. But you don't remember arriving? The celebration?"

Her head spun slowly. She wrapped her hands around the warm mug and took a sip although the tea hadn't steeped long yet. It was enough to clear her mind. "I'd remember a celebration." She struggled to find the memory and came up against the same maddening fog that hid the rest. "Maybe I struck my head?"

Vedran shrugged. "All I know was, you were fine, then people were calling out for Enuwal. You were on the ground, with An—" He choked off the rest of the word. "Someone was standing over you."

"Your head *had* been hurting," Enuwal added.

"Would that explain my passing out and losing memories?" she asked. She added honey to the tea despite the thin set of her mother's lips and disapproving glare. She usually saved the honey for special occasions or guests, but Malia deserved a little something extra to help her understand what was going on.

He shook his head. "No. You don't recall anything at all about the celebration, or the moments before you passed out?"

"Nothing." She took another sip of tea. Ah, that was better. Sweet and slightly lemony. Her stomach grumbled. "Er, which means, I don't remember if I ate or not. I'm guessing I haven't had anything in a while."

Vedran grabbed a basket beside the hearth and set it before her. She pulled back a folded square of cloth to reveal sweet breads and roasted pecans. She fell upon the food, shoving a handful of pecans into her mouth while she tore at the bread. It was crusty on the outside, flaky and chewy inside, and practically melted on her tongue, despite having cooled.

"Vedran, *who* was standing over me?" she asked between mouthfuls.

His gaze shifted to their mother, then lowered to the ground. "I don't think he had anything to do with what happened to you."

"So you've said," Enuwal replied with a frown.

"Tulah already reviewed his memories. They argued, but nothing happened that would have caused her to pass out or lose most of her day."

"He has reason to harm her. Perhaps he slipped her something."

"Tulah couldn't find anything like that."

Malia raised her hands. "Stop arguing."

"We're not arguing," her brother said, crossing his arms.

"You could've fooled me," she muttered.

"What?" Enuwal asked.

She turned. "Mother, would you care to explain?"

Her mother shifted her position against the pillows. A joint popped, and she grimaced. When Enuwal leaned toward her, she held up a hand. "It's old age, nothing more." She sighed. "You said some words to the crowd. We presented you with a couple of gifts. You were tired, you had a headache. I asked you to make the rounds, speak to those who needed it, and then you could retire here for the night. I was about ready to fetch you and bring you here when Paski caught me and started talking my ear off about training the next clan mother, as if he thought I was going to drop dead any moment."

That was another thing Malia had to discuss with her mother. She'd been training as clan mother, but most of that knowledge was gone. The foundation was there, but the details remained behind the fog. She'd have to learn family lineages all over again if she hoped to take her mother's place some day. She bit back a groan as she thought of all that work.

"I knew Andrij was angry with you," her mother continued. "But I didn't think he'd actually confront you, not after I spoke with him just the other day."

"And just who is Andrij?" Malia asked.

Hesitation, then, "He is Dalibor's brother."

The husband she couldn't remember. The brother-in-law she couldn't recall. "Why would he be angry with me?"

At this, her mother looked away. So did Vedran and Enuwal. A chill hand clenched Malia's heart. "What happened? I thought you had told me all there was to know about the war and my life before. Is there more?"

Both men hunched their shoulders, turned toward her mother, and waited.

"Well?" Malia asked, her voice rising.

Her mother took a deep breath. "We didn't tell you everything. Truthfully, I demanded that neither Enuwal nor Vedran speak to you about Dalibor at all if they could help it."

"Why?" Her hands tightened on the mug.

"Tuvin was your friend," she began.

Malia's hand went to the dark gray Jegudun feather hanging from her necklace. It held one of Tuvin's memories of her. He had considered her a friend, and when she held the feather, she brought back a wave of warmth, compassion, trust, friendship. She knew Tuvin through other Jeguduns' memories, but not directly through any of her own. He was the one who had spurred her on to the cliffs, to warn the Jeguduns that a Taakwa army was coming for them.

"Yes," she said cautiously.

"Dalibor tracked you to where Tuvin was convalescing," her mother said. "He wouldn't listen to your pleas, and he killed Tuvin."

The fog shifted; her thoughts tumbled. She couldn't recall the moment at all, but her mother's words rang truthfully. Her hand tightened around the feather. "Go on," she said.

"He enlisted Andrij's help and followed you, despite my and Paski's telling him not to. He caught up to you at Posalo." Sadness washed over her features. "He was a jealous man by nature. You made a bowl for Enuwal, for helping you when you were ill, and Dalibor misunderstood. He destroyed it. Just before Tuvin came along, you set his things outside."

Malia's breath hitched. Dissolution of marriage. "You said he was jealous." Her gaze flickered to Enuwal. "He broke the bowl because he thought I wanted Enuwal? Did he . . . do anything to me?"

"He never laid a hand on you at that time. I would have never allowed him to stay if he'd done such a thing," her mother said quickly. "At the time, I thought I could speak with him, and he would calm down. And, it was still early in your marriage. I thought you were just having a little trouble learning to live with him. So I didn't allow the dissolution, not immediately."

Her mind spun, trying to make sense of it all. "So I set him outside my home, and you made me take him back. Why?"

Her mother winced. "You have to understand, the river had dropped, we were running short of food, and we were relying on hunting more than we had in a long while. Dalibor was a good hunter. A *great* hunter. I thought he could control himself until the harvest, and then we could finalize the dissolution if you still wanted it."

"So for the good of the village, you refused to grant my request for dissolution."

"I'm afraid so. I regret it every day, too."

I'm sure you do. Malia's hands gripped the mug so tightly that her knuckles blanched. She relaxed her fingers one by one as she fought for composure. "So what happened in Posalo?"

"Nothing much," Enuwal said. "You left before Dalibor could do anything. But he was convinced you and I . . . well, he was jealous, as your mother said, and he saw what he wanted to see."

"Had we done anything to give him reason to be jealous?"

"What? Er, no, of course not. You were hurt, and you're not one to break the laws like that. And neither am I."

"And yet I broke other laws. Assisting an injured Jegudun, for one. Helping an exile escape."

"You never broke any bonding laws."

"I still don't see anything that would lead Andrij to such anger."

At this, their gazes shifted away again.

"Mother?" she asked, a warning in her voice that said, *don't lie to me.*

"Dalibor and Andrij caught up with you at the front line," she said. "Dalibor did his best to interfere with what you were doing, to convince the Taakwa *not* to work with the Jeguduns. He attacked you, and you defended yourself."

Malia had to run the words over a few times before the meaning sank in. Her dinner turned to stone in her gut. "You mean . . . did I kill him?"

"Yes." To her credit, her mother looked her in the eye when she confirmed it.

Malia wrapped her arms around herself, shivering despite the warm night. "I killed my husband."

"He was trying to kill you," Enuwal said.

"And Andrij?"

"He was there. He witnessed it."

Her stomach rolled. No wonder Andrij was furious. She would be too, if she'd witnessed somebody kill Vedran, no matter how Vedran had been behaving. Malia scrambled to her feet and hurried outside, gulping the warm night air, one hand against the rough mud-brick wall, holding her up while her legs trembled and threatened to spill her on the ground.

A large, warm hand came to rest gently against the small of her back. Enuwal. His touch had slowly grown familiar to her over the fall and winter. Light, yet firm. Tender. She had often wondered what it would feel like to have that touch all over her body. Then she would shake it off. Her husband had only just died, after all, and even though she couldn't picture him, or recall a single conversation or moment they had together, she still had to go through mourning. She owed it to him, even if she couldn't remember him.

Laughter threatened to bubble up and spill over. Little had she known that she'd been the one to end his life. All this time she imagined him dying bravely at the hands of a Maddion crossbow or axe, or engulfed in dragon flames. She had never imagined for one brief moment that she'd been the one to snuff out his life. She was the reason she wore black mourning beads.

"Malia," Enuwal said quietly.

She almost turned to him, almost tucked her head against his shoulder, almost breathed in his familiar, earthy smell, but the ghost of a man she couldn't remember blew between them, chilling her. The hairs along her arms rose slightly.

"Perhaps you should lie down," he said. "I could get you some tea."

"I've had more than enough rest recently." She shook her head. "You didn't think to even give me the choice of whether I wanted to know the details about his death. You just assumed I couldn't handle it." A tight ball of anger grew behind her breastbone until she found it hard to breathe.

She couldn't be around them a moment longer. Her own people—her own *family*—had kept this from her. If they truly believed her a hero, they would have had the decency to give her the choice as to how much she wanted to know about Dalibor. They were *her* memories; it was *her* life.

She had to get out of the village.

With a frustrated little growl, she left her mother's home, letting the blanket over the door fall with a whisper behind her, and hurried through the nearest alley before heading for the western woods. Pine and fir loomed in the night, dark, jagged shapes against the stars. At least she recalled the terrain, and her bare feet carried her swiftly through the cool, dewy grass across rolling hills as familiar as the pattern of veins on the back of her hand.

A man's voice softly cursed somewhere to her right. She froze, her heart thudding, and strained to hear more. The Jeguduns were camped out nearby. Could somebody be searching for them to harm them?

Another curse reached her. Malia padded on silent feet around a thick pine and found a slim man kneeling on the ground, fumbling with a Maddion crossbow and an arrow. His back was to her, rounded as he hunched over the weapon, bracing it between his knees while he struggled to nock the arrow in it.

"What's this?" Malia asked.

The man yelped. The crossbow twanged, and the arrow fell as he spun around. "What are you doing, sneaking up on me like that?" he roared. Burn scars covered the right side of his neck and part of his face, and disappeared below his tunic. He was so familiar . . . She struggled to recall him. The scars and the worn, wary look about his eyes made him look older. He had to be about Vedran's age.

"What are *you* doing out here with a Maddion weapon in the night?"

He blinked a few times, his chest rising and falling rapidly. "Malia?" His voice was quiet.

She recalled his voice. This was Herule, Vedran's friend. "I'm sorry," she said. "I didn't mean to frighten you. I didn't recognize you."

His hand went to the burn scars along his right neck and face. "Are the scars that bad?"

"It's not the scars. You had your back to me. And besides, I remember you being . . . skinnier. Unbraided. Shorter."

"Such a flattering description." His breathing slowed and calmed. He stood, gathered the arrow and crossbow. A quiver filled with more Maddion arrows lay nearby. Herule tucked it and the crossbow into a narrow, hollow space in an old pine tree, part of the opening hidden by brush.

"What are you doing out here?" Malia asked softly.

He shrugged, and suddenly, despite the braid and his added height and girth, he looked like the scrawny boy who had always been underfoot. "Are you going to tell anybody about this?"

She frowned. "Why would I?"

He waved his left hand in the air. "All Maddion weapons are supposed to go to the clan fathers. Then they decide what to do with them, or who to give them to. There aren't that many, and they've all gone to council members, or men with friends on the council, and I'm neither. I found this one and hid it."

"Mm-hm," she said noncommittally.

"I thought . . . if I figured it out . . . I haven't been able to move my right shoulder very well." He swung his left around, making a large circle, but when he swung his right, it made more of a half circle, and he grimaced. "I banged it up pretty good during the war, and the scars don't help. I don't have the strength to fully draw my bow. But with a crossbow—"

"It would do some of the heavy work for you," Malia finished.

He nodded.

"That sounds reasonable to me," she said. "How about you leave it to me? I'll make sure the men's council grants this crossbow to you, once it's *discovered*." She spoke the last word with an arch of her brow.

A tentative grin wavered on his face. "You would do that for me?"

His words sent a stabbing pain through her. He'd lost much, just as she had. It was certainly the least she could do. "Of course. Now, why don't you head home before you accidentally shoot yourself in the foot?"

"I had the crossbow under control when you snuck up on me."

"Yes, I'm sure you did."

"But . . . what are *you* doing out here?"

She sighed. "I had an argument with my family and Enuwal. I'm looking for the Jeguduns."

"Your first night home, and you've argued with them already?"

"You *do* recall my mother, don't you?"

He pressed his hands together and gave her a shallow bow. "It's not my place to make any comment against the clan mother."

"You've gotten wiser."

Now a solid grin appeared. "As have you. My life in your hands, Malia." He tucked the crossbow back into its hiding place and slipped into the night in the direction of the village.

She watched him until he was long gone, then picked her way through the forest to the Jeguduns' camp, in a small meadow, near the village yet out of sight. She found them easily, a dozen figures strewn around the ground, bathed in the faint starlight. Tulah stood out from the rest with her vibrant white feathers.

Malia's footsteps were silent, but a dozen pair of Jegudun ears swiveled toward her the moment she stepped into the meadow, and a dozen wolfish faces turned her way, teeth glinting.

"Tulah?" she called softly.

Wings rustled. The Jeguduns watched as she picked her way among them to Tulah. The Jegudun trilled, head canted to one side as if to say, *What brings you out here in the middle of the night*?

Malia sat beside her, crossed her arms, shivered. "I'm sorry for disturbing you, but you all left before . . . Well, something strange happened."

She told them about losing most of her day and her headache. "What could it be?" she asked when she finished. "Is it magic?"

Tulah's brows drew down and her lips curled up slightly in an expression that made her look angry, but Malia knew the Jegudun well enough to know it was concern crinkling her face. Tulah spoke with the others, soft whistles, chirps, and chirrups filling the air, their hands darting as quick as hummingbirds as they communicated. Finally, Tulah turned to Malia and chirruped again, then flew her hand through the air, which meant she'd have to ask others back home.

"But what do *you* think? Could it be magic?"

Tulah shrugged, then nodded once. So, she wasn't sure, but she suspected it was.

"Will it happen again?"

Another shrug. Then Tulah gently took one of her hands and patted it. *Don't worry*, the gesture said.

The others settled back down, wings rustling, resting their heads on their arms, bodies curled up tight against the slight chill in the air. With their long snouts and pointed ears, they looked a bit like wolves going to sleep. Anger coiled within Malia. The Jeguduns never complained about being relegated to sleeping in the woods when proper shelter was just down the slope, but they musn't make the few still uncomfortable with the truce between them and the Taakwa have to endure the Jeguduns' presence.

Tulah trilled, raised a brow inquisitively. *What else?*

Malia considered going back home. Or rather, back to her mother's home. And yet, at the moment, she felt more at home out here in the woods with the Jeguduns than she did at the idea of sleeping in the village among her people.

She sighed. "It's about my husband." And she told Tulah what she'd learned about Dalibor. "Did you know I killed him?" she asked when she finished.

Tulah nodded, frowned, then pointed from her head to Malia's. *I thought somebody shared that with you.* Vacir, another Jegudun, had shared many of the war memories with her when she'd come out of her long sleep, but he hadn't shared that particular moment. He could have shared it and spared her finding out this way. She imagined watching the memory through his eyes, watching herself kill her husband. *No.* Perhaps it was best he hadn't. And yet, the feeling of betrayal spread and deepened.

The trees, and the night, hid Selu from her. She'd grown up there, had married there, had built a home for her and Dalibor. When she was younger, she'd dreamed of learning lineages so she could become clan mother, and working her pottery. She'd dreamed of a good man, a good life, a long life, children, peaceful living. She could still have all of that, but her life was cracked, like pottery that had been dropped.

If she'd been in Enuwal's place, or Vedran's, or her mother's, or Vacir's, would she have said anything about Dalibor's death? Would it have helped? She liked to think she would have, but she recalled her expression the first time she'd caught her reflection in a basin of water: gaunt, haunted eyes, dark circles beneath them. She'd jerked back, thinking she'd somehow found a stranger in the basin, only to discover it was *her*. Perhaps they couldn't shake that fragile image of her, and after a while thought it best to not tell her at all.

She stood and brushed the dirt from her skirt. She didn't need protecting from herself, or Andrij, or anybody else. She had faced down dragons, and Maddion. Her family had been scared when she'd been hurt, and so she could understand how they might have been cautious at first, but she was better now, and ready to resume training as Selu's next clan mother. They shouldn't hold information from her, no matter how well placed their intentions.

She was home, but it felt nothing like the place she'd left behind. She asked Tulah, "May I stay with you tonight?"

Tulah nodded, gestured to the ground where the grass still lay rather flat. Malia curled up, breathing in the scent of earth, and the strange combination of fur and bird that was the Jeguduns. An owl hooted nearby, and the wind shushed through the trees.

She made a pillow of her arms and shivered in the chill night. Tulah spread a wing over her. In the morning, she would show her family and the villagers just how strong she was.

CHAPTER THREE

Muvumo sat at a table in the long cavern, shelf after shelf of scrolls lined up on them, the smell of old vellum and ink in the air. Oil lanterns burned on thick wooden tables, casting stars and moons and dragons along the walls. In the cavern, it was easy to lose track of time. It was always dark, always cool, always dry. Muvumo's stiff joints suggested he'd been at his work for a long time, as did his grumbling belly. He pushed back from the table.

He'd been going through the Maddion ancestors' scrolls meticulously, beginning where Kushtrim, the last Most Worthy, had left off. Somewhere in here had to be an answer as to why so many Maddion had begun dying a few seasons before from an unknown illness. Some days, he wondered why he'd fought the other men to secure his place as Most Worthy. He'd taken this role only two seasons prior, and yet felt as though he'd been ruling his people for years. This burden was as heavy as the mountain surrounding him.

"Most Worthy," said Delkis behind him.

Muvumo turned. His personal guard, Delkis, stood as straight as a crossbow blade, wearing long wool pants and a tunic belted with a purple sash. His dark brown hair, twisted in ropes, was pulled back and tied with a strip of leather, and dark half-circles marred the pale skin beneath his eyes.

"You should eat something, Most Worthy," Delkis said.

Muvumo rubbed at his forehead. His eyes felt as if they had grit trapped beneath the lids. "How long have I been in here?"

Delkis had stood guard at the cavern's entrance. "All night, Most Worthy. The sun has risen, and the people have broken their fast."

"Ah, no wonder my stomach complains. And how many died this night?"

Delkis grimaced. "None, Most Worthy, but two more have taken ill." He swallowed hard, the apple of his throat bobbing. "The illness seems to be moving faster."

"I know," Muvumo growled. "There's got to be an answer in here somewhere."

"If you only had more help—"

"We are barely staying aloft as it is. With all those men lost in the war, and then the illness . . ." He shook his head. "If there are men who can be spared, bring them in. But not at the cost of feeding ourselves, or causing them exhaustion."

"Perhaps we could assign more tasks to the unmentionables and free up some of the younger men."

Muvumo's hand sliced through the air. "They're good for one thing only. If need be, we can feed some of them to the dragons. It would at least give us fewer mouths to feed. Besides, we've lost so many men, we can't possibly need that many whores around."

"Of course, Most Worthy."

He interlocked his fingers behind his neck, stretching back. "Where could this illness have started, Delkis? Some people say it's a

Jegudun curse, but I've gone through all our history with the blasted beasts, and there's nothing." He considered the long cavern, the depths where no lanterns yet reached, and shuddered. They'd all be dead before anybody could figure out a cure. He thought of the last person he'd seen die, one of the warriors, Lukus. He'd once been the largest man among the Peerless. At the end, he'd been bones and skin, his clothes hanging slack on him, dried blood and vomit caking his nostrils and around his mouth, seizures racking his emaciated body. A good man, gone.

"My father always had a saying," Delkis began. "'When in doubt, return to the first.'"

"When did he say that?"

"When he was teaching me to wield a dagger. I could never manage to best him, no matter how strong or fast I was. It took me a while, but I finally figured out that he meant I should work on the basics."

"What happened?"

A grin tugged at Delkis's mouth. "I challenged him to a fight and bled him. It was just a nick, but I kept practicing, and eventually I was better than him."

One of the reasons Muvumo had chosen Delkis as his personal guard—besides the fact that Delkis hadn't tried to kill him during the battle to choose the next Most Worthy—was his skill with the blade. Although the Maddion had settled on a new leader, people were still uneasy, what with the war and the illness. They expected miracles of Muvumo. And when people didn't get their miracles, they could turn ugly.

"Return to the first," Muvumo muttered. "Have you ever read the first scrolls?"

Delkis shook his head. "I've read the same ones we were all assigned as boys. The taking of the Jeguduns, the first battle with them and the Taakwa, dragon training and anatomy. I was never one for reading other than what I absolutely had to."

Usually, the first scrolls were assigned to those who didn't pay attention during regular lessons. They had to copy the scrolls and then summarize the contents before the group, and if they couldn't answer the instructor's questions, they faced the dreaded chore of emptying pisspots.

"Who was always in trouble when you were a boy?" Muvumo asked.

A slow smile spread across Delkis's lips. "That would be Kafran."

"Bring him."

~

Kafran walked into the cavern with a swagger and an amused expression. He wore no weapons as Delkis, waiting at the cavern's entrance, would have taken them. He gazed around and said, "I appreciate that you took it upon yourself to take the title Most Worthy. If it includes spending time among these musty old scrolls, better you than me." He swung around to face Muvumo and dipped his head in greeting. The slight tilt to his head, the glimmer in his eyes, all irritated Muvumo more than the screech of dragon talons clawing against rock.

"This is funny, is it?" Muvumo said as he encroached upon the other man. The short axe hung heavy on his right hip, the dagger lighter on his left. His hands hovered near both momentarily.

The cockiness slid off Kafran's face, replaced by wide eyes. The other man took a half step back. "I did not mean any disrespect, Most Worthy."

"What you mean is, you didn't think before you spoke, which is why you ended up in here so often as a boy, reading the first scrolls."

Kafran blanched. "I'm sorry. My deepest apologies, Most Worthy."

A boy's lack of discipline might lead to reading scrolls nobody else wanted to touch, but a man's sometimes led to him cleaning dragon dung, if he was lucky, or serving as a dragon's meal if he was not. Muvumo would've liked nothing more than to hear his own beast munching on this idiot's bones, but he'd called the man into the cavern to help the Maddion.

"See that you maintain a healthy respect for the scrolls and for me while you're in here."

"Of course. Ah, what is it I can do for you?"

Muvumo clasped his hands behind his back and started pacing. While waiting for Kafran, he'd had tea and fried turkey eggs, and he'd snorted a pinch of kasi powder to keep him awake. He now felt simultaneously exhausted and energetic. Even if he laid down right now, his feet would tap, his fingers might drum out a beat. His body sought rest, but his mind was zooming. He typically had no use for the powder, but given the circumstances, he had no choice. He could rest later, once he'd solved this problem.

"I want you to recall the scrolls you read as a boy, the first scrolls. Was there anything unusual mentioned in any of them? Were there any other bouts of this illness, or any other, similar illness? Was there a curse, or some discovery in the mountains? Anything?"

"If there was something about the illness, or anything like it, I would've mentioned it to Kushtrim."

"Think back. Anything unusual could be helpful. How much did you read?"

Kafran grimaced. "A lot. I was in trouble all the time. Most of it was about the weather, and crops. Back then, there were slaves to tend the eastern fields."

The eastern side of the mountains was a smoother, gentler slope, while the western mountains were jagged, stony, treacherous. Once, the Maddion had grown extensive crops along the eastern slopes, but in recent years with a dwindling population and the loss of their Jegudun slaves, they'd given up much of their farming.

"Jeguduns?"

"No. Humans." Kafran frowned. "Solemn. No, that's not right. Sol . . . Solumna." He snapped his fingers. "Solumna. They were living here when our ancestors took the mountains for themselves. They used to worship the sun, if I recall correctly. Bunch of fools, praying to the sun to cast out our ancestors. The Maddion made the Solumna their slaves."

"Was there anything significant about these Solumna, other than sun worship?"

"Not in what I read."

Muvumo poured another mug of tea and drained half of it. It had grown lukewarm, but the minty aroma and taste kept his body going just a little longer. "What else?"

Kafran shrugged. "The scrolls talked about dragons. Breeding, training, feeding. The usual stuff."

"And? Anything else? Even if you consider it trivial or silly, it could be important."

"Ah, well, there *was* something odd in one of the scrolls."

"Well?" Muvumo resisted the urge to slam his mug on the wooden table and wrap his hands around Kafran's neck. Dead men couldn't provide information.

He shifted uneasily. "It sounded more like a fanciful story than any sort of real history. There were people living down south. Desert people. They had a powerful empire. Our ancestors tried several times to take them, but they had magic, and weapons the like of which they'd never seen before. Great wooden arms that flung stone, arrows that flew longer and truer than could be ascribed to simple skill alone." Kafran ducked his head. "I actually got into trouble on purpose for a while there, reading their story."

"Go on." Muvumo didn't care a bit about Kafran's boyhood, save the information he might be carrying around in that idiot head of his.

"One time, our ancestors took a scouting trip down there in preparation for an attack. They found complete destruction. Somebody else had beaten them to it. The scroll I was reading, that man questioned the few he could find hiding in the rubble. He wanted to know who had defeated the desert people." A flicker of fear passed over his face. "He said it was one person. Their enemies from the east had sent one person, and this person defeated them. This person wielded more magic than all the desert people combined."

"Who was this person?"

"The man called this person a changer. Said he had walked into their city as a young, beautiful woman. After she leveled the city, she turned into a man, and then left."

A chill of excitement ran through Muvumo. A changer. He turned the words over in his mind. The changer had leveled a city. The Maddion didn't need destruction, they needed healing. But there had to be more to the story than a powerful changer walking into a city and destroying it, and this was all he had to go on.

"Where was this scroll?" Muvumo asked.

Kafran grabbed a lantern off the table and led the way deeper into the cavern. Muvumo moved to follow, then hurried back to the table. He slipped out the package of kasi powder hidden beneath the scrolls and breathed in a pinch before following Kafran into the dark.

They walked in silence, save for the occasional scuffle of Kafran's feet against stone. Muvumo measured the time in heartbeats, although his heart beat rather fast from the kasi powder. By the time he reached four hundred heartbeats, they'd reached the first of the very oldest scrolls. It wasn't until he counted five hundred heartbeats that Kafran stopped before a shelf to their left, holding the lantern high and squinting as he studied the scrolls.

"Ah, there," he said. He set the lantern down on an old table so he could use both hands to gingerly pull a scroll down. "I remember I had to use a new string to tie it because the old one crumpled away to dust."

Muvumo took the delicate scroll. Sure enough, the string holding it was the color of cream, while the vellum itself was like tea left to steep half a day. The scroll crackled in protest as he unrolled it, like an old man's knees popping as he stood.

The ink had faded, but Muvumo could make out the words. He made a silent note to have several boys come down here and copy these scrolls over again. That is, if they found a cure for this illness.

He began to read, finding the account much like Kafran had said. Then he got to the part about the changer, and the city's survivor talking about her with the Maddion ancestor. The Maddion ancestor wrote the survivor's tale word-by-word.

She was kind when she first entered our city. She had particular interest in our infants and little children, and she spent days visiting those without parents, or those who had been injured or who were ill.

Muvumo hardly breathed as he read. This was what he'd been looking for all this time.

She consoled the orphans and healed the sick. When we saw what she could do for the children, we told her of our ongoing battle with your people, and with others, and we asked for help. She said she could make it so that we never had to worry about your attacks again, and we readily agreed, not knowing what she intended for us. She sent the children and their families away, telling us it was part of the solution, and those unwilling to leave, or those who stayed behind to defend the city, ended up dying, save for a few of us. I do not know whether we should consider ourselves lucky or not. But in the midst of the destruction, she went through an upheaval of her own, leaving behind her youthful, beautiful, feminine figure for that of a man. The changer walked away as the city burned, and may he suffer a thousand horrible deaths for what he did here.

Muvumo straightened, letting Kafran take the scroll and carefully roll it up again. The changer had healed some of their injured and sick children. She might be able to heal the Maddion of their illness. Given the power she showed in destroying an entire city, she must be strong enough to do it if she wished.

He wasn't sure why she would want to destroy an entire city, but the Maddion were far more intelligent than any other people. Muvumo would make the changer cure his people, and he would not be foolish enough to fall for a bad bargain with the changer.

The blood rushed through his veins, not from the kasi powder, but from the certainty that he had, at last, found the answer to the Maddions' troubles. A wide grin spread across his face, the first smile in a long time.

CHAPTER FOUR

Malia lay on her back, her head pillowed in her hands, as the sun's first rays stretched along the valley. Somewhere high above her, the magic barrier covered the entire valley, keeping the Maddion and their dragons out and her people and the Jeguduns safe. She wished she could at least see the barrier she'd helped repair. She tried to imagine dragons overhead, and shuddered. If there was one thing she was glad she couldn't recall, it was the beasts and the Maddion and the terror they'd wrought, although it meant she also didn't remember them falling dead from the sky when she had helped re-erect the barrier. They had deserved death.

And Dalibor . . . did he deserve death, too?

She let out a little growl and rolled over. The meadow was empty, the others having gone to find something to eat. Malia had slept fitfully, when she'd slept at all, thoughts consumed by her dead husband, fueled by anger at her family and Enuwal for hiding things from her. She was supposed to be Selu's next clan mother. She had a right to know everything that had happened, no matter how difficult it might be to speak of it.

A gentle Jegudun chirp came from the long shadows beneath the pines, and a few moments later, Tulah stepped out. She carried a large bunch of flowers, mostly bluebells and daisies in brilliant shades of red and orange. She sat near Malia and began braiding them into a chain.

Malia pushed herself up to sitting. She pulled her fingers through her hair, working out the snarls as best she could. Her comb was in her travel sac, which was in her mother's home. Her stomach grumbled loudly. Tulah glanced up and let out a little growl that was their way of chuckling. Malia's cheeks warmed.

"Have you eaten?" she asked Tulah.

The Jegudun shook her head, then pointed to her.

"You didn't have to wait for me." During her recovery, she'd formed a sort of language using gestures with the Jeguduns who constantly visited her, like Tulah and Vacir, and she'd begun to understand some of their chirps and whistles and growls. It felt good, learning a new task.

The Jegudun's lips curled into a toothy smile, making her look more wolfish than usual. Tulah stood, hardly taller than Malia as she sat on the ground, and held out a hand.

Malia swiftly wrapped her leather strap around her unruly hair, grasped Tulah's down-covered hand, and let the Jegudun pull her to her feet. Tulah reached up and tucked the ends of the flower strand into Malia's leather necklace so that it looked as if her feathers hung from the strand. Their sweet scent tickled her nose, and she smiled.

"Thank you. I'll meet you in the village if you prefer to fly ahead."

Tulah shrugged and fell into step beside her, her rolling gait keeping pace with Malia. They came through the trees and found the village bustling. Men already worked in the fields, and a small group headed toward the northern woods with bows and arrow-filled quivers hanging on their backs. Malia recalled Herule and the crossbow and made a mental point to speak with her mother about him later. Women sat beside the river, washing clothes and setting them out on rocks to dry. Children raced and screamed through the grass, startling pigeons. Older children sat near the river, fishing poles in hand. More people sat inside the village center, or strolled through on their way to speak with neighbors. Smoke curled from flues, bringing with it the smell of sweet breads and fried meat. To one side of the village stood the smoke house, long and tall, and several small flues vented a steady stream of smoke along with the scent of smoked turkey.

A pang went through her heart. It was all so familiar, and yet she still felt like a stranger. She wanted to be home, to *feel* home, to look around her village and her space and her people and remember *all* the details.

Then there was the matter of Andrij. She wasn't sure things would ever be completely peaceful in the village so long as he held onto his anger, but she couldn't simply ask him to drop it. One of Enuwal's favorite sayings came to mind. When she'd grow impatient during her recovery, he'd say, *Give yourself more time.* She supposed she'd have to apply that to this situation, too. Andrij needed time to adjust to her presence, just as she needed time to adjust to living in Selu again. Then again, if she had waited longer to befriend Tuvin, or to warn her people of the Maddions' imminent arrival, she and all of her loved ones would either be dead or enslaved right now. She grimaced. Perhaps a new outlook was needed.

She braced herself, then led Tulah through the nearest alley and to her mother's home. Ayeelah emerged with a basket, spotted them, and ducked back inside. A moment later, her mother hurried out, followed by Vedran and Enuwal. Lines creased her mother's forehead.

"Oh, thank goodness," her mother said. "One of the Jeguduns stopped by to let me know you were with them, but I still worried. Come in, both of you, and have something to eat."

Malia stepped inside the bright interior and breathed in the familiar scents of her mother's home. The others crowded in behind her.

"How are you feeling?" Enuwal asked. "Does your head still hurt?"

"It's fuzzy, but I'll feel better after food and tea."

"Any more memory losses?"

She arched a brow. "Not that I'm aware of."

He ducked his head, chuckling. "Sorry. I can't help but worry."

She gave his hand a quick squeeze. "Actually, it's nice to have somebody worry over me. Sometimes."

Ayeelah bustled around, setting out warm sweet breads and fried sausages, which she told them had just come out of the smokehouse—"It's the first batch, made from venison from the fall hunt"—along with strong nettle and lemon balm tea. For a while, only the sound of munching and murmurs of appreciation filled the space. Malia helped herself to three sausages, two sweet breads, and three cups of tea. Sated at last, she leaned back against pillows and sighed.

"Now I think I can face the day," she said. Her muscles relaxed, and her eyelids half drooped.

"Malia, I'm sorry I didn't tell you sooner about Dalibor," her mother began.

So much for the relaxation. Her shoulders bunched, and she sat straighter. "It would have been nice to have a choice in the matter."

"I know. All winter, Andrij was calm. Composed. I thought perhaps he'd accepted his brother's death. And then he found out he would be a father, and I was sure he'd be too busy and pleased to make trouble. I figured it would be hard enough for you to come home after what you'd been through without adding to your burden unnecessarily."

Malia's eyes narrowed. "Yes, I'm quite delicate."

Her mother shook her head. "It's not that. It's just—" She pursed her lips.

"I suggested she not say anything," Enuwal said.

Malia rounded on him. "You?"

"Your mother has a point. You'd been through enough. I wasn't sure what additional stress would do to you while you recovered, and I suspected returning home might strain your recovery."

She'd had long discussions with Enuwal about her uncertainty with coming home. "Maybe next time I'll keep my concerns to myself."

"That's harsh," Vedran said. "Enuwal was just worried about you, as we all are."

For a moment, her memory of Vedran as a boy, round face and cheeks and mischievous eyes, overlaid Vedran as a man. Pain lanced through her head. She inhaled sharply. Then the pain was gone, as quickly as it came.

"You're right," she said quietly. "I shouldn't be angry with you for caring. But holding things back from me only makes it worse in the end. Now. Is there anything else I should know?"

She was met with shaking heads.

"Well, Tulah isn't sure what caused me to lose most of the day. She thinks it's magic-based, and I have to agree. What else could it be? But she doesn't know anything about it."

Tulah chirruped and again flew her hand through the air. Then she stroked at the tiny, tufted beard beneath her jaw, elongating and exaggerating the movement.

"She'll have to go home," Malia said, "and ask an elder."

Enuwal turned to the Jegudun. “Don’t you all pass down memories from one generation to the next? Wouldn’t you know if there was an explanation?”

Tulah nodded, shrugged, then shook her head. The answers to Enuwal’s questions were complicated.

“Holding all those accumulated memories in one head might be tricky,” Malia said. “*Can* you do such a thing?”

The Jegudun shook her head.

“So everybody knows all the most important stuff, like major history,” Vedran said. “Right?”

A nod.

“But you wouldn’t necessarily have all the memories that, say, Vacir would have?”

She shook her head.

“So some Jegudun, somewhere, might have the explanation we need,” Malia said. “Tulah, do you think you could find out more?”

She nodded, stood eagerly, and bowed to Malia, Enuwal, Vedran, and the clan mother in turn. Then she was out the door, the beat of wings against the air following.

“I didn’t mean for her to bolt out of here,” Malia muttered. Still, the sooner she had answers, the better. She cleared her throat. “Vedran,” she began, “How is your friend Herule? He was in the battle, wasn’t he?”

“He’s not doing so great. He was with a group farther north when some Maddions on dragonback came across them.” He grimaced. “He was burned.”

“I saw. Have you been hunting with him recently? You two used to go all the time.”

He shook his head. “He’s having trouble pulling the bow. He hurt his shoulder, and with the burns on top of that, he hasn’t been able to go.”

Malia's mother sat against a few pillows, finishing her tea, staring into the cup, but she was listening. Malia recognized the slight tilt to her mother's head. Enuwal's knees were bent. He leaned forward, wrapping his arms around his legs.

"Hmm," Malia said. "Are any of the Maddion crossbows still around? Maybe he'd do better with one of those."

Vedran brightened. "Hey, yeah, he probably would. I got to look at one of them, and if some adjustments were made, he'd be able to load it easily." His face fell. "But there aren't any left. Not unless there's one lying around the forest that we haven't found yet."

"Who decides who gets to keep a crossbow?"

"The men's council." Vedran glanced at his mother. "But they've been keeping most of them. I don't see them agreeing to give one to Herule, even if we find another."

She pursed her lips and set down the empty cup. "I left that decision to them. I figured they'd know who best to take one of the crossbows. But if one turns up, I'll make sure to speak with Paski about Herule and see that he gets it."

Malia hid a smile. Her mother had the final say on most matters in the village, so the crossbow, once 'discovered,' was as good as Herule's.

She stood, found her shoes, and grabbed her travel sac from her mother's private room. With that done, it was time to take care of her own business. "I'd like to settle in at my own place," she said.

Her mother made shooing motions. "Go ahead."

She stood in the doorway. "Ah, Vedran?"

"Mm-hm?" he asked, already engrossed in mending a split seam in his quiver.

"Which home is mine?"

"Oh, right." He sprang to his feet. "Come with me."

She gave Enuwal a parting wave and trotted after Vedran across the clearing, nodding at a cluster of older men sitting in the shade as they gossiped. Two of the men sat close together, hands casually resting on one another's knees. They'd been partners as long as Malia could remember. They all returned her nod, studying her beneath hooded eyes, their faces lined and dark like the trunks of old pine trees. No doubt some of their gossip entailed her return to Selu. She resisted the urge to stick her tongue out at them and followed Vedran to the southern side of the village.

He stopped beside a wooden ladder. "Up top."

She craned her neck. The home's lines were straight, the door a dark rectangle covered with a light blanket that wavered slightly in the wind. *Home.* She searched her mind for a memory of building it, of making the plans, of mixing the mud and water and feeling it squish in her hands, of setting out the bricks to dry, and slowly piecing it together and whitewashing the walls once it was built, but there was only the fog. She sighed.

She slung her travel sac across her torso, gripped the smooth wooden ladder, and climbed to the ledge. While she waited for Vedran to follow, she looked north, at the rolling hills, mostly wooded, and the Big River snaking through the valley. The valley was so large that she couldn't make out the immense cliffs that lined it. Selu sat toward the valley's center, and so travel to the cliffs took a few days' time, if a traveler took a sedate pace and was loaded down with goods. She'd made it in two days when she'd left Selu, at least according to what she'd been told, and she'd hardly stopped to rest.

A few dragon bones littered the grass near the river. Further east, dozens of dragons' bones marred the rolling plains. So much death. But it could have been worse if the barrier hadn't been erected again. It was worth losing her memories. Not that she didn't want them back all the same.

Two figures circled in the air to the north and west, too large to be birds. Vedran joined her and followed her gaze.

"Ah, some of the men were talking about hunting with the Jeguduns, the way our ancestors used to. I see they're giving it a go."

The Jeguduns used to help the Taakwa find and trap big game animals. With any luck, the smokehouse would be busy all summer, and they'd have plenty of meat to last through the coming winter.

"Where are the other Jeguduns?" she asked.

"Some are helping with the crops." He shrugged. "I'm not sure where the rest went. The children like playing games with them sometimes."

Malia turned to the blanket hanging over the door to her home. Her heart quickened, and her stomach tickled. She pushed the blanket aside, found the hook just inside the door and gathered it there, and stepped in.

The air held a musty, unlived-in smell, although the walls had recently been whitewashed. Shelves lined those walls, holding blankets, clothes, baskets, cooking utensils and a pot and kettle, bowls and mugs, and pottery. She recognized her pottery work in the attention to detail, both in the structure and in the paintings on the pieces. Wood had already been stacked in the hearth, ready to light, and the kindling basket beside it stood full. Two metal Jegudun lanterns stood on the shelves, feather cut-outs in both. A narrow door beside the hearth led into a pantry. Malia went there first.

It was mostly bare, but dried spices filled some of the shelves along with pecans and a basket holding turkey jerky. There was also a basket filled with smoked, salted trout. It was enough to get her going. She'd have to go into the woods to find greens and more herbs, but she was stocked enough that it was no rush. A small covered bowl held some of the powder the Jeguduns used to make their chocolate drink. Malia took a deep breath of the bittersweet powder, and then covered it again. That she would save for special occasions, although she considered her first night back in her home to be special.

"I thought you could use a little something to get you started," Vedran said behind her.

She startled, a hand rising to her chest where her heart skipped along. "I forgot you were here."

One corner of his mouth rose in a grin. "I could go."

"No." She shook her head. "I don't want to be alone, not just yet."

She peeked into baskets in the main room. One held beads, strips of leather, bone needles and thread, scraps of cloth. Another held her spade for digging clay, bits of dried mud sticking to the bottom and sides. Her heart lurched. She'd gone through the process in her mind over and over. She remembered how to make the clay, how to form it, how to dry it, how to paint it, but when it came time to actually *do* it again, she feared her fingers would freeze. She quickly covered that basket with a square cloth and moved to the next. It held paintbrushes, and tiny, empty jars she used to mix and hold paint.

The final basket held the shattered remains of something she'd made. It had been painted and finished, the color a warm cinnamon. An eye gazed calmly at her from one piece, and the hint of a bobbed tail on another clued her in that she'd made something resembling a deer. Enuwal's clan was represented by deer, just as hers was represented by trout.

Something stirred in her mind. She felt as though she held the answer to a question just before her, just out of reach, and if she could only grab it, everything would fall into place and make sense. She picked up a piece of the pottery.

The fog in her mind churned and roiled like storm clouds. Her fingers tingled where she held the shattered piece. The room began to spin, and a throbbing pain sprang up at the base of her skull.

She cried out and dropped the shard, stepping back from it as if it were a scorpion readying to strike. The fog moved forward.

No. It threatened to swallow her mind. Her memories. Malia staggered.

She was dimly aware of Vedran at the door, crying for help while she fell. She fought against the fog, pushing back with all her will. She clutched her head as if she could reach in and hold it back. Her hand slipped, found one of the feathers around her neck.

Help, she thought, not sure who she asked.

The feather grew hot. She almost let go, but the fog started to roll back. She clutched the feather tighter.

The fog retreated. It calmed, eventually giving no hint as to the turmoil it had just released upon her mind. Malia sat back on her heels, breathing heavily, heart pounding. Talons scrabbled on the ledge and wings fluttered, then one of the Jeguduns, feathers the color of cedar, rushed inside and took her hand. Vedran raced in after.

"I'm all right," she gasped. Her head throbbed, but she retained the day's memories. *Thank goodness.*

Her hand still clutched the feather tight. The extraordinary heat had ebbed. She released it slowly, and when the fog remained calm, reached a finger to it again and touched it lightly.

It was Tuvin's feather. She waited for the stored memory to flow over her, the sense of calm and well being, but there was nothing. She might as well have worn a turkey feather. Her heart constricted. Her only tangible memory of Tuvin, the only piece of him left, and she'd rendered it useless.

She hung her head, and her body shook as she held in the sobs.

CHAPTER FIVE

Muvumo sent Kafran away once he'd finished reading the pertinent scroll and carefully rolled it up again. Kafran's father and oldest daughter were showing signs of the illness. They'd both begun to cough blood and had all but stopped eating. Soon their bones would protrude from gaunt flesh, and then death would follow. With Kafran's wife already dead from the illness, he alone was available to care for them.

Muvumo and Delkis sat alone in the cavern, the only sounds that of their breathing and the rustle of the scroll as Delkis read. Lantern light flickered over the writing, making the words dance on the vellum. Shelf after shelf of scrolls loomed over them, and any of them could hold the key to finding the changer. Muvumo wanted to weep at the futility of it all.

"Have you found anything, Most Worthy?"

"Only the same story Kafran shared with us. After our ancestors found the city destroyed, they went looking for this changer and found nothing." He sat back, letting out a frustrated growl. "There's got to be an answer here somewhere. She—he—could be anywhere."

"You need a break. You've been in here for three days. You've hardly slept, hardly eaten. Go home for a little while, have a hot meal, lay with your wife, clear your mind."

"We're losing time."

"I'll stay and keep reading."

Muvumo's body ached. His mind was like mud, and thoughts came slowly when they came at all. Truth was, he wanted more than a bit of sleep snatched here and there in the uncomfortable wooden chairs. He wanted his hand on his wife's soft breast and his head on a pillow. But admitting that would mean admitting that he was simply a man, and prone to weakness like any other man. Perhaps another pinch of kasi powder would help . . . But the healer had warned him of using too much in a single day. Two pinches, three at most. Already today he'd had two, and his heart skittered along like autumn leaves blowing in a strong wind.

Delkis studied him from across the table. The lantern light cast dark shadows along the narrow angles of his face, most prominent beneath his eyes, already dark from lack of sleep. "Most Worthy, what was the last thing you read?"

Muvumo reached for the scroll, but Delkis laid his hand on his before he could grab it. "Without looking, please, Most Worthy." His voice was infuriatingly calm.

Muvumo snatched his hand back. "That proves nothing."

"It proves you are tired. You wanted me to serve as your personal guard because I'm a good fighter, but it's also my job to give advice. Most Worthy, for your sake, and the Maddions', you must rest. Every man must at some point. I will stay here, and when you return, then I will rest."

"Oh, dragons take you and your logic and burn them both." He stood hastily, the chair scraping on stone producing a painful screech. "If you find anything important, you let me know immediately."

Delkis bowed his head. "Of course."

Muvumo strode out of the cavern and into a sky glorious with pink and orange clouds. Stone rose all around him, reflecting light and looking like a pink fruit sliced open. The air was heavy with the smell of pine and fir and still held warmth, although when the sun set, a cold chill would settle in quickly.

The cavern opened to a large, dirt-covered mesa. A few scraggly weeds and strands of grass grew here and there, but the dragons kept it mostly clear. A low stone wall surrounded the mesa.

Delkis's dragon lay curled on one end, her russet colored hide glimmering in the fading sunlight. As she breathed in, her abdomen expanded and glowed, the light fading as she exhaled. Muvumo craned his neck and found several dragons circling the mountain peak. He let out a long, low whistle, punctuated by three short ones at the end.

One of the dragons broke off from the group and swept down. A deep orange, like the color of aspen leaves in autumn, the beast cast a huge shadow. She slowed as she approached the mesa, her wings stirring debris and dirt and tugging at Muvumo's hair and clothes. When she settled, she stood as tall as an elk. She folded her wings along her side and stretched her neck toward him. She smelled of brimstone and charred meat.

He scratched beneath her jaw, in the tender spot where the scales thinned. She leaned into his touch and grumbled happily deep in her throat. Muvumo's own tension faded as the beast relaxed, and the fresh air cleared his mind. Delkis had been right. He needed a break if he was to continue the search for where the changer could be. At a word from him, the dragon kneeled. He climbed onto the saddle on her back, strapped himself in, and squeezed her sides.

"To home," he said.

Her muscles bunched, and she launched herself into the air, plummeting over the mesa's edge. Muvumo's stomach lurched, and despite his fatigue and frustration, a smile illuminated his face. No matter how often he flew, it always made him feel like a boy again.

He soared over the tops of pines, fir, and aspen. The world was a green blur beneath. The dragon circled around, and the rock face the Maddion called home came into view.

At the top was the entrance to the cavern he'd just come from. Hundreds upon hundreds of tiny dark holes dotted the granite mountain face. Stairs and ledges connected one to the other, people moving along them like tiny ants, and several large mesas jutted out, making excellent landing spots for the dragons. The only mesa not connected to any of the stairs was that belonging to the scroll cavern. It was as if the entire mountain had been made for the Maddion and their dragons.

He thought of his people's history, how they had taken the mountain from the Solumna so many generations ago. The Solumna had farmed the eastern mountain, having built wide steps into its side so that the entire thing looked like a staircase for giants. They once had a series of pulleys and large platforms that carried them and their loads up and down, like spiders traversing their webs. The terraces had long since grown over and blended into the mountain and forest once more, save for a small area that the Maddion farmed.

Those Solumna who survived became the Maddions' slaves. They worked the fields and in the homes for two or three generations before they all died off. *A weak people*, Muvumo thought.

Yet now, the Maddion were dying, and the Maddion were far from weak. There was nothing in the scrolls about what killed the Solumna. It could have been this very same illness, or another altogether, or the hard work that killed them.

Was this changer real? Those who left scrolls behind were sometimes subject to exaggeration. But there was an underlying fear in the words describing the desert people's demise. Would this changer be able to help them?

A grim determination settled upon Muvumo. Someone with that much power had to be capable of helping the Maddion. And if he couldn't, then at least Muvumo could convince him to destroy their enemies. This illness might kill off all of his people, but he'd see the Taakwa and Jeguduns destroyed as well.

His dragon settled on one of the mesas. An apprentice hurried out of the nearest cave to remove the saddle and store it. Muvumo patted his mount's head. "Don't stray far. I may need you at any moment."

The dragon snorted, and twin plumes of smoke emerged from her nostrils. Then she was gone, her departure stirring Muvumo's hair.

He strode up the stone stairs past homes, past a young boy lighting torches for the descending night, past the smells of hearth fires and roasting meat and conversations. A few things were missing, though. There used to be laughter, boasts, stories drifting into the air back before the illness began. How long had it been since he'd heard such things? Three seasons, four? Longer? He found it difficult to recall what life had been like before the illness began taking people. It had taken his own mother, and his younger sister, leaving her baby with only a father to care for him. Muvumo's brother-in-law had quickly remarried, and found a nursemaid for the baby, but nursemaids were in high demand.

Babies without mothers struggled more these days than they ever had before, and not all of them made it.

He passed a door where a gray blanket hung over it. From inside came the sounds of great, racking, wet coughs, followed by someone sobbing quietly. Muvumo hesitated. Early in the illness' progression, they had attempted quarantine to keep it from spreading, but it seemed the illness would take whomever it wished, no matter how much care people took. He'd made it a point, once he'd become Most Worthy, to visit all those who were sick and offer comforting words, but for the past few days he'd been tucked away in the scroll caverns. He thought people felt a little better after he'd spoken with them.

Fatigue and hunger urged him down the steps toward home, but duty moved him to the door, caused him to push the gray blanket aside and step in.

The home reeked of blood and heavy sweat, and less so, of urine and feces. A woman lay curled on her side on a blanket before a brisk hearth fire, and despite enough heat to make sweat pop out immediately along Muvumo's forehead, the woman shivered. She clutched a handkerchief in one bony hand, the cloth stained dark. Her hair, what was left of it, was wispy and gray and flowed in all directions from her head like dandelion fluff. She reminded Muvumo of his own mother, and how the illness changed her from a plump, cheerful woman to a leathery bag of bones within days. He'd endured a day of her begging him to end her suffering before the illness finally consumed her. Being a leader was hard, but sometimes being a son was harder.

Her glazed eyes found him, and she made a funny sound deep in her throat. Her husband, a tiny man curled into himself, looked at her, then followed her gaze. His eyes were red-rimmed, and he, too, held a handkerchief, although Muvumo suspected tears stained it rather than blood. If Muvumo had found a younger man crying over his dying wife, he would've cuffed him for showing such weakness, but old men tended toward sentimentality.

The man uncurled himself, got on his knees, and pressed his forehead to the ground. "Most Worthy," he said, his voice cracking.

"Rise," he said. When the woman struggled, he held a hand toward her. "Not you."

The man stood on shaky legs, his back stooped. "Can I get you something to drink or eat, Most Worthy?"

Muvumo glanced around the small space. Dishes encrusted with dried food sat in one corner, a pile of clothes sat in another, and a fly buzzed around the pisspot. "No, thank you."

The man bobbed his head. "Any news on a cure for the illness, Most Worthy?"

The woman's eyes rolled up, watching him, a tiny flare of hope lighting them. His shoulders stooped. "Not yet. I am searching diligently, though."

The light flickered out of her eyes, and she coughed, her entire body shaking.

Muvumo wanted to flee the home. He'd seen enough death and suffering for a while, and yet he compounded it all the time. Instead, he forced himself to remain still, to look the old man in the eyes as he said, "I'll see that you're brought food and drink. Is there anything else you need?"

"No, Most Worthy," he said.

Muvumo's jaw clenched. "Good evening." He stepped out into the night, letting it cool his forehead, letting it clear his nostrils of the smell of sickness and death. He took in great lungfuls of air. He nearly climbed the stairs and returned to his dragon, and the scroll cavern, but Delkis had been right. He needed a break to clear his head. He continued down the stairs.

He came to a door where a pristine white blanket hung over the entrance. A torch already burned and hissed outside. He pushed aside the blanket and entered a space that smelled of pine and *sprinko*, goat meat rubbed with spices and slow-roasted all day.

Tapestries covered the stone walls, depicting dragons in flight, the mountains, and a hunt in which several men moved in for the final killing blow of a bison already bleeding from several arrow wounds. Muvumo's crossbow and long axe hung over the hearth. A plush rug in geometric red and black patterns covered most of the floor, and a low table sat upon it, pillows piled around. A circle of pine branches hung beside the door, the source of the first smell Muvumo had noticed.

The servant Ankti tended the hearth. When she heard the blanket rustle, she straightened and whirled, and spotting Muvumo, bowed low. She wore a plain shift and a head scarf that draped over one shoulder, hiding most of her dark curls. She was one of the dark-skinned eastern people. She kept her gaze on the floor in front of her feet, hands clasped before her.

"Most Worthy," she said. Her voice was quiet, her accent hardly noticeable.

"Where is my wife?"

"Resting. Shall I let her know you're here?"

"No." He took a step forward. "Has she eaten yet?"

"I was just preparing a plate for her. Shall I prepare two?"

"What a stupid question."

She flinched as if he'd struck her. "I shall do so, then, Most Worthy. Of course you must be hungry."

The woman turned to the hearth again. Muvumo walked past her and through another door.

A down-filled mattress took up most of the space, covered by blankets the same shade as spring grass. More tapestries covered the walls, these chosen by his wife. *Wife.* He still rolled the word around on his tongue, savoring it like he savored a fine wine. He'd taken Chanwa as his bride shortly after he'd taken the title of Most

Worthy. A man in charge needed a wife and children to strengthen his position among his people.

These tapestries showed the forest, a waterfall, and dragon hatchlings. The pictures were soft and delicate, like Chanwa. She sprawled on the mattress, wearing a dress the same blue as a quail's egg. Her hair, light as flax, flowed around her face. Her features were as delicate as if somebody had formed them lovingly from clay, working on them until they were balanced.

"Ankti, is it time for dinner?" she mumbled, her eyes closed. When they were open, they revealed eyes the color of an early morning winter sky.

Muvumo kneeled beside her, leaned over, and kissed her cheek. Her skin was soft and smelled of lavender.

A smile tugged at her lips. "Ankti, you've taken to announcing dinner differently. And is that a beard you're growing out?"

Fatigue slipped away as Muvumo joined his wife, cupping his body against hers. He let out a sigh. He'd been apart from her for too long. He grew hard and pressed his arousal against her.

"My, you *have* changed quite a bit, Ankti," she murmured. "You almost feel like my husband, except he's been gone such a long time that I'm not sure I remember him."

He could not wait any longer. He removed his belt, which held the dagger and short axe, and set it on one of the trunks. Muvumo rolled her over and raised the fabric above her waist, pulling down her undergarments to expose her thighs and the mound of hair growing at their junction. He fumbled with his pants, ripped them off, and pressed himself between those glorious legs and into the warmth of Chanwa's body.

She opened her eyes at last, tilting her head back, and groaning. Muvumo crushed her lips with his, tasting honey and mint. He moaned. It had been so long.

"Slow down," she gasped as he pulled away.

Shudders racked his body as he spilled his seed into her. He rolled off, his tunic clinging to the sweat along his back, and sprawled one arm to the side while the other pulled Chanwa close. He let out a shuddering breath.

Delkis was right; this was what he needed. Already his mind felt lighter. After a good meal and some sleep, he'd be ready to tackle the scrolls again.

"Hello, dearest," he said.

Chanwa turned to him. For a moment, something harsh smoldered in her eyes, replaced so quickly by a smile that Muvumo wasn't sure he had actually spotted anything amiss.

"Are you feeling well?" he asked, brushing her hair behind her ear.

Her smile deepened. "Yes. You?" It had become a question loaded with fear and anticipation among the Maddion.

"Simply tired."

"You've been in the scroll cavern for days. Have you found anything helpful?"

"Perhaps."

She propped herself on one elbow. "What have you found?"

He hesitated. "I'm not sure yet. It could be nothing." He shared almost everything with Chanwa, a habit not practiced by most Maddion men, and yet something held him back.

"That's vague," she said, her lips thinning.

"Frustratingly so, yes."

"Most Worthy," Ankti said from the door. "Dinner is ready."

He pulled on his pants and went into the next room. Two plates of *sprinko* and baked bread sat on the table, along with two bowls of some steaming concoction and two mugs. A closer inspection revealed root vegetables in a thick broth in the bowls, and wine in the mugs.

Ankti kneeled on the stone floor beside the hearth, head bowed and hands clasped before her. Some Maddion dismissed their servants during meals, but Muvumo preferred to have Ankti waiting.

He tore off a hunk of bread and dabbed it in the soup. It was creamy, and spiced just right, with plenty of salt. Chanwa entered a moment later and sank gracefully to her seat. She started with a sip from the bowl.

"Will you be staying the night?" she asked.

"Yes. I've hardly gotten any sleep. I'll be returning before dawn, though. There are still many more scrolls to go over."

Her shoulders rolled down ever so slightly. Was she relieved that he'd be leaving in the morning? Why would she? Chanwa was his wife, and as such, lived to serve him.

"Is there anything I can do to help?" she asked.

He must be imagining things. He'd been gone too long from his wife. He truly needed to be around more often, especially if he was going to get her with child. Then, when she got too big, he could satisfy himself with others. Like Ankti. He could find some uses for that full mouth of hers.

He chuckled. "If only you could read, you'd be a help."

She flinched. "Yes, it's too bad that women are incapable of learning letters."

Muvumo's eyes narrowed. Her tone was genuine enough, but was that the slightest hint of sarcasm beneath? "What have you been doing to fill your days while I'm gone, dearest?"

"I have been visiting my sisters and their children, and I've been working on a new dress. Would you like to see it?" Eagerness infused her voice.

Four large wooden chests sat in their bedroom. Only half of one belonged to Muvumo. The rest belonged to Chanwa. She delighted in clothes, and he swore she could wear a different dress every day for an entire season and never repeat it.

"No, dearest," he said.

She chattered on about her sisters and her nieces and nephews and their neighbors. Her voice was like the winter wind, howling in the background, easily ignored. He could think of other uses for her mouth as well.

He retreated to the bedroom after dinner. An oil lantern flickered in one corner, leaving hardly any light, but he carefully laid out a scroll and dipped his pen into ink. He'd begun his own history and had gotten a mere few lines into it before he'd gone to the cavern to search for an answer to the illness. Chanwa, meanwhile, went to deliver the gift of a pine wreath to their recently-married neighbors. Ankti moved around the other room, dishes and pots clanking as she cleaned up.

Muvumo's pen scratched against the paper. The next room grew silent, and dimmer, and then Ankti appeared in the doorway, her body a shadow against the soft light of the next room. He silently traced the outline of her body against the light, lingering on each curve, and a shudder of desire passed through him.

"If you do not need anything else, Most Worthy, then I will retire to my quarters for the night."

"Is Chanwa back yet?"

"No, Most Worthy."

He considered having her come into the room. She would sit next to him, her body close enough that he could feel its heat through his clothes. She would do anything he told her to do. The possibilities ran through his mind, and his grip tightened on the quill. He caught one of the tapestries out of the corner of his eye. The dragon hatchlings. If he was going to spend his seed anywhere, it would be within his wife. He sighed. "Bring some food and wine to the home up the stairs with the gray blanket. The old woman is sick. Do you know which home?"

She nodded. "Yes, Most Worthy."

"Well, get going, then."

Ankti fled, the blanket rustling in the other room as she left.

He wrote a few more lines, and then the blanket rustled again, followed by Chanwa's light footsteps. The light went out in the main room, and she entered the bedroom.

"I thought you came home to get some rest," she said. "But here you are, working."

"I was waiting for you."

She smiled and arched an eyebrow. "I'm afraid I don't have anything restful in mind."

He carefully scattered sand over the paper, set it aside, and capped the ink. "On the contrary, I think I'll sleep very well afterwards."

She moved to the lantern.

"No," he said. "I want to see you."

She slipped off her dress and laid it carefully over a trunk. Then she stepped out of the undergarments, leaving them to puddle on the floor.

Muvumo's breath hitched. Chanwa was beautiful. He discarded his clothes with less care, the warm air caressing his bare skin, and crossed the room in two strides. He pulled his wife into his arms, pressed his lips against hers, tasting the spices from their dinner. His lips moved down her neck, to her breast. She gasped as he took a nipple into his mouth. He explored her body with his mouth and his hands, biting, squeezing, eliciting more gasps and little moans. Then he pushed her onto her hands and knees and settled behind her.

He entered her and began rocking his hips. He grabbed a handful of her hair and yanked her head back.

“Muvumo,” she cried out.

He shuddered as he spent himself. Then he collapsed onto the blankets, breathing heavily, sated. Chanwa curled up beside him, her sweaty body pressed to his, and lay one arm across his chest. She let out a sigh, and in his drowsy state, Muvumo could have sworn it was filled with disappointment. Before he could ask her if all was well, sleep tugged him under, and he knew nothing.

It felt as though he’d hardly closed his eyes when large hands were shaking his shoulders.

“Most Worthy, wake up,” Delkis said.

Beside him, Chanwa murmured, then pulled a blanket over her head.

“What is it?” Muvumo sputtered as he sat up. The lantern had nearly died, leaving hardly any light, but it was enough to make out Delkis’s furrowed brows.

“I’ve found something,” Delkis said. “I think I know where to find the changer.”

CHAPTER SIX

Malia sat on a blanket spread along the ledge in front of her home. With her legs crossed before her, she leaned forward, slowly working a new clay coil onto the bowl she intended for Ayeelah. The morning sun was warm on her skin, and she could still smell and taste the roasted pecans she'd made that morning to go with her sweet bread.

Every so often, she'd pause her work and scan the northern skies. Only a few days had passed, but Tulah should have word already to explain what was going on with Malia's memories, shouldn't she? Malia hadn't had another episode of . . . whatever that was, but she still didn't know what triggered them in the first place, and every time she tried to make sense of it, her thoughts would swirl, and the fog would start to writhe as if it didn't *want* her to figure it out, and she would do her best to put it out of her mind.

She shook her head. The fog wasn't intelligent. It just *was.* So what was it doing? Why did it eat up her memories?

With the last coil in place, she started smoothing the sides. The wet clay beneath her fingers, rolling the coils, preparing the tiny brushes to paint designs on the finished product, all of that was as familiar to her as breathing, but something was off. She knew what to do, yet the other things she'd attempted to make had come out wrong. Off balance, cracked, too thin in some places and too thick in others. She didn't know if it had anything to do with the fog in her mind, or if it stemmed from something else altogether. True, she'd lost some of her memories of making pottery along with the rest, but she still had plenty of experience behind her, and she'd more than mastered the basics before the time encompassing her lost memory.

She sat back, studied the vase, and sighed. It looked right, for now anyways. The bowl flared nicely and had plenty of room for the columbine flowers and warblers she'd paint on later. First, though, it had to dry almost all the way, and then she'd add the base, and let it dry again.

She brought it inside and set it in one corner carefully to dry, then brought in the blanket and her tools and put everything away. She stood, hands propped on her hips, and considered what to tackle next.

Her broom leaned against the shelves, a small pile of dirt beside it. The floor in front of the hearth had been swept clean, but debris remained near the door. She narrowed her eyes. She didn't recall grabbing the broom that morning. Had she started sweeping last night, before she fell asleep? No, she didn't recall that either, and besides, she'd always swept right after breakfast, so why couldn't she remember that when she could recall everything else?

The ladder creaked, announcing a visitor. Her heart quickened. She snatched the broom and quickly swept the tiny pile of dirt into the corner, then stood the broom so that the bristles hid it. Only then did she notice the basket filled with pecans sitting beside the hearth. Some had been shelled, but the rest remained undone. She hurried into the pantry with it and laid a small cloth over it. Chores left half done, and she couldn't recall starting either of them. She couldn't let anybody know, not when she was trying to return to a normal life. What if her mother found out and insisted she return to living with her? She shuddered at the idea.

Enuwal's head appeared over the ledge. He climbed up easily and stood just outside her door. "I thought I'd go for a walk in the western woods. I haven't explored the herbs growing there yet. Would you like to come with me?"

Malia hastily joined him on the ledge, wondering if she'd left any signs of other abandoned tasks behind her. She scanned the sky again. Her heart hitched when she spotted a distant figure in the sky, but then it tucked its wings and dove. It was only an eagle.

"What if Tulah comes back while I'm gone?"

"You've hardly left your home for days. You would do well to enjoy some of the air and sunshine."

She cocked her head to one side. "Are you speaking as a healer, or as a friend?"

"Both," he smiled. "But mostly my intentions are selfish. I've hardly spent any time with you." His hand slipped into hers.

She flinched, and he pulled back, his smile disappearing. "What's wrong?"

"I don't know. I just . . . I have no idea what caused me to lose more memories that first night home, and it's making me jumpy." She slid her hand back into his and squeezed. "It has nothing to do with you." She pushed aside the guilt that flooded her at hiding the recent little slips.

His warm, brown eyes flicked back and forth as he studied her face, and the skin around them tightened, deepening the lines there. "Very well, then."

She squeezed his hand again before letting go. She longed to go up on her tiptoes and kiss him, breathe in his familiar scent and taste the comfort of his lips, but she couldn't, not with people wandering the village. It might seem as if nobody was paying them any attention, but those old men sitting in the shade at the eastern end, mending bows and making arrows and daggers still had eyes keen as an eagle's, and she still wore mourning beads.

With a sigh, she reluctantly pulled her hand free and went inside for her travel sac. She slung it across her torso before climbing down the ladder. She walked out of the village and toward the western woods, Enuwal just behind her. Swollen gray clouds rolled in from the west, promising rain by the afternoon, just in time to cool off the day. Malia tucked a loose strand of hair behind her ear.

"You've been working on your pottery," Enuwal said. "I'm glad to see that."

"I almost didn't start up again. After I touched the broken piece . . ." She let the rest of it drift away. Enuwal had come running into her home moments after Vedran had called for help. Once she'd finally calmed enough that her voice didn't tremble, she'd told him what had happened.

"How is your hand?"

She held it up. The faint outline of Tuvin's feather stood pink and red against her tan palm. "It stings from time to time, but otherwise it's fine." She still wore Tuvin's feather around her neck, but it held no memories. No life. Tuvin's body had been destroyed, and this feather had been all any of them had to remember him by. He hadn't had a chance to pass his memories on to any other Jeguduns. He was gone, almost as completely as if he'd never existed in the first place.

"Clan mother be praised that Tuvin passed that feather on to you. He saved you in many ways."

She nodded, unable to speak beyond the lump in her throat. "I just . . . I wish I could have passed it on to his family. I should have done that, instead of holding onto it."

They were just inside the woods, the village visible in bits and pieces beyond the pine trees. Enuwal grasped her hand and turned her around. His brows were drawn down, lines creased between them.

"You have nothing to feel guilty about," he said. "Have you ever considered that maybe Tuvin knew you'd need that power someday?"

She reeled. "He couldn't have known."

"There's still much that we don't know about our Jegudun friends."

"Tuvin didn't have the key to the future."

"But perhaps he knew enough about the past to suspect what was coming." He took a step closer. "What I'm saying is, Tulah will find somebody who knows what we can do to stop this from happening again. So don't worry."

"I can't help it."

He smiled. "I know."

She returned the smile. "Now, I might not remember what I was doing this time last year, but I recall plenty of places around these woods that you might have interest in."

Enuwal stepped back and gestured grandly, his tunic flowing as he did so. "After you."

She led them deeper into the woods, up a slope, across a dry ravine lined with juniper brush, and splashing across a spring. The scents of pine and sage filled the air. Malia paused in the shade of a particularly large pine, its trunk dark orange with age, while Enuwal picked sage and inspected the flowers growing around the edge of a small meadow. A warbler sang nearby, and the branches overhead rustled as a squirrel dashed across.

Malia leaned against the pine and closed her eyes, taking a deep breath. Enuwal was right; she needed to get away from the village more often. Perhaps she'd been pushing herself too hard, and that had led to her forgetting a couple of menial chores. Sweeping the floors and peeling pecans were automatic tasks, and it was easy to forget doing them. Her body was sun-warmed and relaxed, and she started to hum an old lullaby she hadn't thought of in years. Her mother had never sung it to her. Rather, her father and her grandmother used to sing it, some song from her father's village, something about the stars dancing.

Enuwal's soft footsteps approached. She kept her eyes closed, picturing him walking across the meadow, his dimpled grin, his hands clutching sage and whatever else he'd decided to pick. His hands were large, firm, but gentle . . . the perfect hands to hold her, to trace every line of her body. She shivered.

He stopped. He stood close enough that she could smell his light sweat and herbs. He always smelled of herbs, and himself. It was one of her favorite scents.

His lips came down on hers, soft at first. His warm breath tickled her face. Her heart responded immediately, hammering against her breastbone, and the blood roared in her ears.

She put her hands on his shoulders and pulled him closer until his body pressed against hers. She deepened the kiss, parting his lips with her tongue. He moaned, and the sound drove Malia to kiss him hungrily. By herself, she was broken, and pieces were missing, but with him, she was whole. She hadn't felt whole in such a long time, and it was so very nice . . .

He pulled away, gasping for breath. "Oh," was all he managed to say. His body trembled beneath Malia's hands.

"Oh," she echoed. She had a difficult time speaking around the emotions lumped in her throat.

"I don't suppose there's any way for your mother to waive the remainder of your mourning period?" he asked.

She laughed shakily. "I don't know. I'll ask, though. It'll be the first thing I do when we get back, and then—" She broke off. She couldn't remember what else she'd been working on. She struggled to find the lost thread and came up against nothing. A blank.

"And then?" Enuwal prompted.

She shook her head. *No, not again.* "Nothing." She stepped out of his arms. "Have you found everything you need here?"

He blinked, straightened. "Yes."

"Good." She started down the slope, toward the village.

"What's wrong, Malia?" Enuwal called out behind her.

She stopped. "I don't know." Her hands gripped the worn leather strap across her torso and squeezed. "I feel like I'm losing my mind," she said quietly.

He stepped up beside her. "What?"

"I feel like I'm losing my mind," she said again.

"What do you mean?"

"The pottery . . . it's all wrong." She winced. That sounded foolish, but she couldn't tell him the truth, that she had these holes in her memory. Then she recalled; she'd been working on a bowl for Ayeelah. She shook her head, relief washing over her. "Never mind me."

"You've been under a lot of strain lately. It's taking a toll."

"Or it's part of this backlash."

"You're not losing your mind. Plenty of people have felt the same way recently, even myself. We're all distracted. We're still recovering from the war."

"I hope you're right and that's all it is."

"Would you like to go home?"

The sun was rising higher. Soon it would be too hot to do much of anything outside. The bowl wouldn't be dry enough yet to add the base. And, she enjoyed being alone with Enuwal. The kiss had been nice. More than nice, really. She'd like another one, although if they shared another like the last, she wasn't sure even the weight of her mourning beads would keep her from going further.

She shifted the travel sac. "Not just yet."

He smiled. "Where to now?"

She considered their options. If they continued on, they'd find themselves in relatively new aspen. She wasn't sure that anything grew there that Enuwal might find interesting. If they angled north and west a bit, they'd come close to the springs. She'd only been there as a child, at least as far as she remembered. They were rumored to be haunted by Jeguduns. Carvings of the creatures covered many of the larger trees. When she was a child, she'd been dared to dip her foot in the spring, and she'd sworn she spotted a monster. Her screams had sent all the children running for the village.

She wondered, now, what purpose the place served. Had anybody been out there since the war? It had grown more forgotten over the years, which seemed appropriate to her current circumstances.

"I know a place," she said, and led the way.

She soon found the stream that led to the spring. It trickled pleasantly over pebbles and a sandy bottom, tiny silver fish darting in its currents. Rosemary grew near it, along with white yarrow. Enuwal murmured something excitedly when he spotted it and began cutting off pieces and tucking them gently into his travel sac.

A faint trail followed the stream. The slope to Malia's left rose steeply, dotted with immense boulders half the size of a dragon. Some clung precipitously; one of these days, a good, soaking rain would cause them to slide down the hill. The thought reminded her of the billowing clouds approaching.

"We should get going," she said.

Enuwal straightened. "Where does this trail go?" he asked, squinting along its depths.

"There are hot springs further down. But it's—" She bit off the rest.

"But it's?" he prompted.

"It'll sound foolish. It's supposed to be haunted by Jeguduns." She chuckled. "I had a scare as a child there, but most likely I just scared myself."

"Does anybody use the springs?"

She shook her head. "Nobody goes near the place, except for daring children."

"Would you mind if we went? I'm curious."

"I am, too," she admitted, and yet a heavy dread crept into the pit of her stomach. Was it the old fears rearing their heads, or something else? The fog in her head was calm for the moment, so perhaps it was simply childhood memories getting the best of her. She shrugged. "Why not?" If the fog acted up, they'd leave. And she couldn't let fear take over, otherwise she'd never set foot out of her home again.

She led the way down the trail. The air was starting to truly warm up, and a light sweat made her tunic cling to her back. Every so often a bird twittered in the distance, but most of the animals were winding down for the hottest part of the day.

She smelled the springs before they came into view. She crinkled her nose at the scent, like rotten eggs. After a few breaths, she acclimated, and it wasn't so bad. She came around one last bend, and the springs stood before her.

One of the nearest pine trees, a massive old thing, held the carving of a Jegudun in flight. The Jegudun was looking up, wings spread behind it. The picture covered much of the lower part of the tree, some areas worn by weather and time, but discernible.

Enuwal laid a hand on it, lips parted, eyes wide and taking it in. He walked around the tree once, slowly. "Amazing," he breathed. "It reminds me of the Jegudun cave with the paintings."

Although the Jeguduns passed their memories from one generation to the next, they also enjoyed painting those scenes most important to them. They had covered the better part of a massive cavern near the falls where the Big River entered the valley. It was partly how Malia had learned of the war, her role in it, and the history between the Taakwa and the Jeguduns.

"These are made by Taakwa," Malia said. "The carving is more like our paintings than the Jegudun paintings. Theirs are far more realistic. This is good, but not as good as theirs." She laid a hand on the carving, wondering who made it, and why. What was special about this place?

Enuwal went to the next tree, and the next. The trees surrounded a clearing, the spring in its center. Grass grew knee high all around, and a few sunflowers were just beginning to bloom. Enuwal went to the spring next, his passage causing cicadas to fly off in all directions, and he kneeled beside it. The spring had no apparent source, nor did it feed the stream that they'd followed.

"I wonder if there are other places like this around the valley," Enuwal said.

"To my knowledge, no, but then again, we hardly talk about this spring among ourselves. We're not likely to share the information with others."

He reached down and brushed away some grass and dirt near the spring's edge. "Malia, look at this," he said excitedly.

She took a few steps toward him. A stone lip came into view, carvings in each one. The one Enuwal had cleared bore the carving of a leaping fish, Malia's clan symbol.

The air in the clearing shimmered. The fog in her mind rolled forward like storm clouds. She cried out and staggered back.

Enuwal stood, his brow furrowed. "Malia?" His voice came from far away, echoed in her head. He reached a hand toward her.

The fog rolled over her. For a moment, she looked at two different days in the clearing. One was today, with Enuwal. In the other day, a gray Jegudun bled on the ground, and a furious man (*Dalibor, that must be Dalibor, he has the same hooked nose as Andrij*) stood over the Jegudun, a blood-covered dagger in his hand.

"Stop!" she yelled.

Then the fog consumed her with a roar, and her head felt as though it would split in two.

She felt as though she stood in the middle of a storm, winds raging and howling around her and inside her head, lightning splitting her skull, thunder rumbling deep in her chest. She couldn't breathe. She reached out a hand, trying to find something to hold onto in the storm.

She found another hand. Dry skin, larger than hers, firm. She grasped it, focused on it. Slowly, the storm ebbed, the wind died, the thunder faded. Her head throbbed, but she could focus.

She stood in a clearing, the sharp odor of rotten eggs in the air, a tall, lanky man standing before her, lines creasing his forehead, his brown eyes searching her face. It was his hand she held.

"Malia, are you all right?" he asked.

"I . . . who are you?"

CHAPTER SEVEN

Muvumo was gone, along with the Peerless, far from the mountains on their search for the changer. He'd hardly spoken a word to Chanwa before he left. He had, in fact, left with only the most perfunctory of kisses, his attention elsewhere. She didn't mind at all. When he was gone, she could be a little more herself.

Her thoughts, at least, were her own, and not his, although if he could figure out a way to invade them, she was sure he wouldn't hesitate. She breathed easier when he wasn't around, but she could never fully relax. That is, until she visited the waterfall.

The first morning he was gone, she told Ankti with a few gestures. *The waterfall. Later.* Ankti nodded and went about her chores while Chanwa left to visit her neighbor, a newly married woman whose husband was out training with his dragon. The usual pleasantries were exchanged. The neighbor was adjusting well to her new life. Yes, it was a shame the men were gone so long. So devoted, you know. The good of the Maddion came before the good of the individual, and that meant dedication to hunting and fighting skills. Yes, the Most Worthy was following a lead on the possibility of a cure for the disease. Yes, she was sure something would be found before the new wife took with child. Chanwa smiled and patted the young woman's hand, amazed her neighbor couldn't hear the hollow platitudes in her voice or notice how Chanwa's smile didn't touch her eyes. But the new wife believed herself in love, and she was dedicated to fulfilling her duties. That is, until her husband raised a hand against her, or came home smelling like one of the unmentionables, or blamed her for bearing him a daughter, slowly chipping away at that love until only crumbs remained.

Chanwa took advantage of their time alone to leak some of the code phrases her mother had taught her into the conversation. The young bride looked amused, and slightly confused, but answered the questions in a straightforward manner. Her family had lost the thread, then. Perhaps her mother had never learned, or one of the only knowledgeable women in the family had died before passing on the skills. Chanwa quickly turned the conversation in another direction, and pushed her secret far, far down and didn't think about it at all. Any hint, any clue, and she'd be dragon fodder by morning. So she smiled until her face hurt and her heart ached, then gave her good-byes.

After lunch, she and Ankti made the trek to the lowest mesa. From there, they took a short, obscure trail to where a stream made a short jump off the rocks, creating a narrow waterfall in front of a shallow cave. There was no way off the mountain from there unless they sprouted wings or turned into fish, and so there were no guards. That combined with the waterfall's noise gave them the protection they needed to speak freely.

"Are you well?" Chanwa asked Ankti once they were behind the falls. She perched on a rocky outcropping, her legs tucked neatly beneath her billowing skirt and her ankles crossed.

"Well enough," Ankti sighed, her voice moderately accented. She'd been with the Maddion for quite a few seasons and knew the language well, along with the trade language spoken by many of the people in the greater world.

Most of Chanwa's friendships were superficial. So many women had lost the secret threads of knowledge. Those who replied to the coded phrases had done so cautiously, and none had encouraged friendship with Chanwa. "These times are especially difficult for us," they'd say. So Chanwa had kept to herself.

Until Ankti.

Ankti had been alone at home while the others attended a funeral rite. Chanwa, feeling ill, had begged off staying and gone home early. She'd found Ankti huddled in a corner as one of the guards, left behind to watch the mesas, tried to force himself on her. A few tart words about negligent duty had the guard apologizing profusely to *her*, not Ankti, and dashing back to his post.

Ankti had been shaking from the encounter. Chanwa sent her to lie down while she tended the hearth and the meal. By the time the others returned, Ankti was back at her duties, with only a slight, occasional tremble in her hands to give her away, and Chanwa was resting, the coiled knots in her stomach more a result of the guard's actions and less from her original illness. If she hadn't shown up when she had . . .

Now, Chanwa reached a hand to Ankti and pulled the other woman down to sit beside her. "Rest while you can," she said.

"Are *you* well?" Ankti asked with a pointed glance at Chanwa's belly.

"I'm drinking the tea. There's no way I'll chance having a baby while this illness is killing the Maddion."

Ankti nodded. "Our supply is good even though many women are using the tea. They feel the same as you."

Chanwa pulled her hand free and fiddled with a loose thread on her skirt. Ankti knew so much more about the world than she did. When she was younger, her dreams of knowing more had been slowly beaten out of her by her father, not by his hands, but by his words. "I don't know why you ask so many questions," he'd say. "It's not like you'll ever need to know much other than how to look presentable and how to listen to your husband." She'd never even seen anything beyond the mountain itself. Oh, she knew the mountains were surrounded by wide open, grass-covered plains, and that herds of elk and bison roamed them, and the world stretched out in every direction, but she had never experienced it for herself.

With a sigh, she drew back to the moment and to the question foremost in her mind. "Have you ever heard of a person capable of changing their shape or appearance? I don't mean wearing a disguise, but using magic to transform completely?"

Ankti sucked in a sharp breath. "There are always whispers of such a being. My father used to tell us—" She bit off the rest. "Well, there are tales."

Ankti hardly spoke of her old life. Too painful, Chanwa imagined. "What do the tales say? What is this being like?"

"Powerful. Long-lived, maybe even immortal. Some of the smaller tribes speak of such a being as a god or goddess. None have actually seen this being in recent times, and so the stories remain just that . . . stories."

Chanwa's shoulders would have slumped, if she ever made such a gesture. "So this search for a changer is as futile as the attempt to enter the Taakwa's valley last summer."

"If such a being exists, they will remain hidden if they choose, and they will be found if that's what suits their purpose."

Chanwa gave a most unladylike snort. "That's a helpful answer."

A smile played about Ankti's mouth. "Do you think such a being would answer to your husband and his men, even if they arrive on dragons?"

"You have a point." She left the thread alone and folded her hands on her lap. "What do we do if they don't find the changer? This illness is killing us all."

"Not all of us."

Chanwa flinched. "No, not you. Not the other slaves, or the unmentionables who come from elsewhere. Only those with Maddion blood are susceptible. So all you have to do is outlive us, and you'll be free."

"Don't misunderstand. I do not waste tears for the Maddion." Her voice softened. "Save one. I would not want to see you hurt, much less die."

"You would cry for me?" Her voice teased, but Chanwa's heart quickened. For a short while, Muvumo had pulled at her heart the same way, but he'd never been tender. He'd never raised a hand to her either, but she'd always felt held at arm's length, her presence wanted only when he sought her to fulfill her physical duties to him or when he needed someone to speak with. But Ankti . . . sometimes Chanwa dreamed of her and wondered how it would feel to hold her close, to feel the other woman's warm breath caress her cheeks as they drew nearer. She ducked her head, warmth spreading through her, and she feared a blush tinged her cheeks.

Ankti laid her hand over Chanwa's. Calluses marred her palms. She squeezed once, her hand lingering a moment, then drew it away.

Chanwa sighed. She hardened her heart a little more every day to protect herself against the deaths, and Muvumo, and what she couldn't have. Things weren't always such for Maddion women. Before the dragons, the Maddion fought little and traded often. Those Maddion lived on the grasslands, near the river, a three days' walk from the foothills, and the Solumna lived on the mountain. There had been more freedom for Maddion women.

But then the dragons came, and several men tamed the beasts, bending them to their will. Then the Maddion raided surrounding people, including the Solumna, and eventually claimed the mountains as their own, living above all others as they believed was their right, and the Solumna and others became their slaves, and their own women became a means to an end.

"What if this changer exists?" Chanwa said. "Would this being help us? *Could* they?"

"If they existed, and if the Most Worthy could find them, then there is a good chance the changer could help. But if they are as powerful as the stories say, they could just as easily make the illness more potent as put an end to it."

"And if the changer doesn't exist, or if they decide not to help, then the Maddion die." Chanwa let her thoughts take her where they willed, with only the gentle roar of the waterfalls intruding, along with Ankti's easy presence. "So . . . who else might be able to cure this illness?"

"The Jeguduns and the Taakwa have magic."

"They also hate the Maddion. They'd never welcome us."

"Hmm. Perhaps they'd be willing to help in exchange for information."

"Such as?"

Ankti cast her a sidelong glance. "Such as the layout of the mountains, or the Maddions' numbers, particularly those men of fighting age."

Her words coiled like a serpent through Chanwa. "You're talking about betraying my own people."

"Not all of them. Only those guilty of killing and enslaving and raping whomever they please. I am certain the Taakwa and Jeguduns would spare women and children."

Chanwa shook her head. "Why would they spare any of us?"

"You grew up surrounded by cruelty. Not everybody lives according to such a code. Did you know that women rule the Taakwa? And own property?"

"What?" There was so little she knew about her people's enemy. If their women ruled, then they must be vastly different from the Maddion. "Let's say they *would* take us in." *Us*. A little thrill passed through Chanwa. By *us*, she meant her and Ankti, not the Maddion in general, although she wanted to see her people survive. "I could live near them, hidden. And you could live among them. Their barrier would only keep me out."

"The valley is a large place. You could find somewhere just outside it. Or, perhaps they could find some solution to allow only you through the barrier."

Chanwa nodded. She imagined passing on information to the Taakwa, and in return, living safely among them with Ankti. It lifted her heart like nothing had recently. Another thought came to her. "There's no way down from the mountain save by dragon, unless one were to spontaneously turn into a goat."

"Then we take a dragon."

"I hate dragons," Chanwa breathed. They stank of fire and brimstone and carrion. Their mouths were lined with sharp teeth, and because they preferred only their handlers, they went on guard whenever somebody less well-known neared them, which included the women, the children, and the servants. Chanwa recalled an enthusiastic child approaching a dragon many seasons ago, and the dragon reacting by letting loose a stream of flame. The screams had etched into her memory, not only of the dying child, but of the child's mother. She shuddered.

"We all do what we must in order to survive," Ankti said. "I hate the beasts as well. They burned my family and my home, and they carried me here as chattel."

As hardened as Chanwa's heart had become, how much worse must it be for Ankti? If she could stand the thought of taking a dragon down the mountain, then Chanwa could, too. She brushed her hand against the other woman's and nodded. "Then if it comes to it, we'll leave by dragon. You and I. Together." She waited, her heart pounding, for Ankti's answer.

Ankti returned the nod. "Together."

CHAPTER EIGHT

The man standing in front of Malia was tall, but not imposing. He stood closer than was polite and, in fact, was holding her hands, but though she wasn't sure who he was (*no, she knew him somehow, she just couldn't pluck his name from the blasted fog in her mind*), somehow she didn't mind his proximity or his touch. He studied her with widened eyes, as though surprised. His eyes were brown, and gentle, as were his hands, but he looked momentarily . . . upset? Terrified? Confused? Malia admitted to confusion herself.

Her head was fuzzy, throbbing, spinning. She moved to a nearby tree and leaned against it, the bark rough under her palm, the scent of pine sap and rotten eggs sharp in her nostrils. Her legs trembled. She let herself down to the ground. Her stomach heaved. She leaned over and retched, but she hadn't had anything for breakfast. Or had she? She struggled to remember, but the fog in her head covered so much.

Push, said a voice. *Her* voice. *Push against the fog.*

That was impossible, wasn't it? The fog was insubstantial, and besides, it was in her head. How could she push it?

But she tried. She sensed that if she didn't, her head would spin faster and faster, and she'd fall into nothingness. She'd become nothing. That sent an arrow of fear through her. She pushed against the fog, fought for her memories, for her sense of self, for this man's name, and how she knew him.

Power surged from deep inside her, from the same place where she drew power for the Jeguduns, from the place where she determined whether a piece of pottery worked or not, from the place where *Malia* stemmed from. It was the deepest part of her, where the roots of her very being grew. She shuddered as she pushed against the fog. It rolled back slowly, reluctantly. She pushed harder, her entire body shaking, sweat breaking out on her brow.

It gave all at once, recessed back to where it had been. Memories surged back. Enuwal showing up at her door in the morning as she was working on the bowl for Ayeelah, and no, she hadn't had much for breakfast other than tea. She'd been terrified when he'd arrived, having just discovered little holes in her memory, as if the fog had been secretly chipping away. The weight of it all sank her deeper against the ground.

She leaned against the tree and raised a shaking hand to wipe away the sweat. "Enuwal," she gasped. "I am sorry. For a moment, I forgot who you were. But I remember now."

He pulled her into his arms. She breathed deep of the familiar herbal scent that always clung to him. His shoulder trembled faintly, then he took a deep, shaky breath and sat back, although he kept her in his arms.

"I should get you home," he said.

"Where are we?" she asked.

He rocked back on his heels. "What's the last thing you remember?"

"You came to see me. We went for a walk. And then . . ." She clenched her hands into fists. "Nothing."

"Look around. You tell me."

She took in their surroundings for the first time. The spring, the pungent sulfur smell, the carvings on the trees. "The Jegudun springs. They're supposed to be haunted."

"They're not, but you had another episode. It was right when—" He bit his lower lip. "Never mind. I just want to get you home as quickly as possible. Can you stand?"

"I think so." She considered pushing him to finish what he was going to say, but if the answer would make the pounding in her head worse, she didn't think she wanted to hear it just yet. "Home sounds good."

Enuwal pulled her to her feet. She let go, took a tentative step, and proclaimed herself fit for travel.

She led Enuwal past the stream and into the woods, then stopped. She could not remember which way Selu lay. She'd always held a sort of map in her mind, with the river and Selu at center, and the earth's undulations and the forest spreading out. It was similar to the map her mother had started teaching her when she began to memorize lineages during her training to become clan mother. But now, when she searched for the map, it was gone.

"Malia?" he asked.

"Just resting," she said. "Is there any water?"

She took his water pouch, putting it to her lips quickly to hide the tremble in her hands. The contents were cool, and she drank slowly as she struggled to recall the way home. She had no doubt Enuwal could get them back, but this was her home. She should be able to close her eyes and find the village without once opening them. The land should rise and fall familiarly beneath her feet.

"Are you ill?" Enuwal asked. "Or having another episode?"

"No, I just need more time to rest." She handed the water pouch back to him and leaned against a fir tree, closing her eyes and breathing deep. The air was warm and smelled of sage and juniper. A flycatcher sang in a nearby tree; the call sounded like *we see.* She focused on the smells and sounds and the feel of the solid tree. She let go of the struggle to remember, instead picturing Selu in her mind and what it would look like in the mid-afternoon, the warmth the walls would hold, the cool respite the shade would offer, the glitter of the sun on the river.

The way home came rushing back to her. Down the slope, south and east, across a ravine, through a final swath of pine, and then she'd be able to see the village. Her knees wobbled as relief flowed through her. She pushed off the tree and opened her eyes. "I'm ready."

Enuwal frowned, but said nothing as he fell in a half step behind her. "As soon as we get to the village, I'm making willow bark tea for you."

"I can hardly wait," she muttered.

"What?"

She sighed. "It will help, thank you." She *did* need something to help with the throbbing in her head. "I hope Tulah has come back. Er, she hasn't yet, has she?"

"She hadn't when we left this morning."

"I don't know how much longer I can put up with these episodes." She rubbed her forehead. Enuwal laid a hand on the back of her neck and rubbed as they walked. She murmured appreciatively and leaned back a little, walking slowly so he could concentrate on the knots in her muscles.

"She'll be back soon, and then we'll have answers," he said.

Malia nodded. She focused on the land. It was familiar now, as well known to her as the creases in her palm. She didn't slow until she spotted Selu through the last of the forest, and then she breathed a sigh.

The sun beat down on her as she crossed the grassy slope. All was quiet. A handful of children squatted in the scant shade next to the village, playing a game in the dirt. A few men worked in the fields near the river, checking the irrigation system. This was the time for rest or staying indoors, waiting out the day's worst heat.

Malia led the way to her mother's home. It was dim and cool inside, and she blinked a few times to adjust. Her mother was gone, probably visiting one of the other families, but Vedran was there, napping in one corner. In sleep his face was soft, reminiscent of the boy he'd been not so long ago. Ayeelah was nowhere to be found, but the kettle sat ready beside the hearth. The spit and the large pot both sat on a shelf, which meant Malia's mother would probably be having dinner with whomever she was visiting, most likely discussing somebody's marriage.

Malia eased onto some pillows and set her travel sac aside. She watched as Enuwal stirred the embers in the hearth and set the kettle over it, then pulled down a mug and searched through the basket until he found willow bark. Her head throbbed a slow rhythm. As bitter as the tea was, she'd welcome it if it brought her relief.

Vedran stirred, mumbled, sat up and rubbed the sleep from his eyes. "Oh, what are you doing here?"

"Malia had another episode," Enuwal said before she could speak. "She lost some of today's memories, and for a while she couldn't remember me at all." He rummaged through the baskets again, his back to them. Even through the tunic, Malia could make out the tension in his muscles.

"Are you well now?" Vedran asked, all trace of sleep gone from his face.

“My head aches, but yes, I’m well. Tulah hasn’t come back yet, has she?”

He shook his head, his lips pressed thin. “I’m sure she’ll return any time now.”

Enuwal set the mug in her hands. Steam rose from it, carrying the bitter scent of willow bark with it, and a faint, lemony smell. She crinkled her nose. Enuwal sighed and added honey.

“Be sure to tell your mother that you were the one using up her honey,” he grumbled.

She sipped, the hot liquid searing a path down her throat and curling in her belly like a cougar after a satisfying meal. With the lemon balm and honey, it wasn’t so bad. She sipped again until she’d drained half of it, then she sat back. Whether it was the tea itself or the expected outcome, the throbbing dulled to more of an unpleasant ache.

“What happened this time?” Vedran asked.

Malia let Enuwal do most of the talking, intervening now and then to describe what she’d gone through. When he mentioned that they’d gone to the spring, Vedran blanched, stood, and began pacing.

When Enuwal finished talking, Malia turned to Vedran. “What is it? There’s something about the spring that you know.”

He rubbed at his forehead as if he were picking up the headache Malia was leaving behind. “It has to do with Tuvin.”

“Tuvin?”

“That’s where he was when Dalibor caught up to you. That’s where he killed Tuvin.”

“Oh.” The fog trembled, but remained put. Tuvin died at the springs. The ghost of an image flitted across her vision—a man, a blood-covered dagger, a Jegudun on the ground. It was there, then gone. Her headache flared for an instant, and she sipped the tea as if it could banish the pain immediately.

"I should have warned you from the springs," Vedran said. "But I never thought you'd go near them. I mean, nobody ever does, which is why you'd hidden Tuvin there in the first place. I just didn't think, Malia. I'm so very sorry."

"No, it's not your fault," she said quickly. Unlike the incident with Andrij, she didn't believe Vedran willingly hid this information from her. Thoughts spun through her mind. Vedran started to speak again, and she held up a hand to cut him off, letting her mind go where it willed.

The first time she'd had one of these episodes, she'd been talking with Andrij. The next time, she had touched a piece of shattered pottery, something she'd made with care for Enuwal, something that Dalibor had broken. Then it happened again at the springs, where Tuvin had been killed. All of these items or people or places held potent memories for her, all of which were hidden behind the fog brought on by magic.

"I think I know what's triggering these episodes," she said.

Enuwal nodded and leaned forward. Vedran sat beside him.

"It's the most emotional memories," she continued. "When I come across any place or person or thing that affected me deeply, but is hidden behind this fog, it pulls. It wants to come out, but it can't." She bit at her lower lip. "Then the fog swallows up whatever triggered it."

"Yes," Enuwal said. "That makes sense."

"What about Tuvin's feather?" Vedran asked. "You grabbed it when you started to have one of these episodes, and it stopped."

Malia hesitated. "Tuvin used magic to infuse a memory into the feather." Her hand rose to grasp it. "Now that memory is gone. The magic is gone. The magic stopped the process, or the memory did, or both. Today, at the springs, I was able to push against the fog in my mind, but it was hard. I'm not sure I could do it again."

"Then we give you more feathers," Enuwal said. "Tulah can put a memory into each one, and the next time this happens, you can stop it."

She traced the faint red lines on her palm. "Yes, but these episodes are still an unpleasant experience. And it seems to be getting worse each time. I couldn't even remember you for a while after the latest one." *And then there's the matter of little holes in my memory, or forgetting the way home . . . those things aren't hidden behind the magic.* She pushed that concern away. Maybe once they fixed this magic-induced memory problem, the rest would fall into place. There was no need to worry anybody about it in the meantime.

He grimaced. "The magic in the feather might be enough."

"Maybe." It might hold off the worst of it, but how many times would she have to burn her hand? She didn't think it would work indefinitely either, not if these little moments were slipping away. "I just wish Tulah would hurry and bring us some good news."

Vedran stood. "In the meantime, I'll see if one of the other Jeguduns can give you a few feathers."

She frowned. "I can't wear a necklace of them, though. Only a clan mother can do that."

"Then wear them on a longer necklace," he said. "Hide them beneath your tunic. Mother will understand. She'd rather you do that than suffer any more." He gathered his bow and quiver and slipped outside.

She finished the last of the tea. "Speaking of clan mothers, I can't resume my training." Her heart tripped as she spoke. It was something she'd been thinking for a while, but she hadn't admitted it until now.

"Why not?" Enuwal asked.

"What if I learn lineages again and then have one of these episodes? It will wipe out whatever I just learned." She shook her head, a little growl building in her throat. "Somebody else will have to train just in case I can't fix this problem with my memory." Her hand rose again to the necklace bearing the old, worn feather along with Tuvin's. She would have to give up the old necklace to somebody else. For most of her life she'd expected to be Selu's next clan mother. What would she do now? The future yawned ahead of her like the mouth of a cave, deep and dark and filled with the unknown. She wouldn't be facing an unknown future if it hadn't been for the Maddion. Her hand tightened around the necklace. She hoped the illness was sweeping through them like a fire across dry grasslands, and consuming them just as thoroughly.

"Let's wait and see what news Tulah brings us," Enuwal said. "Don't give up on it just yet."

Her hand loosened its grip on the necklace. She sat back against the pillows. She might be home, but she'd never been so lost before.

~

Soon after Vedran left, the sky darkened. The scent of rain filled the air, and the wind picked up. Malia sat in the doorway, watching the clouds roll in and trying not to think how similar they were to the fog in her mind. Meanwhile, Enuwal strung together the plants and herbs he'd collected to hang for drying. Their smells—the yarrow and sage in particular—tickled her nose and made her sneeze. She could tell he was as distracted as her by the way he muttered under his breath about the plants not cooperating.

Vedran returned moments before the rain began with one of the Jeguduns in tow, a young male by the name of Aru. The cream-colored down of his body darkened to red-brown feathers along his wings, and his eyes were the deep green of pine needles. He was one of the most adventurous of the group, ready to go anywhere at a moment's notice, and he looked eager now, his feet almost clipping the back of Vedran's as he followed him into the home. Clouds scudded across the sky in earnest, and thunder rumbled nearby.

Vedran said, "Aru is more than willing to donate some memory-laden feathers. But I also found someone else."

Another Jegudun entered, a female Malia had not met before, her feathers a warm brown color, her eyes nearly matching. Her nostrils flared, and she breathed heavily. She'd flown hard and fast.

"This is Umera," Vedran said. "She has a message for you."

Nerves strung tight, Malia gestured for the Jeguduns to enter. "Umera, you look as though you're hungry and thirsty. Can I get you tea? Something to eat?"

Though she looked exhausted, the Jegudun shook her head. Malia's lips thinned. The message must be urgent indeed. She nodded and indicated the pillows. "Sit, please."

Umera settled on the ground but remained upright, muscles coiled beneath the soft down covering her body. Malia sat in front of her, legs crossed, and pulled her skirt over her legs. Outside, rain began to fall, gently at first, and then in fat drops, pelting the dirt like tiny drums. The wind kicked up and drove some of the rain into the home. Vedran hastily pulled the door hanging down and tied it, keeping the worst of the weather out.

"Vedran, why don't you get Aru something to eat and drink while I find out what the message is?"

He looked as though he'd speak, but only went about preparing a plate of smoked turkey, nuts, and berries. Enuwal set the kettle over the hearth to heat up again, and then sat beside Malia, so close that their knees almost touched. She was glad to have him near her.

Umera held out her hands. Malia rested hers lightly within their confines, the Jegudun's palms supple as worn, oiled leather, and the back covered with soft down. She closed her eyes and waited.

A tug came at her mind, inquiring. It was nothing like the fog that barreled through her memories, gulping them up. This tug was polite, gentle, inquisitive; it would never force itself into her memories or coerce her along. Malia let her mind drift, and the tug strengthened, then pulled her along. One moment, she sat in her mother's home, the smell of wood smoke and rain in the air. The next, she was flying.

She was in one of Umera's memories. The Jegudun flew over a large, grassy plain, her shadow gliding beneath her. A flash of white showed on one side. Tulah. Three other Jeguduns flew with them. They pursued dark spots in the far distance. Dragons. Maddion. Icy fear lanced through Malia.

The Maddion were headed for an immense mountain range. The jagged peaks stretched to either side and seemed to go on forever. The plains turned to rolling hills, bison and deer and elk scattering to the horizons, startled by the dragons' passage. Malia could feel the cold air as it had been against Umera's face. They were north of the Taakwa valley, but how far, she didn't know.

The dragons disappeared within the twisting mountain peeks. Umera pulled up, as did the others, and found shelter beneath a deep overhang that protected them from prying eyes. They spoke quietly, then one of them slipped away, most likely to spy upon the Maddion.

What was Tulah doing there? She was supposed to find one of the elder Jeguduns and get answers for Malia. It was important to know what the Maddion were up to, but why did Tulah have to be one of the ones to follow them?

Day drifted to a close before the other Jegudun returned. Rather than relay what she'd seen, she passed on her memories to the others, including Umera, and those images flashed before Malia's eyes.

The Maddion landed in a steep valley, a lake taking up most of it, a grassy shore to one side. Their Most Worthy, flanked by several of his men, disappeared behind a waterfall, leaving behind close to a hundred dragons and men. Why so many of them in this isolated place? What were they looking for? Whatever it was, it couldn't mean anything good for either the Jeguduns or the Taakwa.

They were gone a long while. When they finally emerged, the Most Worthy strode angrily to his dragon, his lips pressed thin, his hand resting on the short axe hanging from his hip. The other men followed shortly, carrying a person between them, arms and legs bundled like a criminal, except the person was a frail man, skin as dark and wrinkled as old, dried leather, and hardly able to walk, or perhaps it only seemed that way since the men were dragging him along.

Who was this man? Why did he live alone in the middle of a wilderness? Why did the Maddion want him? Those questions, and more, snaked through Malia's head. The Jegudun spy crept away, and after a dizzying moment when images spun and twisted, Malia was back in Umera's memories.

The Jeguduns waited until the dragons left. Close to a hundred pairs of massive wings beat the air like so many blankets being snapped to drive the dust from them. They waited until the sounds faded and disappeared altogether, then they crept out of their hiding place and took to the air.

The Maddion were the smallest of specks far ahead of them. The Jeguduns flew, a new urgency to their travel. This man was important, but why? Who was he? Malia couldn't pull free from Umera's memory to ask. Perhaps she'd get an answer in the memory, perhaps she'd have to wait. Something else important happened, otherwise Umera would have let her go by now.

A huge shadow passed over them a moment before Tulah, just behind Umera, shrieked in terror and pain. *Dragon.* A quick glance over Umera's shoulder showed three of the huge beasts, one entangled with Tulah and the Jegudun who had spied upon the Maddion, and one descending directly for her.

Umera folded her wings and dove. The world spun, and Malia's stomach dipped with Umera. If it was possible to become ill while within someone's memory, she was about to find out.

The ground rushed to meet them. Just as Malia thought they'd crash into the earth, Umera snapped out her wings and beat frantically at the air. Her feet brushed against the grass, then she was rising. Behind her, a man shouted, and something large and heavy crashed into the ground. Umera came around. The dragon had been following her too closely, and its rider had been, perhaps, too inexperienced to override his beast's natural tendencies and pull them out of the dive. The dragon lay on its side, one wing bent at an impossible angle, the rider crushed beneath the beast.

A second dragon had landed and stood over Tulah. Bright blood covered much of her white feathers. She crouched on one knee, talons protracted and raised, one wing spread while the other hung brokenly beside her, teeth bared and ears laid back. The dragon's head snaked over her, ready to strike.

Umera leaped upon the rider, clawing and biting. He screamed and reached for the battle axe hanging from the saddle. Umera's claws slashed through the leather straps binding him to his dragon, and she dragged him off and onto the ground where she snarled and buried her teeth into his throat.

Malia was fully immersed in the memory and couldn't pull away. She tasted the hot spray of blood and gagged, noting how Umera enjoyed it.

The Jegudun leaped onto the riderless dragon's back and raked her talons along its sides. The dragon stood upon its hind legs, roaring, but Umera held on. She clambered higher and clamped her teeth onto the dragon's neck, and more blood poured into her mouth. She clung, ripping flesh, until the dragon slowed and then collapsed.

Umera leaped to the ground, panting, and found that the others had taken care of the third dragon. Tulah lay on the ground, breathing shallowly.

Umera hurried to her and took Tulah's hand in her own. Tulah's blue eyes focused on Umera's.

Malia wasn't prepared for the flood of images that came from the dying Jegudun. Births, deaths, celebrations long into the night, flights, battles, couplings, lazy days, joy, sorrow. It rushed through Umera—and Malia—like Tuvin's Falls rushing over the cliff's edge. She gasped, felt as if she couldn't breathe under the weight of all those memories. She tried to single out one and hold onto it, but they flew past.

She caught an image of herself, fleeting. Then another. Then Tulah, traveling over the Taakwa valley, north and west, to the most rugged area, where no villages existed close to the cliffs at all. Multiple springs dotted the area, steam rising from them like smoke from the nostrils of dragons. The land here was rockier and rose sharply to the sheer cliffs, an inhospitable place for Taakwa, but the perfect location for Jeguduns who perhaps wanted to keep more to themselves.

The cliffs towered over Tulah. Where the area around Tuvin's Falls was dotted with hundreds upon hundreds of Jegudun homes, this rock face held only a few dozen. Perhaps the stone wasn't as stable, or perhaps this area wasn't as appealing to Jeguduns. Malia had never been anywhere close to this part of the valley before.

In Tulah's memory, she aimed for one of the cave homes. This had to be where the elder Jegudun lived, the one who might have an idea of what she could do to protect her mind.

Tulah landed on a ledge in front of a home close to the ground. Rasmus had lived among the Jeguduns for the past ten years or so, and he used a rope ladder to get to and from his home. Curled up on this ledge was a different contraption altogether, more like a large bit of heavy cloth attached to three ropes. Malia tried to make sense of it, but Tulah was already entering the home.

Sunlight illuminated most of the cave. Water trickled in through a small opening high on one wall, falling into a small pool embedded in the stone floor, a slight lip around it keeping the water from spilling out. A hearth sat on the far wall, a fire burning in it despite the day's heat. Shelves were lined with bits of thin metal and baskets overflowing with cloth, dried herbs, and tools. A large, plush blanket covered much of the stone floor.

It was the blanket that caught Malia's attention. It was done in the Taakwa style, with tiny figures sewn into it with thread. She might have thought it a recent gift, but it was old, even threadbare in some areas.

A figure moved in the corner's shadows. A Jegudun emerged, back bent, shrunken, wings folded. Gray down, peppered with white, marked his snout, his chest, his ears. His feathers were a light gray, his eyes a faded brown, but still sharp, taking in everything. He moved slowly, and with a limp.

Another figure emerged from the shadows. A person. At first Malia thought the person a man, with his hair cropped short. A few exiles had found homes among the Jeguduns, and so finding someone here was no surprise. But when the figure stepped into the sunlight, her plump, round body revealed an older woman. She was tall and held the softness of her age well, with lines fanning out from the corners of her eyes, and lines well worn around her mouth.

Her eyes were vaguely familiar, as was her walk. Malia did her best to study the woman through Tulah's memory, but the memory faded, and she was back in Umera's mind, watching Tulah die. And then she was back in her mother's home, the smell of rain-soaked earth thick in the air.

She swayed, dizzy from the changing perspectives, and pulled her hands free of Umera's. That woman . . . where had Malia seen her before? The woman wasn't hidden behind the fog, that much she knew. She struggled, searching back and back.

The eyes, so much like Malia's father's. Those arms had held her when she was a young girl.

Her grandmother lived, as an exile, among the Jeguduns.

CHAPTER NINE

Malia rocked back, her heart fluttering as quickly as a hummingbird's wings. Tulah, dead. The Maddion on the move, kidnapping a frail, old man, which somehow meant trouble for the Taakwa. Her grandmother, alive and living with the Jeguduns.

Her grandmother. *Alive.* Not dead of a broken heart as her mother had told her years ago.

Malia searched that memory, probed it as carefully as she might probe a bee's nest in search for honey. A while after her father's death, and her grandmother's supposed death, she'd asked questions. What had happened to her Nana? Where had she gone? She didn't recall a funeral rite for her grandmother.

"She died shortly after your father did," her mother had said.

"How?"

Her mother had hesitated. "She was terribly sad after your father died. He was her only son, and she cherished him. She died of a broken heart."

Now, Malia stood abruptly, hands clenched into fists. "Vedran, see to Umera's comfort, please." She went to the door, pushed aside the covering. The rain had stopped, the ground soaked, the air crisp and clean as twilight approached. The last of the clouds were drifting away, and more people milled about the village center or walked through now that the sky had cleared.

"Where are you going?" he asked.

"I need to speak with our mother."

"But she's with the Grantle clan. Their son is—"

"It can't wait." She strode out, her feet sinking slightly into the soft earth. The blanket rustled behind her, and Enuwal trotted beside her.

"What's the matter?" he asked. "What did you see?"

Anger smoldered like embers in her chest, barely checked. "A lot."

He laid a hand on her arm. "Perhaps you should wait until she gets home."

She shrugged off his hand and kept walking. "This can't wait," she said again. Enuwal stopped, and she walked on alone.

Before she reached the Grantle clan's home, she paused, took a deep breath, and forced her hands open. The Grantle clan did not deserve any of her anger. That was reserved solely for her mother.

She climbed the ladder to their ledge and stood just outside their door. She tried to recall their youngest son's name and came up empty. He sat with his back to the door, his parents on either side of him, and Malia's mother on the farthest side of the room. She was the first to spot Malia. Her face registered first alarm, then annoyance, and finally, a touch of fear. She stood hastily, cutting off the mother in mid-sentence.

"My deepest apologies," she said. "I believe something urgent has come up."

"But . . . we haven't eaten yet," the mother said.

A pot simmered over the hearth fire. Something spicy cooked within, and the smell would have been enticing under other circumstances.

"I will have to get back to you," Malia's mother said.

Malia climbed down the ladder to where Enuwal waited. Her mother followed, more slowly than usual.

"What is it?" she asked warily when she reached the ground.

"I do believe Nana is alive and well," Malia began. "Although living as an exile."

Her mother blinked, and her mouth opened, but nothing came out.

"Perhaps we should go home?" Enuwal suggested.

"Y-yes," her mother stammered. "Let's go home and talk about this there." She started across the village toward her home.

"Not there," Malia said. "*My* home." She walked away, without looking back to see if her mother followed. She might not recall building her home, but it was her space, and she'd rather face her mother in a place where her mother didn't feel quite so comfortable.

She climbed the ladder and entered. While she waited, she lit the lanterns. Her hands trembled. She took a deep, steadying breath, and the wicks caught. She stirred the embers in the hearth, adding kindling until a small fire took form, then hung a water-filled kettle over it.

Ayeelah's wide, shallow bowl sat in one corner. Malia touched it. The bowl was just dry enough that she should add the base, but it would have to wait until she'd spoken with her mother.

The ladder creaked. Enuwal climbed onto the ledge, then turned to help her mother up. Her mother entered slowly, but she met Malia's gaze and stood straight. She'd regained her composure on her way.

Malia sat against a large pillow. "I'd love to hear more about my grandmother."

"May I sit?"

She gestured toward the floor. Her mother settled uneasily on a blanket.

Enuwal stood just outside the door. "Malia? Would you like me to go?"

"No. I need you here, in case I have another episode and don't recall this conversation."

He sat beside her.

"You've had another episode?" her mother asked. "What happened?"

Malia shook her head. "No questions, mother, and don't change the subject. Tell me about my grandmother. Obviously she didn't die."

"You've put some water on to boil. May I have tea first?"

"It won't be hot enough for a while. In the meantime, you can start explaining."

She sighed. "Very well." She shifted her seat. "Your grandmother, as you know now, didn't die." She paused, closed her eyes, then nodded and opened them.

"Your father fell ill during your fourth summer. Nobody could figure out what caused it, or what to do about it. We consulted healers from other villages. Meanwhile, I watched my belly grow with your brother as I watched my husband waste away." A bitter note crept into her voice.

Malia had never really considered the experience from her mother's point of view, other than to realize in some vague manner that it must have been difficult for her. But now she could picture her mother as a younger woman, with one small child and another on the way, and her husband inexplicably ill. Her mother had married later than most since she'd been occupied with her training to become clan mother. Most women passed the knowledge to one of their own daughters, but Selu's previous clan mother had had nothing but sons, and so had chosen Malia's mother to train.

And yet, sympathetic as her mother's situation had been, she had lied about what happened to Malia's grandmother. The anger remained a tight ball in her belly.

"While he was ill, your grandmother spoke of the Jeguduns," her mother continued. "She said things that were considered outrageous at the time, that the Jeguduns might have knowledge that could help your father, that we should approach them. I thought it was her grief and anxiety speaking, and I encouraged her to keep her opinions to herself, or suffer exile.

"She did, for the most part, although she'd mutter something about the Jeguduns from time to time when I was the only one around. But when your father died, she fell into a deep despair. She thought there was something that could have been done to save him had we only put aside our differences with the Jeguduns and approached them."

Enuwal cleared his throat. "I apologize for interrupting, but I feel I must say something before you go on." He turned to Malia. "Having spent time with the Jeguduns, and having some knowledge of your father's symptoms, I'm certain there is nothing they could have done to save him."

She knew he didn't want her to blame her mother for her father's death. She couldn't. She would have to blame the Taakwa in general and condemn them all. No, her father's death was long past, but her grandmother, on the other hand, was alive.

"I know," she said. The water inside the kettle bubbled furiously. She poured some into three mugs, using a dried berry and mint mixture. The tart, sweet smell filled the air when the hot water mixed with the dried berries and herbs. "Please, go on," she said to her mother. It was as much politeness as she could muster.

"She began speaking openly of how she thought the Taakwa were mistaken about the Jeguduns," she continued. "At first everybody ignored it, thinking she spoke out of grief. But one of the councilwomen encountered her early one morning. She had a travel sac, and she said she was going to the cliffs to invite the Jeguduns to Selu." She shook her head. "There was no protecting her after that. The councils met and decided quickly that she must be exiled. She was stirring up the village, and—" She broke off.

"She had to go," Malia said, her voice flat. "Did she ever say what gave her the notion that the Jeguduns were friendly?"

Her mother hung her head. "I think she might have tried. But I never gave her a chance to explain. I was grieving myself, and worried about what I would do with a new baby and another child and no husband."

Malia sipped the hot liquid. It pooled somewhere above the angry knot in her stomach.

Her mother raised her head. "You must try to understand, Malia. How could I explain to a young child that not only had her father died, but her grandmother must be sent away?"

"So you thought it best to pretend she'd died. Of course, you probably assumed she'd die on her own anyway, so it wouldn't be a lie for long."

Her mother flinched. "It was the law."

Enuwal laid a hand on hers. "Your mother has a point."

She pulled her hand free. "Yes, she does. But what about when I was older and could understand the truth? It's the same as her withholding Dalibor's death from me. She doesn't believe me capable of coping with the truth." She carefully pulled Tuvin's feather free from the necklace, leaving only the old, worn feather that marked a clan mother in training. She removed the necklace and held it to her mother. "I was going to bring this up some other time, but I cannot be Selu's next clan mother. These episode are hampering my memory, and until I address the problem, I cannot learn the village's lineages or lead them."

"Please, don't act hastily in your anger," her mother said. "I am deeply sorry I never told you. I will not make that mistake again, you can be sure of that."

Malia shook her head. "I will not be here for you to train anyway."

"What?" said Enuwal.

"Where are you going?" her mother asked.

"I am traveling to the cliffs to speak with the Jegudun that Tulah visited, to find out what can be done for my memories. And, I wish to see my grandmother. I leave tomorrow."

"You can't—" her mother began.

"You shouldn't—" Enuwal said at the same moment.

Malia held up her hands. "I will, and there's nothing you can do or say to stop me. For one, I want to see my grandmother. Secondly, that Jegudun might have the answers I need. Otherwise, why would Tulah have gone there? She wouldn't have known that woman was my grandmother." She stood, brushing bits of dirt from her skirt, remembering how she'd begun sweeping and then had set the work aside, forgotten. She needed to speak with this Jegudun and fix the tiny holes in her memory as well as the bigger one, before they completely rent through her like an old blanket falling apart, turning her into nothing but scraps. "Now, I have to get things ready."

"You can't go alone," her mother said. "You should take someone with you. What if you have another episode?"

She hated to admit that her mother was right, but she was. What if Malia couldn't remember where she was, or why she was traveling? She could end up roaming the forest and getting hurt, or dying from exposure, or from any number of other dangers. She sighed.

"Very well. I'll bring Vedran."

Enuwal cleared his throat. "It might be best if you had a healer along."

"Won't they be missing you in Posalo?"

"Now that the worst of the war injuries have been taken care of, they should be able to get along with anybody trained in healing." He paused. "Unless you don't want me along."

Her mother pursed her lips. "You're in mourning, Malia. If I leave you alone with Enuwal, people will talk. Some might be angry enough to approach the council about it."

"Then let them," she snapped. "We both know the only thing keeping me from marrying Enuwal is the formality of a mourning period. I don't carry a baby, nor do I harbor any feelings for my dead husband, seeing as I don't recall him, and even if I did, I'd probably not like him one bit."

Her mother flinched.

"Besides," Malia continued, "Enuwal and I have taken walks alone, and nobody has complained of it. If those old men insist on gabbing about this after they welcomed me home as a hero, then they can go take a flying leap into a dragon's jaws, and may they snap shut."

"Malia," Enuwal began.

She shook her head. "I will not apologize to her, nor feel guilty about speaking to her in such a way. True, she's my clan mother, but she's also my blood mother, and yet she acts as if I'm some commodity she can use in her power bid. She should be thrilled I'm going to the cliffs, because if I can fix this," she said with a hard tap at her head, "then I can resume training as clan mother, and all of that knowledge and power will remain in the family."

Her mother sighed and stood. "You will not apologize, and that's fine. But allow me to say what I should have said a long time ago." She leaned forward and took one of Malia's hands in her own.

Her mother's hand was soft, the skin thinner and frailer than she recalled, but firm as the fingers tightened on her own. "I am sorry, Malia, for many of the choices I made. In doing what I thought best for Selu, I neglected your needs. I believed you would understand. I thought that was the way things worked. When Oweeda taught me the lineages and the intricacies of the position, I didn't understand what she meant by gaining the village's love but losing those closest. I thought she was speaking some sort of riddle, but now . . ." She paused, swallowing hard. "I do love you, Malia," she said in nearly a whisper, as if she could barely admit it, even now. "I will do better by you from here on out."

She leaned back, withdrew her hands, and nodded to Enuwal. "Now, if you could help an old woman up . . ."

He hurried to pull her to her feet. They bid each other good night, and the rickety ladder announced her progress to the ground.

Malia sank back against the pillows and pinched the bridge of her nose, forcing back the hot tears that stung her eyes. "Sometimes I wonder what she'd be like if my father was still alive. Maybe she would be more honest."

Enuwal moved about, cleaning up the mugs. "More tea?"

She shook her head. "There was something else in the memories Umera shared with me. She and Tulah and a few others followed some Maddion to where they took an old man. I don't know who the old man was, but he was living alone, tucked away somewhere like he didn't want to be found. Whatever the Maddion want him for, it can't be good for us."

Enuwal frowned. "I have a feeling you're right about that. We'll have to find out more." He straightened. "I should go. She's right, those old men will gossip to no end if they know I'm in here alone with you, and I don't see how they couldn't, since at least one of them always seems to be sitting out there, or one of their wives."

"Let them gossip. Unless you're worried about *your* reputation," she added with a wry smile. It faded quickly. "In all seriousness, though, I simply don't care anymore. They call me a hero, I've sacrificed so much for them, and all the Taakwa, the least they could do is keep turning the other way."

"Yes, but, once we're married, I'll be living here, and I'll need the villagers' respect."

She sighed. He had a point. Some people still couldn't accept the Jeguduns as allies. They clung to the old ways of thinking. They would cling to *all* of the old ways. She stood, went to Enuwal, and put her hands on his shoulders. She went up on her toes and pulled him down gently to her until his warm breath washed over her, smelling of tea and mint, and then kissed him, lightly at first, tasting the tea on his lips, then his tongue.

He let out a little moan and pulled her closer. She deepened the kiss, wanting the moment to etch itself into her memories so she'd never forget it, or him. She pressed against his lips hungrily, searching for more.

He pulled away abruptly, his lips slightly parted, his breathing a little faster and heavier. "Malia," he said, his voice hoarse. He cleared his throat. "I really need to go now, before . . ."

She stepped back reluctantly. "Of course. You'll be ready in the morning?"

He quirked a smile. "You still want me to come along?"

"You have to ask? Oh, and I suppose you should tell Vedran to pack his things. Much as I hate to admit it, my mother was right. We should have someone else come along with us."

He dipped his head, then said, "Good night," his gaze lingering on her lips. Then he was gone, the blanket covering the door swinging from his passage.

Malia turned to the room. Its emptiness swept through her, and she trembled. She would travel to the cliffs, meet with her grandmother and the elderly Jegudun, and find some way to fix her memory so she could come back and welcome Enuwal formally into her life and her home, fill the space with children, and take on the duties as clan mother. And she'd find a better way than her mother had, a way to balance the duties to the village and to her family.

She pulled her travel sac down from a shelf and began to fill it for the next day's journey.

CHAPTER TEN

Muvumo brought the old man back under the guise of night, and covered him with blankets as well, so that his people wouldn't know his shame.

He'd gone to find a powerful being, a changer with the capability of destroying an entire people, of reversing the illness slowly killing off the Maddion. Instead, he'd found a simpering, trembling, frail old man who could hardly sputter a few words. Muvumo was surprised the old man didn't die of heart failure during the flight back home.

He had almost killed the old man on the spot, so great was his disappointment, but Delkis had stayed his hand with a few choice words. And Delkis did have a point. How else would this old man survive alone in the middle of a vast wilderness without any supplies? He had to have access to some sort of power.

Muvumo saw the old man settled in one of the empty holding cells and brought some food, water, and a sleeping pallet, along with extra blankets, as he couldn't stop shaking. He set two guards outside, more to keep curious eyes away than from any fear that the old man could actually escape, and then he went home.

He climbed the stone stairs on weary legs. Only a few torches had been left burning, hardly cutting through the dark, but he didn't need them to place one foot over the other on the next step, and the next. His hand went to the pocket inside his tunic and the small, folded paper there. He rolled the gritty contents between his fingers. He'd taken two pinches already that day, and the second had worn off by the time they'd arrived back in the mountains. He considered taking another pinch, but then he'd be awake for the better part of the night, and he needed to be awake early to speak with the changer and figure out what the old man could do for them, if anything. Reluctantly he pulled his hand from the pocket, already counting down the moments until dawn when he could take another pinch of the kasi powder.

Soft, warm light filtered around the edges of the white blanket that covered the door to his home. The smell of roast duck, bread, and oregano and basil wafted out as he reached a hand for the blanket, but Chanwa's soft laughter stayed his hand.

It was late. Who could she be entertaining? He was not prone to jealous fits as some of the other men were, but his wife's laughter was light and carefree, as it had been during their first days together. Lately it had become tighter, forced. Who was this who brought her such pleasure?

A little growl escaped his throat. He jerked the blanket aside and strode in, his hand already going toward the short axe hanging at his hip.

The first room was empty. The hearth fire had burned low, the remains of the meal wrapped and tucked to one side to keep warm for him. Lantern light flickered from the door leading to the other room.

Muvumo hastened to the door. Scrabbling noises came from the second room, and a hushed, quick command. He stormed through, expecting to draw blood, and pulled up short.

Chanwa sat on one of the trunks. Her back was straight, her legs carefully crossed at the ankles and her hands clasped on her knees.

The servant, Ankti, sat on her heels on the floor, head bowed, shoulders trembling. "Most Worthy," she said, the tremble extending to her voice.

"Welcome home," Chanwa said. Her voice was rich, smooth, calm, and carefully controlled, nothing like the bright, spontaneous laugh he'd overheard. "Was your quest successful?"

"What is going on here?" he asked.

Ankti flinched as if he'd struck her with a whip.

"I did not want to wait alone for you," Chanwa said. "Ankti stayed to help me with some of my clothes."

Indeed, bright bits of cloth lay scattered around the floor, and Chanwa's sewing basket sat beside her feet. And yet, he didn't quite believe her. A woman of Chanwa's standing would not stoop so low as to befriend a servant in such a way.

"Ankti, you are dismissed," he said.

The servant kept her head bowed and hurried out, the sharp tang of fear faintly following her.

"Is that all you were doing?" he asked once the blanket fell over the front door with a snap.

Chanwa crossed her arms and frowned. "I haven't taken a lover, if that's what you're asking."

What could he say? That he'd heard her being happy without him and found it suspicious? That it stirred his jealousy, and a strange longing to be the one to make her laugh like that? He rubbed at his forehead. He'd had a long day, what with the disappointment in finding the old man, and losing several men and dragons to the Jeguduns when he couldn't afford losing even a single one.

"You cannot make friends out of servants," he said. "They are below us. They are good for service, and nothing else."

Her frown deepened. "What makes you think I've befriended her?"

"I heard how you laughed before I came in."

She threw her hands into the air. "She is a servant. I don't have to pretend around her. Do you have any idea how difficult it is to be guarded around the other wives? If I say the wrong thing, they scurry off to tell their husbands, who take it as a sign of your weakness. I am worried sick every time you run off, afraid that some warrior will take it as the right moment to challenge you, and all I'll get back is your broken, bloody body, if I'm lucky to get back any shreds of you at all." She turned away, her hair falling over her face.

Her words blew away the frustration and jealousy. He pulled her gently to her feet and kissed her, and the rest of his concerns drifted away as he tasted the sweet tea she'd had after dinner. He pressed his body against hers, eager to lose himself in her completely, but she pulled back. Her blue eyes flickered across his face as she studied him.

"Did you find the changer?" she asked.

He stepped away, dropping his arms to his sides. "Yes."

"You don't look pleased." She laid a hand on his arm. "Why don't we go into the other room? You must be hungry. Eat something, and tell me what happened."

She lit one of the lanterns, prepared a plate for him, and settled on the pillows as he ate. He didn't think he'd have much appetite, but after the first bite of roasted duck, it came roaring back, and he wolfed down the food, not saying much until he'd emptied his plate.

He settled back, the food comfortable in his stomach, his second glass of wine in hand. "We found the changer," he said. "But . . . the changer is an old man. Frail. Weak. He cowered before us. If he was truly some powerful magician, he would have fought us. Instead, he let us capture him easily."

A flicker of disappointment moved across her face. "What has he said?"

"Nothing we understand."

Her nails drummed a rhythm along the wooden table. "What will you do next?"

"I will wait until the morning, when I've had a chance to clear my head and he's had a chance to settle in. Perhaps the dragons scared him."

"Perhaps he is not at all that he seems. He is a changer. What better way to get the enemy to let their guard down than to appear frail and weak?"

"But he let us take him." Muvumo took a sip of wine.

"Yes, right into the heart of the Maddion's land." She raised a hand. "I'm not saying it was a mistake. Clearly we need help. But maybe we aren't the only ones with an agenda here."

Her insight surprised him. "How could he have known we were coming for him, though?"

A slow, sly smile spread across her face, and for an instant, his own wife was a stranger to him. "If he is truly powerful enough to wipe out an entire people that the Maddion couldn't destroy, then he is powerful enough to realize when somebody is coming for him."

He drained the rest of the wine, set the mug aside, and stood. Chanwa hastily stood with him.

"Allow me to clean up the other room so you can lie down," she said. "You must be exhausted." She disappeared through the door, and a moment later came the sound of trunks opening and closing.

Her words echoed in his mind. He stepped outside and let out a quick, sharp whistle, then took the torch from the sconce beside his door and waved it back and forth. He replaced it, and moments later, quick footsteps pattered along the stairs. A boy came running down, breathing heavily.

"Yes, Most Worthy," he said breathlessly as he reached Muvumo.

"Send a message to Delkis. Have him double the guards on our guest in the cells until I give the order otherwise."

The boy nodded. "Yes, Most Worthy." He sprinted up the stairs, the night quickly swallowing him.

Muvumo went back inside and blew out the lantern light, plunging the room into darkness save for the light that filtered through the door to the other room. He extinguished the lanterns in that room, and then settled beside Chanwa, his thoughts consumed by the changer for a long while before he fell asleep.

~

The next morning, Muvumo had a quick breakfast of fried eggs and strong, black tea. With Ankti busy at the hearth and Chanwa in the other room, Muvumo snuck a pinch of the kasi powder in the midst of his breakfast. Within moments, a calm alertness washed through his body, and he gave a little sigh. *Now* he could face the day.

Delkis appeared at his door as the tip of the sun broke over mountains. Birds twittered from the forest, and a dragon roared in the distance. Footsteps climbed the stone stairs outside, some passing slowly, others scurrying like any other normal morning. Muvumo stood, anxious to be off to his own tasks.

"How is the old man?" he asked.

"Awake. He ate breakfast and said nothing when I spoke to him. I paraded slaves through and had each of them speak in their languages. He didn't seem to understand any."

Muvumo sat back with a sigh. How would they accomplish anything if they couldn't communicate?

A woman's wail broke the morning. Chanwa rushed out of the other room, her dress billowing behind her, pale blue eyes wide. "That must be Nanda. Her son had the illness." She grabbed a basket sitting beside the door and hurried out.

Muvumo rubbed his forehead. Nanda's son had been born a few summers ago. The boy would have been old enough next spring to begin basic training with the dragons and other youth. Already their group of new trainees this year was half the size as previous years. Next spring, it would be a fourth, or less, if they even had enough men to train the boys, that is.

He stood abruptly. There was no time to waste. This old man had to have the answers.

Ankti kneeled beside the hearth, washing the dishes in a large bowl of sudsy water, drying them, and setting them aside on the shelf. A basket of clothes sat beside her for washing later. She kept her head down, her hair covering falling over her face and hiding it.

She came from one of the most populated areas the Maddion had ever encountered. Far to the south, trade roads crossed the plains and deserts, and Ankti's people lived among those roads, supplying travelers. They usually lived in small communities, making it easy for the Maddion to pick off those they needed without resorting to much fighting. And, because so many people passed through, they spoke not only their own language, but a trade language and bits of other languages as well.

"Come, girl," he said.

She dropped a plate into the soapy water and turned, although she didn't meet his gaze. "Most Worthy?"

"Are you growing deaf? I said come, you come. Save that for later."

She hastily set the wet plate on a towel and stood, bowing low. "Yes, Most Worthy."

He led the way down the stairs, Delkis just behind him, and Ankti following. Whenever he encountered somebody else, they pressed against the stone wall to his right and bowed their heads. He moved so quickly that at times Ankti's footsteps broke into a run for a few steps in order to catch up.

The air was cool and smelled of pine and wood smoke and fried meat. Voices were unnaturally hushed following Nanda's proclamation that someone in her family had died. Laughter and good feelings didn't last long these days.

The boy tending the mesa spotted them coming and hastened inside the cavern where saddles were stored. He was out with both Muvumo's and Delkis's before they reached him. He bowed his head and murmured, "Most Worthy."

Muvumo craned his head. Only a handful of dragons flew this early. They preferred resting during the chilled nights, and it took them a while in the morning to get going. He let out a long, piercing whistle followed by three short bursts. Then Delkis let out three short whistles, followed by a pause, and three more short blasts.

Two dragons rose from the canopy of trees at the mountain's peak. They circled and flew lower. Muvumo recognized his beast, and Delkis's, a drab brown dragon who impressed none with her appearance but whose ability to make tight maneuvers in the air left all the other riders jealous.

Ankti shrank back as the dragons landed, sending bits of dirt flying in the air. The boy handed the saddle to Muvumo and helped secure it as Delkis saddled his own beast.

Tightening the straps was quick work. A few tugs assured Muvumo that it held securely. The dragon kneeled, and he climbed into the saddle, buckling the straps. He gestured at Ankti.

"Come, girl, climb on behind."

She shook her head, hugging herself tight and trembling.

Muvumo let out an exasperated sound. "There are straps to hold you in. You won't fall."*Although if you keep this up, I'll be sorely tempted to shove you off.*

Delkis hadn't climbed on his dragon yet. He grabbed Ankti and shoved her forward. She took a few stumbling steps, then fell onto her hands. Delkis yanked her to her feet and propelled her toward Muvumo's dragon. Once there, he lifted her while Muvumo pulled her up behind him. Together they strapped her onto the saddle. She sobbed softly and clutched the saddle.

"Quit that crying," Muvumo grumbled.

She bit her lower lip and fell silent, but he could feel her trembling. Her soft body pressed against his back. He could make out the swell of her breasts and the hardness of her stomach. His pants became a little too tight and uncomfortable, and he had to shift his seat. Then he squeezed the dragon's sides, and the beast crouched low before launching into the air, her wings unfurling with a snap, her powerful muscles flexing beneath him as she fought to rise. Ankti's breath hitched, and she pressed even harder against him.

They sailed over pine, fir, aspen, and a few meadows dotted with wildflowers. Then they rose, the cool air pulling at Muvumo's hair, tied back with a leather strap, and caressing his skin. He would have liked to take a long flight to clear his mind, just him and the dragon, and maybe even the soft woman so pleasantly crushed against his back, but duty came first. He sighed.

They landed on the highest mesa with hardly a jostle. Ankti murmured a few foreign words under her breath. She shook so hard that when Muvumo released the straps holding her, she slid to the ground and crumpled in a heap. He climbed down after her and yanked her to her feet.

"What is this?" he asked.

Delkis joined them. "Perhaps she thinks we brought her here to lock her away," he said. "Perhaps she doesn't realize she is simply here to translate."

Her sobs ended immediately, although her body shook a few more times before it steadied. Muvumo let go of her arm, and she stood, head bowed.

"*You* understood what I needed," he said to Delkis.

"Yes, but I am not a servant. They tend to live in constant fear."

"As well they should," he grumbled. He jerked his head toward the cave. "Come, girl."

He strode inside. The cave was large enough for a dragon to pass through, and deep. It delved far into the mountain, with dozens of cells carved into the stone on either side of the passage and thick wood doors leading into each of them. A wide, narrow shelf opened at the bottom of each door for sliding food and drink through. There was a square, barred opening at eye-level in each door. A pair of torches stood on either side of the passage just inside the cave, hardly cutting into the darkness that stretched deep into the mountain. The only resident in the cells was the changer.

The old man was housed in the first cell, scant daylight and a bit of torchlight reaching the small openings in the door. The guards went to their knees when Muvumo entered, bowing and touching their heads to the cold stone floor. "Most Worthy," they said, their voices echoing slightly.

"Rise," he replied. "Has the old man spoken?"

They stood. The guard nearest shook his head. "He's made water, but hasn't said a thing."

Muvumo went to the door and looked through the small, barred window. The cell was just large enough that a full grown man could lie down, but the old man stood, his back to them, his figure a shadow in the cell's darkness. Whereas the day before he'd been stooped, frail, and small, today he seemed as tall as Muvumo, the muscles beneath his filthy, threadbare tunic wiry rather than atrophied. He wore loose pants, and the tunic may have been cream colored at one point, but was now gray. His hair was wispy, white, and sticking out from his head in all directions. He held his hands clasped behind his back.

The man unsettled Muvumo. Power radiated from him this morning. Muvumo hadn't felt that the day before. He couldn't show his discomfort. He straightened instead, and said to Ankti, "Speak to him in the trade language. Ask him his name."

She swallowed hard, her throat bobbing with the movement, and joined him at the small window in the door. The trade language was curt and crude, and the old man didn't so much as flinch when she asked him the question. Without prompting, she asked again in two other languages. She bowed her head and said, "Perhaps he is deaf, Most Worthy."

"Perhaps it is a case of selective hearing," he said. He frowned, considering his options. He could threaten the old man, but if he was a truly powerful magician, threats might backfire. He refused to beg. That left coercion. But what would work on the old man?

They'd found him in solitude. Perhaps leaving him in a crowd would unsettle him enough that he'd respond. Nanda's wail echoed in his head. No, there was something more unsettling.

"Bring him down," he told the guards. "Follow my lead." He whirled and returned to the mesa, blinking in the bright morning sun. His dragon had just settled in a shady patch on the ground, head and tail curled around herself, her sides brightening and fading as she breathed. She snorted when he prodded her, letting out twin plumes of smoke from her nostrils, but she climbed to her feet obediently.

"Most Worthy?" Ankti asked. She almost raised her head to meet his gaze, but didn't quite dare.

"Yes, come along," he said. "I might still need you."

This time, she climbed on more willingly, and without tears. Delkis climbed onto his own beast, and the guards brought out the old man.

The changer blinked in the sunlight, keeping his head down. Once again he looked frail and timid. Had his earlier visage been a trick of the shadows in the cell? Muvumo shook his head and goaded his dragon into the air while the two guards' beasts circled down from the mountaintop toward the mesa.

He and Delkis kept their dragons in a holding pattern while the guards saddled their beasts and climbed on with the old man. Then he led them to his mesa. The apprentice hurried out to meet them.

"Shall I take her saddle, Most Worthy?" he asked.

"Yes," he said. "But leave the guards' dragons saddled."

To Ankti he said, "Run and tell Chanwa that we'll need to see Nanda's boy, and she will have to keep Nanda occupied."

"Yes, Most Worthy." She raced up the steps, taking two at a time in some places, holding up her long skirt and revealing flashes of her ankles and smooth, rounded calves as she did so.

Muvumo turned as the guards landed. They hastened off their dragons and brought the old man toward him. Muvumo ascended the stairs, Delkis on his heels, the guards and old man following.

By now they'd drawn attention. People watched from doorways, or paused with the pretense of adjusting the loads they carried or having conversations with neighbors. Whispers followed. Who was the old man? What was Muvumo doing with him?

Muvumo asked himself much the same thing. What *was* he doing? What if this didn't work? He would be needlessly inflicting pain on a grieving mother if this came to nothing. He faltered on the next step.

He had to do something. He couldn't simply let the old man remain in the cell indefinitely, nor could he set him free before exploring every possibility.

Chanwa met him at the door to Nanda's home. Their usual door covering had been switched out for a red cloth. The red had become all too common recently as more people died from the illness and families mourned.

Her brow furrowed when she caught sight of the old man. "This is him?"

"Yes."

"Why have you brought him here? Nanda is beside herself. She won't leave her son for a moment. We haven't even begun to prepare him for the funeral pyre."

"I can't think of any other way to make this person—this magician—to understand how desperate our need is."

Her lips thinned. At last she nodded and said, "Give me a moment." She slipped back inside.

By then, the guards had caught up, the old man standing between them, back bent and trembling. A few men—Muvumo's own men, whom he'd fought beside—stood on the stairs, watching and talking in low voices. When they realized he spotted them, they hurried on their way.

He knew stories had already circulated. Those with him on the flight to take the old man had said nothing, but he'd read their expressions. They didn't believe the old man could do anything to save them. They thought Muvumo a fool, sending them on a fool's errand. There had to be talk of another man challenging him for his spot. If this didn't work, he would end up in a fight, and either defend his place as Most Worthy, or die trying. His hand went to the short axe hanging from his belt, checking the straps that held it.

The door covering rustled. Chanwa and Ankti emerged, holding Nanda between them. The woman, hardly older than Chanwa herself, looked as if she'd aged decades since he'd last seen her. She had lost her husband during the war with the Taakwa and Jeguduns, and now she'd lost her only son. All she had left were three daughters, and the slim chance that she might attract another man's attention.

She turned green eyes up to him, red-rimmed, with tears shimmering along their bottoms. Before the war, she'd always had a smile on her face, but now it seemed as though she'd never smile again. Her grief was like an icy winter blizzard, blowing against him, chilling his heart. He wanted nothing more than to turn from her. How could his wife bear it, being near her?

He took a deep breath and said, "Your son will be remembered in the scrolls for all time." Without a husband or older son to write her dead son's story, devastatingly brief, she'd turn to an uncle or grandfather to write her son's too-short story.

"Most Worthy," she said, her voice thick with unshed tears. "Would *you* write his scroll?"

"Ah," he began, wanting to tell her he was too busy, he didn't know the boy well enough, he didn't know *her* well enough, but Chanwa watched, and she gave the slightest nod, her lips parting as she waited. "I would be honored," he said, wondering how he was going to fit it in with the myriad other things that needed doing.

But perhaps, if the changer could, indeed, help them, Muvumo would have plenty of time during the upcoming summer and fall to do so. He nodded.

The old man stepped forward. For once, no trace of amusement or fear remained on his face. The corners of his mouth turned down, and there was such sadness in his eyes that Muvumo nearly staggered under its weight.

A tear glimmered in Nanda's eye. The changer reached out, gently touched his finger to it, then traced a line down his own cheek, leaving the remains of Nanda's glittering tear behind.

Ankti gasped. Muvumo glared at her, and she quickly ducked her head. Nanda clutched her hands together before her breast and whispered, "Thank you." Then the three women started up the stairs.

"Ankti, you need to return," Muvumo called after them. Her shoulders tensed. She eased Nanda toward Chanwa and climbed down the stairs.

He gestured for the guards, the old man, and Delkis to follow. Inside, the hearth had gone cold. The family would have no warm drinks or food for the next three days. The tapestries had come down and were carefully rolled and tucked in the corners. The rugs had come up and were put away as well. The lanterns would not be lit for three nights. The family would have no comforts, nothing that would possibly distract them from their mourning.

He found the daughters in the next room. They had laid out the boy in the center, on a plain, white cloth. He wore wrinkled, stained tunic and pants, probably the same he'd died in, but the girls had cleaned his face and settled him so it looked as though he merely slept. The only evidence of the illness he'd suffered was the gauntness of his figure and the state of his clothes. Muvumo didn't want to consider the likely source of the stains, dark and various shades of brown and black. The boy had the same delicate features as his sisters. They had already set stones on his eyes to keep them closed, but Muvumo recalled he had green eyes, the color of new spring grass. He swallowed the lump in his throat.

"I ask for a few moments alone with your brother," he said to the girls.

The three of them were lovely, all with wheat-colored hair and delicate features. Two of the girls had their mother's green eyes, the third had pale blue eyes like Chanwa's, grown even icier with the tears shining in them. They stood, inclined their heads to him, and filed out, muffled sobs following them.

"Bring in the old man," he called over his shoulder.

Delkis came in, followed by the guards and the man, and Ankti trailing after them. With all of them in the room, and the boy laid out on the floor, it was crowded, and stifling. Jars of oil sat beside the white cloth, the pungent smells of pine and fir filling the air, and a pile of folded clothes beside those.

"Ankti, tell the man about the illness plaguing the Maddion. Let him know this is the result. Dead children and mourning mothers."

She dipped her head and began speaking in the trade language.

The old man ignored her. Instead, he shrugged out of the guards' grasps as easily as Muvumo could have broken a dried twig, and stepped forward. He kneeled, without any of the protestations of voice or body that the elderly often made, and laid an age-spotted hand on the boy's forehead.

Delkis started forward, his hand going to the short axe hanging from his hip, but Muvumo stopped him. Ankti's voice faltered, faded. She took a hesitant step backwards.

The old man spoke, his voice quiet but strong. Muvumo didn't understand the words, but they reverberated through him nonetheless, like a multitude of dragon roars echoing off the granite mountains. He sensed that the words were old, so old that nobody had spoken them in countless generations, so old that they carried power, that they connected this old man to the long crumbled bones of those who once understood them. Chills ran through Muvumo, and the pale hairs along his arms stood. He fought against the urge the flee the old man's presence.

Nobody else spoke or moved while the changer talked. Muvumo wasn't sure any of them even breathed. Finally, the old man's voice fell silent, and he rose easily to his feet.

He turned to face them. His skin was leathery, old, and nut-brown, with many lines creasing his forehead and fanning out from his eyes. And his eyes . . . they were brownish-orange, like aspen leaves in the fall, like dragon flanks when they breathed in and lit from within, and they were ancient. Muvumo felt like a child, like an infant, peering into their depths. They were filled with thousands upon thousands of summers, and autumns, and winters, and springs. They were filled with boundless knowledge, malice, grief, love, mischief.

One of the guards whimpered. He fled the home. The other guard gazed upon the old man, his mouth wide open. Confusion swept across Delkis's face, one hand resting on the handle of his short axe, the other reaching toward the old man pleadingly. Muvumo couldn't imagine what his own face showed. Perhaps turmoil, because certainly that's what tore through him as he considered how he'd brought this being into his people's midst. *What have I done?* Only Ankti stood tall and straight, gazing upon the old man without a trace of fear. Muvumo had never seen her so. She was, in that moment, breathtakingly beautiful, and she alone stood strong against this changer.

Muvumo gathered his thoughts. He was still Most Worthy, and *he* was in charge, not this old man. "Ankti," he said, startling her. She immediately dropped her head. "Ask this man—"

The old man raised a hand. "I can speak your language," he said, with only the slightest accent, "and many others. There is no need to treat me as incompetent, or deaf."

Under other circumstances, and faced with other men—*ordinary* men—Muvumo would have reprimanded him for withholding the fact that he spoke and understood the Maddion's language, but this man was beyond scolding. Instead, Muvumo forced himself to stand tall beneath that steady, unsettling gaze and said, "As you can see, my people are dying. Many have already suffered this boy's fate, and the rest of us will, too, sooner rather than later. We brought you here because we believe you powerful enough to help us defeat this illness."

The corners of his mouth curled up. "You do, do you? This is why you barged into my resting place and hauled me away? This is why you shut me in a tiny cell like a prisoner?"

"I was . . . taken aback by your appearance."

"Yes," he said, one eyebrow rising. "Many are."

"My deepest apologies for your treatment," Muvumo said, nearly choking on the words. "And my deepest apologies for the haste, but as you can see, we do not have time to spare." He took in a deep breath. "Can you help us? Will you?"

The old man closed his eyes. Muvumo breathed a sigh of relief. Those eyes nearly glowed with their own light, as if he held the dragons' fire within him. But that must be a good sign, yes, this tie with the dragons?

The old man's eyes opened, once more turning that strange, fiery light on Muvumo. "It is always terribly sad to see little ones die," he said. "For their sake, I will help you."

Relief flooded Muvumo. He believed this man powerful enough to do so. And Muvumo's scrolls . . . every man and boy from this day forward would read them. They would become so popular, so worn, that they would be copied every generation. His acts would live on indefinitely, and he would live among the most famous of those allowed to call themselves Most Worthy.

"But," the old man said, "first we must discuss the payment." He smiled, but it did not touch his eyes.

CHAPTER ELEVEN

The cliffs loomed in the near distance, rosy and shimmering in the morning sunlight. Pine trees grew along the top, a few scraggly ones clinging to the cliff face itself. Malia stood at the edge of the woods in the valley, shaded by aspen. Their leaves whispered in the breeze, and a warbler chattered somewhere in its branches.

Ahead of her was an ugly expanse of land. A field of large, black rocks cut a wide swath in both directions, with no end in sight. A few weeds grew among the rocks, but the field was mostly desolate. If the terrain had been flat, it might have taken half a day, perhaps less, to cross it to the cliffs, but given that they'd have to clamber over the rocks, it would take the better part of that day. If they were still among the rocks when night fell, they would either have to make an uncomfortable and exposed camp, or they would have to try to finish crossing in the dark. Neither option appealed to her, but she didn't relish the idea of remaining in the forest either, not when more little holes had been creeping into her memory. Just this morning she'd looked at a pair of shoes for the longest time, wondering who they belonged to. Only when Vedran had walked by and said, "Aren't you going to put your shoes on?" had she realized they were hers.

A shadow passed over her. Malia shielded her eyes and craned her neck. For a moment, she thought she saw Maddion riding a dragon overhead, and an icy hand gripped her and squeezed, but it was only Aru circling overhead. He whistled cheerfully before coming in for a landing in the tight space between the forest's edge and the beginning of the rock field. He'd been only too happy to join the little group for the journey. Since his cave home was nearby, he'd gone there for the night, and had probably passed on the news that Malia, Vedran, and Enuwal were with him. She wondered if the news had reached her grandmother yet, and what she'd make of it. Would she be happy at the thought of her grandchildren so close, or had she closed her heart to them long ago? Malia's nerves were a mess as she imagined all the possible greetings that waited for her and Vedran.

Unlike her, Vedran was far calmer about the upcoming reunion. Then again, he had no memories whatsoever of their grandmother or their father. Maybe that made it easier for him. Or maybe he was better at hiding his true feelings.

"Good morning, Aru," she said.

He chirruped and gave her a wolfish grin.

"Did you enjoy sleeping in your own home again?"

He yawned and stretched his muscular arms, then feigned sleep, emitting a deep, rumbling snore that made the fur around his mouth puff out. Malia chuckled.

Enuwal and Vedran joined her, both of them shouldering their travel packs. Together, they all looked silently across the expanse of dark rock. During the Dragon War, several of the beasts had fallen nearby when the magic barrier rejoined. Their bones lay scattered over the grass and rocks, mostly whole, although some had shattered.

"Perhaps we should wait until tomorrow," Enuwal said, "and start at first light. I'm worried we won't make it across before today's light fades."

Malia found herself tempted to agree. She could easily spend the day sitting here, studying the rocky field, or the patterns hawks made overhead as they searched for prey. But she sensed that was part of the change taking over her mind. If she gave in for a day, she'd be more likely to wait until the next day, and the next, until she was too far gone, and the fog had overcome her entirely.

"No," she said, "We go now. Aru can take to the air and scout the best route for us."

He trilled and nodded, eager for action. He had been impatient with their progress across the valley, flying in circles above them as they walked, scouting ahead and coming back with reports, hunting, picking up news from other Jeguduns. He seemed dismayed at their slow progress, often looking longingly in the direction they were headed once they'd settled down for the night.

"I don't think one more day will make a huge difference," Enuwal said.

The fog in her mind stirred. Even without the stimulation of a familiar place or person or thing, it had begun to send little tendrils forward. She suspected those tendrils were responsible for stealing the small moments, as if the fog were a hungry beast that fed on her memories. She'd said nothing to Enuwal yet, hoping she'd find a solution soon with the elder Jegudun.

Aru had gladly donated several feathers to her, each one laden with a pleasant memory. They hung from her belt, beside the dagger on her right hip, weapons of a different sort, ready at hand. She didn't want to resort to using one. The faint outline of Tuvin's feather remained on her palm, no longer painful, but still a reminder of how bad things could get.

Then there was the matter of the Maddion and what they'd been up to. She couldn't recall the war, but when she thought of the great beasts flying overhead, letting fire loose on people while their riders shot down the Taakwa and Jeguduns with their crossbows, her blood rushed a little faster, and bitter rage rose. Whatever they wanted with that old man, it surely meant trouble for the Taakwa.

"Aru, did you learn anything new about the Maddion?" she asked.

He trilled sadly and shook his head.

"This is about more than just me or my grandmother," she said. "The Maddion are up to something. We need to find out what, and soon."

"You've been pushing yourself for too hard," Enuwal said.

"All the more reason to get to proper shelter tonight. Besides, the wind has picked up. Most likely it will rain later today, and probably tonight as well. We wouldn't be able to cross, then. It would be too slippery."

Vedran said, "She has a point. Clouds are coming in."

Enuwal scowled at him. "If we get caught in the middle of those rocks when it starts to rain, we have no shelter."

"We should hurry, then," Malia said. She readjusted the travel sac and started forward, not looking back. She scrambled up the first rock, feet sliding and hands gripping, until she stood atop it. The rock ahead and to her right had a fairly flat top. She leaped to it.

Aru's wings beat the air, and a moment later he skimmed overhead, his shadow flitting ahead of Malia. He began to fly back and forth, weaving a progressive pattern in the sky as he determined the best route for them.

"Malia," Enuwal said behind her, exasperation clear in his voice.

She turned. The wind tugged at her hair, pulling a strand loose from its bun. The end stung her face as it whipped around. "Are you coming?" she called back. "You could always wait until the morning and follow then."

Enuwal mumbled something she couldn't make out, but he hoisted his travel sac higher and climbed after her. He moved gracefully for someone so tall and lanky.

"Ah, you're part mountain goat," Malia said when he caught up with her. "That explains the stubbornness."

"In that case, you're more mountain goat than I am."

Vedran snickered.

"That makes you a goat as well," Malia said sweetly to her brother.

His grin vanished.

Aru came back around from time to time, pointing out the direction they should go. Malia leaped when rocks were close enough, but just as often she had to climb into a crevasse, her skin prickling as she thought of snakes and spiders, and then scramble up the next rock. The day grew hotter. She didn't stop often, afraid she wouldn't be able to coax her tired and sore legs into starting again. Instead, she ate and drank as she went. She was so focused that she didn't notice when the wind picked up, and clouds covered the sun. She was only dimly aware that the worst of the heat had disappeared.

She noticed, however, when the first fat, cold drop of rain hit her forehead. She blinked as the water ran into her eye, and looked up.

Gray, ominous clouds rolled in from the west. The trees far behind her whipped and twisted in the wind, and it tugged at her skirt and her hair.

They had crossed more than half the field of rocks. It wouldn't do any good to turn back; they'd be soaked before they made it. There was nothing to do but press on and hope the rain didn't start in earnest until they'd cleared the field. She ignored Enuwal's knowing frown.

She moved as fast as her tired legs and the rocks would allow. A few drops fell, far apart for the moment. Thunder rumbled in the distance. Gooseflesh broke out on Malia's arms.

When the rain began, it was as if someone dumped a waterfall right on them. Malia gasped as the water soaked her immediately. Her tunic and skirt clung to her, making it more challenging to move, and some of her hair came loose, clinging to her face and her neck. It was difficult to see anything through the pouring rain, but she knew they still had a ways to go.

Once the rain began, Aru had chirped once in surprise, given her an apologetic look, and flown off to take shelter near the cliffs.

Malia paused on a wide, fairly flat rock, and allowed Enuwal and Vedran to catch up with her. She hunched her shoulders, hugged herself, and kept her head down as water poured over her.

"Perhaps we should huddle together and wait out the rain," Enuwal said, shouting to be heard over the thunder of falling drops.

The sky was growing darker. Night would come on soon, and even if the rain stopped, they'd still be stuck in the rock field, with only starlight and a quarter moon to guide them. She shook her head. "We go on."

Rivulets of rain poured down Enuwal's face, making his frown look deeper.

"It will get dark soon," she said.

"But at least it won't be raining."

Vedran looked ahead of them and then back the way they came. "It's not much farther. I'm with Malia. We're already wet and miserable. We should just go on. At least somebody will have a warm fire and food for us."

She could always count on Vedran and how he thought with his stomach. She nodded, giving him a tight-lipped smile. Then she studied the remaining rock field through gray sheets of rain. She picked a route and leaped to the next rock.

Her foot slipped. Her arms pin wheeled, and she caught her balance. Her pulse raced, and her head began to throb in time with her speeding heart. She couldn't hear anything save for the rain's constant drum and the occasional thunder.

She made progress, but it was much slower than before, and each time she made it to a new rock, she turned to make sure Enuwal and Vedran still followed. Soon her world shrank to the wet rock before her, and the next, and the next. She grew numb to the chilly rain, and couldn't even imagine what a warm fire would feel like. She felt as though she'd done nothing but cross this blasted rock field her entire life.

Somebody cried out. She whirled. Enuwal lay on the rock behind her, one leg curled beneath him at an awkward angle, his face tight with pain. Vedran, on the rock behind him, leaped forward as easily as a deer bounding, landing lightly. He crouched beside Enuwal, exchanged a few words, then looked up and shook his head.

"He's broken his leg," he said.

Malia bit back the curse that rose to her lips. Part of her mind cried out for her to hurry, she was running out of time, while another part berated her for rushing them at their journey's end. If she'd only slowed down, this wouldn't have happened.

She crawled down the slippery rock and stood beside Enuwal. She grasped his hand. "I'm sorry," she said. "I should have listened to you. We should have waited until tomorrow."

He gave her a weak grin. A few strands of his hair had come loose and plastered to the side of his face. "I will always remember this as the moment you admitted I was right."

Vedran rolled his eyes. "I think he'll be all right."

Malia gently tucked the wet strands of Enuwal's hair behind his ears. She looked at the distance they still had to cover. The end of the rock field was still hundreds of paces away, too far for Enuwal to make it. He'd have to be lifted out by the Jeguduns.

"Stay with him," she told Vedran. "I'll get Aru and tell him what happened. He can round up some help and lift Enuwal out of here."

Vedran nodded and set to work covering the both of them with the sleeping pallets so that the worst of the rain poured off rather than soak them further. Malia's heart, beating a quick tempo to begin with, hastened all the more as she went on alone, jumping from one rock to another, wondering if she'd slip on the next one and break her leg, too. She gritted her teeth and pushed on, determined to see the Jeguduns were ready to snatch up Enuwal once the rain eased.

The sky was a dark, somber gray as she reached a rock and looked ahead for the next, only to find grassy land interspersed with fist-sized black rock. She'd made it to the end of the field. And, the rain was slowing. She climbed down carefully, not wanting to turn an ankle at the very end of her journey, and ran toward the cliffs, her wet skirt sloshing about her trembling legs. The rocky ground gave way to short rows of crops like corn, sunflowers, beans, peas, squash, and husk tomatoes. She pushed her way through them, the air thick with the plants' smells as she brushed their leaves.

"Aru!" she called out as she neared the cliffs.

He emerged from one of the homes near the bottom of the cliffs. He peered over the ledge and trilled inquisitively, glancing behind her and then back to her.

"Enuwal has broken his leg," she called out. "Can you find some others to help lift him out of the rock field?"

He let out an abrupt chirp and disappeared. Moments later, he and another Jegudun emerged, flying into the dying rain. Each one flew to another home, disappeared inside, and reemerged later to fly to yet another pair of homes.

Malia paced, both hands holding onto the strap of the travel sac strapped across her body. The rain stopped altogether. Some of the clouds parted, but it was enough to lighten the gray, and nothing more. Dark was falling quickly. She bit back the urge to call out to Aru again. He was moving as fast as possible.

Finally, six Jeguduns flew out of a cave, carrying a large wooden platform between them. It looked more suited for hauling supplies than a person with a broken leg, but it would do. Malia watched as they slowly lowered the platform, a couple of them joining Vedran to steady it and help Enuwal on. Vedran climbed onto the platform as well. The Jeguduns took up the short ropes attached to it and then took to the air, flying low over the rocks.

They brought it to ground near Malia. Enuwal lay on his back, his eyes closed, the skin around them tight. She hurried to him.

"Enuwal?" she asked.

His eyes fluttered open. "I'd always wondered what it would be like to fly, but I never imagined finding out like this."

"What can I do to help?" she asked.

"Willow bark. Plenty of it. I'll just chew it. And you and Vedran will have to set my leg. I don't think I can touch it myself." He closed his eyes again.

Vedran climbed off the platform. "We should go up ahead of them so we can steady the platform once they get it on the ledge. There's not much space."

Malia nodded. She'd been so busy pacing and watching the goings-on in the rock field that she hadn't noticed when someone had tossed a rope ladder over the lowest ledge. She craned her neck, but nobody stood up there.

She tucked the soggy end of her skirt into her belt and climbed first, the rope scratchy and wet beneath her palms. Nobody stood on the ledge to greet her, and a blanket hung over the door. The ledge was slippery, and she gave a hand to Vedran to help him up.

No time to go inside; the Jeguduns were already lifting the platform into the air. It was narrower than the ledge, allowing just enough space for Malia to press against the stone as the Jeguduns lowered it. The moment it touched down, she and Vedran crouched and steadied it, and the Jeguduns released the ropes. They flew to another ledge to wait.

She kept one foot on the ledge and braced the platform with her other foot. She got under one of Enuwal's shoulders, and Vedran under the other. Together, they helped him stand. Malia knew he must be hurting bad when he put an inordinate amount of weight on her.

A Jegudun pulled back the blanket hanging over the door and gestured them in.

A fire blazed in the hearth, and two lanterns were lit, one already on the floor beside a sleeping pallet and a basket of supplies, including dried herbs for tea as well as willow bark. Long strips of wood also lay on the floor, along with strips of cloth and a clean basin of water.

Malia left behind the fading gray light for a brilliantly lit home, the smell of rain replaced by the smell of root vegetables, venison, and hot peppers bubbling in the large pot over the fire.

"Lay him down," said a woman, emerging from another room Malia hadn't noticed before. "Let's take care of him, and then we'll see to the two of you."

Her body was softened with age, and her face crinkled around her eyes and mouth. She wore her hair as Malia had seen in Tulah's memory, cropped short, more white than black. Somehow, it made her look younger. Or perhaps it was the way she carried herself so straight, and with authority. She moved closer, and the faint smell of wild roses wafted.

Malia's breath hitched, and her heart stuttered. She'd found her grandmother.

CHAPTER TWELVE

Chanwa remained silent and as small as possible so as not to draw Muvumo's ire. She didn't know what happened in Nanda's house, but when Muvumo returned from bringing the changer to his cell, his entire body was as tight and stiff as a new tapestry, his hands clenching and unclenching, and his nostrils flared as if he were an angry dragon about to breathe fire. He strode into the back room and muttered to himself as he paced.

Ankti was hardly any better. Her hands trembled so much that when she pulled down the dishes, they clattered like teeth on a chilly morning. Chanwa took the dishes from the other woman, their fingertips brushing. She set the dishes back on the shelves and pressed Ankti gently to the floor. Then she poured a healthy amount of red wine into a glass for Muvumo, the heady scent rising as she poured. She paused in the doorway to their room. He traveled the length of the room twice before he noticed her.

"What is it," he snapped.

She raised the glass, pleased that her hand held steady. "I thought you could use this."

The lines creasing his forehead eased. "Yes. Thank you." He took the glass and turned his back to her as he drank, a clear dismissal.

She returned to the front room where she poured a smaller amount of wine for herself and Ankti. The other woman raised an eyebrow as Chanwa handed her a glass, but said nothing. She tilted her head back, her neck bared and graceful, her throat bobbing slightly as she downed the wine. Chanwa sipped at hers, her heart tripping, both from Muvumo's dark mood and because of the beautiful woman sitting close to her.

They hadn't planned their escape much beyond what they'd discussed behind the waterfall. They needed a distraction before they could sneak away on one of the dragons and have a long head start. Every day wound Chanwa a little tighter, until she felt like a single thread holding together two halves of a tapestry, on the verge of snapping.

Ankti met her gaze over the wine glass. Her eyes held the same longing that Chanwa felt, and more. Chanwa reached out and slipped her fingers through Ankti's. Her breath hitched as lightning raced through her at Ankti's touch.

The wine glass clinked as Muvumo set it down in the other room, followed by the faint rustle of paper. Chanwa jerked and pulled her hand free from Ankti's hastily. She drained the rest of her glass, and warmth spread down her throat to her stomach and out to her extremities. She sat back on her heels, closed her eyes, and waited to find out what mood her husband would be in when he came through the door.

The cloth hanging rustled, and his footsteps slowly entered. Chanwa opened her eyes to find Ankti busy cleaning their empty glasses in a basin. She turned around.

The worst of the tension had fled Muvumo's body. His pupils were large, leaving only a rim of green around them. He thought he hid the kasi powder from Chanwa, but she knew he'd taken to secreting it away in his tunic's pocket. She'd found it one time as she'd picked up his dirty clothes, thinking she'd help Ankti in this little way. Her hand had crumpled the paper, and she'd pulled it out, taken one look, and knew how he'd kept himself going those long nights and days in the scroll cavern.

She knew some who took a pinch of kasi every now and then, but for others, it became an obsession. For someone whose job was to lead his people, it could be dangerous. She wanted to say something about it, but the words refused to come out. His fury remained, written in the fine lines around his eyes and the tension about his mouth. She'd say something later, when he was calmer.

He strode to the door, and spoke with Delkis who stood guard just outside. "I need to walk." He spoke low, and Chanwa had to step closer to the door to make out what else he said.

"Most Worthy, you said you'd stop using kasi once you'd found the answers in the scrolls." Delkis, concerned.

"I need to think, and it keeps me alert."

"It keeps you awake when you're exhausted. You should sleep, not take a ride on the white dragon."

"Are you my guard, or my mother?"

"It's my duty to protect you, Most Worthy, even if it means protecting you from yourself."

"Such dedication. Very well, make sure you remain at my side. I wouldn't want to turn my ankle on the way down the stairs." The sarcasm in his tone hardly hid the anger seething beneath.

Their footsteps descended and faded into the evening. Chanwa had seen the way other men looked at Muvumo. Calculating. Furious. Envious. Most Worthy was the most tenuous position to hold. A challenge could come at any time, and then Muvumo would have to fight for his very life. And if that challenge came while he was using kasi powder . . . either it would give him a much-needed boost of energy, or it would burst his heart.

"Blasted fool," she muttered.

"Lady Chanwa?" Ankti said from the far corner.

She shook her head. "Nothing. It seems he's gone for a while."

"Should I make a plate for you?"

She grimaced. "I'm not that hungry."

"You should eat. You haven't eaten very well lately." Concern crept into her voice.

Chanwa glanced at the sheet covering the door. As easily as she could hear her husband's conversation outside, anyone standing on the stairs would be able to hear her and Ankti.

"My stomach hasn't agreed with me much recently. I think I'd rather lie down. Won't you come along and keep me company? I believe there are some garments that could use a touch up with needle and thread."

"Of course."

Chanwa let out a deep breath as she entered the back room. It smelled of Muvumo—his sweat, and faint traces of tobacco—but also of the lilac sprigs she'd had Ankti set in the corner. She settled against the farthest wall and gestured for the other woman to sit near her.

Ankti took up a dress that had been draped over one of the chests, then pulled out a box containing bone needles and thread. She set a lantern nearby so that the light fell over her work. Chanwa spent a few moments admiring the other woman's deft fingers as they pushed the needle through cloth and pulled the thread with just the right amount of tension. Her own fingers longed to open the chest and pull out the rolled vellum hidden beneath her clothes, along with the small bottle of precious ink and the pen, but she couldn't be certain of when Muvumo would return. If he caught her at writing, he'd feed her to his dragon. Her mother had driven home the need for secrecy as much as she'd taught Chanwa her letters. She sighed.

"What troubles you?" Ankti asked.

"This changer . . . he showed immense respect to Nanda."

"Mm-hm," Ankti said noncommittally.

"Do you think he'd listen to a woman?"

The needle darted in and out. "As much as he'd listen to any man or child, which is to say, so long as it suited his needs."

For once, Chanwa let her wishes bubble closer to the surface. They carried her to her feet and had her pacing the room. Ankti let the mending drop into her lap as she followed Chanwa's movement.

"What are you thinking?" Ankti asked quietly.

Chanwa went through the front room and pushed aside the white sheet hanging over the door. The stairway was empty save for the torches' flickering. She returned to the back room and stood frozen in its center, her hands clutching each other tight. As much as she savored the idea of running away with Ankti and beginning a new life, it might never happen. She might have to make the best of what she had in this place.

"If he is powerful enough to cure this illness," Chanwa began in a hushed voice, "then what else is he capable of? What other changes could he bring about?"

"What are you suggesting?"

Chanwa's anger normally resided in a small place, deep inside her belly. Sometimes her stomach ached and burned from holding it in. Tonight, she let it loose, let it flow through her veins and set her on a slow, steady burn. It heated her, and if she could catch her reflection, she knew she'd see spots of color high on her cheeks. Her hands clenched, and her breathing grew quick and shallow as it coursed through her.

She kneeled beside Ankti, laid her hands in the other woman's lap, and looked up. A few dark curls escaped Ankti's head covering, and the lantern's light danced across her face, making her features look more delicate than usual, her cheekbones more prominent.

Chanwa fought the urge to reach up and trace the other woman's face lightly with her fingers. She would not try for Ankti's affections, not now, not while the other woman might return them out of a sense of obligation or duty because of her position. But later, perhaps, if things were different . . .

She took a deep breath. "The next time someone brings a meal to the changer, can you assure that it's you who does it?"

Ankti's eyes narrowed. "I could."

"Then would you bring him a meal and a message?"

She hesitated, then nodded. "I can do that. What is the message?"

"Tell him . . . Tell him that the Maddion women would like to have dominion over themselves." Her heart pounded as the words lit upon the air like a bird taking flight. There was no taking them back now.

"If your husband heard you suggest such a thing, you would be in terrible trouble."

"The guards do not speak the trade language, nor yours. This changer understands both, does he not?"

She nodded.

"Then no one needs to know I said such a thing save for myself, you, and the changer."

"You put much trust in me."

"Should I not?"

Ankti shook her head. "No. It's just . . ." She leaned forward. Her eyes, light brown flecked with green, met Chanwa's, and her lips parted slightly.

Chanwa's heart quickened further. She would not impose herself upon Ankti, but if Ankti chose to close the gap between them, then—

Footsteps scraped the stone outside. Ankti snatched up the mending and sat back, the needle moving in and out of the cloth with only the slightest tremble.

Chanwa did her best to shove her emotions deep and smooth her face, but her cheeks burned. Her fair skin would give her away. She went to the basin of water in the corner, cold now that it had been standing there a while, and splashed water on her face. She gasped as it chilled her skin, but it did the job, cooling her flushed skin. She wiped her face dry as Muvumo spoke to Delkis for a moment in the other room. Then he stepped into their room.

"What are you still doing here?" he barked at Ankti. "That can wait for tomorrow."

She set aside the mending and box with needles and thread, her head bowed. "Yes, Most Worthy. Good night." She disappeared into the other room. The light in there disappeared, and her footsteps padded away.

He blew out the lantern in their room. Plunged into darkness, Chanwa gasped. Then her husband's arms were around her, and he was kissing her roughly, his tongue delving into her mouth. He tasted like tobacco, with something bitter underneath. The kasi powder.

He pulled her down to their mattress, tugging at her clothes. Chanwa dove deep into herself, into the same place where she hid her rage and her secrets, while her body opened to her husband.

CHAPTER THIRTEEN

"It's a clean break," Enuwal said. "Setting it will be fairly easy, and it'll heal well."

"But you'll be laid up a while," Malia said. She didn't like how pale he remained, or the slight tremble in his usually steady hands. He was in pain and trying hard not to show it.

One corner of his mouth turned up. "You weren't planning on leaving tomorrow, were you?"

She cast a glance toward her grandmother who was busy speaking with Aru and one of the other Jeguduns who had carried the platform. "I hope it doesn't come to that."

He took her hand and squeezed it, though not with his usual strength. "You were a small child when she was exiled, and Vedran wasn't even born. She won't hold it against you. Now, if your mother were here . . ."

She grimaced. "Don't. I'd rather not think of her right now. What do *you* need?"

"More willow bark." He'd already chewed on a piece, but Malia searched through his travel sac for another. He carried a thick, wool pack lined with oilskin, which had protected the contents from the rain.

Rustling through Enuwal's travel pack released the odor of the herbs within. They tickled her nose, and she sneezed, then sniffled before resuming the search. Her hand closed around a piece of bark, and she handed it to Enuwal. He gnawed on it and grimaced.

"I'm ready," he said. "Vedran?"

He kneeled on Enuwal's other side. "I set a couple of broken bones during the Dragon War." The talon he'd earned during the war nestled between his collar bones. "But show me what you want me to do."

Enuwal directed Malia in laying out the wood and cloth strips, then showed Vedran which way to pull his leg. With that, he took a deep breath, clenched the bark firmly between his teeth, and laid back.

Malia held his hand and chatted, mostly senseless stuff about their journey and the weather, anything to distract him. She kept her gaze on his face, and she knew the instant Vedran set the bone because the muscles around Enuwal's jaw tensed, his hand clamped on hers, and he let out a grunt. Sweat broke out along his forehead.

Her grandmother harrumphed and muttered, "And it's still nothing compared to a woman's birthing pains. Still, he's a tough one. Most men would have passed out."

Malia helped Vedran position the wooden slats along the length of Enuwal's leg and tie up the cloth strips to hold it in place. That done, she poured hot water over a liberal dose of chamomile, valerian root, and peppermint. The minty smell almost overwhelmed the valerian root's musky, unpleasant aroma. Still, when it was ready, she added a dollop of honey to help it go down easier and pressed it into Enuwal's hands.

He sniffed and wrinkled his nose, but said nothing before drinking it. He downed all of it as if it wasn't steaming hot and set the empty mug aside. He lay back and closed his eyes. Moments later, his chest rose and fell steadily.

"It's a good thing he sleeps," her grandmother said. "It's good for the healing." She bustled around the small space, putting the herb basket and other supplies away. "Now, what can I get for the two of you? I take it valerian root won't do. How about chamomile and peppermint? And why don't you step into the other room and change into some warm clothes in privacy? Young woman, you go first." She turned with a wry smile. "It's been a while since I lived among the Taakwa, but I remember the ways."

Malia hesitated. Her grandmother didn't know them. The news hadn't reached her yet, and of course Aru had been too busy seeing that Enuwal was brought safely into the home to let her grandmother know who they were. Still, she'd expected that her grandmother would recognize them, would see a bit of herself in their features. Malia wanted to say something, but her tongue might as well have turned to wood in her mouth for all the good it was doing her at the moment. Days of anticipation and worry, and the moment was so *normal.*

Vedran widened his eyes a little. Malia gave him a small shake of the head. *Not yet,* she tried to convey. Best that they settle in first, have something to eat and drink, and rest before telling her who they were. She went into the other room and let down the door covering.

One lantern lit the space. A few shelves held clothes and blankets. A large, wooden trunk sat in a corner. Two sleeping pallets were rolled up and propped to one side, along with several pillows. The Jegudun and her grandmother shared a space? Malia had never considered such an arrangement before. She'd assumed the exiled

Taakwa would turn to one another, but if they were scattered few and far between, they might not have that chance.

She set aside her leather belt and hip beads, then peeled off the wet clothes, letting them fall to the stone floor with a loud *plop*. She dried herself off and put on her dry clothes. The hip beads went back on. Fortunately, her travel sac was well lined, and there were only a few tiny wet spots on her fresh clothes. She dried her hair as best she could, combed it out, and tied it up again. She brought her wet clothes and leather belt out and hung them in front of the hearth, dried her dagger, and set it aside. She left the feathers hanging on the belt as well, although they were nearly dry already. Vedran disappeared into the room next.

Her grandmother handed her a mug, steam rising from it and carrying the smell of peppermint. She took a sip, cradled its heat in her hands, and slowly warmed up at last.

The elder Jegudun sat against a pile of pillows. The light reflected off his milky eyes, and he gazed into the distance, not quite focused. He canted his head to one side and chirruped inquisitively.

"We hardly ever have company, at least not strangers," her grandmother said. "Forgive me. I have forgotten my manners. This is Ziku, and I am Rina."

Malia laid a hand on Enuwal's shoulders. "This is Enuwal. He is a healer from Posalo." She hesitated. She couldn't very well not introduce herself. She swallowed the lump in her throat and continued, "I am Malia, and the other man is my brother, Vedran."

Something flickered across Rina's face, and she grew somber, looking much older all of a sudden. "Are you and your brother from Posalo as well?"

"No," she said. "We are from Selu."

"Well," Rina said, sinking to the pillows beside Ziku, the lines on her face a little deeper. "Well."

Malia wasn't sure what sort of reception she'd been hoping for when she first met her grandmother after so long. She expected surprise, yes, but not this withdrawal. Her grandmother's demeanor had grown cold, reserved. There was nothing of the faint memory of warm, soft, safe arms here.

"I apologize for intruding like this and upsetting you," Malia said, finding her voice at last. "We have business with Ziku, and then we'll leave."

Rina blinked a few times and refocused on her. "What? No, don't be silly. Unless perhaps I'm not what you expected? Clearly you already know who I am. I just never thought . . . never considered I'd ever see my grandchildren. I convinced myself a long time ago that you were dead. It was the only way I could get through the days, you see. Then there were the other days, when I considered myself dead instead, and this some sort of strange new world for my spirit to wander." She let out a laugh. "I see by your face that you think me mad. I have wondered that many times. But it was never me that was mad; it was the rest of the Taakwa."

"I don't think you're mad," Malia said slowly. "But it turned out you were quite right about the Jeguduns, so the rest of us were all a little blind."

She snorted. "A *little*? I saw that barrier collapse and come raining down, and the Maddion swooping in on their dragons, and I thought, *The fools have brought it on themselves.* But my Jegudun friends tell me someone convinced the Taakwa to fight with the Jeguduns, and that she repaired the barrier when everything else failed."

"That was Malia," Vedran said from the doorway. He hung his wet clothes beside hers and kept his eyes on Rina as he sat. He took the proffered cup of tea from Malia and sipped it slowly.

"Ah," Rina said. "And did it make your mother proud, your bringing the Taakwa and Jeguduns together?"

"It did," Malia said.

"Strange. She was one of the most vocal when it came to exiling me."

"You broke a law. She was the clan mother. She couldn't make any exceptions. And besides, she told me she and the others gave you the chance to change your mind, or at least keep your opinions to yourself." Malia could hardly believe the words as they came out of her mouth to defend her mother.

"Did she also tell you I wanted to seek the Jeguduns to find a cure for your father's illness? She let him die, and—"

"She did not," Enuwal said, propping himself up. Color had returned to his cheeks. His brows drew down, and he glared. Many a disobedient patient had quivered before that look, but Rina merely pursed her lips. "His body was eaten away by disease. The Jeguduns have no cure for it, and neither do the Taakwa."

"You've held onto that anger all these years?" Malia asked.

"He was the only child of mine to survive. Before him, I had seven dead babies. Seven. Can you imagine mourning that many children? I thought I was cursed. And then your father came along, and he was strong, and grew so large, and I thought everything would be all right." She hung her head, sniffed once, wiped at her eyes, and looked up again. "He was taken from me, and then the rest of my life was taken when I was exiled. Is it any wonder I am still angry after all this time?"

"Well, are you angry with your grandchildren?" Enuwal asked.

"Of course not."

"Then may I suggest a proper greeting, and save the arguing for when you all have a chance to know one another properly?"

Malia and Vedran stood, as did Rina, climbing to her feet as easily as a woman Malia's age. Vedran pressed his hands together before him, began, "My life in—"

Rina yanked him close and held him so tight that her shoulder muffled his protestations. Then she released him and pulled Malia to her.

Here were the soft, strong, safe arms that lingered in Malia's memories. And the smell. Wild roses. This was a part of home that had been missing. She wrapped her arms tighter around her grandmother as hot tears pricked her eyes. For a moment, she didn't think about the reason she had come, she just enjoyed this.

And then her grandmother let her go. She beamed, and Ziku smiled as well, a toothy, wolfish grin that lit up his face. He let out a happy trill and ruffled his wings.

The sweet rose scent sharpened, and the room tilted. Malia's stomach lurched. She reached a hand out blindly and found the warm stone above the hearth. The room spun so violently that she thought the very earth would rise up and throw her out the cave, and her body would whirl through the air until it landed with a sickening crunch on the rocky field. She leaned over and vomited tea, her nose and throat burning with it.

The fog in her mind rolled forward, and the tendrils snagged her like cactus spines. *No, not now!* She pushed against it as hundreds of points of pain shot through her head. She screamed, took a staggering step toward her belt and the feathers (*must reach the feathers and stop this, hurry, hurry, HURRY*). The fog swallowed her as she reached out, her fingertips just shy of the feathers.

Fire blazed against her arm, her ankle, her knee, like hundreds of ants at each location biting frantically. She choked on a scream and kicked, trying to get out of the ant pile. She had been in a Jegudun home—Ziku's home—talking to her grandmother, holding her grandmother at last, and then the world had started to spin. Had she somehow fallen out of the cave and into an ant pile?

The fog in her mind had receded, along with the tendrils that had been stealing through her memories like interloping rabbits in a field of greens. She focused, blinked, realized she wasn't in an ant pile at all, she was still in Ziku's and Rina's home with everybody hovering over her, eyes wide and frightened, and they each held a feather in their hands, save for Ziku, who remained seated against the pillows.

A feather had been burned into her left arm, her left knee, and her right ankle, just like the fading red lines in her right hand. These hurt far worse than that one had, maybe because there were more, or maybe because the magic working against her had been stronger this time. She moaned.

She hadn't considered that her grandmother would set off one of these episodes. She thought the person, place, or thing had to be recent and vivid and hidden behind the fog in her mind. Perhaps the sneaking tendrils made it easier for the fog to try to take over, or maybe it wasn't limited to recent, vivid memories, or perhaps the heightened emotion combined with everything else had done her in. Or maybe it was just getting worse.

Her head was fuzzy, and felt as if it were filled with cottonwood fluff. Her stomach roiled, but there was nothing left for it to dispose of, although the taste of bile lingered. Fortunately, the room remained still. She wasn't sure she could stand the spinning again.

"What *was* that?" Rina asked, her voice trembling.

"That's the reason we're here," Malia said. She raised a hand before either Vedran or Enuwal could ask and said, "I'm fine, I remember what we're doing here and what happened just before this episode. But my skin is on fire where you touched the feathers to me."

"There's a salve in my travel sac," Enuwal said.

Vedran handed it to Enuwal, who dug through it and pulled out a tiny jar.

"You should be resting," Malia told him when he took off the lid and made to apply the salve. She took the jar and put a liberal amount on her arm, her knee, and her ankle. The salve took away the worst sting, leaving more of a throbbing, slight pain. It had a sharp odor, with a hint of honey. She sighed in relief as the pain eased, then closed the jar and handed it back. "Keep that handy."

"What was that all about?" Rina asked.

Malia did her best to tell her grandmother about the problems with her memory, with Vedran and Enuwal filling in the gaps, or backtracking to make sure Rina got all the details. She ended with the hope that Ziku, as one of the eldest Jeguduns, would have some sort of knowledge that would help her, especially since Tulah had made sure to highlight her arrival here in the memories she'd passed on before she died.

As she and the others spoke, Rina set out bowls of stew, and bowls of leafy greens mixed with salted nuts and drizzled with lemon juice and oil, a dish she said she'd picked up from one of the people the Jeguduns traded with. It was light and refreshing, a nice contrast to the heavier stew, and for the meal's end, they all had warm chocolate to drink, Enuwal adding dried willow bark to his. He'd gone a bit pale again, but when Malia asked how he was, he insisted he was well enough.

"My goodness," her grandmother said when they'd finished speaking and the dishes sat empty and they all held the warm mugs.

Somewhere in the distance, a cougar screamed, and the sound sent shivers down Malia's spine. She imagined the cougar stalking a smaller creature, perhaps pouncing on it from above like a Maddion guiding a dragon to fall upon someone below. She thought of them taking that old man and wondered what they were up to. The throbbing in her head had slowed, but continued to beat a steady pulse.

Rina turned to Ziku. "Is there anything that can be done for her?"

He cocked his head to one side and stared into the distance, as if listening to inner voices. At last, he straightened and shook his head.

Malia had come all this way, pushing herself, coped with another episode, and Enuwal had broken a leg, and there was nothing that could be done. Her trembling hands tightened around the mug. "Is there truly nothing, no matter how inconsequential or absurd, that we could try? Because I will try anything at this point."

He shook his head again and trilled sadly.

"And so . . . my memories . . . will I eventually lose them all?"

Enuwal grabbed her hand and squeezed. Rina's gaze followed the movement, but she said nothing about it.

Ziku hesitated, then nodded.

Malia sat back. If all of her memories were gone, then who would she be? What would she be like? What would the world be like to her? What would she *do*? She wouldn't be able to ever be a clan mother. She wouldn't be able to care for a home by herself, or even her own needs, not if she was already forgetting the way home, or losing track of chores halfway done, or thinking her shoes belonged to somebody else. She met Enuwal's gaze, squeezing his hand tighter. She wouldn't be able to marry him. It wouldn't be right, asking him to take care of her as the fog slowly consumed her mind.

She withdrew her hand and sat with her legs curled before her, wrapping her arms around them and resting her chin on her knees, as if she could hold in the sheer terror that threatened to sweep through her.

CHAPTER FOURTEEN

The weight of all the Maddions' eyes were like thousands of tiny daggers slicing Muvumo's skin. If this failed, he would be dead shortly after, torn to shreds by his own people. He was numb all over, and felt more like a spectator than a participant in the destruction of his people's history.

And yet, if it worked, his people would live. Their scrolls could start over. *They* could start over. He clutched that idea and held on tight. Still, it did nothing to settle the sick, sinking feeling that had plagued his stomach for the past few days as he took his place on the highest mesa, the rest of the Maddion spread behind him and on the mesas below. Before stepping outside, he'd taken a pinch of kasi powder. Now, he couldn't tell how much of that contributed to his racing heart, and how much came from the storm of emotions within him.

Off to one side, near the cliff face, a sick man, one of Muvumo's youngest warriors, lay on a sleeping pallet. He'd be dead by morning if this didn't work. He'd insisted on joining them.

"Would you care to inspect the cavern?" he asked the old man, who had refused to give a name.

"There's no need," he said, infuriatingly calm. His eyes were the same deep orange of the flames that would soon consume the scrolls. "I would know if you were lying to me and all the men's scrolls were not sitting at the mountaintop right now, ready to burn."

"What do you get out of this anyway?" Muvumo asked. Enough conversations went on around them that they had a semblance of privacy. The setting sun blazed on the granite, turning it shades of pink and orange.

The old man smiled, sorrow pinching the skin around his eyes. "I get the chance to begin again."

Muvumo remained silent. The changer sometimes said things that made no sense whatsoever. And yet, there was a sense of anticipation about the old man, from the tilt of his head to the way his orange eyes burned more intensely than before. It was hard to look directly in those eyes. It felt as though, if Muvumo looked too long, he might fall into them and be burned alive. He shuddered and turned away.

The sun slipped away at last, leaving a few fiery clouds behind as the first stars came out. Delkis stood at Muvumo's side. The women had all gathered at the mesa below, with their servants, waiting. A few of the sick, in the early stages, were among them, supported by servants. One mother held an ill toddler, the child's great, racking coughs cycling with exhausted wails. Those who were too sick to walk were home, waiting.

Sometimes the women's higher, gentler voices drifted up, but he was mostly surrounded by the rumble of his men. His people. He had the same jitters he always got before battles, and he suppressed the urge to shift his weight or check his short axe yet again. Instead, he stood straight, chin high, and met any man's gaze who was willing to look at him. Each one dropped before him, but not fast enough, and not before he caught the hint of a challenge.

A boy brought the cold torch to him. Muvumo took the smooth wood into his hands and hesitated. Once lit, it would signal the men waiting at the top to set the scrolls on fire. His breath hitched in his throat. *All of that knowledge, gone. Our ancestors will be nothing more than ghosts.* Of course, if they didn't give this old man what he wanted, the Maddion standing around him would be nothing more than ghosts themselves. He lowered the torch, and the boy looked at him with wide eyes, as if to say, *Are you sure?*

"Light it," he snapped.

The boy fumbled with the small kindling in the bowl, then brought a flame to the oil-soaked torch with a trembling hand. The flame licked at the torch and took, and the scent of burning pine filled Muvumo's nostrils. He raised the torch high and swung it slowly back and forth.

An answering flame lit up a moment later, swung back and forth, and then touched the base of the pyre. It spread lengthwise first, then licked up, touching the first scrolls. From the women's mesa below came the sound of crying. From the men all around Muvumo, deafening silence.

His stomach knotted tight. His hand gripped the handle of the short axe, ready to pull it free to defend himself, but all eyes were now on the flames high above them, mesmerized. Some men watched with grim expression, others held unshed tears shimmering in their eyes. Delkis alone was impassive, his attention torn between the massive fire and the men surrounding Muvumo, his hand resting near the weapons hanging from his belt.

The old man smiled. Muvumo's hand tightened on the axe. If this didn't work . . . if others took ill . . . he'd behead this old man himself. If Muvumo still lived, that is.

The old man's eyes brightened. The orange swirled around the tiny pinpricks of black in the center of his eyes, deepening to blood red before lightening to the same pink glow of the setting sun on granite. His smile faded, and he doubled over, clutching his stomach and moaning. The skin beneath his tunic rippled as if something beneath fought to escape.

Muvumo shoved his people away from the old man. "Give him space." He didn't know what would happen to anybody standing near the old man. He thought of the scrolls he'd read, describing the destruction of an entire city and most of its people. The changer had promised a cure in exchange for the burning of the scrolls, but Muvumo didn't trust the being one bit.

The scrolls. Muvumo wasn't sure how they fit into this, but their burning was part of the old man's plan. The *changer's* plan. Another ripple went through the old man's body. It was clear that he himself was changing. What exactly would the old man become? Would he even be human?

The air around the changer swirled, brightened, and became the same deep orange as his eyes, as if he were engulfed in flames. A few of the men cried out as their attention moved from the burning scrolls to the scene on the mesa, and they hastened away, taking the stairs two at a time. Muvumo backed against the railing, Delkis tugging at his arm.

"We should go, Most Worthy," he said.

"I brought this thing here. I will be the first to see what he becomes, and what becomes of us." Muvumo pulled his short axe free, wondering if it would be enough to fight this . . . *thing*.

The old man fell to his knees and brought his forehead to the ground as if worshipping. He cried out, and the sound ripped through Muvumo. He'd never heard such pain before, not on the battlefield, not from the sick and dying, not from women birthing. It made him ill to his stomach.

The scrolls were completely engulfed in flames now, collapsing in on themselves. Muvumo only glanced at the conflagration, not wanting to blind himself by staring too long at the light. Full darkness had fallen, with only a few torches lining the mesa and stairs to brighten the darkness. Men ran down the stairs, fleeing the shape changer. The women and children below had fled to the lowest mesa. They couldn't be sure what was happening, but the men's fear was enough to press them all against the farthest railing.

Muvumo clenched his teeth and hefted the short axe in his hand. He would do his best to fight this thing, even if it became a bear, or a mountain lion.

The old man screamed again, his skin rippling faster. The sound began as something guttural and animal, and Muvumo feared he really would be fighting a beast, but then it became shrill. Still animalistic, but feminine, more like a woman in labor.

The orange light that pulsed in the changer's eyes spread and covered his entire form. The shape beneath it shifted, shuddered, slimmed down. The wispy, white hair thickened and became the same golden shade as corn silk. One last ripple passed through the body, then it stilled, save for the deep and rapid rise and fall of its back as it breathed.

The changer raised its head. *Her* head.

Her eyes were still a deep, unsettling orange. The light in them swirled quickly, then slowed to a lazy eddy. Her face was delicate, and young, and beautiful. Oh, it was a beautiful face. It stirred Muvumo's blood even though he knew she wasn't human.

She stood slowly, not from any residual weakness, because power flowed off her like heat from the sun, but with grace and determination. She still wore the old man's clothes, the loose pants hanging low on her hips, the tunic, though baggy, showing the gentle curves beneath, yet somehow she made the clothes look regal. She smiled, and warmth spread from the center of Muvumo's chest out to all parts of his body.

That is dangerous, he thought, but he couldn't quell his body's reaction to her.

She stepped aside and gestured with one arm toward the sick young man behind her. He'd risen from the pallet and stood tall, the pallor gone. His skin flushed with health, and he couldn't hide his smile.

From below, the sick toddler's wails turned into a hearty cry, and the child's mother let out a happy cry of her own. All across the mesa, the ill were shouting, raising their arms and praising Muvumo. More cries came from inside the homes as people realized they were no longer ill. They came pouring out of the caves to join the crowds already outside.

"A promise fulfilled," the changer said. Her voice was deep and melodious and feminine, and spoke of thousands of secrets.

Muvumo closed his eyes, spread his arms, and let his head fall back. He breathed in the air, scented with pine and the sweat of fearful men, and the smoke drifting from the pyre high above. His scrolls would be the first new ones in the cavern, and they would glorify his life. His people had a second chance, and it was all because of him.

He let out a whoop, his voice echoing off the mountain, bouncing higher, and then his men took up the cry with him until their voices filled his head and thrummed in his chest, more powerful than his heartbeat.

CHAPTER FIFTEEN

Malia spent the morning with several Jeguduns in the fields below Rina's home. With every bite of a shovel in dirt and with every weed she viciously yanked out, she felt the tiniest bit better. Vedran had helped her some of the morning and tried encouraging her. "Not all is lost. There might be another way to save your memories." But her fierce silence had finally driven him off, and he'd gone hunting instead.

The sun was overhead when someone cleared a throat behind her. She turned to find Rina standing at the end of a row of young corn. She eyed the basket filled with scraggly weeds. "You've done quite a bit of work. You should come up and eat."

"Thank you, but I'm not hungry."

Rina pursed her lips. Her gaze flickered to one side, and she shielded her eyes with her hand.

Several Jegudun s flew in low from the north and east. Malia squinted, trying to make out who they were, but they were too far away. They landed on Ziku's ledge and disappeared inside.

"Ziku hasn't received so many visitors since he was part of the council," Rina muttered. "And now, we've had a steady stream." She gave Malia a sidelong glance. "Not that we mind, it's just unusual."

"Maybe they have news about the Maddion."

"I'm afraid you might be right." Rina hastened to the rope ladder.

Malia's steps hurried to keep up with her grandmother's. Rina climbed the ladder first, moving as deftly as a young woman, and Malia followed. Before she reached the ledge, she smelled spicy, warm chocolate and sweet breads. Although she hadn't had an appetite moments before, her stomach grumbled appreciatively. The Jegudun s were already talking, excited chirps and whistles filling the air.

She paused in the doorway. Ziku's home was crowded, holding five Jegudun s, Rina, and Enuwal, who had scooted to one side to avoid being a tripping hazard in the room's center, what with his long, splinted leg stretched before him. The newcomers all sat on rugs and held mugs of the warm chocolate drink, with plates before them, the food half eaten. Rina stood just inside the door, one arm crossed before her, the other hand at her chin, her brows drawn down as she followed the Jegudun s' conversation.

One of the Jegudun s had a strange appearance. He was brown, with dark, smeared splotches covering him all over. Malia wondered if he was ill, but then realized the splotches were paint. He slumped while the others sat straight, and he hardly spoke, adding a few sounds for clarification.

Rina inclined her head toward him. "That is Palutzi. He spent the past few days in the Maddions' mountain, watching them. He's brought back some disturbing news."

Icy fingers ran down Malia's spine. "What is it?"

She frowned. "I'm not certain yet. I've picked up something about the illness, and a stranger, but nothing more. I'll have to wait for Palutzi or one of the others to share memories."

The stranger had to be the old man the Maddion had captured. Malia hoped he was safe, but given that he was with the Maddion, he probably wasn't. She wondered what they wanted with him. And what about the illness? Perhaps they were dying off even faster. Even if she lost all her memories, it would be worth it so long as the Taakwa's enemies were completely destroyed as well.

She sat beside Enuwal. "Can I get you anything?"

He shook his head. "I only wish I knew what got them so riled up."

"We'll find out soon enough, I suppose." She helped herself to some of the warm chocolate and sweet bread.

Ziku gazed at the hearth as the others spoke. His milky eyes gave nothing away, but he slumped even further than he usually did. At last, he raised a hand and chirruped, then gestured toward Rina.

She sat in front of Palutzi and laid her hands in his. The Jegudun sighed and nodded his head, then he and Rina closed their eyes.

Malia didn't often have the chance to watch somebody else absorb memories from a Jegudun. Rina's eyes rolled beneath her lids, and her lips twitched occasionally, almost as if she dreamed. One time, Rina gasped, and the lines of her face deepened afterwards as she frowned and her brows drew down.

Malia finished her sweet bread and most of the chocolate drink before Rina and Palutzi opened their eyes. Rina blinked a few times, then turned to Malia and Enuwal, still wearing a frown.

"The old man that the Maddion found is a *mutara*, a changer."

The icy fingers returned to Malia's spine.

"Truly?" Enuwal said. "I thought those were just stories that the elders liked to tell."

"Why would they bring a changer to their mountains?" Malia asked.

"The *mutara* changes places, or other people, or situations," Rina said. "She changed the Maddion."

Palutzi chirruped and shook his head.

"No," Rina frowned. "She didn't change the Maddion themselves. She changed whatever was causing the illness. It was . . . a curse?" she asked Palutzi.

The Jegudun nodded. He turned to Malia and held out his hands, offering to share his memories with her as well.

Malia hesitated. She didn't think a simple sharing of memories would trigger another one of her episodes. "I'd like to see for myself. Thank you," she said, and scooted forward. She placed her hands in Palutzi's. They were small, warm, supple. They gave her hands a reassuring squeeze, and Palutzi's lips turned up in a wolfish grin that seemed to say, *It's all right.* Malia nodded and took a deep breath, her shoulders relaxing.

Palutzi tugged at her mind. Malia closed her eyes and let herself go along.

She was in Palutzi's memories. It was night, and he crouched within juniper brush. He was in the foothills of a massive mountain. A stone face rose in the distance, tiny dots of light showing how a staircase turned upon itself, leading up and up and up, taller even than Tuvin's Falls and the cliffs that surrounded the Taakwa's valley. She grew dizzy contemplating the height.

She smelled what Palutzi smelled, including the juniper, the warm earth, a rabbit hiding in the brush down the steep hill, and even the fading scent of a coyote. A stream flowed somewhere above the hiding place, water gurgling over rocks.

Along the mountain face, men were carrying armfuls of objects out to dragons and sending them to the mountaintop. The objects reminded Malia of the thin, rolled bit of leather the Jeguduns had gifted her with, the one with the painting on it. The Maddion had so many of them. Were they pictures? Did they paint like the Jeguduns? Somehow she couldn't imagine them creating anything beautiful like that. Whatever the objects were, they must be important to the Maddion. Otherwise, why would there be so many? They spent the better part of an entire day moving the objects to the mountaintop via their dragons.

As twilight fell, all of the Maddion gathered on the mesas the dragons had been using to land and take off from. They were quiet, somber.

A white blanket hanging over one of the doors moved. The Most Worthy, wearing his traditional white belt, came out, followed by the elderly man they had taken. The elder walked tall, not at all shrunken and fearful as he'd been. Even at this far distance, even watching through Palutzi's memory, something twinged deep inside Malia in response to the elder. This man was not merely human. He was more; he was magical, and it was powerful magic indeed.

A fire bloomed to life on the mountaintop. All of the objects the Maddion had painstakingly moved up there now burned. The Maddion were still, watching.

And then, the old man shifted into a young woman. Hackles rose along the back of Palutzi's neck, and Malia could imagine her own tiny hairs doing the same at the nape of her neck. This was ancient magic, like the forces that made the world, like the hot, liquid earth that fueled explosions and created mountains, like the grinding of earth itself.

Malia could sense another magic now, through Palutzi. It was the same magic that had caused the Maddion's illness. It flowed away, like water soaking into the earth after a rain, and disappeared. The Maddion were healthy.

Night had fallen. The pyre burned bright on the mountaintop. Dragons circled high above, roaring, the Maddions' exhilaration contagious. The Maddion themselves began to celebrate. More torches flared to life on the mesas, along the stairways. Homes burned bright with light, door coverings thrown back.

Malia pulled away. She'd seen enough. Her enemy was healed while she suffered the slow loss of her memories. The tug on her mind disappeared, and then she was sitting in her grandmother's home again, Palutzi withdrawing his hands from hers.

She found everybody watching her. "The Maddion are no longer ill."

Vedran muttered a curse.

"Their numbers are depleted, though," Enuwal said.

"True. But they still have their dragons, and their rage, and I'm sure they haven't forgotten us." Malia rubbed her arms, chilled despite the warm air and hearth fire. "What do we do now?"

"There's nothing we *can* do," Rina said. "The *mutara* isn't a being to trifle with. Maybe she will take care of the Maddion for us."

"Why would she help them anyway?"

Rina shook her head. "I don't know. They paid her well somehow. I hope they think the price was worth it."

CHAPTER SIXTEEN

Muvumo's night was a blur. He left the revelers initially to check on those who had been ill. All were healed, no longer coughing up blood, or crying in pain, and although the hardest hit were still emaciated, they were eating with gusto, and no doubt they'd soon put the proper weight back on. The youngest had been a baby. He rocked the little girl until she fell asleep, the first good sleep she'd had in days, her mother informed him. She'd been sick a long time, and her mother had all but given up hope when the changer's miraculous cure occurred.

Assured that all was as the changer had promised, he returned to the celebration, Delkis on his heels, although Muvumo was certain that this night, of all nights, he wouldn't need a personal guard. His men greeted him with claps on his shoulder, or outright embraces, pressing mugs of wine into his hand, urging him to join the drinking. The unmentionables were everywhere, and while

Muvumo's cock stirred at the sight of so many women giving and receiving pleasure, he had more pressing matters to attend.

He found the changer on the highest mesa, as far from the revelry as she could have gotten without sprouting wings and taking flight. She leaned against the stone wall, chin high, gazing at the quarter moon. She still wore the old man's clothes, which for all their bagginess, couldn't hide her figure. Muvumo drained his cup of wine and thrust it at one of the guards. The man tried his best to ignore the sounds and sights below, but every now and then, his gaze drifted wistfully.

"Will you become a bird, now, and fly away?" Muvumo asked quietly as he joined her at the wall, careful to keep enough space between them that he could pull his dagger or axe free and defend himself.

She sighed and closed her eyes. "If only it worked that way." Her eyes opened, and she turned them on him.

Muvumo wished to look away from the unsettling, deep orange swirling around her pupil. Instead, he forced himself to hold her gaze. "How does this magic work, exactly? Why did I have to burn my people's history for you to give us this cure? And will this cure last?"

Her lips curved into a smile. Her teeth were white, square, straight. Perfect, like the rest of her. The complete opposite of the decrepit old man she'd been. Which form was true? Was either?

"What did you feel, when you watched your scrolls burn?" she asked.

"Anger. Despair. Sadness at so much wasted. Hopeful that it wasn't for nothing." He surprised himself with his honesty. And yet, he had the feeling that if he lied, this shape changer would know and be quite displeased. He wasn't sure he wanted to know what she was capable of when displeased.

She nodded. "The despair was magnified among the hundreds of your people. I found it satisfying, like a nice mug of wine might be for you after a hard day's work."

He frowned. "You found our despair satisfying?"

"Yes. And why not? Your people have caused plenty of despair over generations. At least this was temporary. What of those you enslaved? What of those women down there right now, the ones you call unmentionable?"

His frown deepened. "You don't understand our ways. It's what they're for. It's what they do, all they've known. They are unsuitable to be wives, or they were captured during raids."

"You're right, I don't understand. You waste so many lives." She studied the night. "I can never change myself, no matter how much I desire it. I have to wait for somebody else's desire for change. Once I have fulfilled their wishes, then I may fulfill my own." She cast a sidelong glance at him. "Would you like to know why I chose this form, this time around?"

He shifted his weight. Under her stare, he felt like a small child being scolded. He couldn't let this woman make him feel that way. "Because it would please me?" he said, half chiding.

She arched an eyebrow. "Yes, actually. I rather thought it would torment you."

He scowled. "What about the cure? Will it last? Or is that another trick of yours?"

"It will last," she sighed. "There was poison throughout the mountain, left behind by one of the peoples you destroyed. Their voices cried out for revenge. It was slow-acting magic, but very powerful. I wish I could have met them."

"Who did this?"

"The Solumna. Your scrolls told you of them, did they not?"

"Yes. They were a weak people, easily captured."

"They were peaceful and far too trusting." She took a deep breath. "But your treatment of them changed all that. If you had just worked *with* them, you would have realized the depths of their powers. Instead, you wiped them out. Now they and their magic are gone forever." She shook her head.

"It sounds like you sympathize with them."

"I do."

"Then why help us?"

Her gaze returned to the moon. Somewhere below them, a man whooped, and then several broke out into a drunken rendition of a hunting song. A woman screamed in fear. Muvumo hoped his men wouldn't damage any of the unmentionables. It would be difficult for a while to replace any of them.

"I wish someone else had come to me," the changer finally said. "But I cannot choose who does so. I can only choose my next form. I was tired of being that old man."

"And why were you an old man?" *What are you, truly*? He wanted to ask, but sensed it would only infuriate her, and he'd get no more information.

"The last person who asked for my help had loved her grandfather very much. He was the world to her, and her enemies had destroyed him. I wanted to know what it might have been about him that inspired such love." She turned her orange eyes on him. "I thrive on chaos. It is my bread, my meat, my tea, my air, my wine, my water. It makes my heart pound and my blood flow. It brings me joy."

Muvumo pressed his hands flat against the top of the cold stone wall. "Why tell me all this?"

"It's been so long since I've spoken with anybody." She turned from him. "When I retired to the cave where you found me, your people had only recently tamed dragons. Your people hadn't yet heard of Jeguduns, or had found the Solumna and ensured your curse. Do you have any idea how I feel sometimes, waiting alone?"

"If you were lonely, why not just venture out into the world?"

"The world can handle only so much chaos. Then things must settle. Balance must be found. Then people get bored, or they become unsatisfied, and that's when they ask me to work magic."

Another whoop sounded below. The men were fully into their cups now, and Muvumo found he had no desire to join them. He was beginning to understand a thing or two about loneliness himself. He was his people's leader now, and losing himself to pleasure as his men were doing felt as if he'd show some sort of weakness. He felt as though he should have more control than them, less abandon. And so, he almost sympathized with the changer. Almost. He couldn't shake the image of how her skin had rippled during the change, as if some immense beast dwelled just beneath the skin. Before, he couldn't wait to find her. Now, he couldn't wait to see her go, preferably some place far from the Maddion.

"Will you leave, now that we've both fulfilled our bargains?" he asked her.

"Not just yet. The chaos is not over."

Muvumo believed that might prove to be a bad thing for the Maddion. He swallowed the lump of fear building in his throat and said, "Then I shall offer a guest's quarters to you. Unless I need to put you in a cell again?"

"There is no cell that can hold me. Not even when I am a frail, old man." She smiled.

A chill ran through him. He turned to the nearest guard. "See her to the best guest room we have available, and see that she's brought some proper clothes. After that, you may join your companions. This is a great night for the Maddion, and I won't have any of my men say they didn't enjoy it."

His eyes lit, and he nodded. "Yes, Most Worthy. Come . . . madam," he said with a moment's hesitation.

"Ah, yes, what shall we call you?" Muvumo asked.

Her grin widened. "I believe this time around I'd like to be called Sersha."

"Well, then, good evening, Sersha."

He waited while the guards saw her to one of the nearer caves. They sent a boy on the errand of bringing her clothes and, Muvumo hoped, something to eat and drink if she wanted. Then the guards hurried to the milling group of people on the mesa below.

"There was a time when I would have been in the thick of such a celebration," Muvumo said to Delkis. "Now, all I can think about is my nice, warm, soft pallet and a fire in the hearth, and perhaps some tea before falling asleep."

Delkis snorted in laughter. "It's a tiring, thankless job that you do."

"True." Muvumo started down the stairs. "Does that mean you have no desire to be Most Worthy one day?"

"I used to think of it all the time. Now that I've witnessed it up close, the position has lost much of its luster, I admit."

Muvumo smiled. "I don't know. Tonight I feel good. I am deeply sorry to have lost the scrolls, though."

"Tomorrow you can begin new scrolls. Imagine, yours will be the first of the new batch. Young men will frown when their instructors assign your scrolls to them. '*They are so ancient*,' they will complain," Delkis said in a whining voice that mocked many of the reactions Muvumo often heard.

He laughed. "I will consider it sweet revenge." He paused outside his doorway. The white cloth hung over, with only the faintest light inside. Chanwa must have gone to sleep already, probably thinking he'd stay up all night with the revelers. "Good night, my friend."

Delkis bowed his head. “Good night, Most Worthy. I will see you in the morning.”

Muvumo ducked inside. The air smelled of peppermint tea and sweet fruit. Chanwa often ate sparingly when she thought she would be dining alone. He slipped off his shoes, hoping to slide beneath the blankets with her, and left them beside the door, then blew out the flickering, fading lantern light.

Another light shined around the cloth hanging over the door to their private room. A faint scratch came from inside. A sigh followed. Chanwa was still awake?

If she thought he’d be gone all night, then she would have time for . . . what? His mind went back to the other day when he walked in and found her flushed, sitting on top of one of the trunks. They were all filled with clothes and fabric. There was no way she could have hidden a man inside one. Or could she?

No, the sounds weren’t right for two bodies moving together. Muvumo’s brows crinkled as he crept closer to the door. He pushed the cloth aside slowly, holding his breath.

Chanwa sat on the floor beside a trunk with a flat lid. On top of the trunk was a long piece of vellum, half-filled with words. She dipped a feather pen into a bottle of ink and bent over the vellum, quickly scratching out another line.

Muvumo’s stomach dropped. *She reads? She writes? It is forbidden! Women take too long to learn such complicated tasks anyway. How did she? And hiding it from me . . .* He recalled his promise to Sersha. What if she found out about this and reversed the cure?

Then he recalled something else Sersha had said, about burning all the men’s scrolls. All of the *men’s* scrolls. She knew.

Cold fury ripped through him as he stormed into the room. “What is this?” he bellowed.

The pen went flying, and the ink spilled over the vellum as Chanwa jumped to her feet.

CHAPTER SEVENTEEN

Malia dreamed of dragons flying overhead. Their shadows passed over her and left her chilled. Then came a fire in the woods, and suddenly she was hot, burning up. People were screaming. *Her* people, screaming in agony. The air smelled of wood smoke and blood and burning flesh. She gagged on the smells. Then all of that passed, and she dreamed of a woman with fiery orange eyes. She dreamed of the Maddion men, surrounding her, death in their eyes, blood on their hands. *Her* blood. It dripped from their fingertips, falling on her forehead, her cheek, leaving hot streaks as it ran along her skin.

She woke with a cry, struggling out of the dream as if she'd been underwater. A cool hand fell on her arm right away.

"Mother?" she gasped.

"No." Rina. Her grandmother. It grew more difficult every time she woke to orient herself to where she was, and who surrounded her. Muffled voices came from the other room. She'd woken

Enuwal and Vedran again. Heavy snores came from the corner. Ziku slept on, oblivious. The air held the lingering scent of their dinner from the night before; Rina had used the last of their venison to make stew.

The fog crept through her mind. Fingers reached out constantly now, digging into her memories and rooting them out as if they were weeds. Soon there would be nothing of her left at all.

She turned her thoughts away from that. She'd go mad if she considered it too long.

"Another bad dream?" Rina asked. "Would you like some tea?"

Faint light showed around the door in the other room. Dawn was imminent, at least, and she hadn't woken everybody in the middle of the night as she'd done before. She'd never get back to sleep at this point, so she nodded.

She brushed out her hair as Rina lit a lantern. When the light spilled over Ziku's face, he let out a little growl and turned over, pulling his blanket higher. Malia didn't like ousting him from his place beside Rina, but her grandmother had insisted Malia needed her far more than Ziku did at the moment, and Rina's close presence did indeed have the ability to ground her when nobody else could.

She followed Rina into the front room and lit a lantern as Rina stoked the fire in the hearth and bustled around, gathering mugs and herbs for tea. Vedran sat up and rubbed his eyes. "Was it the same dream?"

"Yes," Malia sighed.

"You should've never looked at Palutzi's memories," Enuwal said. "The *mutara* would give anybody nightmares."

She frowned. "I appreciate your concern, but I think it's more than nightmares. I think my mind is trying to tell me something." She sat on a rug and accepted a mug from Rina.

"Like what?" Vedran said. He stood and stretched, his fingertips coming within less than a hand span of the ceiling. When had he grown so tall?

She bit her lower lip, uncertain whether to share the idea that had crept up on her. She couldn't wait much longer, though, not if she hoped for some sort of cure of her ailment.

"The *mutara* is powerful enough to cure all the Maddion of their illness," she began slowly. "It would probably be nothing to cure one person of a magic-induced memory loss."

They all spoke at once, a sudden cacophony rising in the cave, and all of them sounded angry. Malia sighed, stood, and walked onto the ledge. They didn't understand what it was like, living inside her head. Every day a little more of her mind slipped behind the fog, gone as if it had never existed. Then there was her failed attempt at pottery yesterday.

She'd gathered everything she needed, then had begun rolling out coils and building them up, intending to make a large, wide bowl that she would eventually paint and leave with Rina and Ziku. But at some point, she'd stopped in the midst of it, sat back blinking, and wondered who was making this bowl and why they had placed it in her way. By the time she remembered, the clay was too dry for her to go on. She had tossed the half-formed bowl over the ledge with a growl, wincing as it hit a rock and shattered.

This morning, dew sparkled on the grass. The sun was squeezing its way over the horizon, lighting the sky with its warm glow, but most of the valley was still in shadow. Fog crept over the ground in a deeper crevasse to the south. An eagle circled over the rocky field, then dove sharply and came up with a small, wriggling form in its claws. Poor rabbit. Malia felt a little like a small creature at the mercy of her mind.

The door covering rustled, and Rina joined her. "The tea is steeping," she said, gazing over the valley. She sighed. "It's a lovely view, is it not?"

Malia made an affirmative noise.

"It was horrible during the war, though. Smoke and fire everywhere, the dragons in the sky. Ziku and I hunkered down, expecting the end."

Malia said nothing. Inside the home, dishes clattered, and voices murmured.

"It's wrong," Rina said.

"What is?"

"The Maddion healed, and you losing your memories."

A host of emotions stirred in Malia. She crossed her arms and frowned. "I agree."

"The *mutara* is dangerous. She enjoys chaos, destruction, violent change. She's like a volcano in that way."

"Yes, I'm aware of that."

"She might restore your memories, but there would be a price for you to pay."

"What could possibly be worse than what I'm paying right now?"

Rina flinched.

"What happens when the day comes and I don't recognize you? Or Enuwal? Or Vedran? What happens then?"

"That may not come for a long time. We'll worry about it then."

"No, *we* won't worry about it, because I'll be such a mess that I won't know what's going on. I'd rather discuss it now, while I still have my wits about me."

Rina sighed. "Very well. Let me just grab some tea for us and we can sit out here."

"No. I'd rather take a walk. Please." She didn't want Enuwal or Vedran intruding and adding their own opinions. She had things she wanted to say, and she wanted only her grandmother to hear them.

She pursed her lips and nodded. "Very well." She rolled the ladder off the ledge. It unfurled with a snap.

Rina climbed down first, and Malia followed. Malia found herself strolling toward the copse of fir trees, the usual target she aimed for when she went for a walk. Now that she had her grandmother to herself, she fidgeted, and found it hard to begin.

"Malia, just come out with it," Rina said softly.

She took a deep breath. "All right, then. This magic has been like a fog in my mind, slowly covering everything. I can't get through it, or push it out of the way. It just keeps coming on and swallowing memories."

Her grandmother nodded, her lips thin.

"I've been hiding problems from everybody, like forgetting my clothes belong to me, or forgetting what I was doing in the middle of a task, or not recognizing the way home. But I won't be able to hide those things much longer, and they're going to get worse, and more common. I'm afraid I'll do something one of these days to hurt myself or others, not on purpose, but because I simply don't know any better."

"I'm happy to keep you with me, and Ziku agrees. You'll be safe with us, and welcome, no matter what."

"I appreciate that, more than you could know. But you and Ziku have yourselves to worry about. My mother has a village to care for. My brother will soon need to find a wife and settle down with his own family, and Enuwal . . . he should do the same. He deserves happiness, not a burden." She swallowed the lump in her throat. "This fog will consume me. When it does—when I'm a shell—then you need to give me to the Jeguduns."

Rina blinked. "What?"

Her hand went to one of the feathers hanging from her belt. She'd spoken with Aru the day before, following the pottery problem. He'd assured her that the Jeguduns would take her in. And more importantly, he'd promised that they would carry out her wish, that when the fog had irreversibly consumed all her mind, they would guide her into death.

Malia said, "I'm telling you this because I don't know what I'll be like when that happens. I don't know if I'll be scared of the Jeguduns or not. So you need to promise me that no matter what, you'll see me handed off to Aru."

"And then what?"

"They will care for me, and I will disappear from Taakwa life."

They reached the copse of fir trees. Malia stepped into the dappled shade and breathed in the trees' strong, sweet smell.

"Malia, you're my granddaughter. I want to care for you. And if you don't want me to care for you, then I know the Taakwa will. You sacrificed so much for them, they would do it without a second thought."

She shook her head. "I'd rather be remembered as a whole person, or nearly so, and not . . . whatever it is I'll become. And besides, it wasn't only for the Taakwa that I sacrificed my memories. The Jeguduns are just as much a part of my life now. But others might think as you do, which is why I need you to stand up for me when the time comes. Don't let my mother or anybody else overrule my wishes. Can you do that for me?"

Rina's mouth turned down, and she looked away. Long shadows and stripes of light overlay her. She looked every bit her age, and more. "You're asking me to give up my granddaughter after we've been reunited."

"You're the only one I can trust to do this."

She sighed and closed her eyes. Then she opened them and smiled sadly. "I suppose our short time together is better than never having known you again at all. Yes, I'll do this for you. I'll give you to Aru and the Jeguduns when the time comes, you have my word."

Malia stood straighter, a heavy load coming off her. "Thank you." She pulled her grandmother into an embrace, sinking into the soft yet firm hug.

"But if you change your mind—" Rina began.

Malia smiled against her shoulder. "I know. I'm welcome at your home any time." She pulled free reluctantly, not wanting to tempt the fog to rile up. "I've kept you from your morning tea long enough." She turned and walked right into a spider web.

Malia grasped at the strands and pulled them off in a hurry, hoping the spider hadn't been hanging around when she'd walked into it. She hadn't even noticed the web, suspended between two trees. It had been as clear as the barrier over the valley.

She pulled off one last strand. That last thought tickled at her mind. It stirred ideas the way a strong wind could stir dirt and leaves into a dancing eddy. She laid a hand against a trunk to steady herself.

"Malia?" her grandmother began.

She raised a hand. She couldn't let go of the trail the first thought had led her down. A clear web, clinging to her. A clear barrier covered the entire valley . . . it took huge amounts of magic and hundreds of Taakwa and Jeguduns to make it. Could a small barrier form around a person? The amount of magic used to make something that small would be nothing compared to that used to create the barrier that protected the entire valley. And with a barrier around oneself, one could leave the valley and go anywhere, including the Maddions' mountain, where a powerful changer lived, and ask that being to cure one's magic-induced memory loss.

She gasped. It might work. It *could* work. She needed to speak with Aru, and quickly.

She straightened. "I'm fine," she assured her grandmother. "It was nothing, really, just a little fright from the spider's web."

Rina laughed. "That *was* unexpected, wasn't it?"

Heart thudding, Malia could only nod. She was silently chanting to herself: personal barrier, changer, Aru. She kept it up the entire way back to Rina's home so that she would remember.

~

That afternoon, Vedran went hunting yet again. Malia knew he was restless. He wanted to return home and help with the crops and the village's hunting. She'd told him he could leave, but he remained out of some sense of duty toward her. She should talk to Rina. Their grandmother could convince him to go back home where he was needed more. Although, he *had* done a fine job of filling their bellies, and making jerky out of extra meat, and he'd been a great help to the Jeguduns with their crops. Still, the Taakwa were just as short-handed as the Jeguduns, and Selu could use his help.

Rina left as well, a basket tucked under her arm, claiming she needed more yarrow root and nettles, and Ziku left with her. Malia couldn't figure out if they wanted some time alone, or if her grandmother thought she and Enuwal needed time to themselves, or whether it was a little of both. Regardless, she was glad to have fewer people around for once. It allowed her mind to settle and mull over the possibilities for casting a magic barrier around herself. The more she considered it, the harder it was to sit still, and soon she was rolling a little piece of clay into a ball, then a snake, then a flower, over and over again. She longed to gather enough material to make a bowl or a pitcher for her grandmother, but she couldn't make up her mind what to make, and she suspected her indecision had something to do with the fog in her mind.

Vedran had found two sturdy, long pieces of wood, and both he and Enuwal had carved them into crude crutches. Enuwal stood now, hobbling on his right leg and the crutches. He held his splinted left leg awkwardly off the ground.

"What do you need?" Malia asked, rolling the clay deftly between her fingers. "You should sit, let me get it for you."

"I hate sitting around," Enuwal grumbled. "I feel so useless."

"Please sit. If you put weight on that leg, it's going to hurt, and then you might pass out, and you'll hit your head on the stone floor or against the wall, and then we'll *really* be in a mess."

This won a tiny smile from him. "But at least you wouldn't have to listen to me complain."

"Oh, don't tempt me into pushing you myself," she muttered.

"What's that?"

"I've heard people say that healers make the worst patients. I always thought that was silly. Healers know exactly what needs to be done. But now I've seen for myself that it's the truth." She spread the clay flat on the floor, then stabbed a depression into its center.

He pursed his lips but sank back to the floor and stretched his legs out before him. "I don't really need anything, I suppose. I'm just tired of being cooped up in here."

"I think we're all starting to irritate one another." She rolled the clay between her hands.

He reached down and scratched his leg, letting out a sigh as he did so. "When my leg is better, we'll go back to Posalo. I know it's not traditional, but I could take better care of you there."

She froze in the middle of turning the lump into a tiny fish. "Take care of me?"

"Yes." He scratched harder. "You'll need someone to watch after you as your memory gets worse." He said it gently, but the words were still like a punch to her gut.

"I've made arrangements already. For when things get worse."

"What sort of arrangements? Your mother is busy as clan mother, Vedran will marry into a family soon, and your grandmother and Ziku are in no position to care for you when they already care for one another. I'm the best choice. And I *want* to do it."

"You can't do that," she said. She squished the clay and set it aside. "Too many people rely on you. And besides, I can't ask you to care for me for the rest of my life, not when you have your own life. You could find somebody else and marry and—"

"Don't," he growled. "I'm not turning my back on you because you're sick. I love you, and that won't change. When your mourning period is over, we *will* marry."

"We *will* marry?" Her voice was sharp.

He squirmed. "Your mother already approved the match."

"That was when we all thought I was fine. And there is nothing saying that it *will* happen if I choose for it not to happen."

He took in a sharp breath, and the lines around his eyes looked deeper, pinched.

"I'm sorry, Enuwal, but what happens to me is my choice."

"What sort of arrangements have you made?" he asked again, quietly.

She took a deep breath. "The Jeguduns have agreed to care for me."

He shook his head. "They can't do that."

"Why not? They owe me their lives just as much as every Taakwa does. I'm merely calling in a favor."

He winced. "Then you may as well let the Taakwa care for you."

"I've made up my mind. This is what I want, Enuwal, and I won't have you or anyone else doing otherwise when I'm nothing but a shell. The Jeguduns understand this, and they *will* fight anyone who tries otherwise. Including you." She could hardly draw a breath through the heaviness descending upon her chest. She went into her grandmother's room, letting the door covering fall across the opening.

In the other room, Enuwal grunted, and the crutches scraped against the floor. He appeared in the doorway a moment later, his expression grim. "Malia, what would you do if the situation were reversed? What if I were the one losing my memories?"

She crossed her arms and kept her back toward him. "I would take care of you," she said softly.

"So why won't you let me do the same for you?"

Because you won't end my life when the time comes. You would keep my body living while my mind died in agony. She couldn't say any of that, though. Instead, she merely said, "I've made up my mind." It sounded petulant, and she hated it.

"You are stubborn, Malia of Selu." The door hanging rustled as it fell back into place, and the crutches scraped against the stone floor. It sounded as though Enuwal had gone out to the ledge.

She hugged herself tight. She'd find her way to the *mutara* and beg the changer to fix her mind. Then she would beg Enuwal's forgiveness, and maybe after that, she'd have a normal life, and a whole mind.

~

Rina and Ziku came back first. There was a chilly wedge between them made of unspoken words and tense shoulders. Malia took one look at Ziku and left him to himself in the back room.

Rina moved about the main room, lips in a thin line, and pulled down a basket. She took out a bone needle and thread and settled against some pillows to mend a small tear on one of her skirts.

"Enuwal is enjoying the sun," she said, with a gesture of her head toward the ledge.

"Mm-hmm," Malia said.

"So why does he look so upset about it?"

"He feels useless. He thinks he can't do anything while his leg is healing."

"He doesn't seem the sort to let that get to him for very long. He looks more like he's lost a dear friend."

"You'll have to ask him about that."

Rina gave her a sharp look. Then her expression softened, and she nodded. "Ah, okay."

Malia sat with a new ball of clay. She rolled it between her hands, breathing in the damp smell of earth. She bent over it, coaxing it into a rabbit's shape. Huddled rabbit, long ears laid back, eyes wide. She could almost see whiskers twitching.

Voices rose from the ledge. Vedran was back. Laughter drifted inside. At least one of them was finding the day enjoyable.

Moments later, Vedran came in with a cleaned turkey. Rina set to work preparing it for the hearth, and soon it was roasting, its delicious smell filling the space. She chatted easily with Vedran about his morning. He had quickly discovered the lay of the land surrounding Rina's home, and they discussed the rock field and the hot springs just south of them.

Malia perked up when Vedran mentioned the hot springs. "Are they like the ones outside Selu?" she asked.

"With carvings?" He shook his head. "No, they're just springs."

Perhaps something about the springs outside Selu was special. She tucked the question away, hoping she'd have time and the ability later to find out what.

Enuwal ducked through the door. "Something smells wonderful," he said. He smiled at Rina and Vedran, though it faltered when he turned to Malia.

She stood and cleared her throat. "I'm going for a walk." She raised her hands as heads swiveled toward her. "Don't worry, I spoke with Aru and he agreed to go with me so I wouldn't be alone. Everybody else has gotten out today except for me."

Rina glanced between her and Enuwal but merely said, "All right. Be careful."

Once on the ground, she breathed a sigh of relief. The days were going to be even longer if this tension continued between her and Enuwal, but she wouldn't change her mind about going to live with the Jeguduns once her mind was beyond help.

She set out for the northern curve of the cliffs, toward the other Jegudun homes clustered along this part of the valley. A couple of Jeguduns worked in their fields, pulling weeds and checking leaves. Gray clouds gathered in the northern sky, bubbling up in a slow boil. A breeze pulled at Malia's hair, sending a few loose strands flying about her face.

She nodded a greeting at the working Jeguduns as she passed. They nodded and trilled in response. Past the fields, she raised her head and let out three short whistles, one long, and three short. The sound pierced the air, drawing more than one Jegudun from their cliff homes, but only one took to the sky, circling lazily until he landed before her.

Aru folded his wings, their apexes rising like mountain peaks behind him. He gave her a toothy, wolfish grin and trilled a greeting, and the smile touched his deep green eyes. Red stained his palms, and for a moment Malia thought it was blood, but closer inspection told her it was paint. He followed her gaze and shrugged, letting out a trill that sounded like a laugh.

"Walk with me?" she asked.

Aru chirped and fell in beside her. She kept the pace slow for his ambling gait. The sun was warm, and cicadas buzzed in the tall grass, but the clouds promised rain before the day's end.

Her heart picked up speed. She was about to trust her idea with Aru, and if he told her grandmother or the others about it, that would be the end of it. They'd make sure she was never out of their sight. But she couldn't do this by herself either. She needed a Jegudun's help. "There's one person who might be able to help me fix the magic that's eating up my memories," she began.

Aru canted his head to one side and chirruped inquisitively.

"I would need your help, though, and your silence. Nobody else can know what we're doing. Can you keep quiet?"

His eyes narrowed as they searched hers. *Is it dangerous,* the look seemed to say.

"It's the only chance I have to heal my mind, Aru."

He blew out his breath, the tiny tufts of hair around his mouth fluttering, and ducked his head. At last, he nodded.

She took a deep breath. "The *mutara* could help."

He half-spread his wings and fluttered them, shaking his head and trilling.

Malia held out a hand. "Let me finish."

Aru folded his wings with a little growl. It was meant for the *mutara,* and not her, but it still gave her a tiny chill.

"I think there's a safe way for me to leave the valley. If hundreds of Taakwa and Jeguduns could form a barrier around this entire valley, then one Taakwa and one Jegudun should be able to form a barrier around an individual. If I had a barrier around me, the Maddion wouldn't be able to touch me, or use my blood. I would be safe."

Aru grasped her wrist. She felt an impatient tug at her mind and allowed Aru to show her what he wanted.

A variety of people flashed through her mind, different sizes and shapes, different shades of skin, different features, but all of them had one thing in common: they were slaves of the Maddion. She saw these people cooking, cleaning, carrying loads, tolerating harsh words and hands on their bodies, and silently enduring the deaths of loved ones and their ways of life. No matter how foul the task, she saw them doing whatever the Maddion commanded. To not do so meant their own suffering, or worse, the suffering of their loved ones. Then the images disappeared.

The fog in her mind roiled a little, like the storm clouds approaching. Her free hand went to one of the feathers hanging from her belt. She waited, but the fog calmed.

"Even if they got one of their servants to bleed me, they'd still need a Jegudun's blood. Look, if the Maddion caught me, I'd have no chance of speaking with the *mutara,* and that would be the end of my chances." She swallowed hard. "There are powders that can end a person's life in moments. Enuwal has spoken of them. Some of that powder in a tiny sac, sewn into my clothes, and I have a way out if I'm captured. The Maddion won't have my blood."

Aru raised his head and let out a mournful trill. He shook his head and then abruptly took to the air. Malia stumbled back, the Jegudun's wings stirring wind that buffeted her, sending her hair whipping around her face and pinning her skirt against her legs. He shot straight up, then circled high overhead, gesturing wildly as he did so. Every now and then his voice reached her.

Malia sighed and set out slowly. He would have to work it out for himself.

She didn't *want* to die. She didn't want to live in a strange limbo, either, a fog-filled mind trapped in a young, healthy body.

Aru's erratic flight eventually slowed. He landed before her, the tall grasses stirring. His nostrils flared, and he gave her a determined look. Malia's heart sank. He was going to refuse to help.

"Here," she said, grabbing his hand. "Take a look inside my head. You haven't done it in a while. Do it, and if you think I'm overreacting, I'll drop this idea."

His lips rose slightly, baring his teeth, not in an angry grimace, but in frustration.

Malia waited. Aru was the most adventuresome Jegudun she knew. If he wouldn't help her, she could be sure no others would either.

He sighed and tightened his grip on her hands. The familiar tug pulled at her mind. She closed her eyes and let Aru into her memories, those he could access, at any rate. She got the overwhelming sense of surprise from him, and dawning horror as he explored her mind. The fog began to roil again, and she pushed him away, afraid his presence might trigger another episode.

Aru's presence faded fast, and she opened her eyes. Sadness filled his eyes.

"You'll help me figure out a way to create a barrier around me? You'll help me?"

He nodded slowly.

A thin smile spread across Malia's face, and she breathed a sigh of relief. She still had a chance to heal her mind.

CHAPTER EIGHTEEN

Malia arranged to meet with Aru early each morning. Since she had trouble sleeping anyway, she might as well make use of her time. And she felt like she was fast running out of it, too, even though the fog had remained quiet for some time now. It reminded her all too much of the calm that preceded storms.

She didn't dare risk creating much magic for fear it would trigger another episode, but all they needed was a small bit to figure out if it would work or not. When the Jeguduns and Taakwa originally created the barrier, every single one of them had worked together, the Jeguduns drawing latent power from the Taakwa to form it much the same way she might have shaped a large clay bowl. She and Aru tried variants on this, with him trying to form a new barrier around her pinky finger, but no matter what they did to create a barrier, it never worked. The fog in her mind would swirl a bit, then settle down, and there would be . . . nothing.

"Do you think it's me?" she asked on the third morning. "Do you think it's because of what's going on with my mind?"

Aru canted his head to one side. The sky to the east was gradually turning orange and yellow, and birds were chattering loudly in the nearby copse of fir. Dew and a bit of rain from the previous night shimmered on the grass like hip beads winking in the light, and the air smelled clean and damp.

The Jegudun shook his head. He pointed to himself, then to her, then swept his arms in a wide circle.

She sighed. "We can't ask anyone else for help." She leaned against a fir tree. They stood beneath the trees, safe from prying eyes both on the ground and in the air. "There has to be a way to get the magic going, like priming the irrigation channels."

Aru shrugged.

Malia let out a mirthless laugh. "You'd be happy if we never figured it out, I know." She fiddled with the feathers hanging from her belt. "You should make one more feather for me to carry if—*when*—we're successful. Put out conversations about leaving the valley, and my plan to find the *mutara* in the feather, so if the magic takes those memories, at least I'll know what I'm supposed to be doing. Clan mother save us, but there's so much to consider." She leaned her head against the tree and closed her eyes. "I'll think of something. You can head home. I'll follow in a bit."

Aru chirped, and moments later came the sound of his wings unfurling. They beat a few times, retreating quickly, and then there was only the birds singing.

She'd hardly slept at all the past few nights, which made it harder to think. Trying to piece together a plan felt like slogging through mud. Irrigation. Priming. Magic. The ideas chased each other.

The next thing she knew, a hand was shaking her shoulder. "Malia," Rina said, concern lacing her words. "Are you ill?"

She fought to wake up. "No," she mumbled. She rubbed her gritty eyes and blinked a few times. Bright sunlight streamed through the trees' branches. She sat upright. "What . . . I fell asleep. Is it morning?" She took a closer look at the sunlight's angle and answered her own question. "Late morning. I'm sorry, I was tired, and I closed my eyes for just a moment . . ."

Rina's face crumpled with relief. "It's all right. I'm just glad you didn't have another episode. I worried when I saw Aru flying home, and you were nowhere in sight."

"No, no, things have been fine. I'm fine, really." The last thing she needed was her grandmother feeling as if she couldn't take these walks with Aru. "I told Aru to go home, that I'd follow, but I guess I couldn't resist the comfort of this tree," she finished with a grimace. Her back was stiff from sitting against the hard trunk.

"Well, comfortable as it is, why don't you come on home?"

Malia followed her grandmother back. Vedran approached from the other direction. When he spotted them, he broke into a run. His brows were drawn down, and as he reached them he said, "Malia, are you all right?"

"I'm fine," she said for what felt like the hundredth time. "I got comfortable and fell asleep before I knew it."

Vedran's face relaxed. "Maybe you should take someone else with you when you go out—"

"No." It came out harsher than she'd intended. "No," she repeated, gentler this time. "I'm not a small child. I don't need your constant supervision. Besides, Aru is always with me." She patted the feathers hanging from her belt. "And I have these, just in case."

They walked to Rina's home together, she and her grandmother leading the way, and Vedran a step behind.

Enuwal sat upon the ledge, head turning this way and that. When he spotted them, he waved both arms overhead. Rina returned the wave. Enuwal stood, leaning on his crutches, and waited. Even from a distance, Malia could read the tension in his body, in the stiff way he held himself upright. If he'd been able, he would have been pacing.

She insisted her grandmother climb up first. She followed more slowly, reluctant to face Enuwal. He would have been worried, just like Rina and Vedran. They'd hardly spoken since she'd told him her plans to eventually live with the Jeguduns, and she didn't look forward to another argument.

She climbed onto the ledge and met Enuwal's brown eyes, expecting lines of anger around them. Instead, he yanked her to him with one arm, the other holding a crutch, and crushed her against him.

He smelled like the sun, and a little bit of sweat and dried herbs. She'd held herself apart from him for so long that his familiar feel and smell sent a wave of homesickness through her. She wrapped her arms around him and squeezed.

"I'm sorry for scaring you."

Enuwal sighed, then kissed the top of her head. "It was foolish of me to remain angry at you. We have so little time left, I don't want to waste it arguing. And of course it's your life to do with as you wish. I respect your decision, Malia, and I won't argue with you again."

If he knew what she was planning, he'd be furious all over again, and she wasn't sure if he'd forgive her for leaving the valley, even if she took every precaution.

"I'm sorry, too," she said, and she meant it for the argument, and for making him worry, and for the anxiety she'd put him through if she managed to leave the valley. She pulled away. "Why don't we go inside?"

Rina insisted that Malia sit while she prepared tea for all of them. Soon they were all settled with steaming mugs in hand, and the smell of chamomile and lemon balm lingered.

Vedran took a few sips, then cleared his throat and set his cup down. "I've been thinking," he began.

"Uh oh," Malia teased.

He frowned at her, then continued, "If you don't mind," he said to Rina, "I'd like to go home to Selu for a while. Being short-handed and all, I think they could use my help. But if you need me," he added hastily, "I'll stay."

Rina smiled. "You've certainly been a huge help. We've eaten quite well, and I know the Jeguduns appreciate the extra pair of hands in the fields. But this isn't the place you call home. Of course you can go back."

"I'll come again before the snows," he said. "I'll make sure you and Ziku have enough food to see you through the winter."

Her smile deepened. "We would love that. You're welcome any time, you know."

He nodded. "I'll leave tomorrow, if that's all right with you."

"Of course."

Without Vedran around, it would be easier for Malia to leave the valley. But she still had to figure out a way to make the magic work for her.

He sat forward. "Besides," he said, "the Jeguduns made this little alteration to their irrigation system, and I'm dying to share it. We could get better flow control and waste less water."

His words stirred Malia's earlier thoughts. Irrigation . . . priming the water flow . . . what if she found a way to prime the magic's flow? She'd need a source of magic first, though.

The barrier itself.

Her breath hitched, and she took a quick sip of tea to hide it, and her excitement. *That's it!* She and Aru could siphon off a tiny bit of the barrier. When the men irrigated the crops, they used quite a bit of water from the Big River, but it didn't make a noticeable dent in the river's level. She could take a bit of the magic from the barrier and never leave the valley, or herself, vulnerable. And, if she didn't have to create a barrier from scratch, she wouldn't even have to worry about losing memories in the process. Her hands tightened around the mug. She could hardly wait to meet up with Aru and try it out. She wouldn't be able to tomorrow because Vedran would be leaving, but they could try the next day.

So soon. The idea squeezed her chest. Leaving the valley was forbidden. Before, when the Taakwa still feared the Jeguduns, the Jeguduns had used that to their advantage and kept the Taakwa from leaving. But the Taakwa feared the outside anyway. They had everything they needed in the valley, and nothing good had ever come from those who lived outside of it.

She had to do this, though. She was taking every precaution. Aru had found the powder she'd asked for, and she had it sewn up tight already in a tiny pocket inside her tunic. Her hand went to the small lump, unnoticeable except to her, and brushed against it. She would succeed at finding the *mutara* and asking for help, or she'd die trying.

Vedran snapped his fingers in front of her. "Malia?" he asked with a frown.

She came out of her reverie and shook her head. "Sorry. Just thinking."

He smiled. "For a while there, you looked like—" He bit off the rest and ducked his head.

"Like my old self," she finished for him. "It's all right. I felt like my old self, too." *All the more reason to put this plan into action.* But she had to do better at hiding her excitement, or they might get suspicious.

"Well, since you're feeling more like your old self," Rina said, "how about a game? You and Enuwal should play."

Rina wasn't being very subtle in her attempt to help mend things between Malia and Enuwal. Malia took the bone dice from her grandmother, who disappeared into the other room with a basket of mending in her hands, Ziku yawning and following.

"Vedran, would you like to play?" Malia asked, rolling the die in her hands, enjoying the way they clicked together.

He shook his head and stood. "I need to pack my things, and I want to clarify a few details with some friends before I leave tomorrow." He went onto the ledge, and a moment later came the sound of the ladder unfurling.

"Vedran sounds happy to be going home," Enuwal said.

"He'll be relieved," she said, shaking the die and tossing them onto the blanket. She grumbled as she lost. Not that she was paying that much attention to the game, but she couldn't let Enuwal know she was so distracted. Rina sang softly in the other room. Malia didn't recognize the song.

"What's wrong?" he asked as he scooped up the die.

"What do you mean?"

"You've been distracted."

So much for not letting him know my thoughts are elsewhere. "Just thinking about Vedran leaving. It feels like our little family is starting to scatter."

"You don't wish to go with him? I know it's hard, being cooped up here with me." He tossed the die.

Malia picked them up and rolled them back and forth between her palms. "I keep expecting word that the Maddion are coming now that they're healed," she lied. "I just hated the idea of Vedran alone if that happened." That last part, at least, wasn't a lie. She didn't want to see Vedran hurt, or worse. True, he wore a dragon claw around his neck now, but if she hadn't worked that magic to repair the barrier, the Maddions would be the ones wearing their victory around their necks.

"They won't any time soon. Their numbers are too small."

"Ah, so it's our grandchildren's generation that should worry." She shook her head. "I'm sorry. I just wish I knew what else they were up to." *And if the* mutara *was still with them.* Each day was one closer to when she wouldn't be able to help herself anymore. The fog in her mind claimed a little more every day. By the time winter settled in, she would have lost most of her memories if it kept going at this rate. *Hurry, I must hurry.*

She tossed the die. "Aha," she said, trying to sound enthusiastic as she won the round.

"They've been rather quiet," Enuwal said.

Which meant it was the best time to sneak into the mountains they called home. "Well, I hope they stay that way. Better yet, they could leave, go far from here, find a people more brutal than them, and end up enslaved."

Enuwal made a noncommittal noise as he grabbed the die and flicked them onto the blanket. He groaned when he came up with a low pair. Malia tossed them, and came up with the same pair.

"A draw," she said, handing the die over. Her hand brushed Enuwal's, lingered a moment. He smiled and gave her hand a quick squeeze as he deftly snatched the die from her. Then he leaned forward. She held her breath a moment before his lips touched hers.

Soft. Warm. He tasted of tea and something spicy. She deepened the kiss, wanting to make sure she recalled this moment, his feel, his smell. She placed her hands on either side of his face and pulled him closer. His breathing quickened, and she drew close enough to feel his heart speed beneath his breastbone.

Rina's song rose and came to an end. Her footsteps scraped against the stone in the other room. Enuwal quickly pulled away, ducking his head, and snatched up the die. He shook them a little too hard and sent them flying halfway across the room. Malia collected them just as her grandmother walked into the room. She raised an eyebrow at Malia scrabbling around on the floor, but said nothing as she put the basket away, her mending apparently done.

"I think I'll lie down for a little nap," she said. "You two will be all right?"

Malia nodded, not trusting her voice just yet.

Rina gave her a little smile, and she was alone with Enuwal again.

She almost told him her plan. The words bubbled up, anxious to come out. But he would never approve, and he would tell Rina, and they would do whatever was necessary to make sure she didn't leave, and she would slowly sink into the oblivion taking over her mind.

Enuwal tossed the die. Low number. Her turn, and she tossed the highest pair possible. She hoped it was an omen of a successful journey, but she couldn't shake the dread trembling in the pit of her stomach.

CHAPTER NINETEEN

Muvumo's footsteps echoed in the empty cavern. The *near* empty cavern. His wife's scrolls, previously hidden beneath a false bottom in her trunks, sat on the shelves that once held the glory of his accomplishments and those of the other Maddion men.

If his people found out that his wife knew her letters—that she could read and write—he'd quickly lose the good graces he found himself in after their miraculous cure. He would burn them before anyone could find out.

He took the first in his hands, the vellum smooth and old, the scroll tied shut with a worn bit of string. There was writing on the outside of the scroll as well as inside, the letters cramped but legible. A few words caught his eye as he held the scroll over an open flame in the lantern.

I had to approach my husband carefully, lest his temper get the best of him, in order to present my idea that hand washing could help those he tended. The midwife told me that they started the practice when a servant spoke of it, and careful observation has shown that the number of women and newborns with contagions has dropped drastically since. It would surely help injured men on the battlefield.

I mentioned it in passing, with a little laugh so that he would not think I was terribly serious. It was enough to plant the idea in his mind. Soon he began cleansing his hands and his instruments stringently. His new method was put to the test when the Most Worthy was challenged and won, though paying the price of an ugly cut across his back. It healed quickly and without contagion, and Benti was elevated above all healers.

Everyone speaks of how wise and clever he was when it was my words, and the midwife's observations, and a servant's experience that brought it about.

The handwriting grew even more cramped and tiny at the end, as if the woman writing it was trying to hold her anger in tight. Muvumo flung the scroll aside and began pacing.

Imagine the gall of the woman, to suggest that her husband benefited from her wisdom. He knew of Benti in passing, only because he'd made several changes to the way healers work, which had saved many lives. It was Benti's careful observations, not the midwife's. It was *his* knowledge, not a servant's. It was *his* accomplishment, not his wife's.

Foolishness. Rubbish. Dragon shit. He whirled with a snarl and snatched another scroll at random. He tore off the string and yanked it open.

His eyes are the stars at night,
His heartbeat the drums that played at my wedding.
His smile carries me higher than any dragon ever could.
His touch sends a river of desire flowing through me.

Heat rose to Muvumo's face. The words were bold, for a woman, and soft, like a woman. The words were . . . nice. They were not Chanwa's, but belonged to another woman in her family.

He rather wished they were hers, speaking of him.

Foolishness.

He held the scroll over the flames, yanked it away a moment later.

Before he destroyed them, he should find out what else these scrolls said. He could not, as Most Worthy, allow any mysteries to exist within his mountain.

He sat at the heavy wooden table and began to read.

Chanwa paced her room, her skirts swirling about her legs. Normally she enjoyed the way the soft cloth caressed her skin and rippled behind her, but all she could focus on this evening was the gnawing worry in her belly. The night the changer cured the Maddion of their illness, Muvumo had ripped away the scroll she'd been working on and torn it, leaving the pieces to flutter around her like snow. She'd only just stopped him from destroying the other scrolls. Her own scrolls, her mother's, her grandmother's. She'd jumped on him, begging him. A sour taste rose in her mouth. She'd *begged* him. She'd gotten on her knees and groveled, cried, pleaded. She'd offered all she had, which according to the law, was nothing. Muvumo had seen fit to remind her of that.

"Even your body is mine," he'd growled, "and I'll take it when I want it, how I want it."

She had cowered, hating herself, and him. She had nearly picked up a broken quill and driven it through his neck. Her hands clenched at her sides, and her pace quickened.

In the front room, Ankti cooked. The spicy smell of *sprinko* wafted through the entire home. It curdled her stomach. Muvumo had forbidden that Chanwa and Ankti speak to one another, save for the most essential commands. He suspected Ankti knew

Chanwa's secret, though he didn't admit it aloud. When Chanwa had disobeyed, seeking Ankti to ask if she knew anything about the scrolls or the changer, he'd caught them. Ankti still moved stiffly from the lashing she'd received. Chanwa would have gladly given up her scrolls for the rest of her life if she had been able to save Antki from the lashing.

A wooden spoon clanged three times against the cooking pot. Ankti had heard Muvumo's footsteps approaching. Even now, having endured the whip, she did her best to watch out for Chanwa. Chanwa pushed all thoughts of her family's scrolls out of her mind and entered the front room.

Muvumo hadn't spoken to her in days, save for chastising her. He hadn't touched her, though, and for that she was endlessly thankful. She wasn't sure what she would have done had he followed through with his reminder that even her body belonged to him.

He shoved aside the door hanging and entered. He made a great show of going to the back room and opening each trunk, then slamming them shut. He moved to the front room next, digging through baskets at random. At last he straightened in the room's center and nodded. He did this each time, as if expecting Chanwa to have produced more vellum, ink, and quills out of nothing.

Chanwa choked back the retorts that rose and instead raised her chin and said, "Good evening, Most Worthy."

He surprised her when he gruffly said, "Come with me."

Ankti straightened at the hearth, her eyes gone wide, the hearth poker in one hand. Her fingers tightened almost imperceptibly around it. Chanwa stepped casually between Ankti and Muvumo, her heart quickening.

"Where are we going?" she asked.

"You'll see."

"I only wondered if Ankti should wait for us, or if she should leave supper warm in the hearth." She was pleased with how her voice didn't tremble, nor her hands, clasped before her.

He turned his narrow gaze on Ankti. "Finish up and go."

Ankti dipped low. "Yes, Most Worthy," she said, using the poker to move a log in the hearth, then setting it aside.

The day's last rosy light faded from the sheer granite rising to Chanwa's left. She had to hurry to keep up with Muvumo. He led the way up the stairs, past torches lit at regular intervals, past homes blazing with light and filled with laughter, a sound that had been rare for much of the past few seasons. The early evening air was cool, and gooseflesh broke out along her arms. She should have grabbed a cloak, but she'd been caught unawares by Muvumo's summons.

He led the way to a mesa. He whistled for his dragon. The beast appeared moments later, its pulsing sides brightening and fading in the night like a giant firefly as it came in to land. Chanwa took a step back, the dragon's wings stirring the chilly mountain air. She hated the dragons, and Muvumo knew it.

An apprentice came running out of the supply cave with Muvumo's saddle. The boy made quick work of tossing it over the dragon's back and tightening the cinches. He was old enough, and skilled enough, that he'd soon be training with a dragon of his own. The boy dipped his head toward Muvumo and then disappeared back into the cave, the torches' flickering light following him in.

"Come," Muvumo said, holding out a hand.

A hundred possibilities spun through her head. He was going to feed her to the dragons for having the audacity to write scrolls of her own. He was going to drop her from high in the air and let her fall to her death. He was going to leave her in the woods, or drop her onto the magic barrier surrounding the Taakwa's valley. Every scenario ended with her dead. But if he'd truly wanted her dead, he would have seen to it days ago. She must appear fearless.

She took a deep breath and stepped forward. He grasped her by her waist and hoisted her easily onto the saddle on the dragon's back, then climbed up after her. He strapped himself in and wrapped his arms loosely around her.

"Hold on," he said in her ear. "Or don't. I won't drop you, but I won't keep you from falling either."

Bile churned in her stomach. He didn't want her dead. Yet. Which meant he needed something from her. And after that?

Her stomach lurched as the dragon crouched and leaped into the air. Its massive wings unfurled, and it rose in the dark. The air was cold as it rushed past Chanwa's face, sending her hair streaming behind her, and sending the chill through her flimsy dress, like thousands of tiny needles prickling her skin. She held back a cry and grabbed the pommel. She wondered if there was a way to release the straps holding Muvumo to the saddle.

But they were approaching a mesa already. Chanwa's hands tightened on the leather as they landed. Muvumo slid off easily, then pulled her after him. Her legs wobbled when she put her weight on them, and she sprawled to the ground.

Muvumo grumbled and yanked her to her feet. "That is why women don't ride."

"Or perhaps I stumbled because it's only the third time I've been on dragonback, and it's night, and cold," she snapped. She clenched her teeth before more words could come tumbling out.

He narrowed his eyes, but only led her into the cavern. The *scroll* cavern. Her steps faltered. Women were never allowed inside.

And yet, here she was, walking into the cool interior. Lanterns lined the walls at regular intervals. About twenty paces inside began the shelves, all of them empty. In between shelves hung more lanterns, and tapestries depicting scenes of war, men caring for their dragons, dragons feasting on their enemies. Their footsteps echoed against the stone.

The cavern wound deep into the mountain. All of the empty shelves . . . Chanwa might have pitied Muvumo once for sacrificing so much, but the last of her affection had disappeared along with her scrolls.

They came to one section with great wooden tables and chairs in the center and a lantern in the table's center. On one of the shelves rested a few dozen scrolls. They looked pitifully out of place in a space that was meant to hold thousands upon thousands.

"I thought they were all destroyed," she said, her voice tiny and echoing.

Muvumo shoved her into one of the chairs. It started to tilt, and she grabbed the thick table to keep from toppling over.

"The changer asked that we destroy all of the *men's* scrolls," he said. "At the time, I hardly paid any attention to the distinction. These," he said with a dismissive wave of his hand, "are your ramblings."

Not destroyed after all. Chanwa closed her eyes, and a great weight lifted off her.

Ankti had assured her that she'd delivered Chanwa's message to the changer. Chanwa didn't know what, if anything, the changer could do to help the Maddion women. True, she'd taken the illness from them. But then she'd commanded all of the men's scrolls destroyed. Chanwa had known right away, when she'd heard that decree, that the changer knew about her scrolls, and those of other women. It was a subtle distinction, but it slipped past all of the men, her husband included. Her scrolls, and those of the women in her family, were safe, but she wasn't sure yet how that gave her power over herself. If anything, this incident had made her more dependent than ever on Muvumo, seeing as he could order her death at any moment. If only she could speak with Ankti about this . . .

"I have read them all," Muvumo said.

She opened her eyes, warily watched as he paced, keeping the length of the table between them.

He shook his head. "How? How did you learn letters?"

Anger surged forward. It was dangerous, being angry at one's husband, and even more so when he was Most Worthy, but she was tired of assumptions. "While you boys and men are off playing at war, us women are left home alone. What should we fill our time with? Sewing? Singing? Gardening? Learning an instrument, perhaps? Discussing pregnancy and babies? That's all we're capable of, isn't it? According to you, at least."

He whirled and slammed his hands on the table. The sound thundered in the cavern. Chanwa didn't so much as flinch. Part of her screamed to stop talking while she still had a chance, but it was too late. The dam had broken, and the words wouldn't stop flowing until she'd had her say.

"And what would you prefer?" he sneered. "To learn how to wield a battle axe? Ride a dragon? Hunt? Maybe you'd like to learn how to piss standing up?"

"Maddion women are no better than slaves, like those you call *servants*, as if that word is somehow less dirty, or the Jeguduns, or the Solumna who brought this illness upon us, or the unmentionables."

He leaned forward, lips raised in a snarl. "Don't you *dare* speak of those filthy women. You are above them, you—"

She stood abruptly, the chair falling back with an echoing clatter, and leaned on the table, facing him down. "Don't *you* speak of them as dirty, not when you come back in the middle of the night smelling like a rutting goat because you've laid with one. If you can touch one of those women, you can speak of her, and so can I."

He pushed back, ran a hand over the twisted ropes of hair. "Where is this all coming from?"

She straightened slowly, keeping her fingertips on the table. "Imagine if, all your life, you were told you weren't that smart, that the only thing you had going for you was your looks, your womb, and what lay between your legs."

He flinched. "Such crude words for a lady."

She ignored him. "Then imagine longing for something more, for knowledge, for a purpose to fill your time, but you're relegated to nothing more than a walking womb. Stay home, watch others leave and take risks. Learn nothing but how to be bitter."

"Who taught you written words?"

"My mother."

"And who taught her?"

"Her mother. And so on, and so on. While the men were gone, the women learned, and we saved our own histories."

The muscles around his jaw twitched. "Yes. I read them."

Silence dragged out, save for Muvumo's ragged breathing. Chanwa was strangely calm. Her husband could do whatever he wished to her, and she would simply disappear, another Maddion woman gone without a trace.

"Why didn't you destroy them?" she asked.

The muscles twitched harder, and the apple of his throat bobbed. He turned away.

Maybe he'd been waiting to bring her here, so she could witness their destruction herself. Her hands tightened into fists. She'd take a torch to *him*, if it came to that.

He faced her. "I don't know," he said.

She didn't know what to say in the face of her husband's uncertainty.

"I will take you home," he said. "You will speak of these," he added with a wave in the scrolls' direction, "to no one, or I will burn them, and you. And you will write no more until—*unless*—I give my leave."

She had no doubt the threat wasn't empty. She nodded curtly, unable to speak around the knot in her throat. So, she'd live another day, but she couldn't write. But she sensed a sort of victory tonight. And so she followed her husband through the cavern, and home.

CHAPTER TWENTY

Malia bid farewell to Vedran the next morning. That night she lay down and feigned sleep as the others wrapped up their days and lay down as well. Her travel sac, surreptitiously packed while the others were busy, sat in a dark corner, waiting for her. The tiny packet with powder remained sewn securely in her tunic. She was ready. She only had to wait for everybody to fall asleep, and then she could slip out and meet Aru. If the magic worked as she hoped, she'd be on her way to the Maddions' mountain this night. That thought alone was enough to keep her heart tripping along and keep her wide awake.

She listened as Rina's breathing deepened into dulcet snores. In the corner, Ziku's breathing rattled and whistled, and from the front room came Enuwal's steady, deep rumbles.

She hated leaving without saying good-bye. She hated sneaking out in the middle of the night without a word about where she was going. She hated the idea of how worried they would be in the morning when they found her gone. She could only hope they'd take solace in the fact that she had Aru with her. When she came back, she would make it up to them, a thousand times over.

The Jeguduns continued to keep watch over the Maddion. So far, the *mutara* remained with them. Malia just had to reach the changer and convince her to help, then sneak out again. *Yes, it's as easy as that,* she thought wryly.

And what if the *mutara* refused to help? What if Malia was caught? Or Aru? What if, what if, what if? The possibilities chased themselves around her mind in circles as she waited.

One thing was certain, though. If she stayed in the valley, she'd lose herself. When it came down to it, she had to go. To stay would be to condemn herself to a slow sort of death. If she left, at least she had a chance.

When she judged everybody well asleep, she slid soundlessly out of the blanket and to her bare feet. She eased her travel sac over her head and around her torso, grabbed her shoes, and stepped quietly into the front room.

Enough star and moonlight seeped in around the door covering to outline Enuwal's face. He slept on his back, the splinted leg jutting out awkwardly, one hand on his chest and the other outflung, head to one side. Sleep erased the lines of tension on his forehead and between his eyes, and he looked younger, happier. This ordeal had worn on him, too. Malia reached a hand toward him, but didn't touch him. She mouthed, *Good-bye, love.* She set the tiny ceramic rabbit she'd made a few days earlier on the floor near him, where he'd find it in the morning, along with a few white and yellow daises she'd picked the afternoon before. Then she slipped out the door.

On the ledge, she put her shoes on, then eased the rope ladder over the side. She climbed down quickly, expecting an alarmed shout at any moment, but reached the ground without incident.

Then she hurried north, through dewy grass, to the trail Aru had told her about.

The steep trail clung to the cliff, and consisted of loose pebbles all along its length. It doubled back on itself several times. It was slow going, her leather-clad feet sending pebbles clattering down from time to time. She'd pause and listen, waiting for Jegudun whistles or shouts, her heart racing. Then she'd climb again.

She reached the top and paused for a moment, breathing heavily. She took a pull from her water pouch and stood with hands on her hips. With all the time she'd spent in Rina's home, she wasn't used to working so hard.

Grass grew hip-high all around. Stands of fir and pine surrounded her, but most of the land here was flat and grass-covered. The night air was warm, bordering on cool, and filled with the sweet scent of night-blooming flowers. The valley stretched out before her, blanketed in darkness, and deceptively still. Somewhere out there, mountain lions and owls hunted, rabbits hid in their burrows, people slept or rocked their babies or made love or spoke of their dreams in hushed whispers. She ached to be a part of it, as a whole person. She'd given so much for this peace; she just wanted a little peace for herself.

Huge wings beat the air. Malia crouched in the grass. Then Aru's familiar form soared over the valley's lip. She stood and waved her arms, calling to him softly. He circled and landed, his passage stirring the grass and a few wisps of loose hair around her face. He wore a small travel sac across his torso, the strap passing under one wing and over the other shoulder.

Aru canted his head to one side and chirruped softly. *Are you sure you want to go through with this*, he seemed to say.

"I'm ready," Malia said. Her mouth was dry. In a few moments, there would be no turning back.

He nodded and led them away from the valley, his gait rolling along. Malia knew when they reached the barrier. The air sizzled ever so slightly, like during a thunderstorm, and the fog in her mind grew agitated. If it wasn't for the fog in her mind, she might have passed through the barrier and thought nothing of the slight tingle. Malia stepped back.

Her hand went to the leather belt around her waist. Her dagger hung over her right hip, and in front of her hung three of Aru's feathers, each infused with a powerful memory that would help fight the fog in her mind if it threatened. The tiny sac filled with deadly powder remained tucked in the hem of her tunic. Warily, she stepped forward until the hairs along her arms stood on end, and the fog began to spin and roll slowly.

"If this doesn't work," she began, "If something happens to me, and I forget who I am completely . . . don't take me back." Her fingers traced the dagger's hilt. "Do what you have to, but don't take me back."

Aru trilled sadly.

"Don't argue. If I lose myself, I won't know that you're a friend and not an enemy. I might try to attack you." She loosened the dagger and sheath and held them toward him. "Here, take this. I don't want to hurt you."

He tucked them into his travel sac, and then held out his free hand for hers.

Malia took a deep breath, nodded, and placed her hand in his.

Prime the pump. She closed her eyes and waited for Aru to get things going. He would use their combined power to siphon off a portion of the barrier. It was such a huge structure, that taking a small piece of it wouldn't make a difference to its stability. *And besides,* Malia thought, *I've nearly lost myself because of it. The least I could do is take a small bit if it will help me.*

Something tugged at her mind. Aru. She tensed as the fog roiled faster. She let him in, carefully. He pulled gently at her, and from deep inside came a well of power, from the same place as joy and love, from the same place where she imagined her designs when making pottery, from the same place that made her Malia. Drawing it out was a slow, difficult, painful process, like an elder kneeling and then rising again on arthritic legs. The power coiled up and out, through her arm to her hand and into Aru. The Jegudun trilled low, and his grip tightened on hers.

The air crackled. It felt as though little bolts of lightning danced across Malia's skin. She gasped, the hairs at the base of her neck rising.

The fog rolled like monsoon clouds. Malia grasped one of Aru's feathers, ready to use it the moment the fog started to take over.

The tingling across her skin intensified. It wasn't painful, not quite, but if it grew any stronger, it would be. She gritted her teeth and held on to her mind, Aru's hand, and the feather. She was still in control.

Her ears thrummed as the air pressed against her, like that of an incoming storm, but more intense. Her grip on Aru's hand strengthened.

A *crack* reverberated in the air and inside her head, and the pressure and tingling eased, then faded altogether, leaving only Malia and the agitated fog. Aru withdrew his hand.

The fog rose higher in her mind, moving forward, threatening to swallow her. Malia grasped the feather tight and pulled on the memory stored within it.

Her hand burned where every tiny strand from the feather touched it. She held tight despite her nerves screaming for her to let go. The magic streamed up her arm, to her head, and pushed against the fog.

Tendrils of dark gray fog shot forward, only to be struck by the magic and sent back. The fog pushed against the magic, something it had never done before. Malia's other hand scrambled for the feathers at her belt, found one, held tight. Burning lanced through that hand, and she choked on a scream. She'd come this far, she couldn't alert anybody that she and Aru were out here.

The fog rolled back, but not far enough, and tendrils of it still shot forward. She needed the last feather. *Aru can make more.* Not that she'd ever survive another episode like this again . . .

She grasped it in her left hand, compounding the burning. At some point, she'd fallen to her knees. She couldn't see, but she could smell the fresh turned earth and the grass and crushed starflower, the scent like garlic. The pungent smell roused her enough to push back against the fog.

"Not . . . yet," she mumbled through gritted teeth.

The fog gave way, rolled back to where it had been. One last tendril shot out, seeking to devour a memory. Malia swatted it away with a burning shot of magic. Then the fog was tame, for the time being, and she collapsed onto her side.

Aru helped pry her hands open. When he removed the spent feathers, it felt as though he peeled a fresh scab off a wound. Malia whimpered. Then he rustled around in his travel sac and rubbed something cool on both hands. After a few moments, the salve began to tingle and sting, and the smell of sunflower oil and honey reached her nose. Aru deftly wrapped bandages around both of her hands, and finally, the burning eased to a dull throb that echoed her heart beat.

Malia shuddered and, with Aru's arms behind her shoulders, sat. The night was as still as when she'd climbed up here, and the stars hadn't moved at all from the time she touched the barrier, and yet it felt as though she'd just gone through days of ordeals. They still had time to get a head start. The original plan had been to travel the rest of the night and through the morning, then rest during the afternoon. But if their plan hadn't worked . . . if she didn't have a part of the barrier around her, then this was it. She couldn't go through that again.

"Did it work?" she asked, her voice trembling.

Aru trilled gently, then lifted her arm.

Her skin glimmered softly, like it was encased in a web of moonlight. If she hadn't been looking for something out of the ordinary, she might have missed it. In daylight, it might not even be noticeable at all. She stood on shaky feet and took tentative steps toward the barrier, one hand held out.

When she touched it, the air crackled, and dozens of tiny bolts of light shot through the barrier, like she'd generated lightning. Malia yanked her hand away and stepped back quickly.

"It worked," she whispered. She threw her arms around Aru and hugged him tight until he grunted. "I'll take my dagger back. You never know what we might come across as we travel."

CHAPTER TWENTY-ONE

Malia made good time as the night wore on. Aru flew ahead, scouting, coming back at regular intervals to report to her and point her in the right direction. The air was cool and smelled of grass and earth. The grasses whispered as she walked through them, and occasionally her passage stirred some small animal, who darted away with a rustle.

The moon set, leaving only starlight to guide her. She walked through high grass, eventually leaving behind the scattered copses of trees, making her the tallest thing on the plains. She preferred the forest and the cliffs rising high around the valley. This was too open. Naked. She shivered and walked faster.

Excitement that the magic had worked energized her initially, but as the sky began to lighten ever so slightly, her legs slowed, and her thoughts became fuzzy. It would be so nice to just curl up right here and sleep. Just a little.

But she was still too close to the valley. The Jeguduns couldn't force her back, not if she didn't want to go with them, and she didn't think they'd allow any of her people to pursue her, but she wanted as much ground between her and the Taakwa as possible.

Wings beat the air. Her heart sped up, and she crouched, waiting to see whether it was Aru or whether it was a dragon. Aru's small, familiar form circled overhead, blotting out the stars, and she straightened as he landed, tucking his wings behind him.

He trilled and held out a water pouch. She drank, making a sharp noise when the icy water hit her throat. It served to wake her a little. She handed it back, wiping away a few lingering drops with the back of her hand.

"Thank you," she said. "I think I need to eat something. I'm getting tired, but it's too soon to stop."

Aru rummaged in his travel sac and presented her with several small, dark beans. She cradled them in her palm and frowned.

"What are these?"

He gestured for her to eat them. Malia popped one in her mouth and chewed. It was crunchy but edible. Immediately, a bitter flavor filled her mouth. "Ugh, what *is* this?"

Aru handed her the water pouch again. She washed down the gritty, bitter pieces and dubiously eyed the remaining four beans in her hand. "This is supposed to help?"

He nodded eagerly and mimed energetic walking. Malia shook her head, but crunched on two more, washed them down, and finished off the last two in the same manner. She pulled out a strip of jerky and chewed slowly on it, letting the salty, meaty flavor wash away the beans' bitterness. She walked on, and Aru flew off again.

The night slowly gave way to the dawn, the stars winking out one by one. As the sun approached, Malia's energy rose.

It began as a tingling all over, followed by quicker, longer strides, and a clearer mind. The fog was still there, as it had been, but her thoughts grew sharper. She could ignore the throbbing in her hands and the fatigue in her legs. If she felt this good when midday came, she would just keep on walking until she reached the Maddions' mountain. A wide smile broke out on her face.

But by the time mid-morning came, fatigue had returned, and so did sluggish thoughts. Aru offered her three of the bitter beans this time, shaking his head when she asked for more. She grimaced as she chewed them and washed them down with water, followed by more salty jerky. They kept her moving until the sun stood straight over her.

Aru pointed out a dry gulch. Yarrow and sage clung to its sides, as well as a stunted willow. The bottom was made of cracked dirt and small rocks. Malia dug into its side, creating a shallow cave that would protect her from the sun, and curled inside, clutching her travel sac to her. Her sweat and the fresh-turned earth hung heavy in the air, as did the day's heat. She didn't think she'd be able to sleep at all, no matter that she was exhausted, but moments after she closed her eyes, she floated away, oblivious to the world, while Aru crouched in the shade in the gulch's bottom, keeping a wary eye on the skies, his wolfish expression and eyes narrowed in worry the last thing she saw.

~

Squabbling chirps and whistles woke Malia.

She sat up, smacking her head against something hard and sending dirt raining on her. She rubbed at her head, wondering if Rina's home had collapsed.

There were bandages on her hands. They throbbed, pulling her further out of sleep. She blinked a few times, found herself at the bottom of a dry gulch. The soft, warm pink light of sunset reflected off the opposite side of the gulch. Heavy, white clouds rimmed with dark gray rolled in from the south and east. The air smelled of sage and dirt, with a hint of moisture.

She brushed dirt from her clothes and her hair, carefully rubbed the last vestiges of sleep from her eyes, and scooted out of her shallow cave. The previous night came back to her in a rush, albeit a fuzzy one. She squinted, searching for the barrier's glimmer on her skin, but her arm looked as it always did, nut brown and hairless, sinewy muscle bunched beneath it. With the travel sac slung across her torso, she peered over the dirt wall.

Aru stood about twenty paces away, arguing with three other Jeguduns. It took her a moment to recognize Palutzi without the spots he'd used to camouflage himself. She didn't know the other two at all.

She'd expected the Jeguduns to send a party after them, but she hadn't expected them to find her so quickly. If she and Aru were that easy to find, they didn't have much chance of hiding from the Maddion and their dragons, either. True, she had the barrier around her, but she preferred to never have the need of testing it out.

The three newcomers surrounded Aru while he crouched, shoulders hunched, head slightly lowered. One of them, slight curves suggesting she was female, gestured wildly as she spoke, her wings half spread. She began to hop around, taking little flights, moving back and forth and sending the grass swirling. She moved closer to Aru, her wings beating around him, and flashed her teeth.

Then she stopped and stared right at Malia. With a sharp whistle, she gestured that Malia join them. Malia silently cursed, then climbed out of the gulch.

"What's going on?" she asked as she strode forward, forcing a bravado she didn't feel into her voice.

The female dropped to the ground, folding her wings shut with a snap. Her brows drew down and her eyes narrowed. She snarled, and Malia's steps faltered.

The fourth Jegudun, another female, trilled softly, and the snarl fell from the other's face, though her eyes remained narrowed. She stepped forward. Her down was dark gray, her wings melding from dark gray and blue around her shoulders to black along the rest of her wings.

She whistled, chirped, and gestured. Malia understood bits and pieces, enough to know that she wanted them to return to the valley.

"I can't," Malia said. "I have a chance to fix my memories."

The other female, her down a sandy color, her feathers dark tan, snorted and looked away, crossing her arms.

Anger flared. "You can't begin to know what it's like. You have memories you can recall with perfect clarity. You can recall your ancestors' memories. What if you couldn't? What if it was slowly eaten away? At what point do you stop being you?"

The sandy female's arms fell to her side, but she didn't quite meet Malia's gaze.

"I don't have much time before I lose myself. I'd rather die trying to fix this than just sit back and let it swallow me."

The Jegudun turned to her, whistling shrilly. *Danger*, it seemed to say.

"I'm not endangering anybody. Aru helped me take part of the barrier and form it around me." At least, she hoped it was still around her and hadn't dissipated during the night. There was no seeing it at all during the day.

The Jegudun stepped forward, sharp teeth glimmering. Malia stood firm, not even flinching when the Jegudun snarled. The female reached out a hand, fingers ending in talons, and grabbed Malia's wrist. A faint buzz went through Malia, and the Jegudun's eyes widened. The barrier remained around her, then. She let out a sigh of relief.

"See?" she said. "Neither the Maddion nor their dragons will be able to get to me through this. They won't be able to use my blood to bring down the barrier." She recalled Tulah's memories of the Maddion taking the changer, and how they swept across the plains. "Please, just go home and make sure Rina and Ziku and Enuwal are safe. Two of us can hide far better than six."

The Jeguduns went off a ways to talk.

She joined Aru. He still stood with shoulders hunched. "How did they find us?"

He held out his hands. Dried blood stood beneath his talons. He'd been hunting, and intent as he'd been on finding prey, the others would have had an easier time following him back here. It was just a reminder that Aru was young, and perhaps not the best Jegudun to be out here alone with her. She pushed aside the guilt as the other three finished their conversation and the darker female approached.

She reached out a hand. Malia shook her head. "I shouldn't. The last time, I nearly lost myself." She thought of the roiling gray clouds consuming her memories.

The Jegudun blew out a sharp breath, the down around her snout fluttering. The horizon sliced the sun in half, and their shadows stretched long on the grass. A flock of quail rose from the grass, wings clapping, before they moved off a ways and settled again. The moment stretched as thin as their shadows.

Then the Jegudun grabbed her and dragged her along. But not toward the valley. She yanked Malia to the gulch and shoved her in.

Malia slid down on her bottom, dirt tumbling with her. She stopped in a cloud of dirt, coughing, and stood. She craned her neck, meaning to call out and ask just what they thought they were doing, when a large shape shot overhead.

A dragon.

She bit back her cry and crouched, searching wildly for a place to hide, her pulse speeding. The dragon's roar reverberated around her, followed by the squeals of the Jeguduns, and the thud of bodies hitting one another at a high speed.

Her sleeping spot wouldn't hide her. The gulch's sides were steep, with thick shrubs clinging to it farther down. She kept low and hurried in that direction, glancing over her shoulder every few steps, heart stammering.

She reached some juniper shrubs and shoved her way inside, stifling a sneeze as she stirred more dirt. She crouched, breathing shallowly, straining for any sign that the dragon was near. She pulled the bandages off her hands, revealing red welts shaped like feathers, and buried the bandages hastily. She unsheathed her dagger and held it ready.

More roars. Jeguduns screaming in rage, in pain. Malia sobbed silently, fingers digging into the dirt. She should have stayed in the valley. She had never imagined any Jeguduns being harmed. She'd always thought *she'd* be the vulnerable one, that Aru could get away if need be. Her hand found the powder, still tucked away safely in her hem. She was as ready as she could be.

Silence fell, save for one Jegudun, letting out a whistling, rattling sound. Then the dragon roared once, swallowing the sound. Malia cringed.

Huge wings beat the air, heading north. Full night fell. Sounds gradually returned: chirping insects, the rustle of small animals in the grass, the distant howl of a coyote. Malia's heart took a long time to slow to normal.

Even when the animals deemed it safe to move about, Malia waited. So long as she didn't go out there, didn't see what became of the Jeguduns, they might be safe. But finally, she couldn't wait any longer. She emerged from the juniper, small branches tugging at her hair and clinging to her clothes, and climbed out of the gulch.

She tightened her grip on the dagger. Not that it would do any good against a dragon, but it gave her enough bravery to walk slowly toward the place where she'd left the Jeguduns.

Something circled in the air. Malia fell to the ground, gasping, heart pounding. *Dragon.* Then she got a good look at the creature and recognized it as a vulture. Dread settled in her stomach. She pushed herself to her feet and forced them forward.

The sharp, metallic scent of blood filled the air. A wide swath of grass had been trampled. Small bodies lay strewn among torn bits of grass and dark pools of blood.

There was the female that had been so enraged at Malia. Her neck was twisted at an impossible angle, her eyes open and staring at nothing. Malia kneeled and closed them. A few paces away was Palutzi, or most of him. One wing and an arm had been torn away and lay nearby.

Hot tears ran down Malia's cheeks. She went to the next Jegudun, the other female, the nicer one who had tried to calm them all. She'd been ripped open from neck to belly. Then there was the other male, the fourth of the group.

She couldn't find Aru. She circled the group, wider with each pass, searching for him, or some trace of him. Had he escaped? Been captured? Was he dead, but lying somewhere else?

She sheathed the dagger, cupped her hands around her mouth and called his name, quietly at first, then louder. He never answered. Whether he was dead or alive, he wasn't here.

The fog spun in her mind, making it harder to think. Should she go back? Go on? Stay here?

Another vulture joined the first, circling overhead. Soon there'd be so many that her presence wouldn't keep them at bay. She couldn't stay here, even though she would have preferred to see the Jeguduns properly cared for. If she went back, their deaths would be for nothing at all. But if she went on, she still had a chance of finding the *mutara* and at least seeing that their deaths weren't completely in vain.

She touched each Jegudun's head and whispered, "I am sorry," then followed the gulch as it cut north through the land. She glanced at the sky every so often, searching for large wings blotting out the stars. The wind kicked up, smelling of dry desert and moisture, and she shivered. Moments later, the first fat drops of rain fell on her.

Malia hugged herself as the rain chilled her and she walked toward the Maddion, alone.

CHAPTER TWENTY-TWO

Malia traveled all that night, then found a place to hide and rest beside another gulch when dawn started to light the sky. The rain lasted a short while, but it was a deluge. She was glad that her travel sac and the tiny sac holding the powder were well lined. She was soaked through from the rain, and water gurgled through the gulch. She curled in the mud, hidden by a willow tree thick with branches, and shivered.

She drifted in and out of sleep, but she kept seeing the Jeguduns, torn to pieces, and gave up on slumber.

Insects buzzed around her face, and she swatted at them. The day was hot and hazy, the sun bright through the willow branches. The ground beneath her was still damp, but had already dried beyond the tree. The mud caking her had also dried, and it cracked and flaked off as she moved, finding a new position. More clouds built up in the south and east, promising another soaking rain later.

Malia didn't have much of an appetite, but she ate anyway, chewing the jerky slowly, and following it up with a handful of nuts. She washed it all down with water.

She was a long way from home. When was the last time a Taakwa had left the valley? Back when they helped rescue the Jeguduns from the Maddion? Just how big was the world? She didn't think she'd encounter Outsiders, not so close to the Maddion, but there were other people out there, somewhere. More questions chased their way through her mind as she wondered what those people were like, what they enjoyed eating or drinking, what they sang, what they wore, what stories they told. She considered them all, because if she didn't, she'd only think about the four dead Jeguduns.

The sun was a little past its zenith. What she really needed was to rest. Better yet, she should sleep, but she was afraid she'd dream of the dead Jeguduns.

Instead, she cleaned her hands with some of the water from her pouch. Her skin, where she'd touched the feathers, was still red. The air felt good on them. Aru had the rest of the salve, wherever he was. An ache went through her, and she quickly pushed away thoughts of him. Maybe he got away. She had to believe he got away. She lay back and left her hands open, fingers slightly curled. The new scars on her hands would join the others on her legs and her arm. Soon she'd be a mass of scars and broken memories.

She dozed fitfully off and on all that afternoon. When the sun rode low, she ate and drank again, then crawled out from her hiding place, warily scanning the sky. The dragon had attacked around sunset yesterday. Perhaps it had been headed home from a routine flight, or perhaps it had been alerted to their presence. Either way, the Maddion would be on the lookout for more Jeguduns, which meant she needed to be extremely careful.

The clouds hung heavy and approached quickly. The gulch was a little wider here than where she'd started following it, and it led toward the mountains. She was close enough now that she could make out jagged peaks. If she pushed herself hard, she could make the foothills by dawn and spend the day there, planning her next move.

Dark shapes flowed across the plains far to her left. Malia watched them a while. Bison. Sometimes the herds found their way into the Taakwa's valley. Out here, they'd make a tempting meal for dragons and Maddion alike. Malia hoped they moved farther from her. She dropped into the gulch, into shadows, and started walking north.

She'd pause every so often to drink and to listen, especially as night fell completely. Once she thought she heard the beat of large wings. She pressed herself into the gulch's side, heart slamming against her breastbone, and waited. Were those dragon wings? Jegudun wings? She didn't move again until they were long gone.

Lightning lit up the sky to the west, and thunder rumbled across the open plains. Usually she loved storms, but she spent them snug in her home, with the hearth fire blazing, and people around her, telling stories of how their distant ancestors harnessed lightning and used it in lanterns, making the night so bright that they forgot what the stars looked like, or that there was even such a thing as night. But out here, she startled at every flash, every boom.

One particularly bright flash illuminated a shape in the sky. Malia froze, waited. Had she really seen that? The fog in her mind rolled restlessly tonight. It didn't threaten to swallow more memories, but it made her thoughts fuzzy.

Lightning flashed again. This time, there were definitely shapes in the sky, large and winged, with riders. Malia counted seven before the dark swallowed them again. Moments later, thunder rolled.

At least seven dragons, probably more, flew nearby. Did they search for her? For Aru? Did they search because they'd found the other four yesterday? Or did they hunt the bison herd?

She kept as close to the gulch wall as possible, hurrying now, and trying not to think about the dragons. She didn't pause any longer to listen or watch. With that many dragons in the sky, she'd never be able to fight them off. True, they couldn't touch her, but the barrier might not stop a short axe or a blade.

The barrier shimmered along her arms, very slight, like the soft glow of starlight on the Big River at night. Did it make her easier to spot, or more difficult? Could they see it at all?

She half-ran at times, her feet spurred by the dragons and the storm. Thunder rumbled more often now, and closer. During one lull, the distant sound of a different sort of thunder reached her. The bison were running. So, the dragons were most likely out to hunt, and not because of her or the Jeguduns. Not that they wouldn't be wary and watchful.

The bison hooves grew louder. Malia cursed under her breath and climbed out of the gulch.

Her heart galloped in time with the hooves. She waited. Lightning lit up the sky, just long enough for her to make out a wide swath of bison heading straight for her, driven along by dragons.

She cursed again. Had the dragons seen her? She slid back into the gulch, dirt and rocks tumbling along. The bison would stumble into the gulch with her, trapped, and the dragons would swoop on them. If she climbed out the other side and ran, she'd still be vulnerable to those bison who made it out of the gulch, and to the dragons.

She began digging at the gulch's side, making a shallow cave for herself like she had that first night. The herd drew closer at an alarming rate. She dug faster, until her lungs and arms burned from the exertion. A dragon roared, and the others took up the sound until it seemed to come from everywhere. The barrier surrounding her flared momentarily, and her skin tingled.

Dirt flew. Malia's breathing was ragged. All she could think of was making as big a hole as she could and hiding in it. *Go, go, go,* she urged her arms. Her hands throbbed. The herd drew closer, the ground beneath her knees and hands shaking from their hooves. She didn't have another moment.

She rolled into the shallow cave, legs tucked up and her travel sac in front of her face to ward off stray hooves. The ground shuddered all around her, dirt falling on her face, in her ear. She clenched her teeth and held on tight to the leather sac.

The first bison tumbled into the gulch. She couldn't see it, but she heard the great body land with a heavy thud, the animal grunting in surprise and pain. Another fell, and another. One bellowed nearby, the sound blending with hooves shaking the ground.

A dragon roared overhead. Hooves scrabbled at the other end of the gulch. Bison bellowed and grunted, and one squealed, sounding like a huge pig. Wings beat the air, then faded along with the squealing.

A hoof landed on Malia's leg, grazing it. She hissed and pulled herself tighter. Dirt flew at her, landing on the leather sac, stinging her legs. More animals tumbled into the gulch, landing on those already there. The noise grew deafening. Malia had gone numb all over, and her ears rang from the din.

Another hoof kicked her leg, but this time, it landed square and hard, and something snapped. The leather sac muffled Malia's scream. The fog in her head rolled faster as pain erupted in her leg.

No, not now. She pushed against the fog, fought for control of her mind, fought to stay alert as the pain threatened to drag her under and into blackness.

Another dragon roared, farther away this time. Hooves scrabbled at the gulch's walls. One of the animals lowed, the sound rising and ending as a squeal. Those who had made it out of the gulch thundered away. The storm had fallen silent. Save for a few animals moving, the only sound Malia could hear was the blood rushing in her ears.

Sounds faded, but the smells sharpened. Blood, churned dirt, stool, the sour stench of fear, the musky animal smell of the bison, Malia's own sweat. She lay still, waiting, wondering if she was bleeding, certain that her leg was broken. What would she do now? She was stuck in the middle of the plains between the Maddions' mountains and the Taakwa's valley. She'd never make it home, hobbling on one leg. She'd have to wait, surrounded by dead bison, which would draw predators. She choked back a sob.

Slowly, she pushed the travel sac aside. A bison had fallen close enough that she could reach out and touch its hide. Maybe it was the same one that had broken her leg. Whether it was or not, she was better off than the dead beast, at least for the moment.

She pulled herself out, and a sharp pain stabbed her right leg between her knee and ankle. She hissed, and twisted around. She didn't really want to see the damage, but better she knew what she was dealing with.

A shallow gash on the front of her leg bled, caked with dirt. No bone protruded, though, which greatly relieved her. Still, there was no doubt that her leg was broken, and she was stuck in a gulch with a dead bison.

A glance told her that she was stuck with quite a few dead bison. Vultures would be on them soon, followed by coyotes, wolves, and maybe even cougars, enticed from the mountains by the quantity of food.

Her one hope was that the bison slaughter would draw the Jeguduns' attention. If they came to investigate, they'd find her. All she had to do was wait. She bit back a laugh. She was well and stuck, that was certain.

She propped herself against the gulch, legs stretched out, and rummaged through her travel sac for the bit of willow bark she'd tucked away. It would at least take the edge off her pain. She found it and started chewing, grimacing at the bitter taste.

She wished Enuwal was here. No, actually, she didn't. She wished she were with him, her year of mourning behind her, alone in their home. It didn't even matter if it was one she built with her own hands, or if it was his. She just wanted to be sitting with him in front of a hearth fire, storms and wolves and dragons outside and far away, with Enuwal's arms around her. She wanted to know he was safe, and her family and friends were safe.

She pulled the cap off her water pouch and drank, washing away the taste of dirt and blood. The water was lukewarm and had a slight mineral taste. She had about half a pouch left, which could last her a day if she was careful with it.

Wings thrummed the air, approaching from the north. Many wings. A chill ran through her. She pressed herself against the gulch, wishing she could sink into the earth. The faint glimmer of the barrier covered her. *They can't touch me.* She kept repeating that to herself.

She slid her dagger free. It wouldn't kill a dragon, not unless she hit the beast at just the right spot, and given that she couldn't stand and fight, it wouldn't kill a Maddion either, unless he obliged her by falling on it, but she wasn't going to just sit here and meekly let them try to hurt her.

A dragon snorted. Another bellowed. They were coming back for the rest of the bison. They wouldn't leave them out here for the predators; that would be a waste.

She scanned the area immediately around her for a bush or shrub to hide in. There was nothing, save her shallow cave. She scooted back inside that, biting her lip to keep from crying out as her leg gave a sharp protest. Maybe, in the dark, covered with dirt, they wouldn't see her. She rubbed dirt all over her arms, her legs, avoiding the already-caked wound, and on her face. With the travel sac tucked against her belly, she waited.

Dragons landed on the plains, snuffling, grunting, snorting. One landed on the other side of the gulch, giving Malia the perfect view of its sides, glowing fiery red as it breathed in, fading as it exhaled. Its rider climbed down, pulled something from the beast's saddle, and unfurled it. A net. Another man joined him, and together, they climbed into the gulch.

Both men wore the long wool tunics, tied with sashes, and wool pants favored by the Maddion. One had light hair, the other dark, and both wore it twisted in ropes and tied back. Their skin was pale, making them easy to spot in the light of the moon and stars. They spoke, their language guttural and harsh, even as they joked and laughed with one another. The light-haired one wore a short axe on his right hip, and the other wore a long blade. Both had daggers on their left hips.

Several more men joined them, and together they laid out the net, then rolled the bison on it. One man climbed on top of the bison, drawing the net together with a ring. A dragon lifted into the air and hovered, taking the ring from the man. He leaped off the bison, and the dragon rose into the air with the prize, flying north.

Malia lay as still as possible the entire time. The men and dragons were so busy, they might not even notice her. She almost admired their efficiency.

They moved to the next bison, then the next, and the next. Before long, they'd sent away all of their dragons with the rest of their kill. The men gathered somewhere up the gulch, out of sight, but close enough that if Malia understood their language, she'd easily eavesdrop on what they were saying.

They spoke rapidly, laughter punctuating their words every so often. They sounded pleased with themselves. They should be, after the kill they'd managed tonight, and after finding a cure for the illness that had plagued them. Their laughter burned deep inside Malia.

Footsteps crunched in the dirt. Two pairs. Low voices reached her, drawing slowly closer, filled with concern, some anger. Malia held still, hardly breathing. *Turn around. Go back*, she thought vehemently.

They stopped, somewhere just out of her line of sight, but close. Their conversation held an urgency that contradicted the easy nature of the rest of the men. Her grip on the dagger tightened.

One voice rose. The laughter in the distance faltered. Then one man resumed walking. He passed Malia, face raised to the sky, hands on his hips. He wore a short axe on his right hip, and a white sash around his tunic. *Most Worthy*. That was what the Maddion called their leader. To gain the right to the title and all that came with it, a man had to kill his challengers, whether they numbered one or one hundred. They were the most brutal of a brutal lot. Malia's blood ran cold.

Another man, wearing a purple sash, approached the Most Worthy. His shoulders drooped, while the Most Worthy's back remained tense. They spoke, weariness suggesting they were going over old arguments. Wary silence fell between them.

The man with the purple sash frowned and looked around as if he'd heard something. Malia hadn't moved, hardly even breathed. He couldn't have heard her. But maybe he felt her gaze on him. She silently cursed and stared at his boots instead. The Most Worthy asked a question. The second man shrugged. In the distance, massive wings beat the air. The Most Worthy started walking back toward the others.

The second man followed, hesitated, looked around again, even at the ground. The bison had trampled all evidence of Malia's presence. He couldn't know she was there. But he suspected something.

He shook his head, then walked on. The men chatted as they climbed out of the gulch and onto their dragons. One by one, the beasts took off, the sounds of their wings and victorious roars fading into the north. Only when it had fallen completely silent, and the crickets had taken up their song again, did Malia take a deep breath and slowly pull herself out of her cramped hiding place.

The gulch was empty, the ground trampled as far as she could see in either direction, the smell of bison and blood fading. She sheathed her dagger and took a sip of water. Her leg throbbed fiercely, and if she moved it, spiked to a sharp pain. She sat with her back against the gulch's crumbly wall and resumed chewing on the willow bark.

She had only a moment to register a scuffle above her head before a man jumped softly into the gulch near her. The man with the purple sash. She dropped the willow bark and yanked out the dagger just as he raised his short axe. He must have recognized she was Taakwa, because his eyes widened, and he let the axe fall to his side. He muttered something, and another man joined him, jumping down. The Most Worthy.

The Most Worthy had a boyish face, or maybe it was the delight spreading across it that made him look boyish. He would have been handsome, if Malia didn't know him to be a monster. She brandished her dagger before her. The man chuckled.

It was the chuckle that fueled the flames deep inside her into something resembling a roaring inferno. Her blood pounded, her lips curled into a snarl that felt as ferocious as any Jegudun's. The grin slid from the man's face, and he started toward her.

The barrier around her glowed brighter when he was a step away. She felt it *push* him, and the air crackled with energy. He stopped, eyes narrowing.

The second man approached, and the barrier flared again, pushing him away as well. Malia worried that they would stir up the fog in her mind, but it remained calm. He raised the short axe. The Most Worthy turned to him, muttering something, and put his hand on the other man's arm, lowering the axe.

Malia grit her teeth and lunged forward on hands and knees to plunge her dagger into the Most Worthy's thigh, the highest she could reach, slicing down and in, toward the large artery that would pump out his life's blood in moments. The barrier repelled him, though, sending him flying through the air just before her blade could reach his inner thigh.

The second man yelled, brandishing the axe, while the Most Worthy shouted at him. He fell to his knees beside his leader, pulling off his sash and tying it around the deep cut.

Malia panted heavily, standing despite the pain, avoiding any weight through her right leg. She put a hand on the gulch wall and began hobbling away, her right foot coming down only enough to help her balance, biting back the cry every time pain shot through her leg.

Something large swooped over her, and a dragon landed between her and the men. The second man shouted, and the dragon took in air, its sides blazing such a bright red that it hurt Malia's eyes. Her skin prickled a moment before fire erupted all around her.

The barrier flared to life again, pushing the flames away. They passed harmlessly by her, without even the slightest hint of warmth. The fire stirred the fog in her mind. *Not now*, she hissed at it. She had no feathers to fight it with. If the fog started rolling forward, it would consume her entirely.

More shouts, the sounds of scrabbling behind her. Malia fought for every inch forward.

Something whooshed through the air. A net settled over her, dragging her down, forcing her to put full weight on her right leg momentarily. She cried out, hating that she showed any sign of weakness in front of these men and the dragon. She took her dagger to the fibers, thinking to cut her way out, but whatever it was made of, it was strong.

Then the net tightened around her. Wings beat the air, and the net jerked up, hauling her off the ground. Her dagger fell, landing in the dirt with a soft thump, and she flew through the cool night, the dragon's sides pulsating rhythmically above her like a strange, giant firefly.

CHAPTER TWENTY-THREE

Chanwa paced her room. The embers in the hearth snapped and crackled as they died, and the lanterns flickered. The other men had already returned from the hunt and were celebrating their success with wine and women and food. But Muvumo and Delkis were still out there. The men returning did not know why, only that their leader told them to go on. The two men had been fine when the others left.

All the bison had been collected. What could have kept the two men out there, other than having a convenient, private place to speak? Muvumo had hardly said a word to her since he'd brought her to the scroll cavern. What fate did he consider for her and her family's scrolls? Her stomach had been a knotted mess since then, growing worse every day until she hardly ate or drank anything. For a little while, she'd thought him sympathetic to her, but his silence since that day had stretched until it hung as palpably between them as the tapestries hung on the walls of their home.

The door cover rustled. Chanwa whirled, but it was only Ankti.

"Do you need anything more, my lady Chanwa?"

She sighed. "No, I don't." She considered asking Ankti to stay simply to keep her company, but the servant still moved stiffly following the whipping Muvumo had given her. Guilt gnawed at Chanwa. The other woman needed rest. "You may go. Sleep well."

Ankti bowed her head and slipped out, but a moment later she scurried back in, eyes wide, and held the door cover back.

Delkis and one of the boys who tended the dragons came in, carrying Muvumo between them. A dark stain covered most of his left leg, and the cloth on that side hung in tatters. He growled at them, "I'm fine, I told you."

"We shall see," Delkis said. "The healer is on his way."

"What happened?" Chanwa asked, straightening the bed pallet as they lowered him. *What the blazes?* Had Delkis done this? No, he wouldn't have helped the Most Worthy back home, he would have finished Muvumo off or died trying. She pushed a pillow under Muvumo's head, but he shoved it away, nearly spilling her.

"What does it look like?" he growled.

Chanwa took a step back, clasping her hands tightly together, uncertain of what to do. "Was it a man? A dragon?"

Delkis let out a snort. "Neither."

Muvumo muttered something she didn't quite catch. He looked as if he'd bitten into a sour fruit.

"Oh, she's going to find out sooner or later," Delkis snapped. He turned to the dragon attendant. "That's all, boy. Take the servant with you on the way out."

The boy bowed hastily, then shoved Ankti out of the room ahead of him. Their bare feet padded on the rugs, then the stone, then faded altogether.

Muvumo stank of sweat and blood, with an underlying hint of bison. A dark sash had been tied around his thigh. Most of the blood on his leg was dried or drying. Given the amount of blood, the cut must be deep. He was lucky it didn't reach the main artery in his thigh, though it looked as though it had come close. Chanwa's heart galloped. Part of her wished whoever had done this had made the cut long enough to finish Muvumo. Then at least one of her problems would have disappeared. But she would have only gained more, in the form of whomever she was married off to next.

A man called out from the front room.

"In here," Delkis answered.

The healer entered. A boy followed, carrying a small bag clutched to his chest, his eyes wide and looking all around. The healer was short and stocky, not at all fighting material, as the warriors liked to say of those they found unsuitable to wield weapons and ride dragons. He wore a dark red sash around his tunic, and his hair, twisted and pulled back, was receding along his forehead.

"What happened?" he asked, his voice soothing.

Chanwa stepped back further, into what shadows there were, and stood still. Usually, she was sent out of the room when the healer tended Muvumo, but she wanted to know what happened out there.

"I was attacked," he said, flinching and tensing as the healer probed the area around the cut.

"That much is obvious," the healer said. "This looks like a clean cut, but from a low angle. Someone on the ground?" He tore the pants, exposing the wound, and removed the sash.

"Yes."

The healer barked orders at the boy who hastily dug out a bottle from the bag and handed it over. Uncapped, it released heady fumes. He poured it along the wound's length. Muvumo hissed and lay back, his breathing rapid and shallow, his eyes rolling up, his teeth clenched.

The healer handed the bottle back to the boy.

"Was . . . that . . . necessary?" Muvumo panted.

"Only if you don't want infection to eat its way through your leg. And this cut is rather close to your manhood. I've seen infections eat away at those. One man lived, but I rather think he wished he hadn't."

Chanwa had always thought Muvumo had sent her away when the healer came because he was afraid she'd faint at blood or some such nonsense like that, but in reality, it seemed he didn't want her to hear how the healer berated him. She bit her lower lip.

"Tagu was summoned to help someone else," the healer said. "I assume it was the man who did this to you?"

"It wasn't a man," Delkis said. "It was a woman."

Chanwa's breath caught. Who had done this? Who would have been out there with them? An unmentionable? Or had they remained on the plains at all?

"A Taakwa woman," Delkis added.

The healer froze in the midst of rummaging through his bag. The boy blinked a few times in surprise. Chanwa's mind swirled. It couldn't have been a Taakwa woman. They never dared leave their valley. But a Taakwa would certainly attack any Maddion they came across.

"A Taakwa?" the healer said. "But . . . now all we need is a Jegudun, and with their blood, we can break down the barrier around their valley. We can take what is ours, finally. We—"

"There is something different about her," Delkis said. "We can't touch her. No Maddion can."

He frowned. "What do you mean?"

Delkis sighed. "You'll see for yourself."

"Then how is Tagu tending her?"

"He's enlisted a servant's help."

Muvumo groaned. "Can we discuss this later, once my wound is sewn up?"

"Oh, of course, Most Worthy," the healer said. He pulled out a small, wooden case. Inside were several bone needles and a heavy thread the healers used for stitches. He had the boy pour the bottle's contents over a needle, the thread, and his own hands. He threaded the needle, glanced at the nearest lantern. His gaze flickered over to Chanwa, and he frowned.

"You shouldn't be in here," he told her.

"But I—"

"I don't need some woman passing out or crying while I'm tending our Most Worthy. Get out."

Chanwa pursed her lips and nodded once. She'd already heard plenty. She hurried outside.

The stairway was empty, with only a few torches lit at far intervals to light the way. The air was cool, and it cleared the bottle's scent from her nostrils.

But her head still swam. A Taakwa woman, here. Where would they take her? To the cells, of course. She leaned against the stone wall that kept people from inadvertently stepping off the stairway. It was smooth from generations of hands running along it and had already lost the day's heat.

Ankti had told her that the Taakwa were led by their women. Their women owned property, had final say in the laws. Men deferred to them. What was that like? What was it like to have an opinion that mattered? To make choices? To hold an important role? To be oneself without hiding it?

She had to see this Taakwa woman, but the only way to the prisoners' cells was by dragon. Women were strongly discouraged from using the dragons, save for emergencies. Perhaps she could entice the attendant to carry her to the cells.

Going to her might be foolish. Word would certainly get back to Muvumo. But after all that Chanwa had been through these past few seasons, she didn't think she could simply go back to her old life, especially not without her scrolls. She couldn't pretend she didn't know how to read and write, or that she was incapable of loftier thoughts. She also couldn't go much longer without having a child, or she risked becoming an unmentionable while Muvumo sought a new wife, but she couldn't stand the idea of having a daughter and never teaching her all that she knew. She couldn't even pretend for much longer that she didn't love Ankti.

Love. She gasped as the realization struck her. Yes, love. She was *in* love.

She grew light-headed and leaned harder on the wall. She forced her thoughts away from Ankti. Later. She'd think more on that later.

Her entire world had turned inside out. But hers wasn't the only one. The men were dealing with the loss of their scrolls. And now this Taakwa woman appears . . . the changer hadn't left yet even though she'd fulfilled her end of the bargain. Things were still modifying, still falling into place. This Taakwa woman had come here for a reason. Perhaps she could help Chanwa, and the Maddion, and not simply by giving them her blood. The valley held no answers, only revenge, and Chanwa was sick of death and war. She was ready for her future, and life, and love.

She hurried up the stairs, holding her skirts so they wouldn't tangle around her ankles. By the time she reached the mesa, she was out of breath. She rarely had cause to move faster than a sedate walk.

Two torches lit the entrance to the mesa's cave, where saddles and other equipment were kept, and where an attendant remained at all times. Chanwa called out, and a moment later, a bleary-eyed boy emerged.

"What is it?" he muttered when he spotted her.

"My husband has an urgent message for the healer tending the Taakwa prisoner."

"Well, what is it?"

She frowned. "I have to take it myself."

"You?" He was wide awake now, and he eyed her from her head to her toes and back again.

She stepped forward, drawing on the same ferocity her husband used to keep people in line, and said, "That's right. Would you care to question him yourself? While you're at it, you can let him know how you delayed his message. He's in an *excellent* mood, what with his leg being sewn up right now and all. I'm sure he would only toss you over the railing to a quick death, and not actually feed you to one of the dragons."

"Oh, no, that's not necessary. I will fetch a saddle and a dragon right away." He let out a series of whistles, then disappeared into the cave.

Chanwa stepped back. Her arms broke out in gooseflesh, not just from the cold, and she rubbed them vigorously. Soon, wings drummed the air, and the pulsating, glowing sides of a dragon came into view, circling and descending, and then the beast emerged fully from the dark and landed in the small glow the torches threw off. The wind churned by its wings tugged at Chanwa's hair, sending tendrils flying around her face, and tiny beads of dirt pelted her.

The boy hurried out, carrying a two-person saddle, and made quick work of settling it on the dragon and tightening the straps. Even in a hurry, he made sure to double check the fit, deftly tugging on the main strap around the dragon's belly, as well as the straps surrounding her shoulders and chest. He was good at his job. Guilt jabbed Chanwa. After this, he'd be lucky to clean up behind the dragons.

He beckoned, and she stepped forward. At a word from the boy, the dragon kneeled, and she clambered into the saddle awkwardly, her skirt tangling around her legs. She gave them a yank, revealing her ankles and perhaps a bit more, and landed in the rear seat with a *thump*.

The boy climbed easily into the forward seat, red burning around his cheeks. He'd gotten an eyeful of the Most Worthy's wife's legs. So be it. He saw that they were both strapped in, then gave the dragon a command.

The beast lurched, and Chanwa grabbed the handles on the front of her seat as the dragon took off into the sky. The dragon carried them higher, circling easily. Warmth rolled off her, even through the saddle, so that Chanwa's legs, at least, were warm. The wind quickly chilled the rest of her, though, and she shivered.

The dragon brought them to a gentle landing on the mesa that led into the cells. Another attendant came running out, but the boy in front of Chanwa waved him off. The one below frowned when he spotted Chanwa.

The boy unbuckled her, remaining in the saddle while she slid off, grasping the saddle's edge to keep her knees from buckling when her feet hit the ground. "I have to get back," he said. "Jemson will bring you back when you're ready."

She started to protest, but the boy had already goaded the dragon. Chanwa had to scramble back to keep out of the way of talons and the great wings. She frowned after them.

The attendant on the ground—Jemson—approached. "What are you doing here?"

The servants showed respect to all Maddion, but among the Maddion themselves, it was up to the men and boys how much respect they showed women. Most showed little to none. Though she'd faced the disrespect all her life, it still rankled Chanwa every time, and she found herself growing sorely tired of it recently.

"None of your business," she snapped.

The boy recoiled as if she'd struck him. "You cannot speak to me that way, no matter whose wife you are," he said.

She ignored him and strode into the caves.

A large passage led straight back into the mountain. Torches at regular intervals lit the way, shimmering off the granite walls and the occasional vein of silver or gold. The air was crisp and chilly and smelled of wood smoke, and more faintly, of sweat and blood.

Chanwa passed a dozen or so empty cells before she spotted brighter light ahead. Voices echoed, both speaking the Maddion language, although one had a strong accent.

Tagu, one of the other healers, stood a good distance outside a cell, his bag, a match to the one the other healer carried, open at his feet. Tagu was tall and muscular, with strong, sharp features. He'd been on track to be a great dragonrider and warrior, but had crushed his leg in an accident. Although he'd eventually walked again, he wasn't fit for battle or long dragon rides anymore, and so he'd become a healer. What only some knew was that he held a fondness for other men's wives. He tended women while other healers preferred to stay away from them, but he addressed more than their ailments.

"Don't get any grand ideas," he was saying as she approached. "The only reason you're doing this is because I can't get any closer to her." He frowned, his arms crossed, one foot tapping at the stone floor. He muttered, "I can't believe a mindless, idiot servant is tending her leg." He glanced up. His frown turned to a round mouth, and his eyes widened. "What are you doing here?" he asked Chanwa.

She sighed. She was getting tired of that question. "I am here to see the Taakwa woman."

"But . . . whatever for?"

"Because I want to."

Tagu gaped and blinked several times. "Does your husband know you're here?"

"He and the other healer wanted me gone from my own home. I am gone. If you're truly concerned, feel free to go tell him where I am, although I suspect he's well-drugged by now." Briefly, she wondered how well the pain-relieving draught would work, given that Muvumo still snuck a pinch of kasi powder daily.

He shook his head. "You shouldn't be here. Come," he said, reaching for her.

She shrugged away before he could grab her, and raised her chin. "I will tell my husband that you touched his wife."

He frowned. "Of *course* I need to touch you. I need to get you out of here." He grasped her arm.

She raised her chin and spoke in a hushed voice. "You will let me go, or I will tell my husband how many women you've tarnished, starting with Cerulia. And then there was Verila, and—"

He blanched. "Stop." He glanced at the servant in the cell, the wooden door left open.

A man was on one knee in the cell, his back toward them, a woman sitting with her back against the stone wall and her legs stretched out before her. He gave no indication he'd heard the exchange, busy as he was tending the Taakwa woman's leg.

"You have no proof," he growled.

Chanwa smiled. "Oh, I don't? Have you taken a good look at Cerulia's boy? He looks so much like her, but as he gets older, he seems to be taking after his father more each day. I'd say he doesn't have Grent's chin or nose, and they certainly stand out, don't they? I think he looks more like . . . well, like *you*. A few other people think so as well. And if the Most Worthy's wife brings up her concern, then people might start looking a little more closely and notice the similarities as well."

Tagu sputtered. His cheeks had gone red, and his grip tightened painfully on Chanwa's arm. She pulled free and took a step back.

He had right to be concerned. Any man found sleeping with another's wife was to be drawn and quartered. And if that union produced a child, then a girl would be destined to become an unmentionable, and a boy would become a servant, if either one was allowed to live, that was. Chanwa was certain that Tagu was aware of his progeny and wanted only the best for his boy. What he *wasn't* certain of was how she wouldn't be able to actually bring herself to put his child in harm's way. She could only hope he would fall for her bluff.

"None of that needs to come to light, though," Chanwa said, "So long as I get to speak with the Taakwa woman."

For a moment, Chanwa feared that Tagu was about to strike her. But then his color faded back to normal, and he took a step back, nodding. "Of course. But she won't understand you, and you her. Unless you've been learning new languages from one of the filthy servants?"

Her anger flared. She pushed it down quickly. "It doesn't matter if we don't understand one another. This could be my only chance to see a Taakwa up close, and alive. When the Maddion invade their valley, I doubt my husband will order any left alive, save for a couple he may want to toy with before killing."

"Very well, then."

The servant's deft hands made quick work on the final strips holding the splint in place. The movement looked easy for him, as if he'd done it many times before. Most likely he'd been some sort of healer before he'd been taken from his people, and that was why Tagu had chosen him to care for the Taakwa prisoner. He stood, giving Chanwa her first good look at the Taakwa woman.

Dirt covered her entirely, save for her splinted leg, which was clean. The lingering smell of spirits suggested the servant had cleaned her leg with the same concoction used on Muvumo's wound.

She wore an animal skin tunic and skirt, both plain, and just as dirty as the rest of her, and simple leather shoes. Her hair was mostly pulled back, but long, dark strands had come loose and hung about her face, or clung to the caked dirt and sweat along her forehead. Her skin was nut brown, and her eyes a deeper brown. Her cheeks were raised and round, her face lovely beneath the dirt, her eyes sharp. They focused on Chanwa, and she had the feeling the Taakwa woman could see all of her secrets: the scrolls, her feelings for Ankti, the special tea she drank every day that kept her from growing a baby.

She took a step forward. Light flared around the Taakwa woman, and something unseen pushed Chanwa back. She gasped.

Tagu chuckled. "Somehow she's erected a barrier around herself like the one surrounding the valley. You can't get any closer. You don't speak her language. Are you satisfied now? You've seen the woman, now come along."

The servant left the cell. He shut the door behind him, locked it, and handed the key to Tagu. The bars within the thick door were made of metal, erected by the Solumna before they'd died. Chanwa could almost feel their lingering hatred for the Maddion. How they must have dreamed of putting their masters behind these very doors. They had come up with a better revenge, though.

The servant was one of the fair-skinned southerners, one of the few that survived a raid years ago. Those who hadn't died from the journey to the mountains had later tried killing themselves. This man had either failed at his suicide and never tried again, or hadn't tried at all in the first place. He nodded at her. "My lady Chanwa," he muttered, keeping his gaze averted. He placed a bottle and leftover strips of cloth into the healer's bag, then stepped back.

Tagu grabbed the servant's arm and twisted it up behind his back. The servant's face went even paler, but he made no noise. Tagu gave the arm a jerk, and something popped. The servant moaned.

"That's enough," Chanwa said, hands outstretched and pleading. "What are you doing?"

"So he doesn't forget his place," Tagu said. He released the servant's arm and shoved him. The man crumpled to the ground, eyes rolling and showing the whites. Tagu met her gaze. "Like you." He advanced upon her.

Chanwa took a step back. Tagu stopped, grinned. No mirth touched his eyes, though. "It's all right. Your husband will remind you." He grabbed his bag, then said to the servant, "Come along, dragon shit."

The man struggled hastily to his feet, clutching at his shoulder, and followed meekly behind the healer.

Hatred burned through Chanwa. This brutality was the reason her people had been cursed. If they weren't careful, someone else would finish what the Solumna had started, and the Maddion would be gone for good.

She found the Taakwa woman standing, holding onto the bars in the door, and watching her. Chanwa startled, took a step back. She hadn't heard the woman rise or approach. The woman's brows were drawn down, her brown eyes narrow and wary.

"That must hurt," Chanwa said. "Please, sit back down." She gestured along with her words. She needed a translator. Would the woman understand the trade language? The Taakwa had been isolated for several generations now, and without the need for another language, they most likely had forgotten it. Would any of the servants speak her language?

The wariness remained in her eyes, but the woman drew back, leaned against the wall, and gracefully lowered herself to the ground, stretching her splinted leg before her. Her clothes, though plain, had been well cared for, save for a few tears that looked recent. She'd need new clothes, and a basin to wash herself, food and something to drink.

Chanwa gave a little shake of her head. She was thinking of this woman as a guest, not a prisoner, and certainly not the person who put a dagger into her husband's thigh. Chanwa should be enraged and demanding justice. She should have marched in here and told the healer to leave the woman's leg to heal crooked as punishment. That was the Maddion way.

Well, may the dragons piss on the Maddion way.

She stepped closer to the door so she could peer through the bars. "What were you doing out there?" she asked softly, mostly to herself.

To her surprise, the woman spoke. The language was lilting and soft, almost lyrical, like a song. *Like Jegudun speech, or birdsong.* Chanwa didn't understand a word, but the urgency was clear, given the way the woman leaned forward and gestured as she spoke. The wariness faded from her eyes, replaced by pleading.

Though Chanwa didn't understand the language, she *did* catch the same word over and over. *Mutara.* It tickled the back of her mind. Then it came to her. That was the word Ankti used to describe the changer. Sersha, she called herself now.

The Taakwa woman had come here because of the changer.

"Mutara?" Chanwa asked.

The woman nodded vigorously. She said something else, and tears welled in her eyes.

Chanwa gripped the bars and leaned close. The faint push of the barrier touched her, warned her away. Her grip tightened. "I will see if I can bring her to you," she said.

The woman sat back, nodded again, and closed her eyes.

She had hundreds more questions, but they would have to wait for a translator. The changer, Sersha, would understand. Chanwa's heart quivered. The changer held so much power. And she'd purposefully struck at the scrolls, saving the women's secret scrolls. What game did the changer play at? Chanwa felt like a tool, serving some greater purpose she didn't know. She wasn't sure she wanted to be Sersha's tool, but she couldn't stand back and do nothing either.

"I'll come back," she said.

The Taakwa woman said nothing. Her breathing had deepened. She slept.

Chanwa moved back, and the barrier's push disappeared. She hurried down the cave to the entrance. She hoped the attendant was still there. She wouldn't put it past Tagu to order the boy away, leaving Chanwa stranded.

Tagu wouldn't dare speak with Muvumo and tell him she was here, not if he wanted his secret kept. Muvumo would be well drugged by now, sleeping, and she could always say she went to visit a friend while the healer was working on him.

She was breathing heavily by the time she reached the cave's entrance. She hadn't run much since she was a small girl.

She burst out of the cave, searching for the boy and the dragon. Instead, she found a wall of dragons, and Muvumo.

Her hands clenched at her sides. She considered dashing back into the caves, but they dead-ended. She could rush to the mesa's side, leap over . . . no. She might yet talk her way out of this.

Muvumo strode toward her, fresh blood seeping through his pants. The healer who had tended him stood behind, wringing his hands, shifting his weight from side to side. "Most Worthy, I really must insist that you return home and let me look at the wound. I'm afraid you've reopened it, and—"

"Of course I've reopened it," he snarled without taking his eyes off Chanwa. She shrank back from the intensity in them. "I had to track down my wife." He advanced upon her. "My *disobedient* wife."

"I was told to leave," she said, her voice shaking. "I was curious about the Taakwa woman. I came to see what a Taakwa looked like, no more. I did not disobey. I was never told not to come here." Her knees trembled. She took another step back and leaned against the cold stone wall.

Muvumo stood over her, close enough that she could feel his body's heat coming off in waves and smell his sweat and blood. Lines creased the skin between his brows. His lip curled on one side in a cruel, jesting smile. His pupils were so wide that his eyes looked nearly black. He'd taken kasi powder. With the draught the healer had given him, he should have been sleeping.

"Of course," he said. "How silly of me not to think to forbid you from seeing the prisoner while my leg was sewn up. How silly of me to think you might have a shred of common sense."

Her heart thudded heavily against her breastbone. Muvumo could easily fling her off the mesa, or feed her to one of the dragons behind him. They shifted their weight and snorted anxiously, as if they sensed the possibility of a meal. Bile churned in her stomach.

"What you need," he said, "is some time to consider your actions." He grabbed her arm, squeezed tight, and twisted. She cried out. He ignored her, pulling her into the cave. "Boy," he called out.

She stumbled, and he dragged her along, the stone scraping the side of her leg. "Muvumo, stop, please."

He dragged her to the nearest cell and pulled her inside. Then he stepped out, and the boy locked the door.

"You will stay in here until you've learned your place," Muvumo said.

And with that, he extinguished the nearest torches and left her in darkness and silence.

CHAPTER TWENTY-FOUR

Malia was imprisoned so far back in the cave that she couldn't tell night from day. The torches were always lit, and when they sputtered low, the boy tending the cave brought new ones. The two torches outside her cell cast a small square of light into her cell so that most of it remained in shadows, encouraging her to sleep, or at the very least, remain inactive.

She shivered in the cold air, but nobody brought a sleeping pallet or blankets. Someone brought her three meals a day, however, and emptied the waste bucket. It was always someone different, and someone obviously not Maddion, although a Maddion always attended them, standing far out of the barrier's reach.

She spoke to each person who brought her food and water. None replied, or even made eye contact with her. She asked for blankets and fresh clothes, and for a sleeping pallet. She asked after the woman who had come to her and seemed to understand she wanted to speak with the *mutara*. She asked for the *mutara*. Some of the servants understood the word. They'd flinch, or make a gesture with their hands as if to ward the being off, or their eyes would widen. Those were the strongest reactions she ever got from them.

From the Maddion themselves, she often received a harsh warning. She recalled how the healer had hurt the man who'd tended to her leg simply to spite the Maddion woman, and so she pushed the matter only so far. She didn't want to be responsible for someone getting hurt.

She kept track of days by the number of meals brought to her. For every three meals, she tied a knot in the leather strap that held her hair. By this, she counted twelve days that she'd been in the cell.

Her clothes stank, as she did herself. Her hair was a matted mess, dirt caked through it, on her skin, in her clothes. With the sparse water they brought, she washed herself little by little until at least her face, neck, and arms were clean. Her entire body ached from the cold and the hard floor.

Her broken leg itched. She welcomed the sensation as it meant the bone was knitting. It was less tender to touch, and the scrape had scabbed over. If Enuwal was here—

She cut off that line of thought. If she dwelled too much on those she'd left behind, she wouldn't be able to focus on her present problem. She'd either get back to them, or she wouldn't. But she *did* ask herself what Enuwal would tell her to do while her leg healed, and so she moved her good leg, stood and hobbled as much as she could tolerate without putting weight on the broken leg, and worked her arms. She'd do well to keep up her strength as much as possible and not give in to the lethargy the Maddion encouraged with the lack of comforts and light.

She constantly checked the little packet of powder. It remained tucked inside the hem of her tunic. She had nearly taken it the first time she'd woken in the cell. She'd been expecting the Maddion to bleed her immediately. Instead, they splinted her leg and were keeping her alive, which meant they didn't have a Jegudun in captivity, so either Aru had escaped, or he had died along with the other four. She fervently hoped for the former. Regardless, as long as they didn't have a Jegudun, they wouldn't bleed her, and she had time.

On the thirteenth day, by Malia's reckoning, one of the previous servants, a lithe woman with fair skin, green eyes, and hair the flaming red of aspen leaves in autumn, brought her food and water and emptied the bucket. The Maddion did not change as often as the servants did. The one standing outside had grown familiar. He inspected his nails while the servant bustled around. They'd even taken to leaving the door open while the servant tended to Malia. They probably figured she couldn't exactly run on her broken leg, so why bother?

The woman kneeled to take away the old plate, empty despite Malia's lack of appetite, and place the new one at her side. She glanced up and formed one word silently. *Mutara.*

Malia blinked a few times, uncertain if she'd actually seen the woman's lips move. She gave a slight nod. A grin touched the woman's mouth briefly, and then she was gone with a swirl of skirts. The Maddion did not bother hiding his lustful glance at the servant's retreating posterior. Malia grimaced. If a Taakwa man had looked upon a woman that way, he would have been pulled before the clan mother by his ears and made an example in front of the entire village. He shut the door and locked it, the sound echoing in the cave.

What did the servant mean? Was the *mutara* coming to see her? Had any of the servants understood her? Who? They were all so different, and it had been generations since the Taakwa had traded with anybody outside the valley. If she could have walked, she would be pacing the cell. As it was, she ate the bland food, choking down every bit. It wasn't horrible. They didn't leave her with stale, moldy bread or tough meat, but the cuts were few and far between, as were the vegetables. Most of what she received was bread and broth. Still, she ate it quickly, drank, and then set to work doing exercises.

She followed Enuwal's example as he was healing from his broken leg. She braced her hands on either side of her rear and straightened her elbows, raising her bottom off the cold stone. She did this until her arms trembled, then rolled over carefully and pressed up, arching her back and enjoying the stretch. Then she lay flat and lifted one leg at a time, rolled onto her back and did the same. By the time she finished the routine, she'd worked up a fair sweat and had warmed up. The only problem was, she'd cool off quickly, and the cave's chill would settle into her bones again.

Several more days passed. The green eyed woman didn't return, and the *mutara* never made an appearance. Malia didn't dare ask about either when the servants showed up to tend her needs. No others gave any indication that the *mutara* would be forthcoming. Every time footsteps scraped the stone, Malia straightened, her heart hammering, wondering if it was the *mutara*, yet each time, she was disappointed when it was only another servant bearing food and water, and a Maddion.

Maybe she'd imagined the exchange. The fog in her mind slowly crept forward day by day, obliterating a memory here, another there. Usually good at faces, she had a hard time recalling her grandmother's, although she could still see the sharp angles of Vedran's, Enuwal's pleasant smile, and her mother's perpetual frown. Her time was running out. Either she'd lose herself to the fog, or the Maddion would kill her.

She sighed and leaned her head back against the hard stone. This had been a huge mistake. She should have remained in the valley and enjoyed as much time as possible with her family and Enuwal before the fog consumed her.

"I am a fool," she said, her voice echoing.

"No more than most," said a woman.

Malia whirled. Somebody's shadow fell across the small, square window in the cell door. Malia struggled to her good leg and, keeping one hand on the wall for balance, hopped to the window.

A woman wearing the Maddion style of a long, sweeping dress the color of a sharp winter sky stood just outside. She was shorter than Malia, with a body that was all curves and softness, even in her face. Her hair was the color of corn silk, twisted back intricately to the nape of her neck. The remainder flowed down her back. Her skin was pale, save for two points of color high on her cheeks. She looked like the Maddions' vision of a perfect, beautiful woman.

Her eyes, however, were red-orange, as if a fire burned inside her. She smiled, and it chilled Malia. The scent of something sweet hung in the air, like honeysuckle, and something else, sharper and pungent, like the smell of a lightning strike.

"Who are you?" Malia said.

"You may call me Sersha. I am known by other names as well. Changer. *Mutara*. Witch. Devil. Angel. Goddess. I've been around for a long, long time."

"And yet you don't look any older than me."

She chuckled. "You have a sense of humor. Lovely. Too many people are afraid of me to ever dream of jesting. I do enjoy it."

"You speak my language."

"I speak all languages."

Malia found herself speechless. She'd spent most of her waking time in the cell going over what she would say to the *mutara*, but part of her thought this moment would never happen. She wasn't sure where to begin.

"You've been asking for me," Sersha prompted.

"Yes."

"Why?"

"I . . ." She licked her lips, gone suddenly dry. Power radiated off this woman—this *being*—in palpable waves. This woman had cured the Maddion of their illness. She could help Malia, no doubt about that now that she was in the *mutara's* presence, but she hesitated at asking for help.

A tendril of fog leaped forward and lashed at her mind. She had until her leg healed, or perhaps a little longer, before the fog consumed her entirely, and then she'd be as good as dead. She'd come all this way . . . she had to ask.

"I need your help," she said. "I worked magic with the Jeguduns last summer, and something has gone wrong. My memories are disappearing. *I* am disappearing."

Some emotion flickered across Sersha's face, too quickly for Malia to make out. Pity? Empathy? She didn't know.

"May I?" Sersha asked, indicating she'd like to come closer.

A wry smile crossed Malia's face. "I'm afraid I don't have the key."

"I don't need keys. Step back."

Malia hopped backwards and leaned against the wall.

Sersha laid her hand across the lock. Something clicked, and the door swung open. She entered, and it shut behind her. "I'm sorry, but I can't have you running off." Her gaze flickered to the splint. "Or hobbling, as the case may be. My hosts would frown upon that, I'm afraid, and I've been enjoying their growing pains far too much."

Malia frowned. She didn't quite understand what the *mutara* was talking about. Enjoying their growing pains?

"Please, sit," Sersha said, gesturing toward the bare, stone floor like a host offering her most comfortable pillows to a guest.

Malia hesitated. She didn't like the idea of giving this woman any advantage over her, even something as minor as height, but there seemed no point in disagreeing, so she slid to the ground, her splinted leg straight ahead of her, and the other tucked in.

Sersha kneeled beside her, the skirt billowing out like a cloud, the smell of honeysuckle and lightning strike growing stronger. Malia tried not looking directly in her eyes. This close, she could make out swirls of deep red in the dark orange. If she looked too deeply, she might lose herself in those eyes, much as she was losing herself in the fog.

The *mutara* chuckled as if she sensed Malia's discomfort. "Let's see what's going on in there, shall we?"

She laid both hands on Malia's head. They were light, hardly disturbing her hair, and yet she still flinched, unsure what to expect.

"Easy, now," Sersha muttered.

Malia closed her eyes. The afterimage of Sersha's eyes blazed in the darkness.

At first, she felt nothing different. The fog in her mind rolled lazily in place, occasional tendrils searching for new memories to gobble up. Then she sensed another presence in her mind.

It eased into her awareness, unlike the adamant tug of the Jeguduns. It didn't intrude, it merely wandered, like a visitor strolling through a village for the first time. The presence moved around the fog, pushing at it, pulling away.

Then the presence pierced through the heart of the fog.

The fog erupted into chaos. It roiled, spreading in all directions. Malia pushed against it frantically, but it was too late. It rolled forward, over everything, over every bit of her. *I was wrong,* she thought. *I should have never let her near me.* The *mutara* had been a Maddion weapon all along.

But the presence shoved the fog back into place as easily as Malia might twist her hair into a bun. It slowly calmed, withdrawing even the tendrils until it was as still as a mud-brick wall, and Malia no worse off than she'd been before.

The presence withdrew, and Malia opened her eyes, gasping. Immediately she turned away from Sersha, who was gazing at her most intently. "That was . . . surprising." Malia said.

"Yes, I can see." Sersha stood in a fluid movement and moved to the other end of the cell.

Altogether, the space was about five paces wide by five paces long, leaving little room, but Malia was glad of the distance. Sersha had entered her mind so easily, and pushed the fog back just as easily. She could probably have unburdened Malia of the fog altogether while she was there, and yet she hadn't. Sersha wanted something from her.

"The magic you hold inside," Sersha said, "is quite interesting. It's very powerful, and yet you have no way to use it except when a Jegudun helps. Very interesting indeed."

Malia felt like a bug squirming beneath a young boy's finger while he poked at it with a stick. Anger flared. "I'm glad you find it *interesting*. It's wiping out all of my memories."

"My deepest apologies. I spend quite a bit of time alone, sometimes for generations, before I'm able to speak with people again. I meant no offense. I've simply never seen something like this before. This symbiosis is fascinating."

Again Malia didn't quite know what Sersha was talking about. What she'd said, *sim bye o sis*, meant nothing to her, but apparently it had to do with Taakwa and Jegudun magic.

"But you used a lot, didn't you?" Sersha asked. "You're the woman the Maddion refuse to talk about. You're the one who defeated them. You raised the barrier. That's why you're suffering with this affliction."

A chill ran through Malia. "How could you know?"

"The servants talk. To them, you are a hero. To the Maddion, you are a villain."

"They would kill me if they knew." Her heart thundered. Her death would be horribly brutal, at that. Barrier or no, they'd find servants willing to do the deed for them.

"I won't tell them."

The assurance didn't comfort her at all.

"I can help you," Sersha said. "I would *like* to help you."

"Can you get rid of this fog and make me the way I was before?"

"Yes."

"And what's the catch?"

Sersha smiled. "No catch. Everything would be reversed, just as it was before this affliction settled in."

"And what do you get out of it?"

"Have you ever kicked over an ant hill just to see what happens?"

"I tend to leave ants be. They sting, you know." She squirmed, not quite sure that she enjoyed being compared to an ant.

Sersha chuckled, the sound mirthless. "Sometimes I do things just to see what happens. I've been around a while. I get bored easily."

Malia thought of her grandmother's words. The Maddion had to pay a price for their cure. Yet they seemed fine, save for getting rid of some scrolls. "Can I have some time to consider it?"

"Of course." Sersha moved to the lock and held her hand over it again, walked out, and locked it behind her. "I wouldn't wait too long, though. If I could figure out which Taakwa you are, the Maddion soon will, too, and then your life will be forfeit."

"Wait," she called out.

Sersha turned to her.

"If you do this . . . if you cure me, can you also guarantee me a way out of the mountains?"

She sighed. "That's asking a lot. I'm afraid you're on your own there."

"What about fixing this," Malia said with a wave toward her broken leg.

She shrugged. "I suppose it would be the least I could do." She nodded. "Yes, I'd fix your leg as well. You'd be as healthy as before you erected the barrier over the valley."

"You'd have to leave the cell door open. That's the least you could do."

She pursed her lips, looking like she was about to protest.

"Being healthy but locked away wouldn't do me any good."

She inclined her head. "True. All right, then. I would fix your head, and your leg, and leave the door unlocked. Satisfied?"

Malia nodded.

Sersha left without a sound, the smell of honeysuckle and lightning strike fading with her.

Malia rested her head against the cold stone and contemplated the ways she could escape the mountain if Sersha helped her.

~

Chanwa slept restlessly on the sleeping pallet in the cold cell. She'd been given blankets, but so close to the cave's entrance, every gust of wind ruffled her hair and brushed cold fingers over her skin. She shivered and snuggled deeper under the blankets. She'd been in here for days already. Muvumo hadn't been to see her. Nobody had, save for a servant three times a day to bring her food and something to drink, or to clean out her cell or bring her fresh clothes, or a basin of water to wash up with. Chanwa wanted to ask after Ankti, to make sure the other woman was safe, but she didn't dare. Muvumo sent his most trusted servants, those who would relay every word she said back to him. She settled for asking after him, instead, and how his leg was healing, how the Maddion in general were doing.

What did the other Maddion women think? Some of them also wrote and read in secret. Did they realize that's why she was in here? She fervently hoped they hid their writings well. Muvumo held onto hers, but others might burn what they found. Or worse, they might bring it to Muvumo's attention, and then he'd have no choice but to burn her own scrolls along with the others. He'd mount a search through every woman's items, and destroy all of their scrolls. That had been one of the warnings her mother had passed onto her. *It's happened before, Chanwa, and it will happen again if we're not careful.*

The fire that had driven her to see the Taakwa woman was slowly dying, although Chanwa fought to hold onto it. She worked through the ways she could take advantage of the sweeping change that had come over the Maddion, but each day she spent in here meant less momentum, and each day her self doubt grew. What could she do? Did she really think she could make things better for herself and the other women? The changer had given her an opportunity, and it was slipping away. She hunched her shoulders and pulled the blankets halfway over her head. She should just give up.

"Chanwa," said a woman, softly.

She rolled over. A woman stood just outside her cell. At first, Chanwa thought the woman carried two small torches. Then she realized the lights were the woman's eyes. They blazed dark orange, like flames. *The changer.* Chanwa stared, unable to pull her gaze away. She slowly sank into those orange eyes until her entire world seemed engulfed in silent flames. She didn't even notice the cave's coolness any longer.

She shut her eyes and looked away, the flames still burning in the darkness behind her eyelids. "You're the changer." Her heart hammered. How close had she been to losing herself to that being?

"Yes. Call me Sersha. I don't mean you any harm. I just wanted to talk."

"You want to talk?" Chanwa blinked a few times, but she stared at a crack where the wall met the floor.

"You're the one who sent me that message," she said. "'*The Maddion women want dominion over themselves.*'"

She shivered at hearing her own words quoted back to her. "Yes. You are powerful enough to cure us of the illness, and yet—"

"And yet, I have done nothing for your cause, except for saving your scrolls."

She nearly met Sersha's eyes. "And for that I thank you. But Muvumo could still destroy them."

"That is true. But he's curious about the women's scrolls, although he'd never admit it. And, he loves you, in a fashion." She canted her head to one side. "But you don't love him, do you?"

Chanwa said nothing. How much did this changer know? Could she read minds?

Sersha chuckled. "Don't worry. I would never tell him. And in case you were wondering, I can't read minds. I'm simply good at reading people. I've had plenty of experience."

"Are you planning on helping us further?"

Sersha sighed. "Change doesn't come easily, or quickly, not unless you're willing to shed a lot of blood to achieve it."

"Are you suggesting a civil war?" Chanwa shook her head. "The last thing we need is more bloodshed, and certainly not among ourselves."

"You know, I almost didn't cure your people of their illness. At least, not in the way I did. I almost wiped you all out."

Her heart grew frigid. She had no doubt the changer could have done it, with about as much disregard as a person crushing an ant beneath their foot. "Why didn't you?"

"Your husband, believe it or not, did the right thing by showing me a child with the illness. I had a child once, long ago . . ." Her voice drifted, sad. Chanwa almost looked up to show her sympathy. "I cannot stand to see children suffer," she continued. "They are at the mercy of the adults in their lives. Sometimes those adults are kind and considerate. Sometimes they are rather idiotic. And sadly, sometimes they are downright cruel.

"Your children suffered from an illness they didn't bring upon themselves. Children are not born hating, or oppressing. They learn it from the adults around them." She paused. "I think it's time your Maddion children learn a different way of life."

"Like what?" Chanwa asked warily.

"Wouldn't it be nice if your scrolls were read by all, and not just by your mother, your grandmother, and your daughters, should you have any? Wouldn't it be nice if your skills were valued as much as your husband's?"

She spoke the very thoughts Chanwa had harbored for a long time, and yet she scoffed. "You're talking about changing generations of patriarchy. Others have tried, and failed, and suffered for it."

"I've wiped the slate clean. The men's scrolls are gone. They have to start over. Why not start by acknowledging women's scrolls? Why not begin teaching boys *and* girls their letters, out in the open and not hidden away in little snatches?"

Chanwa stood and paced. Five steps one way, turn on her heel, five steps the other way. "The men will never do that."

"Hmm. Perhaps. They certainly won't, if that's your attitude."

Her hands clenched at her sides. "You don't know anything about my life. You don't know what it's like to be me."

"I could say the same," Sersha snapped.

The changer had spoken of a child, and spending endless time alone. What if everyone that Chanwa knew and loved was long gone? What if she'd been alone for seasons? Generations? What if she endured her grief while the whole world changed a hundred times over?

"My apologies," she said.

Sersha sighed. "There's no need for apologies. But, why do you think I chose this form?"

"You . . . choose what you look like?"

"Yes. And, why do you think your husband did not destroy your scrolls?" Her voice dropped to a whisper although they were alone.

"He fears you."

"True. But he's read them. Many times. Think of what they say. They are the only scrolls he can turn to now. What are they telling him?"

Chanwa stopped in the cell's center. "They speak of my heart. My mother's. My grandmother's."

"Yes. They speak of what's in a woman's heart. And now he knows."

"And now he knows," she echoed. A shiver ran through her. She wasn't sure if she liked the idea of Muvumo knowing so much about her.

"Begin with one man. The most important man among the Maddion. Convince him of your value, and your scrolls' value, and you may bring about the change you desire, and all without bloodshed."

Maybe . . . Chanwa allowed herself to imagine it for a moment. It might work. If she struck now, while good will was at its peak, she might convince her husband, and through him, the other men, that the girls coming of age now should learn their letters and be allowed to write their own scrolls and speak for themselves. And from there, the changes could keep coming.

But what about Ankti? And the other servants? How could she convince Muvumo and the other Maddion that peaceful trade was far better than looting and enslavement? The Maddion felt entitled to their goods, including human beings. It made her ill to her stomach, thinking that she might gain freedom while Ankti and the others continued to suffer.

"It will take time," Sersha said. "You can bring about the changes you want. And just think," she added with a smile, "young boys and girls will some day read your scrolls as part of their history lessons."

Chanwa scoffed, but she could picture it: boys and girls learning together, and the Maddion working with their neighbors. It could happen.

She'd see that it would.

CHAPTER TWENTY-FIVE

Muvumo lay on his back, head cradled on his interlocked hands, and stared at the dark ceiling as he considered what to do about Chanwa.

The itching in his thigh had woken him early. The only sounds were those of occasional footsteps padding lightly outside as servants went to work or the unmentionables made their way to or from beds. His own bed had been a cold and lonely place recently.

He scratched around the careful stitches the healer had sewn. Several more days, and the healer would remove the stitches, but it would be even longer before he could ride a dragon again. What sort of Maddion ruler was he, unable to ride a dragon? But he'd bled considerably when he'd gone to the caves to confront Chanwa. Fortunately, Delkis was the only one to witness him passing out once he was back home. The kasi powder had kept him going that long, at least.

Delkis's soft snores came from the other room. While Muvumo was injured, he'd sleep nearby, in case any man got it in his head to challenge Muvumo for place as Most Worthy while he recuperated. The general feeling toward him was that of goodwill, at least among the men. The women, however, had become cold and curt, and those who weren't seemed downright terrified, and all because they knew by now that he'd locked up Chanwa. Rumors were running rampant among them, but none included anything about scrolls. Those who knew how to read and write held that secret tight. But there was talk about everything from her taking a lover to having actually been the one to cut him, to her colluding with the Taakwa.

Those servants who saw to her needs let him know that she was slowly cooling. He'd release her soon, but he'd have some work ahead of him to ensure her reputation didn't remain sullied. He should have brought her back here and had her kept in their own home, or removed her to one of the empty homes and had her under constant guard. He could have made up some story about that. But that night he had been simultaneously furious and ecstatic to begin with, and that coupled with the kasi powder made a potent blend that led to questionable decisions. And truthfully, he simply didn't know what to do with a woman who was much smarter than he'd believed.

How many other women could read and write? He didn't imagine for a moment that only the women of Chanwa's family kept that secret. A good leader would search every home and destroy the women's scrolls. A good Maddion would make an example of his own wife.

So why hadn't he done anything?

He'd imprisoned her, yes. She'd used his name to coerce one of the attendants into giving her a ride on a dragon to the cells so she might speak with the Taakwa woman. That, in addition to her reading and writing, should have made his decision much easier.

Instead, he found himself lying awake after a scant half night or so of sleep, as he'd done since he'd imprisoned her, and wishing she lay beside him.

He'd married her because she came from good stock. Her mother and grandmother had had many boys, and their babies had been healthy and thrived. Her mother had been kind and demure and quiet. Her father had been a strong man and a good warrior, and her brothers the same. They'd all been lost either in the recent war, or from the illness. He'd been disappointed that she hadn't taken with child yet. He'd been imagining a strong, healthy boy.

But what if they had a girl? Would Chanwa teach the girl how to read and write? Of course she'd want to, given her history. Could he abide it, knowing she did so in secret?

What if it wasn't a secret?

He rolled onto his side and silently cursed the unending itching in his thigh. *It's a good sign*, the healer was fond of saying, when he wasn't busy scribbling down all he knew, as were all the other healers, so their knowledge wouldn't slip away.

He rose with a sigh. Pain lanced through his thigh. Not for the first time, he wondered just what the blazes that Taakwa woman was up to. Most of the servants didn't understand her. He suspected a few might know some words of her language, but they all pretended they didn't. It didn't matter what she wanted, though. All he needed was a Jegudun, and with the blood from the creature and the woman, he'd bring down the barrier and take the valley, and he'd have revenge for his people. But all of a sudden, it was proving difficult to find a Jegudun outside the valley.

Muvumo let down the door hanging so the light wouldn't disturb Delkis. He lit the lantern, and the smell of tallow filled the air, as did the lantern's soft glow. He went to one of the trunks that held Chanwa's clothes. It opened on silent hinges, and the soft smell of her perfume wafted out, a scent like spring roses. His heart ached, but he pushed aside the pain as he dug through the soft fabric for the one scroll he kept hidden beneath the false bottom. This one he held onto; it was like having a small part of Chanwa remain with him.

He pulled it out carefully and sat with his back to the door, so as to hide it should Delkis walk in. He untied the ribbon that held it rolled. The scroll hissed open in his hands. Tiny, precise handwriting filled it. What had once been an unfamiliar scrawl had become as recognizable as his own, with narrow loops and swirls so as to conserve space. He supposed women didn't have the luxury of using as many scrolls as they needed, and so had to make do with the few they could hide.

About a third of the way down the page, he began reading.

Muvumo is not quite the man I expected. My mother warned me that they were all kind in the beginning, and then grew cruel and common with time, but Muvumo has been steady, even attentive. Sometimes I think he's really listening. I mentioned how my favorite color was robin's egg blue, and he brought some of that very color to me the next time he brought fabric.

I watch him write deep into the night when he thinks I'm asleep, and I have to bite my tongue to keep from commenting on it. I'm afraid I might give myself away.

He spends long nights in the cavern, trying to find a way to cure us. All those scrolls, and so few men to spare to read them. I want to tell him that I could help, that several women can help, but it would be my death, or the deaths of those I care about, and I could not abide that. So I clench my hands and watch helplessly, and I pretend the only things I'm good at are looking pretty and warming his bed.

Muvumo flinched at his wife's assessment. When he first read Chanwa's scrolls, he felt as though he didn't know her at all, that he was married to a complete stranger. But after reading them several times, he felt that he was starting to truly know her, and he found himself thinking, not for the first time in recent days, that she was the sort of person he'd call a friend, had she only been a man.

Must a person be a man for him to consider that person a friend? Considering Chanwa a friend as well as a wife would mean he considered her equal to a man. At first that idea had startled him, and he'd scoffed at it. But now . . . she wrote as well as any man he knew, and with more depth than most. And she had a point when she said the women could have helped read through the scrolls. She'd said nothing because she feared for her life. In the end, he'd found a means to help his people, but perhaps he could have found another solution if only more had been reading the scrolls. Perhaps the men's scrolls would still be sitting in the cavern.

Alongside the women's.

He couldn't quite make that image work. Men and women working together? What would follow? Women riding dragons? Hunting? Fighting to see if they could take position as Most Worthy? He pictured Chanwa brandishing a short axe and chuckled quietly to himself. Ridiculous, all of it.

He rolled the scroll up, tied it, and hid it beneath Chanwa's clothes, in the trunk's false bottom. He took one last, lingering breath of her perfume before shutting the trunk. Then he blew out the lantern and settled down on his sleeping pallet again.

In the morning, he'd release Chanwa and bring her home. She would write no more, and in return he would not kill her. It was the least he could do for the woman he loved.

CHAPTER TWENTY-SIX

Chanwa lay on her side. She was home, beneath her own blankets, with her husband beside her. One of his arms lay across her, and he'd draped a leg over her. Chanwa could hardly breathe from the weight of them, and from his proximity.

You will never write again. If I catch you, I will kill you myself. But not before I torture you and get the names of all other women who perform the same atrocities. Your scrolls will remain hidden away because the changer demanded it, but you are still mine.

She'd been numb since he'd uttered the words. Although his pupils had been wide and dark from the kasi powder, she had no doubt that he absolutely meant what he said and had come to that decision while completely sober. She was trapped, and not only was she no better off than before, but she could no longer fill her own scrolls. There was no hope for changing things for herself, or other women, or the servants.

A snore escaped Muvumo. Chanwa eased his leg off her, then slowly scooted out from beneath his arm. He snorted, and she froze, but he merely rolled onto his back and slept on.

Chanwa slipped into a dressing gown and padded into the front room barefoot. The only light spilled faintly around the door hanging. It was late night, and all was quiet and dark. The air still held the faint smell of wood smoke and the roasted duck that Ankti had cooked for dinner (*no, don't think of Ankti*). Chanwa's toes dug into the plush rugs, but where she touched the bare floor, the stone was icy. She was already shivering by the time she reached the outer door.

She slipped into the cold night air. She leaned against the stone wall, gazing at the stars. They clustered in a river of light and then spread across the rest of the sky like scattered bits of silver. Below her, the mountain descended in a sheer drop. If she jumped from the wall, she would fall a ways before hitting either the tops of trees or the ground, at least the length of several men. The fall would be sure to kill her.

She propped her hands and one foot on the wall, ready to leap over, when a hand grasped her wrist. She gasped and whirled, and another hand clamped over her mouth. The hands yanked her back into a body that was her size, and soft. Not Muvumo, as she'd feared, but a woman.

"Do not yell," the woman whispered. *Ankti.* "When I move my hand, do not speak. Understand?"

Chanwa nodded.

Ankti's hand moved from her mouth and eased its hold on her wrist. "Come," she said, and led her down the stairs. They passed three dark doors and scurried through the light of two torches before coming to a fourth door. Ankti pushed aside the door covering and pulled Chanwa in after her.

It was dark inside, and musty, as if nobody had lived in the space for some time. Chanwa stumbled when her bare feet caught the edge of a rug. Ankti steadied her, then gently guided her to sit. It was dark, with only the rug beneath her and Ankti's hand to accompany her, and Chanwa's heart hammered against her breastbone.

Ankti's clothes rustled as she settled beside Chanwa. She still hadn't let go of her wrist. "What were you thinking, climbing on that wall?" Ankti hissed.

Chanwa stiffened. "Where are we?"

"An abandoned home. Speak quietly, and nobody will hear you. Now, answer me."

"What did it look like I was doing?"

"It looked like you were about to take a flying leap into nothing. Why? You're still alive. I was certain—" She bit off what sounded like a sob. Chanwa dearly wished they had a little bit of light so she could see Ankti. "I thought the Most Worthy would kill you." Her voice was careful, controlled. "Any other man would have done so, after finding . . . what he did."

"He forbid me from doing more, and he's hidden away what I've done. It's as if it never happened." She sighed. "I thought things would change, that maybe I wouldn't have to hide my knowledge, but it's as if all that my people have been through in the past few seasons never happened."

Ankti said nothing. The only sounds were that of her steady breathing. It was so dark and still that Chanwa could easily imagine they were the last two people alive. Being in the caves normally didn't bother her, but in the absolute dark, nearly alone, it left a fluttering sensation in her belly.

"Ankti?" she said hesitantly.

"Do you know what I did . . . before?"

Before she was taken. She never spoke of it. Chanwa said, "No."

"I was a navigator. I lived in the desert, where it was brutally hot during the day. It was best to travel at night, and so I led huge caravans by the light of the stars." Her voice took on a dreamlike cadence. "I led dozens of people and animals across the desert at a time. We'd be gone for days, sometimes for the length of an entire moon cycle. The desert was always changing, but the stars remained constant. I read them as well as you read your words.

"But here, the stars are different. The constellations I knew are either gone, or in a different part of the sky. Here, I'm in charge of nothing more important than cleaning, or meals. I am a shadow of my old self. Maybe I'm not even that. Maybe I'm just a dream. Or that other me was a dream, and this is real."

Chanwa's heart ached. Ankti had been uprooted from her life. Chanwa, at least, still lived among her people. Her life was easy in comparison.

"It was foolish of me to even consider jumping," she said.

"Foolish? Yes. There are things to live for other than your scrolls."

"Such as?"

There came a faint rustling as Ankti neared her. Then her warm breath washed over Chanwa's face. She smelled like soap, like lavender. Before Chanwa could speak, or think, Ankti's lips touched hers, lightly.

Chanwa drew in a sharp breath. Ankti froze. She started to pull back. But Chanwa leaned into the kiss. She gently pulled her arm free from Ankti's grip and placed her hands on either side of the other woman's face. Chanwa pulled back and said, "Just so you know, I have been waiting for that for a long time."

"And I as well," Ankti said, a little breathless.

Chanwa longed to resume the kiss, but she sensed time slipping away. She'd have to get home soon, before Muvumo missed her. "It seems we are both shadows," she said. "I am sorry for what you lost, and I am sorry for what I lost." She slipped a hand into Ankti's and curled her fingers around it. Ankti's hand was warm, with faint calluses along the palm and her fingertips. "So what do we do now? I cannot stand to live like this, so close to you and having to watch how you are treated, forcing myself to be someone I am not."

Ankti shifted, sat closer to her until their hips touched. "My father enjoyed telling stories, and he had many about the changer. She enjoys chaos. She has riled things up for the Maddion, but she won't force them to their end. She'd rather see what your people will do among themselves. She's hoping you will lead your women in a coup against the men."

She recoiled. "I cannot do that! If I tried, they would destroy me, and anybody else who even so much as hinted they agreed with me."

"You need time to organize. If a coup is what you want, at any rate."

Chanwa had never dreamed . . . never imagined . . . how much did she want this for herself and her people? If she had her way, the Maddion raids on other people would stop. She'd open trade with other people. They wouldn't live apart, above, from others any longer.

Ankti squeezed her hand. "There are places where women rule. The Taakwa are not the only ones. It can be done."

"There would be much bloodshed."

"Perhaps. But if you had time to plan, perhaps blood would not have to be shed at all."

"Knowing my people, it would happen, no matter how careful the planning." She sighed. "I can't think of that right now. But . . . I can think of leaving. I can't stay here any longer. This place is suffocating me." She made up her mind, and it felt like the moment before she put her foot onto the stone wall when she contemplated leaping off and into the night sky. "Can you bring a message to the changer again?"

"I think so."

"I will leave, but only if you come with me."

Ankti's took in a sharp breath. "You mean it? You want me to come with you?"

"Yes. At the very least, I can see that you make it to the Taakwa's valley. You'll be safe with them. They hate the Maddion, but they might take you in."

"And you?"

Her grip on Ankti's hand tightened. "Perhaps you are right, and with some time, I can figure out a way to bring about the change I want. Perhaps it's time a woman earned the title of Most Worthy. Or better yet, perhaps we can abolish the term all together."

"There is no turning back once I bring the message to the changer."

"I'm tired of looking back. I am ready to move forward."

CHAPTER TWENTY-SEVEN

Three more days passed for Malia as she considered the *mutara's* offer. Everything could be as it was before. And yet, she didn't trust Sersha. There was a catch, somewhere in there. What would it be? That she'd lose her memories following the war? That she'd somehow go back to the day of the war itself? The more Malia considered the offer, the warier she grew.

But the fog crept up on her every day and consumed a little more of her mind. This morning, she pictured a man, his face lean and brown, with laugh lines cupping his mouth and lines fanning from the corners of his eyes, and gray at his temples. In her mind's eye, she could see him striding confidently in his tunic and pants, his cloak billowing behind him. She could smell the pungent odor of herbs that always clung to him. She knew she loved him, and he loved her. But his name? It eluded her, and the harder she struggled to find it, the more agitated the fog became until she finally had to give up, referring to him only as *the healer*. She curled on her side and cried silently.

Finally, after the midday meal, his name popped into her mind. *Enuwal, Enuwal, Enuwal.* Tomorrow would she remember that he was a healer? Would she even remember that she loved him? She ran through the names of the others she loved: her mother, Vedran, Enuwal, Rina, Ziku, Ayeelah, Aru. She spoke their names aloud, her voice echoing off the cold stone surrounding her, until her voice grew hoarse.

The servant who brought her evening meal was the same green-eyed, fair skinned woman who had whispered *mutara* to her. While the guard watched the servant's posterior as she bent over, Malia caught the woman's attention and mouthed *mutara*. The woman gave a bare nod, set down the plate of food, and straightened. A moment later, Malia was alone again, with only the hiss of the torch and the scrape of the plate against the stone to break the unending silence. How long would she have to wait for Sersha to show up again? It had taken days last time. What if the *mutara* took as long again, and Malia forgot why she summoned Sersha, or even who—or what—Sersha was? She hardly ate her evening meal, leaving half the bread and stew to cool and congeal in the farthest corner where she didn't have to smell it.

At least someone had finally brought her a sleeping pallet, so thin she might as well not have one at all, and a blanket, equally thin and threadbare. She folded the blanket and curled on her side, shivering. She'd grown so used to the constant cold that she hardly even noticed it anymore. She closed her eyes and began to drift off to sleep.

Hushed footfalls approached. Malia's eyes flew open, her heart thudding. It wouldn't be a guard. They made no show of sneaking up on her. It was somebody who wanted to remain silent, and keep the visit a secret. Was it Sersha already? She sat up. She crawled on her hands and knees to the wooden door, then quietly climbed to her good leg, peering out through the bars in the tiny window.

A small man wearing the belted wool tunic and loose pants of the Maddion stepped into the light. Something was strange about him. His hair was tucked beneath a tight, wool cap, even though the weather was nowhere near cold enough for such a thing, and he moved self-consciously, hands constantly checking the daggers hanging from his belt, tugging at the tunic, adjusting his pants.

That's because *he* was a *she*. The sharp lines of the face, and the wide, blue eyes belonged to the Maddion woman who had come to visit just after Malia was put into the cell and her leg was being splinted.

Another figure appeared behind her. This time, Malia picked out that the figure was a woman more easily. For one thing, she had brown skin, unlike any Maddion. But from a distance, at night, the tunic and pants and cap would be enough to hide the fact that a woman—and a servant, at that—hid beneath a man's clothes. She wasn't one of those who'd brought her meals. She carried two travel sacs, one in each hand.

Malia was about to ask what was happening when Sersha joined the other two women in the torchlight.

Unlike the last time she visited, Sersha was tight-lipped and grim. The dark orange and red in her eyes swirled faster, as if agitated.

"What is this?" Malia asked.

"Things are moving rather quickly," Sersha said. "For an old creature like me, it's unsettling, to say the least."

"What does that mean?"

"It means, you called for me, and rather than wait for a more opportune time to help, I must help you now, as well as them," she said with a gesture to the women behind her.

"Who are they?"

Sersha sighed. "The dark-skinned woman is Ankti. She is a servant who, at her mistress' insistence, will be leaving the Maddion and their service tonight. The other woman is Chanwa. She is the wife of the Most Worthy."

Malia straightened. "What? The Most Worthy's wife? What is she doing here? I—"

Sersha held up a hand. "She will not betray you. Doing so would mean her own death." Her lips pursed. "She had Ankti slip a sleeping drought into her husband's tea. She assures me that he is sleeping quite peacefully. For the moment. She wishes to leave him, and she'd like to take her woman with her."

"And what does that have to do with me?"

"They will be safest in your valley."

Malia shook her head. "Ankti would be safe, and probably welcome once my people got over their fear of outsiders. But the other one would never be able to enter the valley. She's of Maddion blood. And even if she *could* live in the valley, she wouldn't be safe. There are too many who wish to shed Maddion blood, regardless of who bleeds it."

"Well, then, you'll just have to make sure she's safe, won't you?"

"What?" Her breathing hitched.

"If you want to return home, healed, you'll bring these women with you," Sersha said. "It's as simple as that. I will take care of the Maddion woman's problem of entering your valley, which I've already told her."

Chanwa and Ankti both watched her silently. They laced hands and stood close. She wouldn't mind taking Ankti with her, but Chanwa was Maddion. She was part of the people who enslaved the Jeguduns and others, who killed many of her ancestors in the first war between the Taakwa and the Maddion. She was the enemy.

But, she wanted to leave, and she wanted to save another. That didn't sound like the brutal Maddion Malia was familiar with.

"How do I know she doesn't want to come along so that she can spy on us and then tell her husband?" Malia asked.

Sersha blew out an exasperated breath. "Because as much as you hate the Maddion, she hates how she's treated."

Malia believed that. She thought about the times she'd wished the illness would take all the Maddion. To her surprise, she didn't wish it for this woman. Perhaps she could convince the councils that it would serve the Taakwa well to have someone among them who could talk about the Maddion in detail. Wasn't it better to have one's enemy close and know what they were about, than to wonder what they did in secret?

She gave a curt nod. "Fine."

"Very well. We are all in agreement. It's best you sit, Malia."

She moved back and sank slowly to the ground, stretching her broken leg in front of her. Sersha laid a hand over the lock. It clicked, and the door swung open. She stepped inside and kneeled. Once again, the scent of honeysuckle and lightning strike filled the air. She laid her cool hands on either side of Malia's head, thumbs pressed against her forehead, and her other fingers splayed around her scalp. The touch was light, and yet Malia couldn't help but think of how easy it would be for the *mutara* to make a quick move and snap her neck.

"Relax," Sersha muttered. "I'm not going to hurt you. Why don't you try closing your eyes?"

She took a deep breath and did so. There was only darkness, the occasional crackle of the torch, and the expectant breathing of the other women.

A presence joined her, so subtly that it felt as though one moment Malia was alone in her mind, and the next the other was with her. The new presence had to be Sersha, but she received no impression of man or woman, young or old, friendly or malevolent. The new presence just *was*.

As before, Sersha moved gently through her mind, pressing on the fog here and there. Malia realized her jaw was clenched, and her hands clasped one another tightly in her lap. She took in another deep breath and concentrated on relaxing those areas, and her neck and shoulders. If Sersha truly wanted to hurt her, she would have done so by now.

Sersha's presence suddenly grew, loomed, like monsoon clouds building, and pushed against the fog, but the lingering magic held tight, like a deeply rooted tree. Malia felt pulled in two, as if Sersha grabbed her by one arm, and the magic grabbed her by the other, and both wrenched in opposite directions. Pain lanced through her mind. The fog bubbled and roiled and fought back.

Sersha shoved, relentless. Malia pushed as well, although she felt like a tiny ant trying to move a boulder. *This is my mind. My memories. I want them back.* She pushed again, and again, and again.

The fog shuddered, paused like a person teetering on the edge of a cliff, and then rolled back. It revealed an expanse so great that Malia felt as though her mind and memories extended on forever in every direction, like the endless sky. The fog faded completely, the last bit of it leaving with an audible *pop* in her head.

The memories flooded back in its place.

Seasons passed in a blur. She paced during the endless nights when Vedran fasted and lived in the woods during his manhood ceremony, consumed with worry for her younger brother. Her wedding to Dalibor, and their first night together, tender, uncertain, filled with awkward laughter and whispers. Then a Jegudun—*Tuvin*—falling injured, and her helping him. Dalibor finding him, killing him, and Malia fleeing. Rasmus, an exile and friend. The fire (*the heat, ash raining, men with arrows trapping them in the fire's path, waiting it out in a shallow trough as it raced overhead, seeking to consume them*). The barrier failing, shards of it falling like snow. Dragons and Maddion swooping in. Dalibor attacking her. Killing him. Blood. Burnt flesh. Screams.

Her finding a Maddion in the woods. Fighting. He almost killed her. She wrapped her leather necklace around his throat and choked him. Her hand flew to her neck, expecting to find the strap there, with the worn Jegudun feather hanging from it, a sign she was clan mother in training. But no, she'd given that up because of her failing memory.

It failed no more.

She leaned forward, gasping as hundreds and thousands of moments washed over her. She remembered kneeling beside the river, outside the valley, with a Jegudun beside her, its wings clipped, and guiding their combined power into the barrier, piecing it back together like shattered pottery. Her blood flowed in that barrier, and Jegudun blood. A little bit of that same barrier covered her. *Had* covered her.

The glimmer was gone. Her protection was gone. But her mind . . . all of it was back. She held back the laughter that bubbled to the surface. Later. She'd celebrate later.

She ripped off the splint. The incessant itching was gone. She stood, carefully testing all of her weight on her broken leg. It was healed. A slow grin spread across her face.

Sersha sighed. "Everything as it was before."

A muffled groan escaped the *mutara*. She bent forward, arms wrapped around her belly as if she were having the worst cramps imaginable. Beneath her clothes, her body quivered, shimmered, writhed, as if large worms crawled beneath her flesh. Malia backed out of the cell, unable to look away, her heart thudding. What was this?

The *mutara* let out a louder groan. She ripped at her clothes, tearing the fabric from her until she huddled naked on the floor.

Her body writhed, the skin bulging, her limbs elongating, growing thicker, more muscular.

Her hair darkened, lengthened, straightened. Her shoulders broadened. Her skin grew darker. The writhing beneath it slowed, then stopped. A shudder passed through her body. No, *his* body. She had changed into a man.

The *mutara* raised his head and turned. His eyes glowed a deep red, with dark orange swirls spinning in them, and they were set in a face Malia knew well.

"Dalibor," she whispered.

CHAPTER TWENTY-EIGHT

Malia's heart pounded. The other two women stared at the *mutara*. They clung to one another, and Malia briefly wished for Enuwal. She was alone and unprotected while in the heart of Maddion territory. And now her husband stood before her. No, that . . . thing . . . wasn't her husband. Her husband was dead.

"Go," Malia said, shoving the women ahead of her. Her word and her touch startled Chanwa into moving, and the three of them hurried toward the cave's entrance.

With the fog gone, Malia felt as though she'd woken from a long, strange dream, except *this* was a nightmare, this racing through the Maddion's caves, with a being that looked like Dalibor behind her. Why did the *mutara* take that form? Her hands bunched into fists as her legs pumped. Her lungs quickly began to burn, her body used to nothing but sitting around for days.

She passed empty cell after empty cell, leaving behind circles of light from the torches. The cave's entrance loomed ahead, lit by torches on either side, a sliver of night sky beyond, stars twinkling. She ached to be out of the caves and under the sky the way a person would ache for food after fasting.

A brightly lit cell sat open at the cave's entrance. Inside, a guard slumped over, his back against the wall and his legs splayed out in front of him. His head lolled to one side as if he slept, and his chest rose and fell slowly. On the wall above him, a row of hooks protruded from the stone. One hook held Malia's belt, sheath, and dagger.

She stepped gingerly over the guard's legs, pulled her belt down, and quickly strapped it around her hips. She sighed as the familiar weight of the dagger hung at her right side. Then she hurried out of the cave and into the night.

She took a deep breath of the cool air, scented with the musky smell of dragons. One of the beasts lay curled on the far end of the mesa, its orange sides glowing and fading with each slow, steady breath.

The mesa opened to the cave, and nothing else. No stairs led away, and when Malia peered over the railing, she was greeted by a sheer drop, the treetops far below, and the ground hidden beneath branches and darkness. Her stomach did a queasy flop.

"How do we get out of here?" she muttered to herself.

Ankti spoke, the language neither Maddion nor Taakwa. But her meaning was clear as she pointed to the dragon.

"Clan mother curse them all," Malia said. The only way off this blasted mountain was on a dragon. She ran back to the guard's room. A hasty search turned up two short axes, a longbow and arrows, a spare saddle, and a short coil of rope. Tied to the railing, it would hardly hang below the mesa, much less reach the treetops or allow them to climb to the ground. She hesitated, grabbed a short axe, and returned to the other women.

"We'll fly out of here together," she said. She pointed to herself, the two women, and then the dragon.

Chanwa's eyes widened slightly, but she nodded. Ankti moaned, swaying on her feet. Chanwa rubbed the other woman's back and murmured softly. A shudder passed through Ankti, and she nodded.

Malia spoke gently, as Enuwal did when helping someone badly hurt. "It will be all right. We'll get through this." An ache passed through her heart as she thought of him. *Not now.* She pushed away his image. She needed to focus on getting the three of them off this mountain.

Malia took in a lungful of air, let it out through her lips. She had led her people through war, she could lead the three of them off this mountain.

Malia turned to Chanwa. "What do we need to do to fly this creature?" She gestured toward the dragon.

Chanwa blinked a few times as she stared at the dragon. Then she shook her head and moved forward. She hesitated a moment before laying a hand on the dragon's snout. She muttered a few words.

The beast snorted and opened one eye. It wore a saddle already, thank the clan mother, or Malia didn't think they'd ever be able to get one secured on the creature. As it was, she couldn't make sense out of the straps and buckles hanging from the leather saddle. There were so many. Some of them seemed designed to hold the saddle to the dragon, others were to hold weapons, and still others were to hold riders.

The dragon uncurled itself, raised its head, then spread its wings and shook them out. Its mouth gaped, revealing rows of sharp teeth, and a plume of smoke slowly curled out as it yawned. The smell of brimstone filled the air. The beast stood and folded its wings. It was easily as tall as an elk, perhaps even larger. Its jaws could surround Malia's head. She swallowed the lump in her throat and tried to remain as calm as possible. Could it smell the sour stench of fear pouring off her?

Chanwa waved Ankti forward. The dragon's eyes narrowed as Ankti slowly approached, but at a word from Chanwa, it bent one leg. Ankti grasped the saddle and climbed onto the dragon's leg, then onto its back. Chanwa helped strap in one of Ankti's legs. They exchanged a few rapid words, gesturing at the dragon's other side.

Chanwa turned to Malia and urged her forward. It was her turn. Despite the cool night air, sweat broke out along her forehead and under her arms. She forced her legs to carry her to the dragon's side where its musky scent grew stronger. She followed Ankti's example and climbed onto the beast's leg before reaching for the saddle. Chanwa boosted her up as Ankti grasped her arm and pulled. She landed heavily in the saddle and immediately spotted what the two women had been discussing.

The saddle was built for two, with straps to hold in two people, yet there were three of them. Chanwa was the only one with any sort of knowledge of how to make the dragon carry them, and so she needed to be firmly strapped in, but that left only two straps for Ankti and Malia to share.

Chanwa hurried to her right side and helped strap that leg in, leaving the left one free. Malia sat tightly against Ankti, the saddle's depression barely holding the two of them in. She tucked the short axe into a strap and wiped her sweaty palms against her skirt. The cloth bunched up around her thighs, leaving her lower legs exposed to the cool night air. Gooseflesh broke out along her legs and arms, not only from the cold, but also from the idea that she would soon be airborne on this beast, and she had no idea what kept it from simply turning around and biting off her head.

A figure moved in the cave's shadows. Malia's heart quickened. "Watch out," she said to the women.

She expected the changer to emerge. Instead, the guard staggered into the torch light. He moaned and leaned against the cave's entrance. He hadn't noticed them yet, but he would any moment, and then he'd raise an alarm.

"Clan mother protect us," Malia murmured as she yanked at the strap holding her to the saddle. She jerked it free and slid to the ground. She pulled her dagger out. She didn't want to kill anybody, but she couldn't leave the guard either.

He was a large man, and even woozy as he was, he could still knock her out with one blow. She had to act quickly, before he cleared his head. She ran toward the other side of the mesa, away from the dragon and the women, and closer to the cave's entrance.

"Hey," she called to the guard. "Are you looking for me?"

The Maddion needed her alive. The guard would do everything he could to keep her that way. She edged closer to the stone wall that surrounded the mesa.

His eyes narrowed, and he said something harsh. His gaze caught the dagger in her hands, and he laughed.

She climbed on top of the wall, careful not to look down into the darkness below, and faced the guard.

He was already hurrying toward her. He didn't realize that Ankti had come up behind him. She brandished the short axe, hefting it in her hands as if she'd carried such a weapon her entire life. Or maybe it was just that she'd imagined this moment so many times.

Malia crouched, ready to jump any direction, save for into the darkness behind her. The guard was nearly upon her when Ankti came up right behind him. Malia was careful to keep all of her attention on him so he wouldn't suspect someone approached him from behind.

He must have heard her foot scrape on stone, or sensed Ankti's presence, because he whirled, reaching for a weapon that should have hung from his belt. Instead, he faced Ankti and the axe empty-handed.

He stepped toward Ankti and grasped the short axe as she raised it overhead, then wrenched it from her. Ankti stumbled back and fell.

Malia jumped to the ground. The guard whirled, and she ducked as the axe whistled overhead. Apparently the guard had given up keeping her alive in favor of keeping *himself* alive. She locked eyes with Ankti.

Fury smoldered in the other woman's gaze, and her lips curled in a snarl. For a moment, she reminded Malia of an angry Jegudun, all teeth and claws and rage. Still in a crouch, Malia slid her dagger, hilt first, between the guard's feet. Ankti caught it deftly in her hands.

The guard spun toward Ankti. The other woman thrust the dagger up, connecting with his abdomen.

Malia leaped up and grabbed the short axe from his hands as his arms collapsed. Ankti yanked the dagger free, and the guard tumbled to the ground. She calmly bent to wipe the bloody dagger clean on the edge of his tunic, then handed it to Malia hilt first.

Malia raised a brow and took the dagger wordlessly, handing the short axe to Ankti. Together they hurried across the mesa to the dragon and Chanwa, who said not a word, but merely helped them into the saddle again.

A long, piercing whistle broke the silence, followed quickly by three short ones.

Chanwa's eyes widened, her hands frozen on the saddle's straps. Ankti was stiff behind Malia, and Malia's heart thundered. *They know, they're coming, we're all dead.* She reached a hand down to help Chanwa into the saddle.

Chanwa stepped back, said something tenderly to Ankti, and then grasped the dragon beneath its jaw. She jerked the dragon's head up. Its wings unfurled, and it dove over the railing and into the night. Malia's own screams mingled with Ankti's. *Calm, calm, calm*, she told herself.

This beast could carry us anywhere it pleases, including back to its roost. She looked over her shoulder.

Ankti's eyes were wide, and she scanned the mesa, quickly falling away behind them. A lone figure stood on the mesa. Chanwa. Another, familiar figure ran out of the caves. Malia's heart hitched as she expected the changer to attack Chanwa, but he merely ran to the stone wall and leaped over it into the dark forest.

"How do we guide the dragon?" she said.

Ankti said nothing.

Malia tapped the other woman's cheek. "Don't let her sacrifice be in vain," she growled. "How do we turn?" She pointed south and west. "That way."

Ankti blinked a few times, then nodded. She pointed to her legs, then leaned over and pressed Malia's right leg against the dragon's side. The beast began to turn.

Malia let out a surprised squawk and grabbed at the saddle. She was glad for all the times Jeguduns had shared flying memories with her. She wasn't nearly as terrified as she might otherwise have been. Still, her pulse galloped.

Her control was tenuous, but eventually, through pressing her legs against the dragon, she aimed its head in the direction of home.

Home.

Once she was home, she could figure out what to do about Ankti, and Chanwa. The Jeguduns would help. Her people would help. Soon she'd be home, and everything would be all right.

Chanwa knew those whistles. They were Muvumo's signal for his dragon. The sleeping draught had worn off, and he was coming.

Her thoughts raced, considering and discarding a dozen possibilities at once. Weighed down with three riders, the dragon would be slower than the others. Besides, if she remained behind, her husband would have to take the time to deal with her before finding out that the Taakwa woman and Ankti were gone. She could give them time.

"Ankti, my love, go as far from here as you can. Think of me when you look at the stars," she said as she backed away.

Ankti's eyes widened as she realized what Chanwa was about to do. Before she could change her mind, she dug her fingers into the tender spot beneath the dragon's jaw and urged it into the air. *Fly, you ugly beast, fly far from here*, she thought.

The dragon took to the air, its flight as staggering as a drunkard's walk, and quickly disappeared into the night. Her husband's beast swooped down on its way to answer his call, close enough for her to hear its wings flapping. Somewhere far below her, men were shouting. Torches blazed to life.

She forced herself to remain standing, to keep her chin up, to clasp her trembling hands before her. She waited for her husband as the blood rushed in her ears and she fought down nausea. Her revolution might not last beyond the length of time it took Muvumo to bring an axe down on her, but she would see it through.

Below her, a dragon roared. A tear burned a trail down her cheek. She wiped it away and waited.

CHAPTER TWENTY-NINE

The dragon flew low, stirring grass with its passage. Malia leaned forward, silently urging the dragon on faster. She glanced behind them often, wondering how much of a lead they would get if the Maddion pursued. Starlight made everything shimmer in faint silver. She still couldn't believe Chanwa had sacrificed herself like that for them.

Dried tears had formed narrow, chalky lines down Ankti's face. Earlier she had pressed against Malia, sobs shaking her body. Now, her face was as impassive as the carvings of Jeguduns in the trees around the hot springs, save for her eyes. Deep in them shone a fierce determination, alternating sometimes with terror.

She caught Malia watching her, and her eyes narrowed.

Malia had a pretty good idea of why Chanwa sacrificed herself. It was awkward, twisting back slightly to pat Ankti's knee, but she did so, saying, "We'll figure out some way to help her, but first you need to get to safety. She'll be all right." Malia wasn't sure at all that

Chanwa would be all right, or that she was even still alive, but Ankti looked ready to explode in all directions.

Ankti gave her a tiny nod and wiped at her cheeks with the back of her hand. Malia turned back around.

They passed over a dry gulch. Malia couldn't be sure in the dark, but she thought it might be close to where she'd been found after the bison slaughter. Fear sharpened the memory, making it seem as though it had happened only the night before, and not more than half a moon past.

How long had Ankti been a slave to the Maddion? Where were her people? Malia had a hundred questions for Ankti once they could communicate. The Jeguduns could help, sharing memories between the two of them.

Chanwa, however, was a true mystery. Wife of the Most Worthy, and yet she had planned to sneak away in the middle of the night with her servant. Malia had even more questions about Chanwa.

Memories washed over her now, of images that Vacir had shared with her. During the first war generations ago, the Maddion had brutally killed the Taakwa before they erected the barrier over the valley. They'd hung Taakwa by their wrists from large poles in the ground, leaving their feet dangling and their weight held by nothing but their arms. Dragons went from one to the next, disemboweling them, feasting on their intestines even as they still screamed. The Maddion did not hesitate to destroy their enemies, and the *mutara* had strengthened them again.

Where could she take Ankti until things were sorted out? Rina. Her grandmother would take the woman in without hesitation. Guilt stabbed at her as she thought of leaving without a word. Rina must be so worried, not to mention Enuwal and Vedran. Who else knew that she'd left? Surely the Jeguduns knew, but did her mother? She had a lot of making up to do when she got home.

At some point one of the servants had removed her hip beads. She didn't know where they were; perhaps they were in the same room with the dead guard, tucked away, although more likely they'd been thrown away. She recalled every moment with Dalibor now, including when he'd killed Tuvin and when he'd attacked her, and her plunging Tuvin's talon into his neck. The intensity of his hate had burned in his eyes. Just recalling it made her ill. And the *mutara* had taken his form. The *mutara* had been in her mind, had seen everything, and obviously had wanted to unsettle Malia, otherwise why take Dalibor's form?

She checked behind them again. Nothing. They were halfway to the valley, and dawn would start to lighten the sky soon. She would be home by the time the sun rose over the horizon. *Home.* She almost sobbed with relief. The stars sparkled overhead like the barrier had glimmered on her skin. The air was cool, without the sharpness held in the mountain, and smelled faintly of sage. *Home.* They were closing in. She couldn't wait to hold Enuwal, to feel his arms around her, to kiss him, to breathe in his familiar smell mingled with that of the herbs he was always drying or the seeds he crushed. His leg must be healed by now.

The dragon snorted, and a shudder passed through the beast. It rose into the air as they approached a wide swath of trees. Malia's grip on the saddle tightened. Ankti, who had been still and silent, her head resting on the back of Malia's shoulder, tensed again.

Nobody followed them. *Thank the clan mother for Chanwa.* Malia meant what she'd told Ankti. She'd figure out a way to help Chanwa if it was at all possible. As the dragon rose higher, Malia thought she could make out the rim of the valley and the Big River far in the distance. They were going to make it.

They passed over the trees, and from below, a dozen dark figures burst out of the cover, screaming.

Jeguduns.

Malia's heart leaped with happiness a moment before she realized the Jeguduns didn't know who rode the dragon, only that one of the beasts was approaching their home. She cried out, but her voice was swallowed by the roar of the dragon and the cries of the Jeguduns.

"Don't hurt them," Malia cried out even though the dragon didn't understand. The beast's sides pulsed faster and grew warmer beneath her legs. Its side glowed brighter with each inhalation. It was circling, getting ready to breathe fire.

Malia turned frantically to Ankti. "How do I keep it from breathing fire?" There had to be some command.

The other woman shook her head. She yelled at the beast, but it seemed to be acting on its own now. The Jeguduns were threatening it, and the dragon was going to defend itself.

The Jeguduns darted past, flying almost straight up. Their talons tore at the dragon's belly, legs, the saddle. The beast shuddered and jerked, and Malia squeezed her legs tighter. The dragon snapped at the Jeguduns and grazed one. The Jegudun cried out and tumbled slowly toward the ground.

The others circled around, faster than the dragon, and dove for another attack. Their cries echoed in Malia's head, along with the dragon's roar. Its sides pulsed even faster, burned hotter. She kicked with her free leg, trying to distract it from breathing fire. She waved with one arm at the Jeguduns, still holding the pommel with the other.

"It's Malia," she cried out. "Don't harm us."

Her voice was tiny among the Jegudun and dragon cries. The Jeguduns dove toward them. One more pass, and they might rip off the saddle or mortally wound the dragon, and either way, they'd all fall into the trees below.

Malia waved with both arms. "It's Malia," she called again, her throat aching with the strain after days of hardly speaking with anybody. "Don't harm us."

The dragon's sides bellowed, and a low rumbling came from its abdomen. It was about to breathe fire on the Jeguduns. Malia yanked her legs free from the straps. Ankti yelled at her. She ignored the other woman and, as the dragon snaked its head around, crawled forward along its neck and shoved its head down, grunting with the effort. The beast was strong.

She recalled how Chanwa had dug her fingers into the bottom of the dragon's jaw. Malia slid further along its neck and kicked at its jaw. Her foot connected with the soft flesh.

The beast whipped its head around, growling, as smoke poured from its nostrils and its gaping mouth. The movement sent Malia sliding. Her hands and feet scrambled to grab onto something . . . anything. Ankti's fingers grasped hers. She curled her fingers, seeking a better hold.

Ankti's fingers slid through hers.

Malia fell, the stars above her spun, and the ground rushed up to meet her.

~

Malia screamed as she fell, the wind whistling past her. Her blood pounded in her ears. She was spinning, the stars in her vision one moment, the trees' outlines the next. Her only chance was for the trees to break her fall without breaking *her*. She struggled to slow her spin, making herself as big as possible, as the Jeguduns did when slowing down for a landing.

Tuvin had shared one of his memories with her. In it, she had flown near the falls, felt the spray on her face, the air rushing past, seen Tuvin's shadow on the ground. But this was nothing but darkness, spinning stars, a sickening tumble in her stomach, and her pulse galloping out of control. She hoped she hadn't gained back all her memories only to die shortly after.

Overhead, the dragon roared again, and the hiss of flames filled the air, followed by screams, both human and Jegudun. She didn't dare look, in case the movement threw her into another spin. Besides, the trees were approaching fast. She flexed her hands, ready to grab any branch that came into reach.

Talons hooked her shoulders, digging into her flesh. She cried out. More talons hooked into her legs. Wings beat the air, and Jeguduns grunted overhead. Her descent slowed.

"Don't fight the dragon," she gasped. "The woman riding it is under my protection."

One of the Jeguduns let out a surprised chirp, then whistled to the others. The dragon gave one last roar, and then the night was filled with beating wings and the heavy breathing of the Jeguduns carrying Malia.

They had slowed her descent, but they couldn't completely control it. They approached the ground faster than Malia was comfortable with. The last of the trees passed just beneath her, close enough that she might have reached out and tugged off a pine needle. Something wet trickled along her leg. Blood, from the talons digging into her flesh. She could cope with some blood if it meant a softer landing.

The waving grasses came up beneath her, then tickled her. She collected her wits so that she was ready when the Jeguduns let go. She fell the last few hand spans, rolling over once before coming to a stop. Her breath came fast and shallow, and she clutched herself, shaking all over.

"I made it," she whispered. One last shudder passed through her. She slowly sat up, scanning the dark sky.

Several Jeguduns landed beside her, their wings whipping the grass every which way. Overhead, a large, dark shadow passed, a woman sitting atop it. She was safe, then. Malia let out a sigh of relief.

The dragon circled around and landed a good distance away. The Jeguduns half opened their wings, fluttering them and hissing. Malia made a quick check of her legs. Bleeding, but not badly. They shook when she stood.

She didn't recognize any of the four Jeguduns surrounding her. More circled in the air. One broke off from the group and dove rather quickly for the ground. He moved into a hopping run as he landed, then he threw his arms around Malia, chirping and whistling rapidly.

"Aru!" She squeezed him back. "I thought . . . I didn't know what happened to you. You're alive, thank goodness."

He stepped back, looked at her inquisitively, the starlight glinting along his sharp teeth, and canted his head to one side as he trilled. *What happened to you*? he seemed to say. He turned to the dragon and Ankti and hissed.

Malia sighed. "It's a long story. The woman on the dragon, Ankti, is under my protection. The dragon can fall over dead so far as I'm concerned. But we need to get to the valley as quickly as possible, so I supposed we need the beast a little longer." She glanced at the other Jeguduns. "Was anybody hurt?"

Aru shook his head. Malia closed her eyes momentarily in relief. Enough Jeguduns and people had died already. She only wanted to get home to Enuwal and her family and find out what Ankti could tell them about the Maddion.

She hated the thought of climbing back on the dragon, but they could cover so much more by air. If she walked, she'd be out in the open when the sun rose. And who would explain the sudden appearance of an Outsider woman in the valley?

She hurried to where the dragon snorted and shifted its weight uneasily. Ankti sat rigid in the saddle. The cap she'd been wearing had come off at some point, and dark curls framed her face. She spoke when she saw Malia, and gave her a tremulous smile.

"Let's go. We're close to the valley," Malia said.

She grasped Ankti's hand and clambered into the saddle again. She went to buckle her legs into the saddle. They trembled violently, and she couldn't so much as line the strap up with the buckle. Ankti murmured something, leaned forward, and slowly buckled Malia in. Malia settled in with a sigh.

"Now what?" she asked.

Ankti spoke a word and dug her heels into the dragon's side so hard that Malia could feel the movement through the saddle. The beast lurched, and then they were in the air, the ground slowly falling away. Malia clutched at the saddle. They were almost to the valley. She kept repeating that line to herself.

The Jeguduns split into two groups, one in front and another behind the dragon. The beast snorted, its head swinging back and forth as it tried to keep all of them in its sight. Malia's grip on the saddle tightened. The dragon's muscles remained coiled tight beneath her legs, but it didn't threaten to breathe fire or attack.

As the sky lightened to a deep blue in the east and the first stars twinkled out of existence, Malia spotted the valley's rim, and the Big River snaking its way across the grassy plains to where it plummeted into the valley. Her heart ached with the sight. *Home,* she thought again. Back in her cell, she thought she'd never see it again, and now that she returned, she vowed never to leave again. She would keep the secret of making the personal barrier to herself, and she'd make sure Aru never spoke of it either.

She guided the dragon to an area near the place where the river crashed over the cliffs and into the valley. She didn't want the dragon flying too close to the barrier and being repelled by the magic. To come this close and be thrown off . . . She nudged the dragon with her legs and words, and the beast descended. Then they were on the ground.

Ankti scrambled off the dragon, fell to her hands and knees, then stumbled a few steps away. Malia followed, a little more gracefully, though without any less haste.

The dragon shook itself like a bear spraying water from its fur, then leaped into the air. Half the Jeguduns had landed, but the others remained aloft. They held the space between the dragon and those on the ground. The beast reluctantly circled away, back toward the mountains.

Malia led Ankti to the cliff's edge. They reached the head of the trail that clung to the cliff face and led to the valley floor. Malia paused for a moment. Here, at last, they were safe from the Maddion and the dragons.

Long shadows stretched across the valley with slivers of light breaking through as the sun just emerged over the horizon. A pair of eagles circled the clearing on either side of the river as it cut a swath through the valley. The forest stretched away along rolling hills, lighter aspen mixed in with dark pine and fir. The air carried the scent of the forest, and occasionally a light spray from the waterfall. The sound of the rushing water was a pleasant roar. *Home*, she thought again. This time, to stay.

The only difference was the dragon bones that littered the grassy swath of land between the base of the cliffs and the forest. They were thickest here, where most of the Maddion had been when the barrier formed again. The dragons had fallen silently from the sky, dead. She recalled it now, as clearly as if it had happened the week before. She heard the screams of the dying, felt the river's clay in her hands as she worked the magic between them, reforming the barrier. Then there was a great rush as the barrier came together again. She cringed, expecting her mind to rebel as it had so often recently, but there was no fog to swallow her memories. She took a deep breath.

She led Ankti down the trail, taking it slow although her heart and mind urged her to hurry to her grandmother's. Loose rocks littered the trail, and her feet slid every so often. She paused on flatter areas to catch her breath and let the other woman rest. Ankti walked stiffly, like an older woman.

Aru approached, carrying a water pouch in his hands. He came closer until his wings stirred the dirt and Malia's hair, then tossed the pouch.

She caught it, letting out an *oof* as the full pouch hit her. She passed it to Ankti before taking a long draught herself. Cold water blazed a trail down her throat. When it hit her belly, her stomach grumbled, reminding her she hadn't eaten since the day before, and not well at that. She tied it to her belt and continued down the trail.

One of the Jeguduns must have gone ahead to tell of their arrival because, as Malia reached the valley floor, a familiar figure hurried toward them.

"Rasmus," she called out, waving.

He'd started growing his hair. It hung over his ears, revealing scattered gray that, along with the scar down his cheek, made him look even older than the last time she saw him, but the lightness in his steps and the smile on his face softened the harshness about him.

"Malia," he said as he approached. "Enuwal visited me a few days ago. He said you had disappeared, and nobody knew where you were. Are you . . . well?"

She flinched, imagining the fear Enuwal must have felt. "I'm sorry for running off. I'm well. Better, actually. I found a way to return my memories."

He grinned. "That's wonderful. I'll send messages out immediately. Enuwal and your brother have been searching for you." His words faded as his gaze caught Ankti standing behind her. His brows furrowed. "Who is she?"

"She escaped the Maddion."

His attention returned to her. "Where *were* you all this time?"

"It's a long story, and I'm sorely tired."

He stepped back and truly took in her appearance for the first time. She wore unwashed clothes, her hair was matted and unkempt, dirt covered much of her skin, and she bore puncture marks on her legs from the Jeguduns grasping her, dried blood caking her skin.

"Let's get you taken care of. There's plenty of time to discuss what happened later."

"Please, send out the messengers first. I don't want the others worrying any longer than they already have."

He gave a curt nod.

Malia turned to Ankti, about to gesture for her to join them, when a large shadow passed over the grass. It was too large to be a Jegudun. She shielded her eyes against the bright morning sun.

It was their dragon. It flew over the valley, unimpeded by the barrier.

Her heart thudded. She hadn't felt the same little tingle of magic this time like she had when she and Aru had walked through it. But that hadn't meant anything; she'd barely noticed it when she'd left the valley, and only because she'd been seeking out the barrier. It couldn't be gone. She hadn't removed enough to disturb it when she left, and the Jeguduns would have said something about it right away if there was a problem with the barrier.

Then she recalled the *mutara's* words. *Everything shall be as it was before*. Whatever the definition of *before*, it meant no barrier over the valley.

It meant the Maddion and their dragons were free to enter.

ABOUT THE AUTHOR

Rebecca Roland is the author of the Shards of History series, The Necromancer's Inheritance series, and *The King of Ash and Bones, and Other Stories*. Her short fiction has appeared in publications such as *Nature, Fantastic Stories of the Imagination, Stupefying Stories, Plasma Frequency*, and *Every Day Fiction*, and she is a graduate of the Odyssey Writing Workshop.

You can find out more about her and her work at rebeccaroland.net, her blog Spice of Life, or follow her on Twitter @rebecca_roland.

SHATTERED FATES

SHARDS OF HISTORY, BOOK 3

Rebecca Roland

The magic barrier protecting the Taakwa from their enemies, the Maddion, is gone. Malia, who led the Taakwa against the Maddion in the Dragon War, must convince the magical being, the changer, to repair the barrier before the Maddion invade to take revenge on her people and the winged Jeguduns who also call the valley home, even if it means reversing the healing the changer wrought for her.

Chanwa, the wife of the Maddion leader, uses the disorder created by the changer to lead a coup against her husband in a desperate attempt to ensure she and the other Maddion women are treated as equals. Her life, and the future of every Maddion woman, depends on her success.

Both women know the only way to succeed is to come together in an unlikely alliance.

THE KING OF ASH AND BONES AND OTHER STORIES

Rebecca Roland

An exiled man returns to his family and the life he left behind. A king is determined to avenge his people. A man doomed to die gives his wife her greatest wish. A suspected affair leads to a shocking and wondrous surprise. Roland works her magic again in this four-story collection of eerie and enchanting works, including Rasmus's story from after *Shards of History*.

OPAL

Fae Of Fire And Stone, Book One

Kristina Wojtaszek

White as snow, stained with blood, her talons black as ebony…

In this retwisting of the classic Snow White tale, the daughter of an owl is forced into human shape by a wizard who's come to guide her from her wintry tundra home down to the colorful world of men and Fae, and the father she's never known. She struggles with her human shape and grieves for her dead mother—a mother whose past she must unravel if men and Fae are to live peacefully together.

Trapped in a Fae-made spell, Androw waits for the one who can free him. A boy raised to be king, he sought refuge from his abusive father in the Fae tales his mother spun. When it was too much to bear, he ran away, dragging his anger and guilt with him, pursuing shadowy trails deep within the Dark Woods of the Fae, seeking the truth in tales, and salvation in the eyes of a snowy hare. But many years have passed since the snowy hare turned to woman and the woman winged away on the winds of a winter storm leaving Androw prisoner behind walls of his own making—a prison that will hold him forever unless the daughter of an owl can save him.

CHAR

Fae of Fire and Stone, Book Two

Kristina Wojtaszek

Fire is never tame—least of all the flames of our own kindling.

Interwoven with elements of Hansel and Gretel and The Seven Ravens, Char is the stand alone sequel to Opal, and second in the Fae of Fire and Stone trilogy.

FAE

Rhonda Parrish's Magical Menageries, Volume One

Meet Robin Goodfellow as you've never seen him before, watch damsels in distress rescue themselves, get swept away with the selkies and enjoy tales of hobs, green men, pixies and phookas. One thing is for certain, these are not your grandmother's fairy tales.

CORVIDAE

Rhonda Parrish's Magical Menageries, Volume Two

In Corvidae birds are born of blood and pain, trickster ravens live up to their names, magpies take human form, blue jays battle evil forces, and choughs become prisoners of war. One thing is for certain, after reading this anthology, you'll never look the same way at the corvid outside your window.

SCARECROW

Rhonda Parrish's Magical Menageries, Volume Three

Within these pages, ancient enemies join together to destroy a mad mommet, a scarecrow who is a crow protects solar fields and stores long-lost family secrets, a woman falls in love with a scarecrow, and another becomes one. Encounter scarecrows made of straw, imagination, memory, and robotics while being spirited to Oz, mythological Japan, other planets, and a neighbor's back garden. After experiencing this book, you'll never look at a hay-man the same.

SIRENS

Rhonda Parrish's Magical Menageries, Volume Four

Featuring stories by Kelly Sandoval, Amanda Kespohl, L.S. Johnson, Pat Flewwelling, Gabriel F. Cuellar, Randall G. Arnold, Michael Leonberger, V. F. LeSann, Tamsin Showbrook, Simon Kewin, Cat McDonald, Sandra Wickham, K.T. Ivanrest, Adam L. Bealby, Eliza Chan, and Tabitha Lord, these siren songs will both exemplify and defy your expectations.

The Falling Of The Moon

Moonfall Mayhem, Book One

A.E. Decker

In the gloomy mountains of Shadowvale, Ascot Abberdorf is expected to marry a lugubrious Count and settle down to a quiet life terrorizing the villagers. Instead, armed with a book of fairy tales, her faithful bat-winged cat, and whatever silverware she can pinch, Ascot heads east, to the mysterious Daylands, where her book promises she can find True Love and Happily Ever After, if she only follows her heart.

Determined to win the hand of Prince Parvanel, Ascot storms the Kingdom of Albright. With the book's guidance, she's confident she'll overcome any obstacles the imperious Queen Bettina Anna throws in her way, be they witches, evil stepmothers, or Big Bad Wolves.

Unfortunately, the book doesn't cover reluctant princes, wolves who read Dostoyevsky instead of blowing down houses, or a guild of Godmothers whose motivations may not be as pure as three drops of blood on a sweep of snow. Most annoying of all is the captain of the guard who swears he'll see the moon fall before she weds Prince Parvanel.

There are stories … and then there are *stories*, and if this parade of shifty shenanigans continues, Ascot might have to rewrite her own tale lest she end most Unhappily Ever After!

AVAILABLE NOW FROM WORLD WEAVER PRESS

Beyond the Glass Slipper

Ten Neglected Fairy Tales to Fall In Love With

Some fairy tales everyone knows—these aren't those tales.

Annotated by Kate Wolford

Bite Somebody

Paranormal Romance

Immortality is just living longer with more embarrassment.

Sara Dobie Bauer

Bite Somebody Else

Paranormal Romance

Coming Soon!

Sara Dobie Bauer

Campaign 2100: Game of Scorpions

Political Satire Science Fiction

A third party, and an alien, take on a corrupt world government.

Larry Hodges

Char

Fantasy

Fae of Fire and Stone, Book Two

An isolated fae must travel a century into the past to rewrite the book that will save her people.

Kristina Wojtaszek

Corvidae

Short Story Anthology

You'll never look the same way at the crow or raven outside your window.

Edited by Rhonda Parrish

Far Orbit Apogee
Science Fiction Anthology
More speculative space adventures.
Edited by Bascomb James

Frozen Fairy Tales
Short Story Anthology
Winter is not coming. Winter is here.
Edited by Kate Wolford

The Haunted Housewives of Allister, Alabama
Cleo Tidwell Paranormal Mystery, Book One
Who knew one gaudy Velvet Elvis could lead to such a heap of haunted trouble?
Susan Abel Sullivan

Heir to the Lamp
Genie Chronicles, Book One
Young Adult Fantasy
A family secret, a mysterious lamp, a dangerous Order with the mad desire to possess both.
Michelle Lowery Combs

He Sees You When He's Creepin': Tales of Krampus
Short Story Anthology
Twelve new tales of Krampus to help you gear up for the most "wonderful" time of the year.
Edited by Kate Wolford

The King of Ash and Bones and Other Stories
Short Story Collection
Rebecca Roland

Omega Rising
Wolf King, Book One
Paranormal Romance
Cass Nolan has been forced to avoid the burn of human touch her whole life.
Anna Kyle

Opal
Fae of Fire and Stone, Book One
Fantasy
A wizard will guide the daughter of an owl to the colorful world of men and Fae.
Kristina Wojtaszek

Scarecrow
Short Story Anthology
Hay-men, mommets, tattie bogles, kakashi, tao-tao.
Edited by Rhonda Parrish

Sirens
Short Story Anthology
Sixteen siren songs that will both exemplify and defy your expectations.
Edited by Rhonda Parrish

Skye Falling
Wolf King, Book Two
Paranormal Romance
Skye, a Fae-shapeshifter halfing, could die if she doesn't find out how to wake her dormant wolf.
Anna Kyle

WORLD WEAVER PRESS

Publishing fantasy, paranormal, and science fiction.

We believe in great storytelling.

Made in the USA
Las Vegas, NV
24 May 2024

90322865R00184